MindField

A science thriller

by

Tim Dub

Published by New Mill

Copyright: Tim Dub 2016

The moral right of the author has been asserted.

All characters and events in this publication are fictitious and any resemblance to real persons, living or dead, is purely coincidental.

All Rights Reserved.

No part of this publication may be reproduced, stored in a retrieval system,
or transmitted, in any form or by any means,
without the prior permission in writing of the author.

Find out more about the author on
www.timdub.com

Cover by Freda Dub

Sky in cover image courtesy of STScI

For the few

September 21st

Chapter 1: mind's eye

(6:55 am)

There was nothing in the speckled half-light of dawn to suggest it was an unusual morning; apart from the piece of paper. The woman's fingers found it tucked beside the cushion in the window alcove as she sat huddled against the thickness of the cottage wall.

There are things you know are false but choose to believe; and things you know are true but are impossible to . . .

It was her handwriting, but with no recollection of having written it or any memory of its scribbled content, she dismissed the discovery as unimportant and crumpled up the note to toss it at the bin. She sighed, and turned to peer at the face that stared back at her from the gloom of the window, wondering if the whitened image reflected in the glass lacked character . . . *like a plot without a twist.*

A stray twig fanned by a gust of wind tapped on the window pane, as if to summons her. Now fully awake she looked again, through her reflection and across the patchwork of countryside to a line of distant hills, their contours dappled by patterns of light and dark, cut through by an accusing finger of black cloud that reached across the sky.

So 'real' - and yet its boundary is . . . she paused, irritated by the elusiveness of the description, *. . . so 'imagined' - like the line between the present and the past.*

The woman inhaled deeply as if to gather her resolve and swung her feet sideways to touch the floor, slipping out of her pyjamas as she stood up. She crossed the room to the full length mirror that swivelled around a midpoint in its heavy frame of mahogany and flicked back her bob of thick black hair, turning slightly to accentuate the outline of her naked figure.

Surely I'm . . . how can he . . . ?

Her phone sounded, interrupting her thoughts.

Seven o'clock . . . who on earth?

'G'day Chris.' Like many Australians, her boss's voice held the promise of humour. 'How's it goin'?'

'Oh . . . Ian, hi. I was just thinking of you,' replied Dr Christine Reynolds, fumbling to wrap herself in a towel.

Chapter 2: dr lineker I presume

(7:01 am)

'Look . . . sorry to disturb you . . . but it's important. I was wondering if you managed to finish those graphs?' asked Dr Ian Lineker.

Chris hesitated, still distracted by the memory of Lineker's good-natured smile and sinewy ease. 'The graphs . . .' she said, as she refocused her thoughts, 'well . . . sort of. They're pretty much done.'

'Good. I want to compare notes before the meeting. Can you get in by eight?'

'If I hurry, but there's still some fine tuning to do. I'm afraid I was up late looking at how Modular Forms might contribute to apparent kinks in the direction of time.'

'Time?' Lineker interrupted. 'Time is what we haven't got at the moment, so spare me the details. It will be the new guy, Bill Grafton, chairing the committee. We can't afford any mistakes.'

'Grafton,' she laughed. 'To be honest, I have trouble taking Dr Grafton nearly as seriously as he takes himself.'

'Well . . .' Lineker sounded irritated. 'You better. If they cut the budget - we're buggered.'

'Don't worry - we can handle Bill Grafton,' Chris replied, unsettled by the urgency in his voice.

'Sure we can . . . no worries,' he said. 'See you at eight.'

She smiled to herself, more in resignation than amusement. She knew she was attracted to Lineker for reasons other than just admiration for his 'radical' physics, but she also recognized that any form of romantic involvement with a work colleague would be risky, especially one who was more than twice her age.

For a second time, Chris glanced at the heavy green chronometer on the bedside table.

Ten past – must hurry.

After a quick shower, Chris rifled through the neatly ordered rows of blacks and greys in her wardrobe and selected a business suit still enclosed in the plastic sleeve from the dry-cleaners. Unsure whether she would need a raincoat, she crossed the room to look up at the approaching cloud and so didn't see the tall man in the shadow of a tree who watched her with his one good eye as she appeared briefly at the window. As soon as she had gone, the stranger strolled to a Mercedes saloon in the car park nearly opposite the cottage, and sat behind the wheel, waiting.

Chris retrieved her briefcase from the table and pulled an umbrella from the hall stand, then knelt to stroke the cat that was rubbing against her legs. 'See you later Erwin - be good,' she murmured, grabbing the keys to the 1970's Citroen Deux Chevaux for the quick descent from the Hills to the sprawling complex of ex-government buildings on the Worcestershire Plains some thousand feet below, and the meeting that both she and her boss had dreaded since they'd received the notice demanding a progress report, just a few days before.

Chapter 3: net drive

(8:50 am)

Saul Baedeker adjusted his aubergine tie over a black shirt. His brown aquiline face was lightly powdered just enough to subdue shine, something he did every morning as a precaution in case he was interviewed under camera lighting. He chose platinum cuff links to accent his immaculately pressed light grey Paul Smith linen suit, and squinted at himself through glittering eyes, pleased at the overall effect that accentuated his subtly coiffured thick silver hair. He was 65, but was frequently mistaken for a 45-year-old, so free was his face from the wrinkles and creases of the vast majority of his contemporaries and so easy his lithe elegance as he moved.

The speaker crackled. 'Fifteen minutes from landing, Mr Baedeker sir, so we'll be there at 9:05 am local time,' the captain announced. 'Temperature in Birmingham is 10 degrees Celsius - that's 50 in our money - skies are clear, at least for now anyways. But this is England, so don't rely on it,' he chuckled.

'Okay Ben, thanks,' said Baedeker, pressing the button on the vanity unit in front of him. He returned to his seat feeling the familiar warmth of self-congratulation, fuelled by his confidence that another jigsaw piece was ready to slot into place. 'Clinton, bring me the briefing papers on these New Physics people, and make sure Paula has got to the point this time. I don't want waffle.'

'Yes sir, Mr Baedeker. Dr Valence assures me the revised paper is very succinct,' replied Clinton. Baedeker's assistant had an eager polished look, the scrubbed exuberance of obsessive good health illuminating his aura of Aqua Brava and talc.

The plane taxied to a halt, its shrieking jets suddenly dropping in pitch before the pilot flicked his switches and the noise collapsed to expose the baleful entreaties of a solitary gull which had been practising its scales under cover of the jet-powered din. A short walk away was a sleek car, grey and discreet, waiting on the tarmac.

'How are our people finding the new Audis?' asked Baedeker.

'They like them very much sir,' replied Clinton.

'Yes, thought they would Clinton - one of the few things the Europeans do better than us,' volunteered Baedeker, as he followed Clinton across the tarmac.

'Malvern please, driver - and how long to get there, avoiding the freeways?' asked Baedeker as he approached the parked Audi.

'I estimate 60-70 minutes, sir,' said the chauffeur. He was short, stocky, handsome, but with the sort of badly broken nose that said either 'tough guy' or 'loser'. It would take a tough guy, or a loser, to call him either to his face.

'Good. And what's your name driver?

'Mike Aziz sir,' replied the man.

Chapter 4: crunch time

(9:00 am)

Just as the many former titles of the Malvern Research Institute had reflected the political priorities of previous eras, a raggle-taggle collection of buildings were testament to its struggle to keep pace with a rapidly evolving technology. Post-war Nissen huts, modern prefabs, huge radio telescope dishes and utilitarian sheds dressed in red brick ordinariness, were grouped around the only structure remaining from the original nineteenth century complex, which housed administrative staff in its minor rooms, and a rarely-used 'Committee Room' in its largest. This room, poorly lit by tall windows latticed with smaller panes, was almost empty except for a heavy table, some chairs, and the smell of must.

Three men were seated behind the table, in front of a substantial disused fireplace. On the dark oak panelling above the fireplace were photographs of elderly dignitaries captured in frozen condescension, like the entrance lobby of a stuffy school clinging to pretensions of a long-lost grandeur.

Dr Grafton, the Director of Research at the Malvern Research Institute, was wearing a beige jacket and black trousers, with a pale green tie draped across a clearly-defined potbelly. His straggly hair was off-white with an untidy circle of baldness framing a pug-like face, its expression of puffy irritation as fixed by habit as an old shoe is by a bunioned foot. He was polishing his spectacles vigorously as Dr Ian Lineker and Dr Chris Reynolds approached the table across the solid timber flooring.

'Congratulations on the piece in New Scientist, Lineker,' Grafton greeted them fulsomely.

'Thank you Dr Grafton, yes, we were very pleased to find such an open minded reporter.'

'I'm sure you were,' replied Grafton. 'Perhaps 'gullible' might be a more accurate description of your young friend's state of mind.'

Ian Lineker looked confused for a moment. 'Tim Parry is well credentialed,' he began, 'he has written extensively on . . .' Lineker got no further.

'Yes, yes, Lineker - we have a lot to cover. Of course you know Dr Billings,' Grafton gestured toward the portly man seated on his left.

'Hi Ian, Chris,' Dr Billings smiled reassuringly at them, his double chin softening his collar in buffers of stubbled pink.

'Dr Janbir Chatterjee from New Materials Science has kindly volunteered to assist the committee as an observer,' Grafton continued, indicating the man on his right. Chris suddenly remembered her friend, Chatterjee's wife, had suggested they meet for coffee, a message as yet unanswered. She decided to say nothing as the thin Indian man, with a prominent hooked nose and an air of patrician haughtiness, nodded briefly before returning to the papers in front of him.

'G'day guys,' said Lineker, greeting them with a friendly wave as he and Chris took their seats.

'Let's get some things understood from word go here', Grafton resumed, 'so we are all on the same page - parameter wise.' He spoke in a cultivated monotone, as if disposing quickly of something he found tiresome. 'We are accountable as a cost centre and we will be looking at all our projects, not just yours Lineker, so no-one can expect special treatment and no-one can complain at the fairness of the outcome.'

Grafton paused and peered over his spectacles, fixing Lineker with a belligerent stare before continuing.

'Now about your work, and of course the lovely Christine Reynolds your . . . ahem,' Grafton stopped and coughed quietly as if clearing his throat, 'your 'research assistant.''

What the . . . A pulse of anger ambushed Chris as she felt a glow suffusing her face. *For God's sake, don't blush,* she admonished herself, pursing her lips in an effort to control the reaction . . . *not in front of 'Rant Gob Fill'.* The label had popped into her mind.

Even as a child Chris had cultivated a habit of finding an anagram in everyday words, a skill which later she had perfected as a crossword champion. The hand raised to cover her mouth at first to conceal her irritation, was now trying to suppress a smirk as she savoured the words for a second time. *'Bill Grafton' – 'Rant Gob Fill'. Hmm, . . . how very appropriate.*

'Yes . . . my collaborator on this project - Dr Reynolds, Sussex and Cambridge - one of the leading research mathematicians of her generation.' Lineker spoke clearly and loudly 'We're very lucky to have her here in Malvern.'

Chris glanced across at Lineker who turned as if sensing her attention, and clearly winked at her. This was more like it. They were going to put up a fight.

Chapter 5: bare hill

(9:05 am)

'Ah yes, Mike Aziz. Our new driver. I've heard about you. You're the one with an interesting background. How old are you Mike?'

'Thirty-five sir,' said Aziz, holding the car door open and standing upright next to it.

'A good age - I have fond memories of thirty-five,' commented Baedeker, as he eased into the back seat of the car. 'And what do you know of us at PORTAL.com?'

'I've been told you're the First Minister of what I understand is a sort of web-type Church,' replied Aziz . . . *and you're worth a heap of money*, he thought, remembering the article he'd read about PORTAL's phenomenal growth that had brought evangelism well and truly into the age of the internet.

'Yes, well. That's a good start,' said Baedeker, distracted by a policeman who saluted as they were waved through a security gate in the high fence at the back of the airport. 'Nice touch, Clinton,' Baedeker said to his fresh-faced assistant seated next to him in the austere Germanic comfort of the rear seats, both men hidden from the policeman's gaze by the heavy tinting of bullet proof glass.

'Thank you, sir,' said Clinton 'This mission has been facilitated by Assistant Police Commissioner Lawson. He's a believer.'

'That's very affirming to hear, Clinton. Now Mike, where were we?' continued Baedeker. 'Ah yes . . . your last name - Aziz - is that an Arab name? Are you a Muslim?' he asked, a fleeting suggestion of disapproval passing quickly across his otherwise serene face.

'No sir. My father was a Lebanese Catholic, my mother an English Quaker. They divorced early on. I was brought up a Methodist in Cornwall then spent several years in the British military here, and then for a while in Australia. Religion plays no part in my life these days,' explained Aziz peering briefly into the rear-view mirror to check on his passengers.

'I'm sorry to hear that,' said Baedeker, appearing to lose interest in Aziz as he took some papers that his assistant had handed him, and started to study them in silence.

It suited Aziz to be ignored. He could drive in peace, and think. Mentioning Cornwall had reminded him of his recent visit to a former school-friend who even after twenty years still lived in the same tiny Cornish hamlet where Aziz had grown up. Aziz had come away with mixed feelings; his usual reaction to anything related to the past, polluting his recollection of a young boy's simple pleasure with the complicated ache of a grown man's sadness.

Not that it was all bad, Aziz decided, comforted by the knowledge that he had got on well enough with his mates even if he was always the outsider, the boy with the funny name; the boy who never quite felt he really belonged to the community of his peers.

'We are a very modern community. There are many Semites who are followers, though no orthodox Jews of course,' added Baedeker as he finished reading a page and selected another. 'We at PORTAL are open to all.'

Open to all . . . repeated Aziz to himself, surprised at the relevance of Baedeker's comment, as if somehow the man had read his thoughts. Hustling the car at speed through the countryside, Aziz drifted into re-imagining, tasting once more the bitter-sweet solitude of day-break walks through tranquil fields, where rivers of mist marooned hilltops to create magical islands that spoke to him of integrity, isolation and dignity. He remembered too the dog that was his closest companion; and the stabbing sadness of his death.

Baedeker had finished perusing his papers, and was looking at Aziz in the mirror. 'We think we have something unique, especially for those who have somehow faltered in their journey with the older religions, and for those to whom life has been unkind.' Baedeker was beaming unctuously at

Aziz. 'I'm aware you have had a troubled history, especially in the last few years.'

Careful, thought Aziz, adjusting his hands on the steering wheel to relieve the weight of tension suddenly creeping down his neck toward the solid ledge of his shoulders.

Must be careful.

Chapter 6: light speed

(9:07 am)

'Yes, yes, Lineker. I am well aware of Dr Reynolds qualifications, though we may be discussing some of your own in due course, perhaps starting with why the Australian Institute of Physics refused to renew your membership. So, if you'll spare me the lecture I'll continue.' Grafton had noted Lineker's wink and was clearly not amused.

'Now . . . let me see.' Grafton turned over a piece of paper on the table in front of him. 'The Malvern Research Institute was commissioned by Sincom, the third biggest Chinese telecom provider, to design a pattern for their new fibre optic infrastructure. You assured us that your team could contribute efficiencies using theories on neural networking - brain patterns if I can call it that - which you had worked on as a researcher at the University of Darwin in Queensland.'

'Northern Territory and I was Professor of Physics there,' interjected Lineker.

'Whatever Lineker . . . It was on the other side of the world - I think we can agree on that. As I was saying . . . I was chatting to an old Oxford friend who it turns out is now a visiting professor at the ANU, a somewhat 'better known' Australian university. He tells me you couldn't get a renewal of your research funding. Forgive my bluntness but he said you were generally regarded as a bit of a 'kook.''

'If I may . . .' interjected Lineker, more forcefully. 'I've been looking at a number of experiments carried out over the last hundred years into how light behaves. Interpret the data properly and these experiments show that the speed of light varies depending on its direction of travel.'

'I read your assertion Lineker.' There was an ominous calm to Grafton's delivery. 'You could say that is why I've called this meeting. If - and that's a bloody big 'if', given that a certain Albert Einstein says it isn't so - if you're right - then surely the speed of light would be affected by the speed of the earth travelling around the sun.'

'Not only that . . .' started Lineker. 'The whole of the solar system is moving too, which would also have an effect.'

'Just give me a moment to understand, if you would be so kind Dr Lineker,' asked Grafton, his voice dripping with sarcasm. 'The solar system is moving relative to . . . to what exactly?'

'To deep space,' Lineker replied cheerfully.

'Deep space?' Grafton sighed.

'Absolutely. The whole solar system is moving through space at over 400 kilometres per second - 3,600 times quicker than the fastest supercar.'

'But there isn't anything in 'deep space," Grafton spluttered. 'How can you say something is moving relative to nothing?' He looked genuinely perplexed.

'Space is made of stuff too!' said Lineker, beaming like a generous child sharing candy with a friend. 'But look - all that is just the tip of an incredible iceberg of new science.' Lineker was animated now. 'If light has a variable speed the implication is, as you mentioned, that Einstein was wrong, and the whole concept of space-time was an invention to fit the maths and nothing to do with reality.'

'Whoa, Lineker hold on,' exploded Grafton, standing from his chair. 'You're saying Einstein got it wrong? Wrong!' He held his head in a caricature of exasperation. 'You're supposed to be a scientist, man. You of all people must be aware how far cosmology has come in the last hundred years - thanks to Albert Einstein?' Grafton was waving his hands slightly above his head, jerking them back and forth. 'I can't believe I'm hearing this - what exactly are you saying for Christ's sake?' The word 'exactly' was delivered with exaggerated emphasis as Grafton ran with the momentum of his own melodrama.

'Well - it's all been a colossal bungle,' replied Lineker.

Chapter 7: open heart thuggery

(9:12 am)

'Have you discussed your situation with one of our outreachers?' asked Baedeker, smiling amicably at Aziz's reflection in the rear driving mirror.

Aziz had suspected it was touch and go getting a job without signing up to the Church, but as ex-SAS and bodyguard for three years to Marguerita Dion the cosmetics heiress, he had been confident that he was as well qualified as anyone to be a driver in the world of celebrities where personal protection was a key consideration to counter the vulnerability of transport by car. He had researched PORTAL, the 'Parish of Reason Truth and Love', before saying 'yes' to the job offer and had learnt approvingly of their educational and aid programs, pleased at the opportunity to be part of an outfit that held to some sort of ethical base rather than the 'following orders' amorality of the military, or the 'drug and party' vacuity of an air-head socialite.

'Yes, sir. I did speak to a . . . err . . . a consultant. I certainly found it all very interesting,' replied Aziz. Baedeker was reading again and appeared not to have heard what Aziz had said. 'Just not ready yet to fully commit,' Aziz concluded, his voice trailing off in acknowledgment of the apparent lack of interest in his reply.

Like father like son, Aziz added to himself, suppressing what would have been a wry smile before it made it to his lips as he thought again of the void left by his father, and the resentment it had spawned. When Aziz had matured to resemble him, his mother's loathing of her departed husband grew into a fault-line in her son, as Aziz's own manhood gradually became an object of her hostility. Deep down, in a place he often visited, Aziz felt betrayed by them both.

'Not ready to commit eh?' Baedeker surprised Aziz by repeating his words, whilst continuing to browse through the documents on his lap.

'No sir,' replied Aziz, the reflexive response reminding him of how effectively his military training had marked him, and wondering if he should try harder to disguise it.

'But you joined the army,' observed Baedeker smiling. 'That was a commitment.'

'Just a chance to play with bigger toys sir,' quipped Aziz, repeating the half-truth he had always used to conceal the real attraction of the military - his quest for an authority entitled to his respect - something he had never found at home or at school.

'With us - all you need do is open your heart, Aziz,' continued Baedeker.

'I'll try sir,' replied Aziz. *The fuck I will* . . . he added under his breath.

'Commitment is of the mind and we are not interested in your mind.' Baedeker's voice seemed distant; Aziz was hardly listening to him anymore. As he did every day, Aziz was remembering his deployment in Afghanistan.

'Stop the struggle,' Baedeker commanded emphatically, suddenly demanding all of Aziz's attention.

Shit, thought Aziz. *Is he onto me?*

'Let the love enfold you - that's all,' concluded Baedeker, his face diffusing the benign calm of an apparently pleasured distraction.

Love! Aziz felt a twist inside, the image of the naked backside of a reclining woman flashing for an instant into his mind.

Oh well - fun while it lasted.

Chapter 8: no chance

(9:15 am)

'Oh dear - I think we have a problem here.' Grafton slumped back into his seat, his body language designed to broadcast exasperation. 'Gentlemen - I need a moment's recess.' He stared around the room with an unfocussed truculence like a boxer before the bout, inviting conflict, relishing a challenge.

'That'll be all for now Mr Lineker,' Grafton snarled, emphasising the 'Mister'. 'But you Reynolds - could you wait outside for a couple of minutes - until we call you back in?' He twisted his face into a phoney smile. 'If it isn't too much trouble,' he added.

'Look I'm happy to take you through the evidence . . .' began Lineker, 'anyone can check my work.'

There was a sudden bang at the window as a blast of wind heralded the machine gun clatter of hailstones against the glass.

'Not just now Lineker, thank you.' Grafton barked. 'Though, I will be in touch - you can be sure of that. Just shut the door please,' he said, 'on the way out.'

When Lineker and Chris had left, Grafton immediately started to speak. 'This is even worse than I feared - the man is talking absolute gibberish. And his nonsense is appearing in the press - we'll be a laughing stock.' The words were delivered quickly and without inflection, as an actor on his own might rehearse his lines without the need to consider an audience.

'There may be a medical dimension in this. We may even be liable for an action of negligence in failing to deal with his instability.' Grafton's tone suddenly changed. 'You're Lineker's boss Billings - why in God's name have you allowed the situation to get this far?'

'But Bill, some of his observations are remarkably plausible,' began Dr Billings, his palms in front of him in a gesture of appeal.

'Don't tell me you've gone native?' demanded Grafton angrily. 'We're supposed to be designing a bloody comms network - not rewriting the textbooks with fantasies.'

Grafton rose to his feet and with his hands clasped behind his back, began striding up and down as he talked. 'Amazing a Cambridge scholar like Reynolds being so impressionable. A woman of course - who would have guessed it? Sort of groupie hysteria I imagine.' Grafton was heading toward the door. 'But I want to see if we can pull her back from the brink. Either of you got anything to add before I get her back in?' he asked over his shoulder.

'Not really Dr Grafton, no. I couldn't agree with you more,' said Dr Chatterjee evenly.

Chapter 9: a world of pain

(9.20 am)

Aziz slid the car down a gear, easing its bulk around a bend before he accelerated smoothly down the narrowing ribbon of stipple-grey tarmac, the muted sun adding a sheen of glitter to a gunmetal surface recently washed by a morning shower.

'I am sure we can find something for you better than just driving. Some employment more suited to your particular talents,' said Baedeker, as he continued to work through the papers on his lap.

Finding jobs had not been easy for Aziz since he had been invalided out of the army five years previously with the physical injury which had so emphatically closed a chapter in his life.

'We know more about you than you might suppose.'

So Baedeker knows about me does he - he must know about Afghanistan. The image returned - a memory that haunted him and gave nothing in return, except the pain of those who witness evil and do nothing.

When discharged from hospital, a faltering limp when he walked was all that outwardly revealed the legacy of Aziz's ordeal. The moral confusion that disfigured him inside was more discreet, suggested only by a line of cynicism in his conversation and the regular nightmares from which he would awake covered in sweat, still screaming, still powerless to avoid the calamity that he revisited so often in his sleep.

'You should understand we are here in the UK on a very important mission for everyone.' Baedeker's tone was conciliatory, almost confiding, 'To rekindle the flame of love.'

Why would he say that? The weight of anxiety had now clamped itself onto Aziz's back, more heavily than the pack of claymores he had hauled through the desert.

Does he know I can't even fuck any more? That fuckin' shrink must have told them . . . Aziz was furious. *Bastard . . .*

'We are working toward no less than a re-formulation of the notion of God, for the followers you understand. We want the concept to be more accessible in the digital age. An extraordinary opportunity for those who can contribute.' Baedeker seemed to suddenly remember his audience as he continued. 'We have time Aziz, the eternity of the present is on our side. You will join the fold when you are ready.'

That's just what I ain't got – time, thought Aziz, his anger subsiding as he dared to believe that he was not about to be fired for his non-belief. *Not if I'm to make the sixty minutes to Malvern.* Aziz banged the car down into third gear, revelling in the muffled sound of the diesel engine as it roared in protest.

'We pride ourselves on our alchemy - we take the base metal of human misery and turn it into the treasure-trove of God's love.'

The car rushed past the line of traffic to cut sharply in at its front before a fast approaching hill crest, the sudden move serenaded by the Doppler distorted fusillade of an offended car horn honking a furious protest in his wake.

Jesus H thought Aziz, stamping again on the accelerator. *What the fuck have I got myself into this time?*

Chapter 10: not everything is relative

(9:20 am)

In the oak-panelled foyer outside the committee room, Lineker sat slumped in a leather chair, his head in his hands, elbows on knees, as if the weight of Grafton's hostility was a burden he could only carry with a physical support.

'I'm not sure that went well at all,' he said. 'I didn't really get a chance to do justice to the research. He seems to have made his mind up already.'

'Of course he has, but don't worry about it,' comforted Chris, feeling an unfamiliar tug of tenderness. 'The man is just a buffoon.'

Lineker looked at her and smiled. 'You can lead a dork to laughter but you can't make him think.' He shrugged, his mood lifting. 'I wonder what they want with you? Probably trying to drive a wedge between us.'

'Well there's no chance of that,' she replied.

'Didn't think there would be,' he smiled at her. 'Look, if by any chance you were considering working from home could you give me a lift to my place when you're done. I need to be out of here for a while.'

'Of course – I feel pretty much the same way.'

'Thanks,' said Lineker, reaching over to squeeze her hand before he stood up suddenly and added. 'You know I went through something very similar to this in Australia.'

The memory seemed to rekindle Lineker's sense of frustration; he drew his fingers through his hair, then sat down again. 'There are physicists who will go to any lengths to defend Einstein's theories, despite it being obvious they don't actually understand how his physics works.'

Chris was looking at him with concern, surprised again at the novelty of her own reaction, a confusing amalgam of compassion mixed with the disappointment of seeing someone she usually relied on to be strong, seeming so agitated.

'Really, it's more like arguing with a religious cult than anything to do with science,' Lineker continued. 'Of course, Galileo had a similar problem taking on a faith-based belief system all those centuries ago.'

Hang on, Chris thought. *Wasn't Galileo forced to recant his 'sun at the centre' theory, tried by the Inquisition and spent the rest of his life under house arrest?*

'Is that good?' she asked ruefully, a slight smile playing across her features.

'These people just ignore the results that don't suit them.' Lineker, shaking his head in disbelief, had not heard her remark. 'It really shouldn't be happening to a scientific theory in the 21st century.'

'Not to worry, truth will out eventually,' she comforted, trying to hide her unease that this time it was she who had to provide the reassurance, a feeling made more poignant by the suspicion that he too would be very aware of how their roles had suddenly reversed.

The hail and rain outside had sputtered to a halt, and with the morning light of an English autumn streaming from a window behind her, Chris was illuminated in an outline of gold as Grafton's lined face peered round the door.

Grafton paused, staring at her, for a moment seeming lost for words before he scowled and demanded; 'Still here Lineker?'

'Yes, I was just . . .'

Grafton ignored the reply. 'A couple of minutes with you Reynolds, if it's not too much trouble.'

'See you in a bit, Ian,' Chris said quietly, following Grafton back into the room.

Chapter 11: you don't know what you've got
(9:30 am)

As Chris entered, Dr Billings was the first to speak. 'Look Dr Reynolds, let me just explain that things are reaching a crisis with the funding. We all appreciate the sincerity and the hard work that you and Lineker have put in - I myself have been very excited about some of the concepts.'

'Thank you Billings. No need for a preamble,' interrupted Grafton, his face turning angrily toward his colleague as he resumed his seat. 'This is how it is - off the record you understand Reynolds.' Grafton was facing Chris across the table. 'I like you, I really do. You remind me of me, when I was your age.'

Chris noticed Dr Billings' eyebrows rise suddenly, his hand reaching to conceal what she thought was an involuntary smirk.

'I was young and impressionable too,' continued Grafton. 'We're all looking for glory and the next big thing. I understand that - I really do. But - and this is very important - you have to realize Lineker has lost the plot.'

Chris was sitting with her arms crossed in a failing attempt to ignore a tingling sensation that was spreading from her chest toward her fingertips.

'I don't mind telling you, I am concerned he may actually be mentally unstable.' Grafton was calmer, and hadn't noticed the anger now glinting in Chris' eyes. 'It's important we are all completely frank here. There's nothing 'personal' in this is there?'

I don't believe it . . . Chris could feel the churning inside . . . *the little shit's doing it again.* 'It's important you understand . . .' she began, but Grafton raised a hand to silence her and giving her no chance to continue, he announced:

'You deserve to know that I'm recommending we pull the plug on this nonsense as soon as we can get out of it contractually, but I'm pleased to tell you - I may be able to reassign you, even if Lineker has to go.'

Her face reddened again, but this time not from embarrassment place? - Dr Christine Reynolds was furious as she rose to her feet. 'Ian Lineker is probably the most original thinker any of us will be privileged to meet in our lifetimes. He has revived a moribund physics that has been in crisis, a physics committed to cherry-picking the evidence.'

'Hang on a minute . . .' began Grafton.

There was something about the swaggering assumption of dominance in Grafton's tone that triggered an explosive reaction in Chris, though she had little time to make any conscious connection with its source other than the image of her father haranguing her mother at the dinner table, a ritual she had endured every Sunday throughout her childhood. Chris was not going to allow another bully to abuse his power and diminish someone she cared about, at least, not without opposition. Her forcefulness lent a tremor to her voice as with her hands clenched into fists at her sides, she shouted over Grafton.

'If I may finish . . .'

Grafton fell silent, his mouth still shaped to form the now abandoned word.

'The assertion that light has a constant speed has been confirmed by experiment as wrong. Using a 'process' rather than an 'object' based approach, Dr Lineker has shown that space is itself a dynamic entity, something real, not just the 'absence of anything." Taking a deep breath, Chris resumed more quietly. 'And Dr Lineker has succeeded in resolving the inconsistencies between Relativity and Quantum Mechanics that have incapacitated modern physics for the past fifty years. The suggestion that such an outstanding scientist has some sort of mental problem is absolutely preposterous.'

'I see,' said a momentarily chastened Grafton. 'Quite a speech Dr Reynolds. So you and Lineker have come up with yet another so-called 'Theory of Everything?"

'No - this is Process Physics. It's been around for some time and this is a development from that. There are extraordinary philosophical implications too, but it's all there in the maths.' Chris sounded excited, her anger dissolving in her enthusiasm to explain something important. 'We've mapped a mind-like network as the ultimate nature of reality . . .'

'Enough, Reynolds, stop,' insisted Grafton, seeing that the tide of her fury had ebbed. 'Answer me one question?' Grafton paused, looking round to his colleagues, as if conscious he was about to deliver the killer blow. 'Do you believe in homeopathy?'

Chris recognized Grafton's strategy as a crude manipulation – the sort her father might have attempted as he routinely ridiculed her mother in front of his friends, a spectacle Chris had witnessed on countless occasions, until her mother had grown silent and withdrawn. This time the understanding engendered pity, not anger.

Chris pictured the last time she had seen her father, an hour before he died. She saw his shrivelled hand reaching out to clasp her arm with the little strength it still possessed, as if one heartfelt gesture could annul the legacy of a lifetime of distance. She remembered too that she had refused to let him touch her, and the guilt that followed.

'Believe?' repeated Chris, distracted by the image and a sense of futility. 'Well for me it's not a question of belief. But yes, I do take homeopathic remedies for some conditions.' She sounded oddly calm, and somehow indifferent. 'Is that relevant?'

Rolling his eyes upward to the ceiling in a look of exaggerated exasperation Grafton replied. 'That'll be all Reynolds. I think we've heard all we need, thank you.'

Chris looked at the three men seated in a row behind the table, her calm appraisal somehow conveying a disdain that teetered unambiguously close to contempt. 'Gentlemen,' she said, her voice now measured and firm, 'if a theory is shown to be false but you choose to believe it, you betray not only the Truth . . . but your own integrity as men of science.'

She strode toward the door, knowing Grafton would be watching her and resenting him for it. As she pulled at the door to close it behind her, she raised her middle finger vertically, in view of the seated men. With precise timing, she withdrew the finger a moment before the door clunked shut.

Chapter 12: letting off steam

(9:45 am)

'Did you see that?' Grafton demanded. 'Was she . . . was she gesturing at us?'

'Sorry, I wasn't looking,' said Chatterjee.

'I really can't believe she would gesture at us,' began Billings. 'Really . . . I think maybe you're getting too steamed up here.'

'Steamed up is it?' Grafton interrupted quietly, a menacing determination resonating in his voice. Billings fell silent, looking dejected, as Grafton stood, talking as he walked around the table.

'Billings - you are Head of Communications Design at MRI. That makes you the direct line manager for Lineker and Reynolds.' He suddenly stopped, and turned to lean across the table. 'I'm holding you responsible for this farce.'

Dr Billings opened his mouth to reply but Grafton gave him no opportunity. 'I'm afraid there's no room for discussion - I'm going to have to let you go. Don't you agree that's for the best Dr Chatterjee?'

Chatterjee didn't bother to look up, as he made a note in the margin of the paper in front of him. 'Absolutely, couldn't agree with you more Dr Grafton.'

Chapter 13: the folly of men

(10:00 am)

'I don't think Grafton can just shut us down without some notice period even if he wants to,' reassured Lineker as they crossed the car park toward the Deux Chevaux. It was a desultory drive to Malvern Wells, with neither he nor Chris finding much to say.

'Look, why don't we meet up later,' Lineker suggested as he got out of the car. 'We'll go through the options . . . discuss the best way forward.'

'Okay, 7:30 ish my place?' she smiled.

'I'll look through your time-loop stuff about Modular Forms, it sounds like it could be a welcome distraction. See you later.'

The little Citroen struggled up the hill to Chris' home, Victoria Cottage at the Wyche Cutting, its mood echoing hers. Suddenly everything was too hard, and she was concerned that even Lineker's normally irrepressible optimism had seemed so muted. The interview with Grafton had troubled her, and so had her reaction to the unwelcome memories that it revived of her mother's unhappiness, and her father's behaviour.

Miserable bastard . . . always undermining us . . . but I never really gave up trying to earn his . . . She hunted for the right expression, dismissing the notion of 'love' as too self-indulgent - *his approval. Maybe still haven't, maybe that's it.*

Chris stopped, remembering the turmoil she had felt as a child, distressed that even now it seemed unresolved, the realisation renewing her determination to avoid her mother's fate. She knelt to give the cat a perfunctory stroke before entering the cottage, then immediately went up to her bedroom to change from her suit before throwing herself on the bed and hugging the pillow to her as she rolled onto her side. The heavy green chronometer on her bedside table was only inches from her face.

Damn . . . maybe I'll just post it back to him, she thought, remembering she hadn't yet replied to Kim Zazie's recent text requesting return of his valuable timepiece that he had left behind, *wouldn't want to give the wrong impression.* She thought back to their first encounter when he served her drinks across a trestle table at the party after the 'New Math' conference at Sussex University where she'd been invited as a guest speaker. She remembered his arms, dark with the trace of bluish veins and his hairy maleness. She pictured too his brilliant blue eyes, and the laughing quizzicality that she'd found so hard to resist; at least, for the first night.

Cute . . . damn cute. But just not right . . . and I bet he left that watch on purpose. The last thing I need right now is someone clingy.

'Especially if I'm goddam pregnant,' she added out loud, feeling a stab of concern at the memory of the broken condom revealed when the spent Kim Zazie had rolled off her.

She sighed, confused by the sense of gathering pace in her life, and an unfamiliar instability. *Must get a grip . . .* she admonished herself, strolling into the kitchen *. . . must get back to work. A bit more on the Modular Form proof then I'll go for a jog.*

She made a cup of tea, and sitting at the kitchen table, stroked the cat on her lap, while adding to her mental list - let Kim know she didn't want a relationship with him, stop thinking about Ian so much, start looking for another job, eat better - and see more of Nandini, the only real friend she had made since moving to Malvern, who had now left two messages in the last few days.

Suddenly aware of the tension in her jaw, Chris went to the airing cupboard and surveyed the innumerable bottles of tiny pills, each homeopathic remedy a memento to the minor complaints over the years. She eased the dropper from the darkened bottle of Rescue Remedy, feeling the reassuring drops of brandy underneath her tongue.

If only Grafton could see me now.

Chapter 14: elementary my dear doctor

(12.30 pm)

The sun had already passed its zenith when Chris pushed her chair back from the computer desk, changed into her running gear and after some dutiful stretching, launched herself through the door. She barely registered the man sitting in a car at the Wyche car park, as she turned in the other direction, taking the lower, more level path toward the southern end of the Malvern Hills. Before long her breathing regularised, the strumming of her feet settling her mind as she entered the woods below Pinnacle Hill.

A slight increase in concentration for the ascent and a freewheeling ease on the downhill sections disposed of the easy slopes for the first fifteen minutes of the run, before she burst onto the grey expanse of a second car park, a soulless wound in the dense green cover that had shrouded the track. There were just two cars parked there, one of them with the driver still seated behind the wheel and another man behind him. A trace of concern troubled her but was quickly dismissed as Chris sped across the tarmac to resume the slight rise of the winding pathway on the other side. The obelisk, a whimsical folly from a minor nineteenth century aristocrat beckoned in the distance.

Men, she thought, a ripple of amusement on her lips.

Before her were the huge concentric undulations of the Stone Age fort known as British Camp that ringed the hill at the apparent end of the Malverns.

People have lived here since before history . . . Comforted by the sight of the flowing earth sculptures, the idea lessened her anxieties, as if they were no longer hers alone but shared with the unseen community of past lives, and she could rely upon not just her personal strength to face the difficulties in her life but also the resilience of the human spirit emanating from the hills themselves . . . *but the Malverns have always been here. Always changing, always the same – the archetypal 'process'.*

With the cool of the breeze upon her skin, she felt a surge of happiness as like a meditation, the rhythm of running dispersed the chatter, leaving her mind as little more than a monitor to maintain equilibrium in her body, now sensed as a machine, an automaton, powering through the landscape. *I'm going well,* she decided, relaxing into the simple joy of being, and the chance once more to think without distraction about her latest paper, 'Physics as a Complex System'.

'Process and function . . .' she said out loud to herself, '. . . must make . . . more of that,' grabbing the words between breaths, each syllable timed to coincide with the rhythm of her running. *So much more useful than 'objects and form'.*

As she ran, gaps in the trees revealed the pretty fields, coppiced woods and farms of the Herefordshire countryside, stranded by history as if in tribute to a simpler time and a different way, like limpets in an ebbing tide which cling to the rocks and remember what was. Along the indigo swath of the horizon she could just make out the Welsh mountains, spot lit with occasional beams of light piercing the white and grey of clustering clouds.

Chris was sweating freely, but slowing noticeably with the sudden gradient. She would be struggling by the time she passed the bench at its summit, where a man in a grey suit was seated, looking across at the view before he suddenly turned and looked down at her. Unusually, she decided to turn round and avoid the unequal encounter with the stranger.

As she turned she saw someone else, a stocky man with a slight limp, quickly ascending the slope toward her, and a third man following behind as he too, rapidly approached up the track. Her chest thumped with the immediate fear and the certainty of the hunted that this was not right, they were surely working together to corral her. *One above, two below.* She thought back to her self-defence course a year ago - *get away if you can, but kick if he makes a move, then run, and shout* - as she turned back up the hill to face what she prayed was the lesser threat, and the inevitable confrontation that awaited her.

Chapter 15: water works

(Nigeria)

The wing of the banking plane lowered to reveal the crenellated skyline of Lagos city-centre receding into the distance and Magnus felt himself relax for the first time in twelve hours, relieved he would soon be back in the USA.

The rest of the PORTAL delegation had flown out two days before, frustrated by the outcome of their week-long negotiations to provide investment funds for a State Water Board project to build a new water purification facility in Nigeria, the second such scheme they had planned in Africa. PORTAL had been successfully opposed by a Dr Okeke, a board member who had argued persuasively that funding would be preferable from the World Bank rather than an American-based private fund, and had convinced his colleagues to delay further consideration of the deal with PORTAL for at least another twelve months.

Assigned the task of resolving this impasse, Magnus had arrived in Nigeria three days ago. It was his first solo assignment and he had planned it well, researching his target carefully. Magnus had learnt that Dr Okeke was an ascetic man with a gourmet's appreciation of quality over quantity in his cuisine and that he lived alone, but was visited six days of the week by a maid servant who cooked and kept house for him. Magnus called round to visit Dr Okeke at six o'clock in the evening of the maid servant's day off, and introduced himself before asking if he could be allowed to argue the case for acceptance of PORTAL'S manifesto. The Doctor had been reluctant to let him in, but Magnus put a proposition to him that was as unusual as it was appealing.

Walking in the local market, Magnus had noted that cod was routinely imported into Nigeria from Norway, and had brought 500 grams of the fish with him which he showed the doctor, explaining he wanted to cook him a meal of cod, using a traditional Icelandic recipe he had learnt from his mother.

The young man's charm and vivacity, and the prospect of a gourmet feast rather than the cold meal that had been left for him, persuaded Dr Okeke to accept the young man's offer, and the Doctor had stood back from the door and allowed him entry.

All had run smoothly for Magnus as he prepared the meal until, to his surprise, the maid servant entered the kitchen at the very moment that Magnus was shaking the white powder of tetrodotoxin poison into one of the fish meals. Refusing to be thrown off course by the interruption, Magnus asked her calmly why she was there on what he understood was her day off. She explained that because the doctor didn't cook for himself, he had phoned her to tell her that Magnus had visited and to ask her to switch her day off and come round immediately to learn the recipe on his behalf. Seeing Magnus had already started on the preparation of the food she apologized for being late.

'What's that you've added to the meal,' she had asked, pointing toward the small bottle that Magnus had just set down on the bench.

Staring dreamily from the plane window at the lights reflected in the black water of the lagoon next to the diminishing speck of the airport, Magnus replayed the incident in his mind. *Interfering bitch . . .* he thought . . . *it was her own fault.*

'Actually it's a poison extracted from the puffer fish - also known as 'zombie powder' - a type of neurotoxin with no antidote - part of my travel kit,' Magnus had replied, the broad smile on his face confusing the girl, who assumed she had either misunderstood him or he was joking. 'Here, see for yourself,' he invited, gesturing toward the container.

As she turned away from him to pick up the phial Magnus quickly reached out and gripped her with his arm so her throat rested firmly in the bend of his elbow, which he progressively tightened around her neck, locking his arm by pulling his hand closer to him. Unable to make a sound, she was unconscious in just ten seconds. He bound, gagged her, and tied her quickly to the kitchen table.

Magnus re-joined the doctor in the dining room and told him that the girl having been shown the recipe, had left for the night and though the Doctor was surprised she hadn't said goodnight as was her custom, he accepted Magnus' explanation that she'd wished to avoid disturbing them. Magnus served the poisoned meal to the Doctor and taking his seat opposite him, started to eat the other dish whilst engaging the doctor in conversation.

'And how are you enjoying your fish?' Magnus enquired when he noticed the doctor flexing his fingers as if in some discomfort.

'Very much thank you,' replied the doctor, though I fear I may be allergic to the dressing you have used - I have a tingling in my hands.'

Magnus explained his recipe in detail, assuring the doctor that there was nothing he could think of that would induce allergy, but the doctor suddenly interrupted to complain he was now finding it very painful to move and was extremely concerned that it must relate to something in the meal, asking Magnus to fetch his bag from the surgery. Magnus suggested that first the Doctor extend his hands so Magnus could look at them. The Doctor held out his hands with difficulty. Magnus grinned at him, then reached out and swiftly encircled the Doctor's hands with a thin cord he had concealed in his clenched fist before pushing the doctor violently so as he fell to the floor. Magnus bound him with more cord and when he was satisfied the Doctor was immobilized, hauled him back onto the chair and tied him to it.

'Still a bit of wiggle in your fingers Doctor – enjoy it while you can,' he had said, patting Okeke on the cheeks before seizing a napkin from the table and stuffing it brutally into the doctor's mouth.

Magnus returned to the kitchen quietly, observing the girl from behind a bench. She was conscious and completely silent, as if against the odds the only strategy available to her - hiding - might somehow work. When she saw Magnus, she started to struggle furiously, kicking out and twisting so as her legs were between them, ready to strike at him if he approached. Magnus sneered and strode toward her, sweeping her legs aside contemptuously, and delivering a violent slap across her face.

It was enough - she gave up her struggle, as if resigned to her part in the script that Magnus had written and with no-one to appeal to, unable to find the strength for even token resistance. Magnus carried her into the room where she could be seen by the doctor. When he saw what was happening Okeke started a fearful grunting, his eyes bulging in terror and beads of sweat standing out on his forehead, as he struggled unsuccessfully to regain movement in his limbs.

The girl looked across at Okeke without expression, her will now so broken she seemed almost cooperative with Magnus as he carefully, in a cruel parody of tenderness, pulled up her skirt to expose her naked legs. Removing his trousers and underwear he lay with her, with her neck cradled in his arm to control the flow of blood through the girl's carotid artery. Magnus gazed intently at her, keeping her on the border of consciousness until her breathing became more urgent and her mouth moved as if to frame some communication. Magnus eased the pressure on her neck and transferred his hand to grip himself, hard. He allowed her one word, 'Please . . .' then strangled her to death, timing the moment the spark of life was extinguished to coincide with his own orgasm.

Magnus carefully wiped away the tears that had formed in her eyes and retrieving the phial from his pocket, sprinkled some of the poison on her hands. He removed her binding and the gag, and dragged her over to the doctor to slash the doctor's face with her left hand, taking care the fingernails grazed the doctor's skin. Magnus dumped the girl at his feet before he untied the doctor, who was now close to death, and lowered him carefully to the floor next to her. By adjusting the doctor's arms, Magnus managed to lock Okeke's paralyzed hands around the girl's throat until the marks from his fingers were visible around her neck. Then he released Okeke who slumped in a heap next to the girl, confident that it would look as if the doctor had managed to strangle the girl before the poison she had administered rendered him completely immobile.

Magnus had cleaned up as carefully as he could, wanting to show respect for the situation; wanting everyone to play their part. He suspected if the police were any good they would be able to find evidence to link him with the scene, but not enough to convict him of the murders. *I'll be long gone.*, he grinned to himself. *Maybe now these people will understand we are serious.*

Magnus had walked back to his hotel before catching the flight to Los Angeles just a few hours later. Now he pressed the button to order another drink, looking back down the aisle to check how the stewardess was progressing. He was lucky. He smiled with the deep satisfaction available to only a privileged few, savouring the certainty that with his posting to PORTAL's Clean Team, as his new posting was known, he had found his chosen path.

Lífið er gott, he smiled to himself. *Já, lífið er gott.*

Chapter 16: sweater

(2:15 am)

'Dr Reynolds. Please . . . don't be alarmed, we mean you no harm. I am a minister of the Church,' came the shout from the seated man, now rising to greet her.

What the fuck . . . how does he know my name?

'What do you want?' she demanded, aware of a different urgency in the pounding of her heart. 'Who are you, where are you from?' At first, she hardly recognized her voice, it sounded too much, too pleading, the voice of fear.

'I am Saul Baedeker from the Parish of Reason Truth and Love. We are known as PORTAL. This is my driver Aziz, and my assistant Clinton - and I want to talk to you about God.'

'About God! I think you've mistaken me for someone else. I don't have a god.' Baedeker was rapidly closing the distance between them. 'Or know anything about . . . Her,' Chris added aloud, thinking at the last moment to throw in at least a token of her own power, though this didn't sound quite right either.

'Well you and I agree God is no longer a 'him', so there's a start, but I would wish to go a little further than just a gender change.' Baedeker chortled in appreciation of his own joke, his perfect teeth displayed like an orthodontist's dummy, then, with a smile of genuine warmth on his face, he gestured to the bench behind him. 'Rest for a moment while Aziz brings up a towel.' Not pausing for a reply Baedeker continued. 'The old anthropomorphic notion of God is really too primitive to be tenable any longer. We know your work. I believe we have more in common than you might imagine.'

Chris ignored his invitation to sit. 'What do you know of my work?' she demanded angrily.

'You see we are a modern Church and we have a scientific outlook to our faith,' continued Baedeker. 'We have followed Dr Lineker's papers - with difficulty I may add, they are not widely published - and believe that you have a theory which confirms our view that the ultimate nature of reality is in effect the mind of God - God is in everything. You have a scientific formulation that could be very useful to us.'

'Whoa, hold on here,' protested Chris.

'Would you like this Miss?' Aziz was handing her a towel, distracting her.

'Err, thanks,' she said, suddenly aware that Aziz was staring at her. She was used to the attention of men, and normally dressed to discourage it, but her tight running shirt, wet with sweat, and her lycra tights made her feel vulnerable. Chris glared at him with the exaggerated disapproval of schoolyard outrage, and he looked away. She immediately felt a softening of her anger and studied Aziz carefully to check whether the sense of familiarity meant they had met before. Unable to place him, she turned back to Baedeker.

'There aren't many who have read our work, I'll give you that.' The information had aroused her curiosity, and reassured her that this encounter was unlikely to be dangerous. 'But you must understand that a religious interpretation is not what we're about at all. We've taken a quantum mechanical formalism and introduced a reiteration of a randomly introduced variable. We're trying to reproduce complexity from very simple relationships with very few axioms, rather than start with complexity and understand it by breaking it down into components.'

'I see . . .' said Baedeker, supercilious patience written across his features.

'Rather than using a line, 'time' is represented much more as we actually experience it, with a 'now', and an uncertain 'future' and a known 'past.'' Chris was becoming more animated, her enthusiasm for the new physics replacing her initial anxieties. 'It's true if you represent the model graphically it maps a network of nodes and connections that has parallels with a neural network, but we're scientists not theologists.'

'That's wonderful Dr Reynolds. I won't pretend I have a clue what you're talking about but I'm very happy you're taking care of the details. We each have a role to play. It's the 'neural type network', or 'brain pattern' we would call it, that has caught our attention. To me it implies everything has a degree of consciousness; and if the deepest level of reality is structured like a mind, from which everything else emerges, then I am happy to give that mind the label 'God.''

'Well . . . that's a conversation we can have . . . but this is Ian Lineker's baby - not mine,' protested Chris. The word 'baby' stopped her for a moment, aware of its resonance, and the possibility she might be pregnant. 'I'm just his number cruncher,' she resumed more quietly. 'It's not a trivial task producing testable outcomes with a new paradigm, but he's the brains behind all this. Why aren't you talking to him anyway . . . and why didn't you phone?' she asked, her anger building again. 'You scared the bejesus out of me.' She faltered briefly, thinking she should make some concessions to the sensibilities of a man of God. 'I mean, you scared the hell out of me'.

'I think perhaps you underestimate your own contribution Dr Reynolds,' replied Baedeker soothingly. 'As to why I didn't phone - there's no privacy in modern communications as you will know, and I like to experience directly what I term the 'aura' of my associates. We are a media type organisation. You would be a more amenable public face for PORTAL.com than a fifty-year old scientist in a baggy jumper. Dr Lineker could appeal to a particular demographic but our research suggests that . . .'

'Stop right there,' interrupted Chris, her expression leaving no doubt that this time Baedeker had gone too far, 'I gave him that jumper.'

Chapter 17: payoff

(2:45 pm)

'We live in interesting times, Ian,' Chris said over the phone, *her* long legs draped over one end of a settee, and a towel wrapped over her shoulders to support her neck. Her running vest was wet with the sweat that had pooled between her breasts and was now spilling with an imperceptible flow to collect again in her bellybutton.

'Tell me about it,' he replied.

'I'd rather do that in person if you don't mind. We've been invited to a presentation at Llanthony Priory hotel at four pm so it's a bit rushed. I can pick you up in thirty minutes.'

'That's very little notice Chris. I'm still working on a report for Grafton. Making it punchier, taking out the more radical interpretations, emphasising the potential for commercials spin-offs . . .'

'Ian - listen - this is something else. I've met some people who are going to make Grafton history. It's a Church.'

'A what?'

'A Church.'

'As in cathedral?' he asked.

'No - as in internet.'

'Sorry Chris, I'm not with you at all.'

'I'll see you in a bit, Ian. Just trust me on this.'

'Hang on. You do realize Llanthony Priory is a three-hour drive at least. No way can we make it by four pm.'

'They're sending a helicopter for us.'

'A helicopter?'

'Yes a helicopter. The Church people - the internet Church people. They believe we can help them with a formulation of God, and they're talking about funding our research which they say suggests an ontology that they find convincing.'

There was a pause, slightly too long to be natural, before Lineker spoke.

'Do you know Chris, recently I've been starting to feel just a bit . . . old almost.' His tone had changed. 'Confused by things.'

For a moment, it fooled her.

'Don't worry you poor old sod. Pack enough for an overnighter, and I'll look after you,' she laughed, the beading sweat gently coalescing into a tiny rivulet that trickled across her belly to etch a glinting trail on the inside of her thigh.

'Just lie back and enjoy it'.

Chapter 18: three's a crowd
(4.00 pm)

Chris was staring through thick Plexiglas at the tessellated regularity of rural England when her daydreaming was interrupted as the neatness of the green pastures gave way to the tussocky summit of Hatterall Hill just west of Offa's Dyke - the mediaeval border between Anglian Mercia and Welsh Powys. Far below she saw three men jump from a landed helicopter and scurry toward the ruins of Llanthony Priory, its moss-softened arches more closely resembling the giant ribs of a dinosaur than any possible habitation of man. A sudden change in the thwacking rhythm of the rotors above her announced the start of their own chopper's gradual descent as it circled slowly, to land with a jolt beside its parked twin.

Chris shielded her eyes from the lowering sun, squinting at the remains of the nave and the picturesque hotel which emerged from the relics, as if the living present had been grafted onto the bones of prehistory. By the time she and Ian had clambered out of the helicopter, Baedeker was striding towards them across shadows that mapped the outline of the priory onto a closely-manicured lawn.

'Dr Lineker - welcome to Llanthony Hotel - I'm Baedeker. Call me Saul. Very privileged to meet you.' Baedeker's arm was outstretched in greeting. 'Come in, come in. We've booked the place for the weekend, so make yourself at home. This is a wonderful chance for us all to get acquainted.'

'Oh, . . . look . . . great to be here. Very pleased to meet you too,' Lineker replied, shaking the offered hand.

'And the lovely Dr Reynolds - what a pleasure to meet again,' Baedeker said addressing Chris, before indicating to Clinton to deal with the luggage that the pilot was lifting from the nearer of the two machines crouched bug-eyed like dragonflies resting in the last warmth of the late afternoon.

'Lovely Dr Reynolds' is it, she mused, recognizing this was not an ideal beginning.

As Baedeker turned away, Lineker looked tentatively across at Chris. She smiled and this time, it was she who winked at him. He smiled back, then declining the offer of help, turned to stroll toward the helicopter and collect their luggage himself.

Breathing deep of the country air and loving the bustle and excitement of their glamorous arrival, Chris felt good again, basking in the feeling that life could deliver the unexpected, and the novelty of unearned good fortune. The sun was warm on her back, comforting, sensual. She glanced at Baedeker, acknowledging his showy charisma, his calmness and the air of authority that wealth and its grooming can bestow. From the corner of her eye, she saw that Aziz was looking in her direction, but he quickly looked away.

Has he been staring at me again?

She had not thought of him that way before, but now she felt a tingle of pleasure.

Tough guy, she thought, *mm . . . interesting.*

In a display of female sexiness as fleeting as it was spontaneous, she slightly arched her back and hoisted her jeans a little higher so as the material would cling more tightly to her shape. But her attention settled on Ian, now returned with the bags. Tall and lean, his stubbly jaw and his face lined with the sun from another hemisphere, he was looking at Baedeker with a boyish curiosity and the generous smile characteristic of so many Antipodeans. She felt a surge of compassion for him, for his modesty and immediacy. But there was another strand of feeling mixed with the familiar sense of admiration - she wanted to hug him, feel the hardness of his body, kiss him, know his response.

'A penny for your thoughts, Chris?' asked Lineker as the helicopter that had brought them there curved up into the sky with a clattering crescendo and disappeared over the rounded top of the great hill behind them.

'I think you can get a much better offer than a penny,' said Baedeker, smiling. 'Have you been here before?'

'Actually, I have,' Chris replied. 'When I was a student I came here with my boyfriend. We camped in the field for a few days. I remember a cow tried to eat the end of the tent and frightened the . . .' she paused, searching for an acceptable expression, 'bejesus . . . out of us.'

A flicker crossed Baedeker's face.

'We treated ourselves to one night in the hotel, I remember the tower and the four-poster bed.' Chris also remembered, but omitted to mention, how good, and bad it had been. How she and her boyfriend had walked and had sex on the hill. How they had come back, drunk a little too much then gone to bed early for more greedy lovemaking. She remembered, guiltily, the sense of a missed opportunity that he had not been more forceful, and how her frustration had turned to irritation with him. She had ended the relationship shortly after returning to Sussex. 'The joys of youth,' she said.

'And the follies,' added Baedeker as if he had read her mind. Ian gave a strange unconvincing laugh, as if preoccupied with something. She offered him a questioning smile, but he averted his gaze, and her heart gave a skip of joy, suspecting that for her boss too, their relationship enjoyed more than merely a professional tension.

I'll bet he's thinking of the four poster, she smiled to herself, imagining the possibilities, and feeling the quickening inside.

Chapter 19: pearls of wisdom

(4.*10* pm)

They descended the concave steps, as countless travellers had before them, into what was now the bar of the Llanthony Priory Hotel. Brass pots on the thick stone walls, old landscape pictures and striking modern photographs in black and white punctuated the matt texture of layered whitewash, brilliant against the blackened wood of the flooring. Solid oak tables and chairs had been arranged as if for a conference, with glasses and bottles of mineral water next to writing pads and expensive pens, carefully presented to greet them.

'I love this place,' Baedeker said waving them in. 'It's what we lack in the New World, don't you agree Dr Lineker? The very ancient, a bedrock to our culture.'

'Well yes,' Ian replied, 'though of course in Oz we have aboriginal relics that are 35,000 years old.'

'Of course, of course,' replied Baedeker dismissively. 'Mankind, though a very recent species, has left evidence of its activities in many places. I was speaking of our own ethnicity, and I think you will concede how much more rewarding is say, Stonehenge, than a bunch of stone shards in an outback paddock.'

'Well, the Aboriginals had no need of developed technology. They were able to sustain life without sophisticated tools, living off the bounty of the land itself, but they did have a highly developed society,' Lineker smiled.

'Yes, yes. The pearl is created in transformation of discomfort that is true. No challenges may have generated no impetus for innovation or civilisation. Let us just note there were far fewer Aboriginals than would populate even a medium sized city these days so there was precious little society to 'develop'. But your point about sustainability introduces a topic of overwhelming interest to me, that I had intended to discuss at the end of a presentation I have arranged. However, now is as good a time as any, and it will set the context for what I hope will be your contribution to our mission.'

Lineker and Reynolds were concentrating now. What did this unusual man want with them?

'What would you say Dr Lineker is the biggest challenge facing humankind today?' asked Baedeker.

'I'm tempted to say dishonesty in science, but maybe I'd be grinding too personal an axe,' laughed Lineker. 'I imagine it would have to be climate change. Or famine and poverty - the inequitable distribution of wealth in the world.'

'And you Dr Reynolds, what would you say?'

'You could add lack of education for women, lack of clean drinking water for many. I don't know, I'm sure it depends on your perspective. Transitioning away from oil, obsession with growth. You could sum it up as human greed. Where does one end?'

'Very good, Dr Reynolds. Your thinking mirrors much of my own. I agree with both of you but would suggest there is one factor underpinning every one of the concerns you have itemized.' Baedeker paused for effect. 'The human population of the world is grotesquely out of balance with the resources needed to sustain its lifestyle. All the other problems flow from that simple and awful fact, even one might argue, the harm that emanates from human greed.'

'Well yes,' said Reynolds. 'But what of the argument that if there were not corrupt governments then it would be possible to feed an even bigger population than we have now? And an economy not based on growth could be sustainable.'

'A population that was four billion 35 years ago, and is already closing on twice that now. So, change human nature and we can fit another few billion on the planet is that the answer?' said Baedeker calmly. 'And what happens in another 35 years do you imagine, even if the population numbers level off? The problems you cite have acquired a catastrophic momentum.'

'I think we're in for disruptions of the current status quo,' said Lineker. 'But how to deal with it, I really don't know.'

'We at PORTAL.com do have a plan to 'deal with it',' said Baedeker portentously. 'I agree we are heading for major upheavals as competition for water, food and land intensifies. Unless that is, we take immediate and effective action. This is partly why you are here.' Baedeker was strolling about the room, relaxed and at ease. 'I want you both to work for our 'Truth' division. I see your work as vital in informing the consensus in society.'

'Truth division? Doing what exactly?' asked Chris, her voice uneven with concern.

'Let me explain. A new world will need a new ethics,' continued Baedeker. 'For instance, certain universal assertions about the sanctity of life must now be qualified.'

'Surely any notion that life is not sacred is a very slippery slope,' began Ian tentatively.

'And I don't quite see which problem you will be addressing or what we can do to help?' continued Chris.

'Human beings are overrunning the planet. Something must be done before there is an apocalypse of horror. We at PORTAL have found a way - an obvious way - birth control.'

'Aren't there already programs to promote that?' started Lineker, exchanging a glance with Chris.

'We plan several initiatives beyond the conventional approaches. It will all become very clear in my presentation. Why don't the two of you take a little while to refresh and I'll see you down here in, say, half an hour or thereabouts. Just bear in mind what we're talking about here.' Baedeker laughed as if sharing a joke that he was enjoying.

'We humans have become vermin. We are now a verminous species, Dr Lineker.'

The laughter vanished as suddenly as it had appeared. Baedeker stared impassively at Lineker before turning to approach Chris. 'Tragic but true.'

His face now only inches from hers, Baedeker's delivery was so emphatic he almost spat the words. 'Vermin, Dr Reynolds. Vermin.'

Chapter 20: hard graft

(4.30 pm)

Dr Grafton's life seemed shrouded by trouble. He had been given financial targets that would require the closure of at least two of the RMI's six programs, unless someone came up with a serious money-earner on a par with the world-changing discovery of radar in their predecessor organisation, some seventy years previously.

Less likely than winning the Euro lottery, thought Grafton, staring at the neat lines of books covering the wall while he fiddled with one of the pens arranged with clinical precision on the desk at which he was seated. The more he had investigated Lineker's project after the meeting, the more his confidence in his management team had been eroded, though a quick look at the background papers had given him a begrudging admiration for not only Chris' mathematics, but the scope of Lineker's theory too.

If only it were right, the guy would win a Nobel prize.

Grafton was troubled by his reaction to Lineker. Even if he was deluded, the Australian was clearly very clever, but with his easy going nature and his athletic physique - Lineker just riled him. Grafton was sixty-two, lived comfortably, and was widely respected in the scientific community, though his role for the last twenty years or so had been as a manager and administrator. His training in Mathematics and Statistics at Oxford had by chance found an unusual application early in his career, when he contributed to development of an epidemiological model on the spread of foot and mouth disease in cattle. It had not sounded glamorous, but it had been exciting work. For several heady weeks, during a terrible outbreak of the disease across the UK, he'd been a media star, a status that had culminated in his election as a Fellow of the Royal Society and given him a taste for celebrity that these days found fulfilment on the local radio station HW758, where he was occasionally invited to comment on science issues as the resident expert.

There was the more complicated issue of Dr Reynolds. Grafton was attracted to her, captivated by the contrast between a sexuality that her business suits could only partially disguise, and her confident efficiency in a world he had always associated with men. With little experience of women, it never occurred to Grafton that Chris's life might be less straightforward than she made it appear, so he concluded that she had fulfilled her potential in a way that had always eluded him; and he resented her for it. There was no refuge for him even in the possibility of claiming any intellectual superiority. Her career had been more distinguished than his, and was of far greater contemporary relevance. She was brilliantly gifted, he could see that, startling the world of mathematics when four years earlier she had reportedly adapted Perelman's proof of the Poincare conjecture, and applied it to a Mobius strip, a novelty that had excited string theorists across the globe and seen her profiled in New Scientist as 'a face of the future'. Grafton no longer had the energy, or the time, to closely follow 'new science', his time was more than taken up with managerial responsibilities, and he resented the thought of his own professional disaffection, in contrast to the enthusiasm of Lineker and Reynolds.

During his lunch break ten minutes later, Grafton was absent-mindedly surfing eBay looking at model airplanes and wondering how best to break the news to his wife if he were to buy the latest aircraft that had caught his attention. Not that it was an issue of money, just of how to deflect or tolerate the inevitable scorn that the purchase would attract when added to his existing collection of fourteen models, which had already displaced the cars from the garage. When the phone rang Dr Grafton felt the usual wash of panic - he did not expect the call to bring good news. These days, it rarely did.

Chapter 21: russian roulette

(4.35 pm)

'Dr Grafton?'

'Yes.'

'My name is Emelienko – You not know me - I represent SRS'

'SRS?'

'Society for Responsibility in Science,' came the heavily accented reply.

Oh dear . . .. 'Yes?' said Grafton cautiously.

'You have Dr Lineker working on Physics project?'

Oh Christ, thought Grafton, *this I do not need.* 'That's correct,' he said, keeping his voice as neutral as he could manage.

'We saw report - New Scientist. Science professors not believe you, yes? We find more papers, support your side better yes, . . . on MRI website.'

Shit, thought Grafton, his head sinking onto a hand for support. *I told Billings to make sure that stuff was removed from the website. SRS - why have I never heard of these people?'*

'Very little informations, much more we have found on heresy.com,' Emelienko was continuing.

Jesus - heresy.com. What's that? Grafton's internal monologue was increasingly anxious. *'Who would put stuff on heresy.com?* He was thinking with a growing sense of panic how best to contain what he feared would become his public shaming.

'It is of course our policy here only to publish research once it has been thoroughly scrutinised in-house, and properly peer reviewed, as I'm sure you will appreciate. Any publication by 'heresy.com',' he made a guttural sound that was supposed to convey contempt, but was immediately concerned that it had simply made him sound afraid, 'is entirely without authority and is completely inappropriate at this stage.'

'Of course,' agreed Emelienko evenly. 'SRS only interested in truth too. We want encourage good science, deny to bad science.'

'Well look, you need have no disquiet about our rigour here in Malvern. All of our projects are subject to a procedure of continual review.' Grafton was speaking too quickly, too defensively.

'Very good Dr Grafton' replied Emelienko smoothly. 'What review you have in mind for this physics?'

'Well, I think it's no secret that I myself am sceptical of some of the theoretical assumptions that Dr Lineker has made. Of course all this will be closely scrutinized by a committee, but my initial feeling is that the project is unsuitable for us here at MRI. Look . . . I'm sorry . . . but who did you say you represent again?'

'Ah . . . interesting . . .' said Emelienko, ignoring the question. There was a short pause, as if he was considering the information. 'I not know how you thinking before. Good we speak. Easy for both benefit. I want purchase rights for Process Physics'

'What on earth!' replied Grafton involuntarily, trying frantically to assimilate what he was hearing. 'Well, I will have to evaluate the implications of all this . . . I'm not at all sure what you mean by 'purchase rights' . . . of course I can make no guarantees of anything at this stage, but . . . well . . . did you mention what sort of figure you have in mind?' he asked tentatively.

'Three million pounds - if everybody in research sign secrecy covenant,' replied Emelienko.

'Three million pounds? Three million for Lineker's . . .' blurted Grafton suppressing the word 'bullshit' just in time. 'Who did you say you are . . . and why on earth, may I ask, would you be so interested in Process Physics, which you have just implied is bad science? Is this some sort of joke?'

'No joke. Your opinions not mine Doctor. I have no opinion with bad science,' Emelienko sounded impatient. 'We have client. Client wants control timing informations for this science. They want such informations, only accurate informations.'

'Okay,' said Grafton his mind racing, 'and do you mind me asking who your client is?'

'You can ask but I no tell you. Even I not know.'

'Are you serious? How can MRI possibly do business with someone when we don't even know who they are,' spluttered Grafton, his instinct for bureaucratic closure rising to the fore, and his ingrained respect for authority sounding every alarm bell in a fluster of fresh anxiety.

'You might be engaged by Iran or Korea or the Russian mafia . . .' Grafton's voice tailed off as it occurred to him that he might have stumbled on the truth and that Emelienko might not be the sort of academic or bureaucrat he was used to dealing with. 'Or anyone,' he added lamely. He pulled at his tie to loosen the neck, feeling the sweat start under his shirt.

'Tell me Doctor. You look into SRS if you want. You know background everyone you deal with? I offer three million to avoid - how you English say - 'rock the boat'. You negotiate make everyone happy. I was authorised to pay more. You try to shut anyway. The three million is all you get now.'

'Higher than three million,' gasped Grafton. 'I don't understand. Are you trying to bribe us?' he was careful this time to present a collective face.

'Official deal only. Lawyers must agree. Must clarify intellectual property copyright,' continued Emelienko his voice now icily controlled. 'Three million is limit. We pay to own research. This not game - my client powerful people. You have 24 hours, then tell your decisions. I email you details now. Have nice day, Dr Grafton.'

Grafton stared at the receiver, listening vacantly to the dial tone that had replaced the stilted voice that Grafton was sure had sounded Russian. He tried to collect his thoughts rationally. Was that a threat? The three million sounded like a preposterous offer, and therefore must be a hoax. Who would even think to play such a prank? Lineker and Reynolds were the most probable candidates - perhaps trying to gauge the future of their Process Physics obsession. Had he given too much away, been too indiscreet too early?

On the other hand: If this offer were real, and there had been a serious tone about Emelienko that made it difficult to dismiss without at least investigation, then selling the whole thing for someone else to worry about would solve many of his problems in one go - he would be hailed as a hero at MRI and with that much money available, his life would definitely become easier. He would surely be able to negotiate a better employment package for himself, perhaps even retire early, without compromising his integrity by directly accepting anything that might be construed as a bribe.

Either way, Lineker is key to all this, he reminded himself with annoyance, as he started typing SRS into google with one hand and reached for the phone with the other.

Chapter 22: publish and be damned

(4.40 pm)

Lineker had just concluded the conversation with an agitated Grafton over his satellite phone when there was a tap on the door. 'Come on in,' he shouted.

Chris entered breezily. 'I was studying the spiral carving on the wooden bed posts and it made me think of the space flow vorticity in our new gravity theory...' she began.

'Wow...' Lineker's exclamation had been involuntary. She was wearing a black muslin dress, so fine that against the light of the window that the curves of her figure were clearly visible through the sheer material. Her makeup was emphatic, just the respectable side of gaudy.

'I was just saying you need to look at this wood carving ...' her voice tailed off, realising the topic was now secondary.

'Looks like we're ready to meet the man,' Lineker resumed, a feeble smile betraying his attempt to disguise his surprise at seeing her in something other than the formal suits she favoured for work, or the jeans and baggy sweaters she normally wore for leisure.

She gave a mocking half curtsey, the coquettish subtext at odds with her normal demeanour. 'Ready ... yes,' she beamed, 'and willing.'

'Oh . . . right . . .' Lineker coughed to clear his throat, embarrassed, acknowledging the power of her sensuality, but also his own awkwardness in the no-man's land between the impetus of desire and the restraint of convention.

She could see his discomfort, and felt a flutter of panic in her belly at the possibility of ridicule, made worse by her own suspicion that her experiment with a new identity might be a mistake.

Am I being too much? she worried, flustering to backtrack to the more formal efficiency of their work time exchanges. 'Yes . . . I'm eager to see what our host has to say for himself,' she said, 'it should be interesting.'

'Absolutely.' Lineker laughed unconvincingly, clearly relieved to return to safer ground. 'Look, some interesting news. I've just had a call from Bill Grafton. He's found someone who may want to fund our project.'

'Really?' she paused. 'That's wonderful!'

'Well . . . it's all very vague,' he replied. 'Apparently there are issues about control of information or timing of publications and other stuff to be agreed, so I'm really not sure - but Grafton sounded very serious - as usual you might say.'

'Well, that's fantastic, amazing.' She paused. 'Who is it?'

'Something like Association for Responsibility in Science Education.'

She frowned. 'Ian. That spells ARSE - you're kidding right?'

'Sorry Chris, yeah, I'm kidding . . . couldn't resist it. It's SRS - Society for Responsibility in Science. To be honest I'm not taking any of this too seriously. Heard of them?' Lineker opened the wardrobe to retrieve his jacket.

'No,' she said. 'Sounds like the sort of people we need on our side though. I knew it could work out,' she added wistfully. 'I believe if you retain your integrity things will always work out.'

'Well, hopefully,' he agreed somewhat reluctantly, looking out of the window at a cow munching on the long grass, resigned to the company of a goose a few feet away from her head. 'But let's not celebrate till the money is in the bank. I'm afraid I told him if its censorship then basically, I'm not interested.'

'Censorship! Is that a note of cynicism I detect in your voice? she laughed.

'Maybe.'

'Well whatever - it's a beautiful evening and we're in Wales for the weekend!' Let's just enjoy ourselves . . . and worry about all this tomorrow.'

'You're right – we need a break.' Lineker was grinning back at her. 'Lay on McDuff,' he concluded.

'*McDuff* . . .?' she smiled to herself, believing she recognized the source of his animation. *So he is interested after all. I knew this dress was worth it.*

'I thank you, kind sir,' she said, accepting his invitation and exiting the door onto the landing. The combination of her high heels and the tower's narrow spiral staircase forced Chris to proceed cautiously. Disappointingly, she felt her mood change, as if somehow synchronized with the physical descent so that what had been cheerfulness was with every step, progressively replaced by apprehension. There had been an unsettling quality to Baedeker's zeal, and though her intuition could not foresee what awaited them, a strong sense of foreboding was warning her that any change was unlikely to be for the better.

Chapter 23: long division

(4.55 pm)

'Ah - The good doctors. Come on in.' said Baedeker as they pushed open the heavy oak door to the great hall on the ground floor, 'You look absolutely stunning Dr Reynolds if I may say so.'

Chris felt a flush of pleasure at the compliment, and an irritation with her own gullibility in being so easily charmed. But this time, she knew his flattery was more than merely routine.

'You're too kind, I'm sure,' she replied, amused by the Edwardian Englishness of her response, something she assumed was a balancing reaction to the brash self-confidence of this forceful American.

'Clinton has put together a short introduction for your benefit,' continued Baedeker. 'I believe if you know who we are and something of our aims, it will make much more sense to you when I explain how you can help our organisation.' Baedeker was beaming at them, his hands clasped together in front of his chest. 'I have asked Mr Aziz, my driver, to sit in with us too, as part of his own induction program' As if to invite him into the conversation Baedeker gestured toward Aziz, who was seated at the bar, staring into a half-full glass of beer. 'We haven't discussed it yet, but I'm sure Mr Aziz won't mind me telling you: he is being considered for a task that is a better fit with his natural abilities.'

Chris smiled at Aziz as he looked up. Clearly embarrassed, Aziz waved back in an exaggerated parody of greeting. He was in luck. Chris sensing the origin of his clumsiness, recognized the subtly miscued mimicry as the strategy an adolescent might employ who whilst seeking to disown his reaction, at the same time yearns to be understood.

She tossed her hair back with one hand, surprised that something about Aziz made her feel different, an unfamiliar lightness she could not explain. *Must stop acting so . . . girly, when he's around,* she thought, watching the two men as Ian reached out to shake Aziz's hand.

'Then dinner . . . later,' continued Baedeker. 'I discovered my chef in Bedarra - in your neck of the woods Dr Lineker I believe. He's been with me ever since.'

'Not really my scene I'm afraid. I grew up in outback Queensland but haven't lived there for over thirty years now. Tropical island resorts were never quite my thing.'

'Ah yes, always the dedicated professional. Well perhaps we can help you there. You see, for us, money is the earthly route to God's will, a facilitating energy, a tool to accomplish a task. Speaking of which, I wonder would you and Dr Reynolds be interested in a starting package of, say, twice your current remuneration to join us? Perhaps then, you too could occasionally enjoy the delights of a tropical hideaway.' He laughed, cheerily; the sort of laugh that left his audience unclear if they were listening to an unusually nice guy, or just an unusual guy.

On hearing the money offer, Lineker, sucking his lower lip into his mouth and frowning, looked questioningly across at Reynolds. Her eyebrows were raised, her cheeks slightly indented from a gentle inhalation. She was staring pointedly downwards, as if aligning her nose with Baedeker's feet in a studied emulation of indifference. She looked up suddenly and gave Lineker a flashing smile of such brilliance and warmth, Lineker's head jerked back slightly as if in surprise, before he beamed back at her as they took the seats that Clinton had arranged for them.

So confident was he that his offer would impress, Baedeker took no interest in their reaction and looking to his assistant clicked his fingers, like a magician at the start of an act. A screen slid down automatically at one end of the far wall of the cellar-like room.

'Think of how film is immeasurably advanced compared to the parchment and quills used by the men who built this ancient chamber,' announced Baedeker grandly. 'The presence of the Church you are about to encounter is even closer to God than was ever attained by the worship once practiced in those mediaeval ruins outside. Clinton - you may start.'

To the stirring crescendo of Wagner, the screen lit with close-up images of smiling faces, youthful and vigorous, alternating with scenes of crowds roaring approval at a silhouetted image of a lone figure in the distance, the logo PORTAL displayed in gold, before the image suddenly shattered into a cascade of shimmering lights.

The light receded leaving the man viewed from behind. 'We are the way, we are chosen, we are as one. Our time is now, we are the moment, we are forever,' he shouted as the camera zoomed toward him, his fist punching the air in a gesture of defiant victory.

The camera panned quickly closer to the figure, then circled around him to reveal the unmistakable face of Saul Baedeker. The 'blockbuster' narrator – his voice deep, relaxed, and calming - began with the history of the Church supported by a litany of statistics, emphasising how PORTAL had grown from a fundamentalist Christian brotherhood to a membership of 42 million. The voice-over detailed growth rate, countries of operation, monies given to charity and so on, all intercut with images of office-like glass buildings, with happy besuited staff smiling amicably in a fabulous display of immaculately whitened teeth and subtle tans.

Baedeker was shown greeting the US President visiting PORTAL HQ in California. A whistle-stop tour of several of the world's less well-known nations showed Baedeker equally relaxed with a succession of important-looking individuals introduced as presidents or prime-ministers, many in national dress against exotic backdrops of mountains, pastoral scenes or rural villages.

The mood suddenly switched. An organisation chart was thrown up with Baedeker explaining the church's five operational divisions; Word, Manna, Wellbeing, Transformation and Truth. As the narrator detailed the role of the 'Truth Division' and its responsibility for philosophy and research, Baedeker smiled at the scientists. 'This is your area,' he assured them. They nodded, grim-faced, discomforted at the improbability of the synthesised wholesomeness they were invited to admire.

The film ended with Baedeker extending his arms to the camera as it panned toward him. 'We are the Universe, God bless America, we are the One, God bless America, you are forgiven, come home, share the love. God bless America. God bless America.'

The closing shot zoomed forward to the scintillating azure of his eyes, framed by laughter lines that etched a filigree of humour and good nature in his handsome face.

Baedeker, the real-life Baedeker, was staring intently at the screen, his eyes moistening with emotion. Slowly he recovered himself and turning, reached out to Chris to grip her hands in his. 'Welcome to our world my child, welcome,' he said.

Chapter 24: iced tea

Lineker, sensing his turn was next, moved quickly away from Baedeker to lean on the bar next to Aziz. 'Well, that was . . . overwhelming,' commented Lineker loudly, breaking the mood with a tone that trod the dangerous border between jocular and sardonic.

'That's a normal reaction, first-time,' replied Baedeker, either unaware of or choosing to ignore, any suggestion of cynicism.

'You were saying we would be involved with the Truth Division, and that was somehow related to overpopulation. I'm afraid I'm not at all certain how we can assist,' said Chris, gently pulling her hands away from Baedeker's persistent grip.

'The Truth Division has several sections. We have theology and philosophy teams for example, but most of our funds go into practical research labs in areas like genetic modification, new virus vaccines, cyber networking and others, that may be of some use in the future.'

Lineker opened his mouth to interject but Baedeker gave no ground.

'Your research is more fundamental to us than a mere technology. We are a modern Church and I think you can give us the science to support what has been revealed to us spiritually. Imagine the benefits of kids being taught our truth in science lessons? It could chop a generation off our mission time.'

'But our work is not religious,' protested Lineker.

'Everything is religious Dr Lineker,' observed Baedeker smoothly. 'The classical expression of God as in some sense an entity presiding over his creation, is simply not palatable to the modern age. We believe God is everything, in everything and of everything. We think a key misunderstanding is the nature of time. We believe in God as 'now', the eternal moment. We can have heaven on earth now, rediscover Eden now. There is no need to wait.'

'Well it's true our work started by reformulating time away from a simple geometric time line . . .' started Lineker but Baedeker ignored him to continue.

'Your work representing reality as connectedness, the processes of interaction and relatedness as the building blocks of what is - that sounds right to us. Rationalism and science have destroyed much of value. There is no ethical base to society anymore. Your work could help us redress that.'

'You have to be cautious not to over-interpret a mathematical formulation as evidence of a physical reality,' insisted Chris.

'Exactly right, 'added Lineker, 'It's called 'misplaced concreteness."

'We are interested in a spiritual reality, not clumsy metaphors. Isn't a 'misplaced interpretation' as you suggest may happen - isn't that already happening? Isn't science the new religion?'

'Look, I'm no fan of what is happening to science at the moment . . . but . . .' began Lineker.

'All you need know is that your research can carry on unimpeded in the Truth Division.' Baedeker continued as if he had not heard the interruption. 'The Word Division would take your work and teach it.'

Baedeker gestured at the barman. "Iced hibiscus, please,' he ordered, turning away to continue the conversation and unaware of the apparent distress his impossible request had prompted.

'And the Well-Being division does what?' asked Chris gently, deciding it prudent to move the conversation along, concerned that Lineker might be heading for open confrontation with their host. She noticed Aziz, implacable at the bar. She was certain he had been watching her again.

'Well-Being looks at how we translate our insights into actions to solve the practical problems in society - they have just started a new Clean Team which is already reporting some success.'

'Problems like overpopulation,' suggested Chris.

'Exactly so and that is why we are here,' said Baedeker with a clipped emphasis. 'Let me show you another short film - it was developed as an internal training video but we find it serves as a very useful recruiting tool to put us all on the same wavelength in the shortest possible time - I think you'll find it a powerful piece of work.'

Chapter 25: rats

(5:30 pm)

The screen at the end of the room lit up again. This time it was Clinton who held centre-stage. He was shown in front of a clock, its hands pointing to noon. He suddenly yanked on one end of a large black cloth to reveal a cage of glass. Inside the cage was a miniature landscape of hills and flowing water, small toy houses grouped around a village pond, a kitsch rendering of English rural life as it might have looked centuries ago, in a re-creation of the idealised worlds of Constable or Gainsborough. There was however, a major difference between this scene and the world portrayed by the English Romantics. White rats were living in the cage, some feeding from troughs of pellets, others grooming themselves, some just sleeping. A counter next to the clock, the word 'Population' above it, showed the number 'thirty'.

Chris looked at Lineker anxiously. His returning half-smile offered little reassurance. Aziz, occasionally sipping at his beer glass, remained implacable in the background.

Clinton pressed a white button and a small hatch opened on the left of the cage, and two more rats appeared, sniffing tentatively as they inched forward into the playpen, waiting to be greeted by its occupants. The counter clicked over to 'thirty-two'. The picture dissolved to recommence with a close up of the clock, now showing '12:10'. When Clinton pressed the button again and four more rats appeared, the counter changed and the newcomers followed where the first couple had tentatively entered into the miniature country scene awaiting them. Two more activations of the shutter, at intervals the clock indicated to be of five minutes each with a doubling of the newcomers at each interval and the immigrant population already equalled the original population with the counter showing 'sixty'.

There were signs of tension in the cage. Squabbling amongst the rats occasionally erupted into briefly vicious fights as the agitated creatures roamed incessantly back and forth. At 12:30 on the clock, Clinton was shown pressing a black button next to the white button, and a large trap opened on the right of the cage. A boiling melee of black rats, spitting and snarling, burst into the cage as the counter sprang to 'one hundred and twenty'.

The effect was immediate and disastrous. There was an explosion of chaotic violence as the creatures tore at each other in a frenzy of panic and spontaneous fury. Blood spattered the walls as rats started to die, their contorted bodies heaping up on the floor of the cage. Clinton pressed a third button, and a white mist released from the ceiling of the chamber hissed gently down on the frantic rodents. They died quickly, a brief spasm prelude to a sudden seizured stillness. In a few tortured seconds, the mayhem was replaced with silence.

With a fourth button, the ceiling and the floor descended and the carnage was replaced from above with an exact replica, as the clock and counter reset to their starting values. The scene again revealed thirty rats in their playground, peacefully occupied in a life of apparent trouble-free leisure before the screen went blank.

'A wonderfully apt allegory for our times,' announced Baedeker. 'Don't you agree?'

'Absolutely not - those creatures suffered appallingly,' Chris remonstrated angrily. 'Surely there is a less cruel way to represent your point?'

'Shocking, I know,' said Baedeker 'But that precisely IS the point.'

Chapter 26: something in the water
(5:45 pm)

'There is no longer a 'business as usual',' said Baedeker. 'War, famine, poverty - we're not saying one cause is responsible for all of the current challenges to our world - but nothing can ease the situation as effectively as a drastic reduction in the population of the planet. We are in crisis not just as a culture - but as a species.'

'Surely, it's the rich who consume most resources, it's not just numbers of people. We need to even out consumption . . .'

'And aren't the poor trying to become wealthy too?' interrupted Baedeker.

'Studies suggest empowering women is the best way to control birth rate, 'insisted Chris.

'We already run several highly acclaimed education programs, as you saw on the film. But that would take many generations, time we do not have,' replied Baedeker.

'Well what do you propose?' demanded Lineker.

'Our plan is simple,' Baedeker smiled at the two scientists. 'We will acquire strategic infrastructure, starting with water supplies in carefully chosen locations. Everyone drinks water - the rich and the poor.'

'You're buying up water companies?' asked Lineker, puzzled.

'Acquiring, yes, sometimes by purchase. It's ironic that the developed nations are more willing to sell, but the less developed nations are more open-minded. In certain African states for instance, we have been invited to design and build the facilities from scratch.'

'You can't mean you intend depriving people of water?' asked an incredulous Lineker.

'Of course not,' Baedeker said, looking horrified. 'No - we're treating the water to improve male fertility. We have a fully equipped bio-lab working on this and we anticipate dramatic results.'

'I'm sorry I don't get it,' said Chris. 'Improving male fertility will surely tend to increase overpopulation.'

'We add synthetic endocrine enhancers to the water - a more effective variant of those already found in plastics - the male sperm count becomes far better regulated for reproduction rates that harmonize with the current needs of the world.'

''Enhance', 'regulate' 'harmonize'. Maybe we're using words differently here. Are you in fact saying you aim to sterilize the male population?' Lineker protested.

'We avoid unnecessarily emotive language.'

'Surely governments wouldn't permit that?' added Chris.

'On the contrary. Enlightened regimes welcome it. We are recognized as visionaries in the nations where we've started our trial programs. The royalties already represent a useful income stream to us and local birth rates are plummeting. We're getting an encouraging reaction from our first Chinese province too.'

'Do the local populations know of this?' asked Lineker.

'The relationship between a people and their government is of no concern to us,' replied Baedeker. 'We, ourselves, are used to handling adverse publicity. There are simple techniques that are very effective, provided one acts early and decisively.' He smiled warmly at them. 'We must all be prepared to sacrifice something to rescue the world.'

'But if you succeed in removing a generation, who will look after the old?' asked Lineker.

'There are promising developments to encourage that problem to be self-limiting too.'

Lineker and Chris were silent as they exchanged an anxious glance. Aziz was ordering another beer. Chris thought she had seen him shaking his head, but couldn't be sure.

'Look,' said Lineker after a moment. 'You've raised some big issues here - we need time to discuss it. I have to say, I find aspects of what you're telling us deeply unsettling.'

'Absolutely, me too,' added Chris.

'Of course, of course, as much time as you need.' Baedeker registered no emotion. 'There's a lot of radical innovation in our program. Take your time to think it over. I must leave in a couple of hours but the hotel is yours for the weekend.' Baedeker turned on his heel and was striding toward the door.

He stopped for a moment to add; 'Aziz will chauffeur you home tomorrow morning, and members of my staff will stay on to look after you until your departure. But as you consider my proposal, I urge you to set your prejudices aside. Try to think of what's at stake. We are at a turning point in history - think of future generations.' In an instant he was gone.

The remark jolted Chris like an electric shock.

'Come on Ian, let's walk. I'll just get a jacket and change my shoes.' She gently gripped his palm and with a tiny tug indicated they should leave.

As they entered the garden a few minutes later, Chris looked up at the Priory, a solitary crow perched on a wall which caw-cawed a plaintive lament to an unseen companion, somewhere amongst the ruins.

'Think of the history here - the human stories - the aspiration and the sorrow written in the stones,' she said. 'And now this. It all seems a bit bleak.'

'I don't mind admitting It's left me kind of unsettled.' Lineker said glancing sideways at Chris. 'The guy's a . . . lunatic.'

'I reckon . . .' she said, her fist clenching at her side. She felt afraid, threatened by the unknown. It was an unfamiliar sensation for a woman who normally welcomed the future as a place of opportunity. This time it was different. This time she felt unsure of her ability to identify the evil woven into the fabric of the mundane, and of her resolve to oppose it.

Chapter 27: what to do

(6.00 pm)

The wind freshened to quicken the dance of billowing clouds across the sky, again darkening with the threat of a gathering storm. They walked silently for a while, across the field where chickens scuttled and clucked with momentary indignation, and Friesian cows dedicated themselves to the endless meditation of feeding.

'Well . . . I don't know whether he can be really serious about all this. Maybe Mr Baedeker gets a bit carried away with being centre stage,' suggested Chris, eager to break the silence.

'Just because someone is ridiculous doesn't mean they're not dangerous. What did he mean by being prepared to sacrifice something? Was that some sort of threat?' Lineker was asking, as he helped Chris over the stile.

'To be honest, I think Mr Baedeker is his own biggest fan. I'm not sure we should take absolutely everything he says as the literal truth . . .' she replied, again trying to reassure them both.

'Maybe, maybe. The world's full of them isn't it - and we seem to be attracting more than our fair share these days.' Lineker grinned, before they fell into single file to concentrate on the steep ascent through a tree-lined pathway to the hilltop above Llanthony, where the remaining traces of Offa's Dyke still marked the boundary between invisible kingdoms.

A helicopter rose from the valley. It passed near them with a deafening roar, then hummed its way north like a giant dragonfly, diminishing to a speck in the distance before disappearing altogether into the dark blue of the sky.

'Where I grew up near Charlestown in Queensland they always used to say: 'You can't win,' chuckled Lineker, 'but you've got to laugh!' He smiled at her.

She smiled back, knowing he was concerned and appreciating his courage. *Almost the same age as my dad,* she thought, looking at the laughter lines on his craggy features, like the scouring of brush marks that add texture to the canvas of a Van Gogh painting. The comparison revived the unwelcome legacy that had formed throughout her childhood, and was never very distant, like the acrid sweetness of a mouldy house.

The blackmail of the beggar, she thought, picturing her father and remembering how he had cultivated his inadequacies as an emotional weapon. *And of the little man,* she added, recalling the excited fuss they had all made when they had measured her against her father, back to back, on her fifteenth birthday . . . *he was even resentful of that.* For the moment Chris had forgotten Ian, thinking back to when she found her brother sobbing in the garden and his unhappiness under the assault of a lifetime of scorn, and how he had tried to kill himself at eighteen. *Poor little bugger - never managed to escape,* she sighed, lost in the familiar replay of the unresolved *I was lucky.* She remembered the thrill of winning a scholarship, a thrill she couldn't share knowing her brother had never excelled at school. She could feel the anger building, irrational, universal and unfocussed. At *least I learnt not to rely on some goddam man.*

'He seems as mad as a dingo in a wasp nest,' said Lineker, unaware of her preoccupation. 'That thing with the rats was just gratuitous, surely?'

'Oh Baedeker . . . yes,' she replied, jerked back to the welcome relief of the immediate. 'Appalling. And the white - black thing was a bit sus too. But, I hate to admit it, some of the things he said I agree with - the analytic part, even the possibility of a new conception of God could be very exciting, and . . . we would be funded for the research.'

'Aligned with an outfit that has an agenda to crash the world's population by poisoning the water - even from what we know - it isn't a good look. And what's his plan for the old for God's sake? Heart attacks all round at sixty?' asked Lineker rhetorically. 'I think 'PORTAL dot crazy' has a more committed position than I'm in any way comfortable with.'

'Yes, of course you're right,' she replied, her brief flirtation with the possibility of joining PORTAL rapidly dissolving in the common sense conclusion. 'Anyway, it's good to be here, even if things aren't going to work out with the Church.'

'I think so too - it's important to review what you're about in life every now and again,' agreed Lineker, smiling at her with the effusive goodwill that she found so attractive.

'And take care of unfinished business,' Chris thought, prompted in part by her recollection of her last visit and content to ride the tide of her response to this attractive man. She turned to stare absent-mindedly into the distance at the lowering sun. The glow of the light added golden flecks to the hazel of her eyes and dusted subtle shadows across her face, accentuating the angled beauty of her features and highlighting the shine of her forehead scar, a memento of a childhood slip. Remembering the scar, she turned her face away from the light, embarrassed at her own vanity but hoping he had not noticed. 'Come on, let's go down,' she said.

They walked until the greys had moved closer to their night time pitch and faint pinpricks between the clouds had begun to shape the constellations. Only the return of the helicopter disturbed the tranquillity of the evening.

'The helicopter was only out for half an hour or so – wonder where it went?' shouted Lineker over his shoulder, as Chris followed him down the hill.

'Some errand for Mr B I wouldn't wonder,' she shouted back, thinking of how pleasing it was to watch Lineker move, how fit and youthful he seemed. By the time they saw the outline of the humbled Priory in the distance, Chris had decided what she was going to do.

Time for a little fun around here, she thought.

Chapter 28: tough stuff

(6.15 pm)

'Aziz,' called Baedeker. 'You've seen the video - how do you feel about it?' Aziz glanced briefly at his watch, then crossed his arms in front of him, hand on wrist.

'Never did like rats,' he replied.

There was a pause as Baedeker looked Aziz up and down. Aziz, motionless, stared in front of him, as if on parade.

Baedeker continued. 'I'm looking to recruit people for duties requiring more decisive action than is within the scope of the good scientists. I understand you were in the SAS?'

'Yes, I was involved with special operations, sir'. The 'sir' had been involuntary - it still surprised Aziz, he had thought he had the reflex under control; but it did not appear to surprise Baedeker.

'Good. So what are your feelings regarding our Church, Aziz?'

'To be honest, I've always avoided an opinion on religious matters,' replied Aziz, 'And politics.'

'That's fine, just fine but . . . you do understand the threat of over-population?'

'Sure, I think there are too many people.'

'So you support our efforts to improve the situation.'

'Well the overall objective sounds okay to me, as to your methods - frankly, I don't think I know enough to comment.'

'Well said, Aziz. Perhaps you should come over to the States, and look around our facilities. We have several programs that I wasn't able to touch upon today, many of them in their early stages. Some of the ideas might still be regarded as radical.'

'That sounds very interesting sir,' replied Aziz. He motioned 'yes' to the barman who was asking him with sign language if he wanted another beer.

'We're always looking for good men with the right background. We want people who share our goals and passion. People without prejudice.'

'Just one thing. Why start with Africans and the Chinese?' asked Aziz. 'Weren't you saying you want to control their populations first?'

'Absolutely. Blacks because their leadership is the most, shall I say, compliant. The Chinese already take the problem very seriously. It's important to address the Jewish problem too.'

'The Jews?' asked Aziz. 'Why the Jews?'

'Because they control the current status quo. It's the Jews who own the financial system. They don't care about the fate of the world as long as the 'Tribe of Israel' prospers. They believe they are God's 'chosen people'. If you want to change the world you have to tackle the Jews. With a Lebanese father, you of all people would know that surely?'

'I never really knew my father,' said Aziz quietly. 'And how would I fit into all this?'

'Let's take a stroll in the Priory - it's even more beautiful in the twilight of the evening,' Baedeker suggested. 'An emptiness abandoned to time and dreaming,' He turned to smile at his companion.

'Like a Council Estate,' added Aziz.

They were already amongst the ruins before Baedeker replied.

'We are dealing with a practical problem here, not a theoretic one. To answer your earlier question - how would you fit into all this. A number of African leaders are amenable to financial inducements.'

'Do you mean bribes?' asked Aziz.

'But not all,' continued Baedeker, ignoring Aziz. 'Sometimes we just can't agree terms. To deal with that we're recruiting for a unit - the Clean Team - designed to eliminate problems at source. We've got one very promising young man already and you would work with him.'

'Do you mean to kill people?'

'I like your directness, Aziz. It's important there are no misunderstandings here. This is a mission to reshape the future and save us from an apocalypse of chaos and anarchy. We need an entirely new ethical code. The world is an inconceivably different place from the mythic time of the Ten Commandments. Beautiful isn't it?' continued Baedeker, as they entered the heart of the Priory, extending an arm in invitation to Aziz to admire the soaring nave. 'Desolate and dignified,' he added.

'How I feel in the mornings sometimes,' joked Aziz. It was the formulaic offering of a man's man, its value in the reassurance that cliché can lend, with the cheap communion in the safe and the known. Aziz regretted the remark even before he had finished it, but was reassured that Baedeker registered no reaction.

'The first modernisation that is essential is that life can no longer be regarded as sacred. As an SAS soldier you would understand that?' he asked.

'Perhaps,' replied Aziz cautiously. 'But Hitler thought he was right too - and some of your ideas sound . . .'

'Hitler was a strong leader at a time of crisis for his people,' blurted Baedeker, his normally calm delivery betraying a hint of heightened emotion. 'Of course we know that Hitler made the mistake of confusing his own ego with the greater good and lost his way. But that was a different era with different challenges. He was wrong about gays for instance - now we recognize their social responsibility in reducing the birth-rate as an inspiration for the future - we're not hung up on race either.'

'But you're starting in Africa . . . and you mentioned the Jews.'

'Why wouldn't we start in Africa? Don't go soft on me Aziz. Be honest with yourself - who do you want to populate the planet - them or us?'

'And the Jews?'

'Well of course Hitler was right about the Jews.'

Chapter 29: respect

Aziz was uncomfortable.

Killing for this cunt - I don't think so. He had led an eventful life and his training had taught him that the key to effectiveness was action; and to keep his feelings to himself.

'I'm sorry sir, that's just not right for me at this stage in my career. I'm very happy to provide personal protection as your driver, but your other requirements are really beyond my current capabilities.'

He was pleased with his reply, he thought it sounded professional and gave no hint of the growing contempt he felt for what he believed were yet another bunch of crazies, but he had no view whether or not their project would succeed, and long ago had recognized that for his own emotional survival the best reaction to the immorality of others was a cultivated indifference.

The change in Baedeker was subtle, minuscule clues signalling his displeasure.

A rogue's preference for operating alone had often made Aziz very effective in the field of combat, but it had also seen him reprimanded by his superiors and criticized by his mates. But even if not gregarious, Aziz had always retained the sensitivity for mood of any creature that has evolved to hunt in packs, and it was clear to him Baedeker was not pleased.

'Okay, so be it Mike. I appreciate your frankness.' The slightest frown replaced Baedeker's relaxed openness, his voice hardening with a clipped finality to his speech as he continued. 'We have a joint security arrangement with the US government – actually, with an intelligence agency. I'll arrange for them to have a chat with you before you leave tomorrow. They can explain more effectively than I could the need for the absolute confidentiality of our mission.'

'Of course sir - I understand the delicate nature of your task.' Aziz instantly regretted using the word 'understand', and the word 'delicate'. Baedeker would only want that he did as he was told, not that he would presume to either judgement or interpretation. There was a delay; Baedeker sizing him up. Aziz felt uncomfortable again.

Baedeker seemed suddenly to arrive at a conclusion. 'There is no action without consequence Mr Aziz.' He was staring at Aziz, unblinking. 'We will accept no compromise in fulfilling our purpose. You must understand the needs of the family of God will take precedence over all others - even over the well-being of our nearest and dearest here on earth.'

Aziz wasn't sure, but he thought he was being threatened, and it annoyed him.

Chapter 30: close for comfort

(6.30 pm)

By the time Lineker and Reynolds re-entered the grounds of the Priory, the subtle chill of the autumn evening was in the air. As they approached the Hotel, Aziz stepped through the French windows onto the lawn.

He approached them quickly. 'I understand you want a lift back to Malvern,' he said and hardly pausing in his stride delivered what sounded like an ultimatum: 'I'll collect your bags at 9 am tomorrow morning, and will be leaving 9.30 am - sharp.' Not waiting for a reply, he strode brusquely past them with his awkward limping gait toward the flat above a converted stable the other side of the dry-stone wall that bordered the entrance drive to the Priory.

'He seems a bit agitated,' Chris said, watching Aziz walk away. 'I can't quite fathom Aziz - there's something about him.' A fleeting frown flickered across Chris's face, revealing her preoccupation like the ripples on a lake suggest a sudden breeze. 'He seems very ... alone.'

For the second time in as many hours, her appearance demanded Lineker's attention. This time the contrast surprised Lineker, the childlike puzzlement somehow emphasising the symmetry of her features and the clarity of her complexion. He found he was staring at her, trying to understand what were the components of such beauty. Chris noticed his stare and in the same instant, Lineker realising his attention was inappropriate, looked quickly away.

'Let's go inside,' she said, glancing at him, eager to cover his embarrassment.

Sipping on an iced tea, Baedeker was waiting for them.

'Ah, the good Doctors,' he exclaimed standing briefly to acknowledge their arrival before resuming his seat at the bar. 'Join me for a hibiscus tea – very good for blood pressure. I had to send out for it. Shame I can't spend more time here. The service is first rate.'

'I wondered about the helicopter,' replied Lineker, an eyebrow raised in implied disapproval.

'May I ask if it's too early for an indication of whether you will be joining us?' Baedeker enquired.

'Well we have come to a decision and I'm afraid the answer is 'No'. We understand your concerns, more than that, we share many of them,' replied Lineker. 'We believe though that any interventions must be properly sanctioned through a global consensus with publicly accountable entities, and with the consent of the people affected.'

'I see. Is it a problem that could be resolved by adjustment of the remuneration package?' asked Baedeker equably.

'No, it's not a question of money,' replied Lineker. 'Your program seems just too radical for a private corporation, and I have to say it, too ethically compromised.'

Baedeker rose from his seat to confront them. "Global consensus', 'sanctioned', 'entities' - you've attended too many committee meetings Dr Lineker. Well your 'global consensus' just isn't going to happen I'm afraid - you can fiddle while Rome burns – I'm afraid I cannot.' Baedeker sounded cross and was making no attempt to conceal it.

'To be frank we're worried too about the racial dimension to your proposal . . .' began Chris, but Baedeker interrupted her brusquely.

'So be it - I respect your decision. But I don't have time to debate with those who fail to appreciate the urgency of the crisis we are facing.' Baedeker seemed to relax a little, as if his irritation was already dissipating after their rejection of his proposal. 'I believe in the power of positive thinking, I don't waste energy either on regret or on looking back, so if you change your mind - either of you – feel free to give me a call. I'll have someone watching your research as it develops.'

'Yes of course,' said Lineker, surprised at Baedeker's abruptness.

'Please respect the confidentiality of what we have discussed. I can't overemphasise how important that is to us.

It would be a matter of grave concern if our discussions became public knowledge. Nice to have met you Dr Lineker.' His tone and expression suggested he didn't mean it.

'And you Dr Reynolds.' Baedeker suddenly reached out and gripped her fingers, pulling them toward him to ostentatiously kiss the back of her hand. His eyes looked up at her with a determined and theatrical stare. The effect was brazen, audacious, the phoney homage of an alpha male to a selected mate. He turned without waiting for any response, snapping his fingers at Clinton, who issuing hushed instructions into a bullet-microphone near his mouth, followed Baedeker quickly toward the door.

Chapter 31: five poster

(6.35 pm)

As Baedeker left the Hotel to walk to the helicopter, Lineker and Chris moved toward the bar's French windows to watch him leave. A burly man emerged from the recesses of the thick stone wall and flanked Baedeker across the lawn then hopped easily into the helicopter behind Baedeker.

'Where did he come from?' asked Lineker.

'Security type I suppose,' mused Chris. 'Was he unusually good looking or am I just in a good mood?' This was an unfamiliar role for her, flirting with her boss, but she had made up her mind.

'Oh . . . I think he . . .' began Ian, before his attention was distracted by a dapper young man, wearing a chef's whites and hat.

'Sir, madam, pardon my intrusion. My name is Pierre and I am your chef for the evening. Tonight, deer baked in hay with sauerkraut and chocolate, flame-grilled mackerel with smoked eel, or culled from the hills behind us, we offer a rack of lamb, oven-roasted on a bed of herbed mograbieh, baby carrots and chilli jus.'

'Well that sounds . . . fantastic,' said Chris, in an easy simulation of the species of sophistication that mocks as it admires.

'Or something vegetarian, as you might wish.'

'I'll go for the lamb please,' said Chris.

'Me too,' said Ian, 'local is best.'

'Not always sir. If I may recommend a nice Pinot Gris from Church & State in British Columbia.'

'Err yes, . . . that sound's great,' said Ian 'don't you think Chris?'

'Well . . . yes it does,' she grinned.

'Bon, parfait,' said Pierre, 'I'll ask Silvio here to take your drinks orders and discuss hors d'oeuvre. When would you like dinner served?'

'What do you think Chris?' asked Ian.

'How about an hour from now? The anticipation of pleasure enhances the experience, don't you think?' she said, smiling at Ian, openly flirting with him.

When they were alone again, she stretched out with the easy languorous grace of a cat awakening from a fireside nap, and had begun 'I think I could get used to this sort of lifestyle . . .' when the sudden roar of helicopter engines outside briefly shattered the tranquillity. 'Well, there goes our host,' she continued. 'I don't want to be ungrateful, but I can't say I'm sorry to see the back of him.'

For the next two hours they ate, drank and chatted, enjoying the atmosphere that a fine meal can establish until, pampered and satiated, a feeling of well-being enveloped them in a cocoon of comfort. The easy torpor was abruptly fractured when to her surprise, Ian pulled back his chair, and stood up. 'Well, a momentous day. What would old Grafton think of all this I wonder'.

What was in his mind was less prosaic. He was strongly attracted to Chris, but was equally determined to avoid anything resembling his brief involvement three years previously with an assistant who had worked for him. She had been gifted, and sexy. She had also been married. Ian was single, his wife having died five years before in a car crash, and for nine weeks they revelled in frequent opportunities for illicit sex. Though Ian's conscience was troubled by the furtive tension of her infidelity and his own complicity in deception, so irresistible was the attraction that he chose to ignore it. He hadn't understood until too late, that what at first had seemed his lover's freshness and spontaneity, in part had derived from the erratic unpredictability of a bipolar condition.

When their liaison had been discovered, there followed a cycle of accusation and recrimination, that had spun into tragedy when the husband killed himself. At the inquest Lineker had been criticised for using his status as her boss to take advantage of a vulnerable and sick young woman. The criticism, and his anguish at the outcome, had seared a resolution in his mind never to risk inappropriate closeness with a colleague again.

He summoned his resolve. 'Well I'm off to bed Chris - it's been lovely spending the day with you, and I'm sure all this will work out all right in the end . . . I'm off then . . . err . . . goodnight.'

Knowing nothing of Lineker's thoughts, Chris watched in dismay as overly eager to leave, he banged into a chair then strode unevenly to the small door at the base of the tower, stepping through onto the spiral staircase beyond, and in an instant was gone from sight.

'Um, night-night . . . Ian,' Chris sighed, leaning back in the comfy sofa wondering what next. By now, she had consumed enough fine wine for the restraints of convention, and the earlier uncertainties about her appearance to have long since dissipated.

A bit of romance would be nice, she mused, her brain fogging with alcohol and desire, *but sometimes you have to make do with what you can get.*

She was used to feeling distanced from men - her first sexual encounter had been much later than for her contemporaries, and it was some time before a friend had explained that though few men would fail to notice her, her combination of striking good looks and bookish aloofness would deter most from even trying their luck. But throughout the evening her rapport with the awkward Australian had strengthened, and she felt sure he was as attracted to her as she was to him. On top of all that, she wanted a fuck.

Bugger . . . what now . . . she muttered to herself as she climbed the stairs, her movements overly purposeful like a tightrope walker on a windy day . . . *that book I read on the plane . . . Summer of . . . something . . . about that woman who got herself well and truly seen to in five capital cities?* She chuckled and burped loudly, leaning heavily on the door as she fumbled for a key. *Why the fuck not? It worked for her.*

In her room she undressed slowly in front of the mirror, her hands rising to cup her full breasts, a perfect parabola on the lower side, the slightly flatter upper surface lending a natural uplift to nipples that her thumbs now briefly crossed, the delicate touch rewarded with an instant response.

Yeah . . . it looks as if my Mr Ian needs a helping hand.

She showered, changed into a simple white sleep shirt and fixed her hair then she detached one of the cords securing the heavy curtains away from the window. She tied her wrist to one of the four uprights of the four poster bed and reached for the house phone to dial Lineker.

'Ian, I need your help, urgently.'

As she put the receiver down, it occurred to her this could all be a very bad mistake. The effect was immediately sobering. She reached for the phone again but could already hear the muffled thudding of Ian's feet on the stone stairs.

What the hell, she thought, as a loud knock on her door announced Dr Lineker the moment before he stumbled into the room, . . . *in for a penny.*

Lineker appeared about to say something, but no words emerged. His eyes travelled quickly from her face, now infused with an aura of dreamy sensuality, down the plunging line of her shirt and the narrowness of a waist that emphasized the curve of her hips and the sensuality of finely shaped legs, then back up to the underside of her outstretched arm and the velvet muscle above her breast, in a display of perfect contour, and of femininity.

The position left her vulnerable physically and emotionally, so direct, unambiguous and explicit was the invitation to sex. Lineker felt his prick stiffen and beneath the fuzzy clamour of his racing mind, a burgeoning sense of excitement. But, drunk though he was, he remained aware this voluptuous fantasy was none other than Dr Chris Reynolds, leading mathematician and work colleague. Clearly she was not sober. It would be wrong - it was wrong.

'Don't worry I'll have you undone in a second,' he muttered, avoiding her gaze.

Inclining her head slightly to present the graceful lines of her neck more clearly to him, Chris replied with a mix of tenderness and patient resolve; 'No Ian, I want you to tie the other one.'

September 22nd

Chapter 32: aftermath

(8.30 am)

Chris Reynolds was awoken by a tap on the door. She saw the still sleeping Ian Lineker next to her, his lean body covered by just a sheet, the stubble starting on his chin. The sight pleased her, as did the memory of the previous night - a fleeting concern whether she had been too wild quickly dismissed as she recalled Lineker's frantic excitement at their love making.

'Who's there?' she asked.

'Aziz.' His tone was no nonsense, authoritative. 'We leave in thirty minutes. Are your bags ready?'

'No . . . we'll hurry,' she shouted. 'We can take care of our bags.'

'See you downstairs - thirty minutes.'

'Okay,' she called back.

'Who was that?' asked Ian, waking from a deep sleep.

'Aziz says we've got to leave,' Chris told him, throwing open the window to encourage the fresh morning air to disperse the musk of stale sex that permeated the room. 'He sounds kind of emphatic,' she added, 'and he's not the sort of man I'd like to keep waiting.'

'Oh Christ,' said Lineker, swinging his legs onto the floor.

'What's up?' asked Chris.

'Headache that's all.' He gave her a wry grin, responding to the haze of self-congratulation as he recalled the unexpected pleasure of the night, and a level of sexual abandonment he had assumed was consigned to memories of youth. Chris smiled back as she gathered her things for a shower.

But for Lineker the satisfaction of a particular kind of exhaustion was tainted by the acid taste of more than just a hangover, so that when Chris emerged from the shower wrapped in a towel, a serious-looking Lineker began: 'Look, we need to talk.' He paused to clear his throat. 'Thing is - don't get me wrong . . .'

Starting in her belly, Chris felt a pulsing wave, that for a moment left her reeling as it flowed into her head. Her reaction confused her on several levels. This time someone had beaten her to it, an injury to her vanity for which she was unprepared. But there was another element, something additional to the reflexive discomfort of being rejected. Over the years, the pattern had been easily rationalised, but recently the whisper of concern had become more persistent. She was troubled, not for anything that was happening but the suspicion that if Ian were not ending the relationship, she would have done so herself, just as she had with Kim Zazie, and everyone else before.

'You don't think we should do this again right?'

'Um . . . it's . . .' Ian replied, surprised by her accurate anticipation of his intent. 'If I were twenty years younger then . . . who knows.' He persisted. 'But our research is more important than . . .' He faltered again, unsure of exactly what he wanted to express. 'You're a very beautiful woman . . . I just don't see it would work if we were to . . .'

'Ian, sshh.' she stopped him, gently. 'It's . . . I understand . . . really . . . and you're a very attractive man. Just best friends again right?'

'I reckon . . . best friends with a secret,' he was saying, 'one helluva secret.'

They laughed together, and she kissed him efficiently on the forehead, again feeling the distant gnaw of guilt that she was not more upset, before looking at her outline briefly in the mirror as she started to dress.

Chapter 33: flying high

(9.00 am)

Grafton was depressed.

He slipped on his Polartec jacket, and unloaded his bag from the boot of the car to begin the trudge up the Hills. It was a beautiful morning but Grafton was unaware of it, though he sucked heavily on the chill air as he struggled up the slope, lost in thought and wondering what more he could have done.

He had investigated SRS thoroughly, checked with the charity commissioners, done lengthy google searches, database searches and with Companies House for their accounts. There was little to discover.

The organisation was only 18 months old, and appeared largely dormant. Emelienko's offer had placed him in a quandary on how best to act, and provoked the inconsistencies within his own character. Nothing good had happened in Grafton's life that he had not worked hard to achieve, an experience that had crystallized into a personal philosophy. He was therefore highly sceptical of any offer of something for nothing, seeing it as not just implausible but almost immoral.

Grafton had given his life to science, turning his back on commercial corporations to make a career in public service, and had faith in science as the ultimate expression of the Enlightenment and the Age of Reason, humanity's greatest intellectual endeavour. That was why so-called Process Physics was an anathema to him, usurping the language of the science he had learnt and so he believed, denying the empirical facts. To Grafton, Lineker was a peddler of pseudo-science and a charlatan. He was offended by the suggestion that he should be part of any process that perpetuated Lineker's nonsense.

On the other hand, he was equally offended that someone could believe that Dr W Grafton BSc, MSc, PhD, FRS might suppress scientific enquiry for base commercial reasons.

Anyway, it was obvious to Grafton that Lineker was uncontrollable - the idea he could be silenced was laughable - the man was the worst sort of fanatic, a delusional maverick with a mission. But Grafton was tired. The ideals of scientific enquiry and of knowledge for its own sake seemed to have evaporated long ago. These days there was the drudgery of budgets, commercial relevance, selling of 'product' and the inexorable exodus of the most talented of his staff to the USA or more recently, China. The idea of just taking the money and easing up in life was very attractive to him.

These internal conflicts had taken their toll; mired in indecision he had sought compromise in the best way he knew how. He had written to Emelienko by email offering full sponsorship rights and a place on a review committee to examine Lineker's work internally. He had offered to set up a trust. He had emphasised to Emelienko that in his view the science was ill-founded and its focus would in all likelihood be altered, but he had found the resolve to stress that as a scientific institution, the primary commitment of MRI was to the truth. He promised that every endeavour would be made to best accommodate the commercial interests of sponsors, but the requirement for external peer review made it very difficult to contain information past a certain point, especially with theoretical research. In view of the creative nature of the staff involved it was anticipated, so Grafton had written, discretion would be difficult to maintain.

Grafton had also written a full report and sent it to the MRI Board. He fully expected nothing to come of any of it but, as he saw it, he had at least done the right thing by everyone, resisted temptation for direct personal gain, and left the way open for further negotiation. But the workload that had consumed the whole of his day far into the night, and the effort of protracted indecision, had left him drained.

As he neared the top of the hill Grafton felt the bile that the exercise had released in him. He felt a flash of anger as he reviewed the charade that substituted for family life – how he and his wife led virtually separate lives, how they had no shared interest since their youngest child had left home eight years previously, and how his wife made no attempt to hide her contempt for him, a derision that had grown to fill the vacuum of habit and forgotten desire.

Fuckin' bitch.

He gathered up the resentments he had nurtured; of her smugness, her self-important bustle and her friendships with similarly self-satisfied women, a circle he was excluded from but nevertheless that was used as a yardstick, to condemn him as peculiar and a misfit.

Hateful fucking bitch.

At the top of the hill Grafton unpacked his bag and primed the motor on his S&B ME163c radio controlled plane. He felt the rising excitement gradually displacing his hostility as the buzz increased to a shrill screech and he felt his heart lift too as the little aircraft zoomed into the sky far above the Worcestershire plain. On impulse he diverted it to briefly harass a crow before reminding himself this was improper conduct, looking around sheepishly to see if his mischief had been witnessed.

Damn - just my luck, he thought, seeing a tall man walking purposefully toward him across the hill.

Chapter 34: aziz

(9.05 am)

'The needs of the family of God will take precedence even over the wellbeing of our nearest and dearest here on earth.' Aziz had considered that remark too long, the thought revolving like a pig on a spit. *Was that little prick threatening my girl?'*

His teenage daughter was all that remained of Aziz's family. Her mother, an Australian he had met in Earls Court, had died three years previously, her death hardly registering with Aziz who had not spoken to her for the last ten years of her life. He had attended the funeral in Nottingham, as much to meet his daughter as to mourn the loss of her mother, and he had not seen or heard from his daughter since.

Aziz insisted on carrying Chris' luggage to the car, and she and Lineker were following him across the lawn when three men in suits appeared from behind the stone stables the other side of the entrance drive.

So that's who they sent. Aziz had heard their car purring up the driveway twenty minutes earlier. He had noted the car was an Audi identical to the one he drove. Though the morning sun had barely escaped the horizon, all three of the men were wearing dark glasses. Their hair was close cropped at the temples to lend a squarish look to their heads, one fair skinned, the other two dark.

Surely, they must be joking, thought Aziz. *Americans just take themselves too goddam' seriously.*

The blonde man, about the same height as Aziz was almost unnaturally broad, his arms seeming disproportionately short held slightly apart from his sides, as if the bulging muscles evident beneath his sleeves prevented them from hanging loosely in the normal way.

Typical steroid abuse, thought Aziz. Another man was tall, more naturally proportioned, solemn and taciturn; *The dangerous one,* thought Aziz. The third man was young. 'College rookie,' noted Aziz.

'Aziz,' the blonde man shouted, his voice heavily accented. 'Spare us a moment. In private.'

'Sorry about this,' said Aziz to Chris, returning her bag to her and handing her the car keys. 'You'll see two grey Audis. Just press the button. I'll join you both in a moment.'

Two of the men fell in either side of Aziz, the third was behind him. It made him uneasy. It made him think of captured civilians being marched somewhere away from view to be shot in the back of the head, the moment of opportunity when some gesture of defiance might enable their escape or at least the chance to die without acquiescence, lost forever in resignation to their fate. By temperament and by training, Aziz was not that kind.

Fuck with me and you're fucked, he repeated to himself, like a mantra to empty the mind, feeling the tremble in muscles that with the intelligence of the body prepared themselves autonomously for action.

'Just step into the Priory for us,' said the tall man.

'For us'. What the fuck is 'for us', thought Aziz.

They walked in silence until they stopped amongst the nearby ruins, its floor a lush carpet of tightly mown grass between the ragged walls of time-worn stones that sheltered them from view beneath a ceiling of open sky. The three men were arranged in a loose semicircle in front of Aziz. They were relaxed, insolent, the tall man chewing gum.

'It's about your daughter.'

The remark hit Aziz like a hammer blow.

Chapter 35: tough shit

(9:06 am)

Grafton watched immobile, somehow mesmerised, as the man came right up to him, stopping slightly too close for comfort. He was over six feet tall, standing erect with the controlled precision of a dancer. The appearance of a natural refinement suggested by the prominent cheekbones and concave cheeks was marred by a thin scar starting just below his hairline, that traced a slightly raised seam to his right eyebrow above an almond-shape eye filled with a blank, like the white of fried egg. The line resumed below the sightless eye to tangle with his upper lip, twisting it into the appearance of a permanent sneer, its menace enhanced by a crudely drawn tattoo of a dagger on the back of his hand. Grafton noticed too, the sinewed solidity of his frame and the bunched arm muscles with the unyielding hardness of beef jerky rather than the pudgy softness that Grafton had long since assumed was the normal condition for flesh beyond the age of thirty.

'Dr Grafton play good game . . .' the man said in a rasp that emphasised his foreignness. After an awkwardly dramatic pause, speaking slowly, he added 'fly plane buzz buzz, Dr Buzz Buzz fly plane.'

'Now look here . . .' began Grafton, but spluttered to silence as the man swung his arm in an arc of blur as if to punch Grafton in the face. Perfectly judged, the fist stopped just an inch from Grafton's nose. Grafton raised his arms in a reflex to protect himself, though had the strike been intended he would have been far too slow. In the same instant the man reached out with his other hand, and tweaked the end of Grafton's penis, pulling on it hard as a calf yanks on its mother's teat.

Grafton gasped more in surprise than pain, then was pushed to the ground, tripping over the man's foot that had been placed as a lever behind him. He lay there perplexed and humiliated, too afraid to move, while the man fumbled unhurriedly with his fly and casually extracted his penis, positioning himself with legs slightly apart looking down at Grafton. He took aim and released an arc of urine, playing with its direction to wash over Grafton's hair, in his eyes and then his mouth. Grafton spat and spluttered, peering up through the pattering stream, speechless, shocked. When the man had finished he shook off the last few drops, returned his penis to his trousers and without warning, took a sudden flying kick at Grafton, striking him in the belly.

The man turned on his heel and strode off quickly, leaving Grafton curled in a foetal position staring bug-eyed at his receding back and consumed with agony as he fought for breath through the vomit and the tears. A crashing sound jolted him into the present. By the time he had crawled and stumbled to the splintered remains of his plane, Grafton was shivering uncontrollably.

Chapter 36: goes round, comes round
(9:07 am)

The remark hit Aziz like a hammer blow. *'You fuckers . . . what about my daughter?'*

Paradoxically, his anger was fortified not by his closeness to his daughter but by his estrangement from her. The assumption in the American's threat of what he would value, served only to remind him of what in fact he had lost – how he had missed her childhood, and of how little he had given her. And, if they knew of his daughter - what else did they know? The memory returned, uninvited, of what he had witnessed. The murder of a girl who could have been his daughter. And how he had done nothing.

'We want you to understand the situation here. It's very important to Mr Baedeker you don't go round talking about his plans okay?'

'Sure, he told me that,' replied Aziz keeping his tone as neutral as he could, trying to control his twitchiness by stroking his chin briefly with one hand as if smoothing a beard, a 'tell' that 'Beaky' Jones, his combat instructor, had failed to eradicate in training.

'We want you to understand right? If you talk about this to anyone - someone will have to pay.' The blond man was leering at Aziz. 'It will be your daughter.'

It came as an implosion, his vision flashing with a white light of intense brilliance that collapsed to a small black point, leaving Aziz stranded as if in space - timeless, without location, mindless; an exquisite release from the pain of the world - before the dot expanded with a rushing bark to reconfigure as before. This was the ecstasy of blind fury.

In one movement Aziz had kicked the blond man between the legs with sickening force. The tall man was scrabbling for his gun when Aziz grabbed his arm, wrenching it against the movement of the joint, using his own arm as a lever. The man's face drained of blood, and his tongue protruded grotesquely from whitened lips as the cracking sound, like splintering wood, gave macabre confirmation with the unnatural angle of his arm, that the injury was traumatic. Aziz seized his gun with his other hand as he smashed the man's nose with his fist, the blood exploding like a squashed tomato across his face. His own weapon still pointing to the ground, the third man, the young man, was stopped in his tracks as Aziz pressed the Glock 23 pistol to his forehead. The whole confrontation had taken less than two seconds.

'For fuck's sake. Jesus man! There's no need for that shit . . . for fuck's sake man. What the fuck did you do that for?' The young man was sobbing, the adrenalin wracking his body in a bubbling confusion of reflex and fear.

Aziz took the young man's gun, pressing quickly on the magazine release. He fired a shot to clear the chamber and listened to the whining bullet that shattered chips from the rock and left a shiny gash on the stone next to him, before the singing ricochet whistled up and away as he hurled the Glock across the lawn.

Aziz knelt over the man he had kicked. He was moaning gently, his contorted face purple with pain. Aziz pressed a sharp thumbnail into his neck. It was a trick he'd been shown as part of his SAS training by an old man, a Kung Fu master and healer, using a pressure point to enable rapid recovery from physical trauma. By the time the fallen man began to calm, Aziz was striding away, his limp more noticeable than before.

'Threaten my daughter again and I'll kill you all,' he shouted over his shoulder.

'You just assaulted agents of the United States Government - you fuckin' crazy - you're in deep shit man, deep shit,' hollered the young man.

'Well fuck off back to America then,' shouted the retreating Aziz, 'this is fucking Wales.'

Aziz had walked just fifty feet, and was almost at the perimeter wall when he heard the frantic clicking of a gun trigger. Unconsciously seeking reassurance, he ran his hand over the outside of his trouser pocket to feel the spare magazine he had removed from the young agent's Glock before he had thrown it across the grass.

Bloody amateurs, he thought, slightly quickening his pace, as he stepped through the gate and out of sight.

Chapter 37: grafton

(9.10 am)

Grafton was in shock. He had just been assaulted, but it was so quick, and so unexpected, that except for the searing pain still cutting across his stomach it seemed more nightmare than reality. He moved gently, fearing anything sudden might worsen the damage and risk permanent disablement. He was frightened and humiliated, the taste of another man's piss still in his mouth. He realized how vulnerable anyone unsuspecting is to a purposeful attack and how reliant personally he was on the boundaries of civilised behaviour. For a moment, with the purging clarity of fear, even if he had never been physically violent, he regretted his own use of power to intimidate. With the realization he too had acted as a bully, something within Grafton was changed forever.

What really worried him though was that the man had known his name, so this was not some random assault, being in the wrong place at the wrong time. Someone was trying to intimidate him and the only possible candidate he could think of was Emelienko. But why?

With hindsight he was forced to concede that what he had presented as a counter offer, could have been interpreted as a rejection to anyone insistent on their own terms and conditions. Was his first suspicion correct and he was dealing with some sort of criminal organisation like the Russian Mafia?

Why in God's name would they want control over Lineker's bad science? he asked himself.

By the time he had stumbled down to St. Anne's Well, Grafton had calmed a little. He had decided not to go to the police, not yet at least. It wasn't an experience he wished to recount in public, not the detail anyway. Instead, he would let the security chief at MRI know what had happened, and ask his advice. He resolved two more things.

First, if these thugs thought that Bill Grafton Ph.D. FRS and Head of Research at the MRI could be dictated to by crude intimidation, then he would show them they had seriously miscalculated. He would send an email terminating all negotiations as soon as he got to his office.

Second, he needed to talk to Lineker urgently.

Chapter 38: honest to god

(9.12 am)

Chris Reynolds was sitting in the back of the Audi and Lineker was waiting next to their bags, when Aziz walked quickly from the Priory.

'Was that a gunshot we heard Mr Aziz?' asked Lineker, a frown of anxiety leaving two deep lines in his forehead, like furrows across a ploughed field.

'Yes, a weapon was discharged - in order to make it safe you understand - no-one was hurt,' replied Aziz, lapsing into military-speak. 'The keys please?' Aziz caught the keys that Lineker tossed toward him, and threw their luggage into the boot. 'Please, hurry,' he said.

As Lineker clambered into the rear seat, Aziz crossed to the other Audi. Out of sight of Lineker and Reynolds, he crouched behind the car to stick the blade of a penknife retrieved from his pocket, into two of the tyres. Aziz returned quickly to his own car and hopped into the driver's seat. He gunned the engine, the tyres throwing a spume of mud and leaves into the air as they scrabbled, then gripped to propel the Audi forward, its rear dipping slightly as it accelerated away with a powerful whoosh.

'Everything alright Mr Aziz?' asked Chris, concerned at the speed they were travelling and Aziz's apparent preoccupation with something.

'Not entirely,' replied Aziz. Aziz was trying to assess the safest route to Malvern, and when, and how, the Americans would come after him.

Chris glanced at Lineker and he responded by raising his eyebrows slightly in acknowledgement of their shared concern.

'Do you mind me asking - who were those men who wanted to speak with you?' asked Chris. 'Are we in danger Mr Aziz?' she added, reaching out to grip Lineker's hand.

Aziz was trying to figure out if his actions had worsened the threat to his daughter. The sudden intrusion of the possibility that others might be at risk jolted him from his introversion. It occurred to him he was probably not alone in his opposition to the Church, he had seen the scientist's revulsion at the 'Rats' movie.

'No, not at all. No need for you to worry. Those guys back there . . . well, they were CIA, working as the security detail for the Church. PORTAL has influence.' He offered up a smile, perfunctory and unconvincing, as he checked the side mirror and the possibility someone was following, before turning the hurtling car into the sharp bend that was rapidly tightening before them.

'And why are they after you Mr Aziz?' asked Chris. It was a bold question, it got to the heart of the matter, but as the screeching tyres testified, it was an unavoidable line of enquiry.

Aziz looked at her in the mirror and saw the worry on her face, different from the expressions he had already seen, but written in the same language of perfect proportion. Something about her intrigued him, just as it had when they had first been introduced. There was nothing he could specify, it was too subtle to be categorised - a sort of wistful detachment and a melancholic delicacy that her lingering look and sideways glances had hinted at. To Aziz, she seemed the essence of femininity, and so desirably different from the world with which he was familiar that he felt the floodgates of repressed emotion straining to contain a tide of feeling.

'Call me Mike,' he said.

Chris glanced again at Lineker, the gesture prompted by a woman's sensitivity to the rivalry of men, and an intuition of how sometimes, so little can signify so much.

'Sure, Mike,' she replied.

Aziz was wondering how much to say. Whether he should buy intimacy with another's secrets, whether it would make him seem too much like an overeager schoolboy anxious to impress. He decided to risk it.

'They said they would hurt my daughter if I talked about what they're up to.' 'Hurt your daughter - good God - that's . . .' said Lineker, before lost for words, he stopped in mid-sentence.

'What do you mean 'up to'. . .?' asked Chris curious.

'You do realize they're neo-fascist loonies don't you?' replied Aziz.

'Well, we rejected their offer to work with them so that kind of speaks for itself,' replied Lineker, 'and I understand they have an idea for population control starting in Africa and China, but apparently the governments agree with it, or so he says. So I got the impression that it's an issue of practicality rather than ideology.'

'Err . . . did you? I've seen what happens when the 'holier-than-thou' interfere in other people's countries. It's a fuck-up.' Aziz sounded truculent, unattractive.

The car was speeding up a narrow lane between hedges and tree tops that still heavy with foliage, were turning to shades of yellow and tints of red. They slowed for a junction and turned left onto an even smaller road.

'I probably got a less prettified version than you did,' said Aziz.

'I thought you already worked for them?' asked Chris.

'Only for a couple of weeks as a driver . . . but I think I just resigned. Baedeker wanted me to join a special team.'

He paused, wondering again if he should risk what he wanted to say. This time he felt compelled to do so.

'They wanted me to kill people for them.'

'What!' exclaimed Chris. 'Are you sure?'

'Yes. I think I got that bit right,' replied Aziz sardonically.

'Jesus, why are you telling us this?' asked Lineker, shocked.

'Because you need to know what you're involved in and . . . you may be able to help me,' replied Aziz.

He was looking in the rear mirror again, as he had done often before to check if they were being followed, at the same time Chris looked up. Their eyes met, and Aziz was certain her eyes smiled at him. In that moment Aziz knew the reason he had given was only part of the answer and he was not about to disclose the rest. It was a choiceless compulsion, whether more than sexual or a new dimension to the power of sexuality, he didn't know. He only knew he had to get to know her better – much better.

Aziz banged on the brakes as rounding a corner, the car hurtled toward a young woman on a horse waiting at the lowered gates of a level crossing, steam rising gently from the muscled flanks of the great beast between her legs. She touched a riding crop to her hard hat, a country greeting of gratitude at their consideration in slowing, her gesture stolen from the moment, as the horse demanding her full attention, bucked and whinnied at the disturbance.

'Look, this is not good,' said Lineker. 'You were saying we might be able to help you. What do you have in mind?'

'I figure the best way to protect my daughter is to take the fight to them,' said Aziz.

'Why don't you just keep quiet about it all, as they ask?' suggested Chris.

'Firstly, they didn't 'ask' and secondly, our relationship has gone downhill a bit since then,' replied Aziz, his clenched jaw adding prominence to its outline.

'And, anyway, how could we help you?' asked Chris.

'You have something they want, that may be some sort of start.' Aziz sounded determined.

'But where would you start against a global organisation?' asked Lineker.

'Well first I want to know why they are interested in you. If you can pull them in, then maybe I can fix some of them.'

'Do you mean persuade them to change their minds?' asked Chris.

A small train trundled by. Shortly after, the gate swung up to allow them over the railway tracks.

'You could put it like that.' Aziz was concentrating, driving carefully to avoid distressing the horse further. 'Probably only need to do the boss - he seems the main man - so that could be enough.' He sounded distracted, the resulting casualness initially camouflaging his meaning.

'Do you mean . . .?" Lineker asked, incredulous at first, then almost amused at the outlandish improbability of what he was hearing. 'You can't go round murdering people if that's what you're talking about, just because they're . . .' began Lineker.

'Psycho new-age Nazis who have threatened my daughter,' finished Aziz, 'well I can try.'

Chapter 39: never wanted to, can't help it

(9:20 am)

Aziz was sounding more than a little crazy himself, and dangerous, thought Chris, exchanging another anxious glance with Lineker. Aziz saw it in the mirror.

'Believe me - like a lot of life - this is not a situation I would have chosen. These people have threatened my daughter and to be honest,' he continued, 'I've had more than a gutful of people telling me what to do. Have you got any better ideas?' he demanded.

'We can't help you kill people,' said Chris, 'we'd be worse than they are. No, if they've done wrong what you do is expose them, discredit them, get them arrested, imprisoned.'

'The world isn't just split into right and wrong where all you have to do is tell teacher and everything's okay again,' said Aziz, shaking his head, less in exasperation at the situation than at the childlike naiveté of the two scientists. He continued, his tone more conciliatory, 'From the little I've seen, they have powerful friends.'

'If you don't believe in the possibility of 'goodness', how can there be . . .' she paused, searching for the right expression, 'how can we end suffering, how can we bring about the transformation that the world needs?' asked Chris, the intensity in her voice revealing that the remark was heartfelt and spontaneous. 'How can we make it a better place for our children?' Her comment surprised Aziz. He might have dismissed it as pathetic from a man. But spoken with such candour from a young woman, it touched something within him. Aziz stared at her in the mirror, the power of opposites drawing him further into its spinning vortex.

How wonderful, that she would say that to . . . to a fucked-up old bastard like me, he thought, enjoying the same sensation of heightened awareness that he had known when awaiting enemy engagement, the experience of prepared readiness which is living at its most alive. It softened his anger, unravelling his initial certainty with the possibility that Chris could be right and wondering if there was a better way to protect his daughter, Isabel, than by killing Baedeker. He did have another weapon, though he was unsure how to use it.

Oblivious to the subtle transformation within the granite-like exterior of her driver, Chris continued, 'They're an internet Church, so maybe the internet can be used against them.'

'However you proceed, you'll need proof,' added Lineker.

'The internet is not my speciality,' said Aziz wryly, seeing an opportunity to keep contact with Chris. 'Maybe you can help me out there. I recorded everything that arsehole said to me - this is more than just a pretty watch, here - see.'

He held up his wrist ostentatiously. The heavy green timepiece seemed familiar to Chris, her attempt to place where she had seen it suddenly rewarded with the recollection of the chronometer next to her bed, still awaiting its return to Kim Zazie, the man she had met in Brighton.

A ring tone shrilled and Lineker fumbled for his phone.

'Ian Lineker,' he said into the mouthpiece, then paused listening.

'What, look . . . that's terrible mate . . . haven't got a clue unless . . . I'll come and see you as soon as we get back - should be in a couple of hours. Yes, I may know who's behind this - no I don't think it's Russians – most likely it's an American Internet Church - look don't worry okay. No . . . no absolutely not. There's nothing in our research except theoretic science. See you soon, and don't worry.'

A camera in a yellow box dutifully photographed the cars' transgressive speed but could not record the baritone roar from its tyres or their sudden change to a falsetto scream as they flashed across a speed sign embossed on the tarmac, a warning that Aziz pointedly ignored as they hurtled down a dual carriageway at twice the legal limit.

'Jesus, someone's threatened and assaulted poor old Grafton,' explained Lineker to the others. 'He's really shaken up. He thinks it's the Russian Mafia - he thinks it's connected to our work in some way.'

The tyres shrieked again as the car slowed to turn into a side road where before long the hedgerows fused into a solid blur of wriggling stripes and panels of green.

'Russian Mafia for fuck's sake!' said Aziz incredulously, 'I think you need to tell me what the fuck your work is about . . . and why the fuck everyone's so interested in it?'

Chapter 40: rubbish

Magnus was bored. He had finished the test paper for the 'Faith in Science' seminar before the others, ticking the boxes of the multiple choice answers without too much thought or concern at the eventual outcome.

The tutor, Cindy Lopez, had deliberately included a quirky option in the answer choices, her intention to convey some moral principle or to be humorous. Occasionally, Magnus had marked the wrong box, deliberately choosing 'oncology' instead of 'ontology', or 'irritator' rather than 'iterator'. What did he care what she thought of him? She didn't know who he was, or what he could do.

The Peregrine Falcon that nested near the PORTAL compound was cruising in the sky then dived suddenly to lunge at a pigeon. Magnus watched the drama through the window, disappointed the bird had missed. He consoled himself by crushing a beetle that had wandered close enough for him to reach it with his foot.

His phone warbled for attention. The message said, 'Pack for aboard. Briefing in two hours.' Magnus pushed his chair back from the desk, and rose to his feet.

'Got to go Cindy,' he said loudly from the back of the classroom. 'Something important come up.' The thought sparked an image.

'Sure Magnus.' She smiled her assent. 'Next class is this time next week.'

He imagined Cindy's face, split and bruised, wet with tears, his cock pushing into her mouth. As he stood up and strode for the door, he crumpled up his answer sheet and tossed it into the bin with an exaggerated throw. 'Yeah,' he said, 'see you then.' He knew they were all looking at him - *Pygmies* he thought - and he knew it felt good.

Chapter 41: a friend in need

(12.30 pm)

Chris watched the car accelerate down the narrow road. She pushed the business card Aziz had given her into her purse, and retrieved the keys to open the door to Victoria Cottage. Erwin, the cat, squeezed gracefully through the wrought-iron bars of the garden gate and entwined herself eagerly around Chris' legs, demanding to be noticed with an insistent purr. Chris fed the cat, had a light lunch, and relieved she had no pressing commitments decided she needed some fresh air and an opportunity to unwind from the bruising turbulence of the last twenty-four hours.

She jogged for a while, trying to clear her thoughts. This time, the therapy that exercise normally provided didn't work, so she turned back early. After showering, Chris lay on the settee to rest, but unable to settle, she reached for the phone.

'Hi. Chris here - how are you?' she asked when her best friend, Nandini Chatterjee, answered her call.

'Chris – fantastic, long time no see,' said Nandini delightedly, in the singsong voice of the Indian subcontinent. 'I am very well, and how are you?'

'A bit all over the place I'm afraid. I was hoping to catch up with the gossip. Are you doing anything just now?'

'Come on over for a nice cup of tea and we will chin-wag. I have a scrummy cake I baked just this morning.'

Thirty minutes later, outside the Tudor red brick house in the tiny hamlet of White Leaved Oak, Chris embraced her portly friend dressed in an incongruous sari and wearing her 'John Lennon' specs, before following her into the kitchen. After a few minutes, carrying trays of tea and cakes, they re-emerged into the garden, still verdant in the muted midday light of an English autumn. The women stopped for a while on a bridge, which Nandini explained had recently been completed from recycled materials by her husband, Dr Janbir Chatterjee. Its single arch spanned a small ornamental pond carpeted with lilies that formed canals for the ducks to punt along in a leisurely dawdle, occasionally flipping over to present a cone of feathered backside to the watching women. They strolled across the bridge until, settled in the gazebo and serenaded by the gentle cooing of a pigeon and the reassuring response of its mate, Dr Reynolds felt almost safe again.

'Now how have you been keeping yourself dear?' demanded Nandini.

'Up and down, you know . . . the usual.' Chris frowned. 'To tell you the truth, everything seems to be unravelling a bit - I'm worried I may be pregnant – I'm over a week late.' she added as an afterthought.

'Joy of joys, my dearest friend,' began Nandini. 'When is the little angel due?'

'Well, it was only a few weeks ago . . .'

'Ah' interrupted Nandini, suddenly more serious. 'In the lap of the gods, but a woman knows. So it's all going swimmingly with that handsome Italian man I met at your place?'

'French not Italian. No, I've finished with Kim – haven't told him yet but its settled and anyway I've met someone else since.'

'Oh, I see,' said Nandini sharply, with an intake of breath. 'If you don't mind me asking - are there a few candidates, how shall I put it . . . seeking your hand?'

'Nandini please . . . nothing like that . . . no . . . It's just I spent last night with Ian Lineker.'

'What, the smiley chap you gave that beautiful sweater to?' asked Nandini.

'Yes, my boss - Dr Lineker.'

'Well, good heavens – you've 'met' with your boss!'

Chris wasn't sure if Nandini was being sarcastic.

'Who would have thought? He is very clever and from New Zealand too . . .'

'He's Australian,'

'Yes that's right dear . . . same idea,' continued Nandini unfazed. 'Always seemed to me a very . . . mature sort of man. Do you mind me asking? How does he feel about you being, possibly, . . . pregnant?'

'Well of course, we haven't discussed anything like that yet.'

'Yes, best to wait till you know, no need to put the cart before the apple upset.'

'We had an awful lot to drink I'm afraid and didn't really bother with precautions,' said Chris. 'If not Kim it could be Ian.'

'Spare me the details dear,' Nandini interrupted, as she took another slice of cake. 'I have visited Konark in Orissa and seen the carvings, and Mr Chatterjee has been a veritable tiger in his time, I don't mind telling you. But you are in love with Dr Lineker.'

'Well no, not really in love - no,' said Chris. 'I had become a bit obsessed with Ian but not in love. In fact, we already agreed to go back to being just good friends - I suppose you could call it a 'one-night stand." She smiled guiltily, anticipating her friend's disapproval. 'It's what we both wanted,' she added, 'and we're still very close.'

'Oh,' said Nandini 'My, oh my, a very quick flash in the pan! But you may be having his baby . . . or the Italian man's baby . . . someone's baby anyway.' Nandini suddenly looked serious, her smile replaced by a frown of concern. 'Have you ever considered dear you may have a bit of a problem with men, a problem with commitment?'

Chris felt a stab of anxiety - the sudden understanding that a private suspicion may have become public knowledge. Nandini was continuing. 'It seems to me that whenever a man is interested in you, you finish with them.'

'Ian wanted this . . . not me,' protested Chris, knowing this was not all of the truth.

'You only seem to want what you can't have dear. Remember that married man, the rich one who had bags of money and a Rolls-Royce?'

'Phil and his wife were very unhappy together,' argued Chris.

'Yes, and when he left his wife . . . you dumped him. More tea dear?'

Chapter 42: and don't it always seem to go
(12.35 pm)

Nandini sounded cross, frowning at Chris. 'And then the Italian boy gets keen and he's out too,' Chris was staring glumly at the ducks. 'And, anyway, there is rarely a right time to become a mother, dear. The little ones decide for themselves. Here try these if you don't like the ones I made. They're gluten free. I got them from the health food store.' Nandini rotated the plate a little to make the cake portions easier for Chris to reach. 'I have to say - what's going on with you and Dr Lineker I just don't understand,' Nandini concluded.

'Well . . . neither Ian or me wanted to risk our working relationship, though work isn't going too well either at the moment.' There was a subdued tone to Chris's voice.

Nandini Chatterjee had given much of her life to raising her family, but when the three children had grown up and left the family home, she had enrolled on a correspondence course in Astrophysics, recently completing the PhD that she had abandoned twenty years previously when she married.

'Didn't you say you had made real progress explaining light lensing without Mr Einstein's General Relativity?' queried Nandini.

'Yes, I mean no . . . no, that's all fine - it's just funding as always.'

'Ah yes – funding. Janbir said you were at his latest committee meeting, dear. We discuss the Process Physics sometimes very hotly, but sadly, I don't think you can be relying on his support.'

'That's a pity. It won't help if Dr Chatterjee isn't on our side.'

'Well, I have tried to persuade him dear but he is such a stick in the mud,' said Nandini, '. . . like a bull in the haystack.'

'Actually, we have been approached to work for a very peculiar outfit with a radical agenda to reduce world population,' replied Chris. 'They're really creepy so we had to turn them down.'

'Yes yes, my dear, there are too many zealots these days,' observed Nandini wistfully, giving her head the lateral shake so typical of her continent of origin, as she stared absentmindedly into her Worcester porcelain tea cup. 'Best to stay well away from extremists. Now back to you and Dr Lineker - what are you going to do?'

'I don't know . . . nothing really.' said Chris. 'Just carry on I suppose.'

'It's important we learn from our mistakes dear. You can't go on as a single item all your life.'

'I imagine not, but work takes up all my energy. I don't have time for relationships,' protested Chris, a remark that did little to interrupt her friend's torrent of advice.

'I'm not talking about how you earn your money. I'm talking about who you are - I'm talking about balance. For starters, you could wear a bit of colour now and again, and not just jeans all the time.'

'Actually, I recently bought a lovely dress,' began Chris, 'it really suits me . . .'

'And I bet it's black dear. A bit of nail polish and showing off your body isn't being feminine. A woman must trust, she must allow herself to be vulnerable. If she doesn't, how can she love, and without love dear - what is the point? You're no spring chicken any more either. Time you sorted out this man-problem of yours, time you thought about settling down,' said Nandini.

'I'm only twenty-six,' Chris was saying plaintively, 'maybe I'm just waiting for Mr Right.'

'Mr Right is it?' Nandini demanded sternly, though she seemed suddenly lost for a reply, looking distracted for a couple of seconds until she resumed with a more conciliatory tone. 'It was so much simpler for Janbir and me. We did what we were told and everything worked out fine. You must understand that sometimes your feelings are less important than what is right, especially when there might be a baby on the way.'

'Well - I'm not ready to give up a life of my own - I've seen what can happen,' Chris blurted out, picturing one of her first memories - her mum collapsed on the kitchen floor, howling in despair, blood streaming from a cut above her eye. And how her mother had tried to stifle her crying when she saw her daughter peeping around the kitchen door. Chris stopped abruptly, realising how silly it might sound, and suddenly aware of how upset she had become.

Nandini realized too, pulling Chris closer to wrap an arm around her as she stroked her head. 'There, there . . . you'd be surprised how different things can look . . . once you accept the need for change.' Nandini held her for several seconds then gently released Chris from her comforting embrace and stood up. Chris snuffled a bit, and smiled, confused by her own emotions but reassured by Nandini's air of maternal authority.

There was a loud quacking as the ducks hoping for more food, jostled with each other to secure the best position for the crumbs that Nandini scattered on the ground.

'And how much fun is a different willy every night, if you're honest with yourself?' added Nandini, unable to resist the question, shattering the harmony that had briefly been re-established between them.

'Nandini, please . . . it's not like that . . .' Chris got no further.

'Well that is what it will become if you're not careful,' Nandini interrupted in a no-nonsense voice. She inhaled ostentatiously, straightening her back as if about to embark on a difficult physical challenge and continued. 'This is what you do. First - you wait another week to ten days then you test for pregnancy. If you are pregnant you speak to Dr Lineker. You ask if he loves you and wants to be your husband. If he says yes - you marry quickly and have the baby.'

'But Kim has black hair and Ian is blonde,' sniffed Chris.

'And you are dark my dear - so no problem there. It's as old as history, just look at that nice Prince Harry.'

'But I told you - neither of us has any interest in marrying.'

'In that case you tell him you're pregnant and he must pay while you bring up the child until you can work again. He has a good job, he won't notice. Anyway, I think you will find that a mature man like that will be glad to marry and you will change your mind too with a new baby around.'

'I don't know . . .' began Chris.

'And if you're not pregnant,' interrupted Nandini again. 'You henna your hair.'

'Henna my hair? Why would I do that? I thought you liked my hair?' By now, Chris intrigued by her friend's analysis, was looking and listening intently as Nandini disposed of the options with authoritative certainty.

'Maybe time for something a little less boyish,' said Nandini sternly. 'Then you go shopping for clothes with a bit of femininity in them too. I'll go with you, and I can let you have some nice jewellery - I have some lovely pieces.'

'Oh . . . I see. . .' said Chris, wounded by the implied criticism.

'Then you forget all this nonsense about your past; your childhood and who said what to who - you find an Englishman your own age, and you marry him,' concluded Nandini undeterred. 'Now hold your cup out for a top up dear.'

Chapter 43: pissed

(2.00 pm)

'Is Lineker with you?'

'Is that you Dr Grafton?'

'Of course it's me Reynolds. I need to speak with Lineker.'

'Well he's not here I'm afraid,' said Chris, stirring a pot of boiling rice on the cooker for the sushi she was preparing for tomorrow's lunch and wedging the phone under one cheek.

'We were supposed to meet half an hour ago but he hasn't shown.'

'He's normally very punctual,' observed Chris. 'I'll tell him you were looking for him when I see him next.'

'There's something serious going on Reynolds - I'm being threatened.'

'What . . . who is threatening you?' she asked, concerned.

'I've been assaulted . . . horribly assaulted.' Grafton replied. 'I think it's the Russian Mafia. Lineker's stupid non-science is very important to someone and that someone has no respect for the law.'

'Excuse me Dr Grafton,' interrupted Chris. 'I really am growing tired of your cynicism. Our work is not stupid non-science, maybe you should take the time to understand it. Maybe I can help you.' The anger accumulated from a series of recently unanswered provocations was now audible in her voice. She continued forcefully.

'Process Physics uses an equation derived from Quantum Mechanics. The equation represents changing connectivity patterns – it's an equation of 'interaction' or if you like, of 'process.' It does this by adding a random element to its variables, and then recycling the results back through the same equation to represent the next 'moment' in time – that's why we call it an 'Iterator Equation'. Because of this there is no need for a rule put in by hand to explain why time only has one direction - how shocking!' she said sarcastically. 'The 'present' – the 'now' moment - is treated as real, not dismissed as some sort of psychological illusion. Because of that the notion of 'simultaneous' is allowed its proper place. And above all, light is not arbitrarily required to have one speed, unlike every other natural phenomenon.'

Chris was trying to remove the pot from the cooker with the phone still under her chin but as she lifted the heavy container, the phone dropped to the floor. By the time she had retrieved it Grafton was speaking, but she chose to ignore him and recommenced where she had left off. 'We account for all the experimental evidence, not just the bits that suit us, without the invention of a bunch of things that no-one can actually detect, like the 'superstringers' with their 'multiple dimensions' or 'space quanta.'' Further irritated by the difficulties of cooking and talking at the same time, and unaware of the extent of the trauma that Grafton had endured, Chris's mood was deteriorating even further. 'It's all there in the Maths. Anyone can check it. Gravity is explained, and you don't need Dark Matter and Dark Energy to get the equations to balance, or even Higgs bloody Bosons or Gravitons or any of the other sci-fi bullshit of modern physics,' she added furiously.

Grafton, distressed himself at the rapid erosion of the certainties that had sustained him for so long, was having none of it. 'You'll be telling me next the Hadron Collider is a waste of money I suppose, Reynolds,' he shouted at her. 'The world's leading physicists are all wrong, except you and Lineker. Your arrogance is unbelievable - and now you've involved these madmen - you don't realize what you've started.' Grafton's voice had the choking sound of a man losing control. 'If you hear from Lineker tell him I need to see him very, very urgently - and tell him I'll have his guts for gaiters.'

Chapter 44: stan the man

(2.10 pm)

'Are you all right Dr Grafton - I thought I heard shouting?' Grafton's secretary asked, popping her head around the door.

For fucks sake just piss off, Grafton thought, grimacing with the nearest he could achieve to a smile. He dabbed quickly at his face with a tissue, fearing a tear might have escaped the corner of his eye. 'Fine Margaret, thanks, everything's fine.'

It was some time before he was able to make his next call. This time his call was to Stanley Warner, the retired policeman in charge of security at MRI.

'Any progress?' asked Grafton.

'I've contacted a friend who is now in Special Branch, and he is running checks. But it's only been a few hours, Bill, these things take a while.'

'So nothing to report?' demanded Grafton.

'Well . . . the local fuzz say there was an incident with a man matching your description of the guy who attacked you. Apparently when an old fella accidentally obstructed him on the pavement he pushed him violently out of the way and swore rather unpleasantly at some bystanders who protested.'

'When was this?'

'Yesterday evening. But to me it just sounds like you've been unlucky. The local police want you to go in and file a complaint.'

'Unlucky!' He knew my name for God's sake. A random thug doesn't know your name.'

'Oh yes, of course . . . well, the local station are onto it and so is my contact in London. In the meantime - just check from the window before you go outside, keep the car in the garage, vary your route to work. You know all the usual things.'

'So you think there is some danger Stan?' Eager to hear a third party's assessment of the seriousness of his ordeal, Grafton pushed a pile of papers to one side to make space to sit on the edge of his desk. The papers cascaded around the bin, some falling directly into it. Grafton was gripping the phone hard, pressing it to his ear.

'No not really,' Stan was saying, his Devonian accent complementing his naturally laid-back delivery, 'I think this guy is just a nasty pasty who overheard your name in town and followed you to the hills, and has long since moved on because he hasn't been seen since. However - these are sick times - and a little bit of caution never hurt anyone - I'll let you know if anything turns up.'

'But doesn't it seem more than a coincidence that I've just been speaking to someone with a Russian accent who offers me a lot of money for control of one of my research projects? Then I'm attacked - by someone with a Russian accent.'

Warner had taken the MRI job to supplement his retirement pension in the belief that there would be nothing to do. Grafton was persisting, missing the cues that the elderly man on the other end of the phone wished only to conclude the conversation so as he could return to his copy of Ice Station Zebra, that he was re-reading for the fifth time.

'There may well be a connection, Bill. But like I said, it's not illegal to have a foreign accent. We're not Nazi Germany are we? Get down to the station and let the local boys fill in a report sheet okay? Sometimes it's the pattern that catches these morons and you can't spot a pattern without information.'

'Of course - thanks Stan - I hope you're right.'

'Take it easy Bill,' said Warner, hanging up.

Grafton was pacing across his office when Margaret knocked, entered the room and handed him a post-it note. 'Took this while you were on the telephone,' she said breezily. 'The man had a foreign accent - sounded phony to me - he said you'd know what it was about.' She left without waiting for a reply. The words popped into Grafton's vision with a shocking urgency.

'A friend phoned. Wants to meet 2:15 pm entrance Winter Gardens, Priory Rd side. Dr Lineker will be there.' The note was timed at 2:00 pm.

The bastard. I knew bloody Lineker was in this up to his goddam Aussie eyeballs . . . Grafton stopped himself, unable to complete the thought. He clenched his fist, drawing a deep breath in an effort to remain calm and strode for the door. *That guy is finished - I'll have his fucking balls . . . how dare he deny his involvement - how dare he.*

Chapter 45: long and winding

(2.10 pm)

After dropping the scientists off, Aziz had eaten a late lunch before returning to the Audi to drive along the back roads from Malvern, heading west, to look up Phil 'Beaky' Jones on his organic herb farm ten miles out of Hereford. Beaky had been his unarmed combat instructor before he became a friend, and Aziz knew Beaky was a good man in a crisis.

Must get to Izzy . . . before they do. The memory returned; the same memory that woke Aziz in the depths of the night.

Aziz had been withdrawing from a reconnaissance mission in a rural area east of Kabul in Pashtun Afghanistan, when through the window of a damaged house he had seen the shooting of a girl who like his own daughter, Isabel, was not yet adolescent. The girl had been cradling the head of her father just a few metres from Aziz, so close he had seen the flecks of gold in her green eyes and the proud dignity of her dirt-stained face. Though hideously injured, the man was still alive as he lay on the floor in what had once been their living room. An allied soldier appeared at a gaping hole in the mud wall opposite and levelled his assault rifle to take aim. The girl had looked up at Aziz, both of them knowing – she resigned to her fate, he screaming to deny it - and the family which had so little other than life, lost even that, when the face of an angel was shattered to blood and bone.

The day after, Aziz and his sergeant Phil 'Beaky' Jones, had been pinned down by an AK47 and grenade attack in a prolonged fire fight. They had both been hit, a bullet tearing through Aziz's upper thigh before lodging near his spinal column. Despite his injuries, Aziz had fought to reach Beaky, now bleeding badly from a shrapnel wound, and had bandaged him, whilst returning enemy fire. He had called in an air strike and under its cover had dragged the unconscious Beaky for two miles on a roughly fashioned sled before they were rescued by an Afghani squad dispatched to help them.

Six months later Aziz had been awarded the Conspicuous Gallantry Cross, which he had sold to a collector when finally, the doctors had given up on him.

Must stay calm ... must think it out.

Aziz gripped the wheel, shaking his head to dispel the dizziness that was emerging from the back of his head, like a spider crawling from beneath a rock. The intention to kill Baedeker, that Aziz had shared with the scientists, had been forged in the heat of the moment with the adrenaline still coursing in his veins. But now, Aziz was no longer sure. Even if stopping Baedeker had the collateral benefit of bringing down the Church, it was uncertain it would help Isabel. Aziz felt his enthusiasm for the plan starting to wane.

He had attacked and badly injured two security men, who looked to him suspiciously like the type of US agents he had been briefed by before covert operations in Afghanistan. Whatever the reality of their threats to him and Isabel, even if they had been bluffing before, he was sure he'd pissed them off big-time, and he had to assume they, and the police, would be looking for him now.

They'll come in hard, with the cavalry - now they know I'm no fuckin' pansy.

Aziz tried once more to piece together the jigsaw of recent events but he lacked answers to some important questions - why had this Grafton character been threatened, what was the connection with Lineker's work, were the Russian mafia really involved or was all this down to PORTAL.com? Without knowing who the players were, Aziz decided he couldn't properly assess the nature of the threat to his daughter, and that was his major concern. He had given her so little of worth in her life, it was abhorrent to him that his only effect on her now should be to place her at risk of harm.

I need more intel – I've got to find out what the fuck is going on here, thought Aziz, not yet admitting that the reason he was looking forward to his mission was he believed it would take him closer to the woman he had just dropped off at her Malvern home; the woman he was realising he so much admired - the woman he was beginning to hope, one day might bring him peace.

Chapter 46: on the table

(2.30 pm)

Grafton had left the office almost immediately after he received the note of Emelienko's phone call and was waiting impatiently at the door to the Winter Gardens when a black Mercedes with tinted windows pulled up. The driver hopped out and walked quickly around to the kerbside to open the door for the seated occupant. The driver was whippet thin, with a scar running down one cheek and the fluid movements that Grafton immediately recognized as belonging to his assailant on the hills. The man grimaced at Grafton, in a mockery of a smile, the gold top to a front tooth glinting in the sun. He opened the rear door to enable a thick set man to ease himself from the leather and chrome interior of the executive saloon and approach Grafton, one hand held out before him, inviting a handshake.

'Dr Grafton I presume,' he said in the heavy accent that confirmed this was Emelienko, head of SRS, the Society for Responsibility in Science. On seeing the chauffeur, Grafton's anger had subsided immediately, to be replaced by a gut-wrenching fear at the shameless proximity of someone who could assault him with casual impudence and against whom he lacked any defence.

'My apologies for calling you with false messages. We meet quickly, before matters get out of hand.'

Grafton meekly took the man's hand giving it a light squeeze.

'Where is Lineker?' he asked.

'This is problem Dr Grafton. Dr Lineker not able be with us.'

'You said. . .' began Grafton.

'I sorry to misleading you. Important we meet. More likely you come see Dr Lineker than meet with Shirov again.' A wide grin split his chubby features as he swept a podgy hand through the foppish flop of grey hair that wandered across his face. 'Dr Lineker I'm sure, he sends regrets.'

'Where is he and what do you want?' asked Grafton, grim-faced and nauseous from the bile rising in his throat.

'Dr Lineker with client. Client require you publish retraction of Lineker's work. Dr Reynolds will help do this.'

'What on earth!?' protested Grafton.

'My client understand you not believe Lineker's claims - so task easy for you, Dr Grafton.'

'This is outrageous,' insisted Grafton summonsing his courage. 'I will not be intimidated like this. I wish to speak with Dr Lineker immediately.'

'Dr Lineker cannot speak just now. He released when client says works not a threat.'

'A threat . . . what do you mean . . . you're holding Dr Lineker as a hostage?' said Grafton incredulously, the full horror of the situation emerging from the residue of the mundane.

'Not me Dr Grafton. Client. I think you better assume my client bad people.'

There was anger in Emelienko's voice. 'Understand - Dr Reynolds also - if contact police about situation, will cause Dr Lineker great harm. Cause you great harm. Yes - is right yes?' He turned to his driver, and the two men laughed, with the casual amiability of those who have power without the distractions of empathy. The sound chilled Grafton and he gave an involuntary shudder, as he felt the tickle of goose bumps racing across his skin.

Emelienko continued with the cheerful tone of someone arranging a garden fete at the vicarage. 'You must do public retraction of work in seven days. Please understand - client are ruthless people. You have seven days before Lineker . . .' He drew his finger across his throat, in a parody of menace, then turned on his heel and walked quickly back to the car. Shirov, his driver, made a sudden lunging gesture toward Grafton. For the second time, Grafton fearful he was about to be struck, hunched, cowering with his arms held protectively over his head, feeling the sudden dampness of urine around his groin, compounding his humiliation and feeding his despair.

The man smirked the gloat of the school-yard bully before crossing the road in time to open the car door for his boss. Grafton watched as the car surged powerfully away up the road. The whole encounter had taken only slightly more than two minutes, but Grafton had lived an eternity, the condition outside of time, that is an unwelcome side-effect of terror.

Chapter 47: time out

(2.45 pm)

As he drove toward Hereford, Aziz was replaying his first memory of Chris. He remembered her running on the Malvern Hills, flustered and furious, her skin damp from exertion, a vision of sexiness and radiant good-health. *She'd look like that after fucking.* The thought excited him.

A tractor and trailer had just lumbered onto the road from a rain-soaked field. Aziz slowed the car, enjoying the slight thudding reverberation of the tyres as they squashed the mud clots to discs of dirt, before he overtook the slow-moving vehicle with a cheery toot and resumed his daydreaming . . . *have to say, cutest little arse I've seen for a long, long time.* He imagined his fingers, and his tongue, probing, pushing in; and he imagined her pushing back, her breathing becoming louder, her eyes slitted with desire.

But . . .

The self-doubt that stalked him was suddenly at his side, ridiculing his fantasy, reducing him to a voyeur of another man's pleasure. Behind it came the anger.

Smug Australian prick . . . fuckin' bastard.

When night sweats had interfered with his rest, exhausted and confused, Aziz had tried sleeping in the cupboard under the stairs. The arrangement had brought him some relief. But when people's faces had transformed into leering masks in the street, Aziz had finally sought help for the 'post-traumatic stress disorder' diagnosed when he was discharged from the service. His psychiatrist, a lisping slightly effeminate young Buddhist, had warned him that 'erectile dysfunction' could become more than just a physical handicap, that penetration was symbolic of manhood representing conquest, overcoming, and power, as well as a route to union and completion. He remembered he had asked: *'So it's all my fault from now on is it?'* but he couldn't remember the response.

The furious honking of a car horn behind him wrenched him back into the present.

So who's this cunt? thought Aziz, checking the side mirror.

A black Mercedes was pressing to overtake, though the road was narrow and windy. Aziz increased speed a little, studying the driver in the rear view mirror. He thought it unlikely to be the Americans from Llanthony but begrudgingly admitted if they had caught him that quickly, they were entitled to a degree of respect. The familiar knot was forming in his gut as his mind calculated how best to respond, and his body gathered itself in a reflexive preparation for action.

'Never underestimate the opposition.' The thought was immediately strangled as the Mercedes suddenly accelerated past his Audi, cutting sharply in front of him, the driver's arm raised vertically from the window with a totemic finger pointing insolently above it to form a continuous line with a dagger tattoo on the sinewy forearm.

A spasm of blind fury exploded in Aziz. 'You fuck!' he yelled at the retreating car, stamping on the accelerator, his own car surging forward in pursuit. Shaken by the unexpected intensity of his reaction, Aziz remembered again the advice he had been given by his psychiatrist - that impotence would engender a sense of inadequacy, and frustration might find an outlet in resentment and rage.

Aziz smiled to himself, his foot easing off from the pedal, and the Audi slowed once more to a sensible pace. *'Wanker,'* thought Aziz, watching the Mercedes disappear into the distance.

The driving incident, and the release of pent-up emotion had brought focus to Aziz's mind, and a clearer appreciation of the dilemma that was building around him. Even if he wished to, he could not simply ignore the events of the last twenty-four hours, the Church's security agents and the police would see to that.

Could he perhaps get close enough to Baedeker to snatch him, use him as a bargaining chip, trade him for his daughter's safety? Did he need Chris Reynolds to help him? How could he get the Church investigated when the police would arrest him if he went to them? Any disclosure he made about the Church, if it became public, must surely increase the danger to his daughter. How could he protect his daughter when he didn't even know where she was?

The Church appeared eminently capable of being ruthless. If Chris Reynolds helped him, wouldn't she be placing herself at risk, especially now that she had refused the Church too?

Shit, he thought, banging the steering wheel with his fist. 'Shit, shit', he shouted, feeling the strain at the back of his throat, feeling the invigoration of anger contesting the draining realization of defeat. For the moment at least, he had lost - it was time not to attack, but to retreat. For his daughter's sake, he had to be quiet about the Church. For Chris Reynolds's safety he had to stay away from her, whatever his feelings, until one way or another the Church was no longer a threat. He would arm himself against the people who would come looking for him, and he would lay low . . . *ditch the car, trade the American's gun with Beaky,* he reminded himself, as he drove gently down the track to Beaky's farm.

Aziz made one error in his deliberations, but it was not a mistake that would affect the future - it was the error of imagining the future was his to control.

Chapter 48: mood shift

(3.00 pm)

The row with Grafton over the phone had left Chris feeling frazzled, so she had taken refuge in the distraction of work. She was hunched over her monitor, trying to pinpoint what in the computer code had caused her modelling of 'borehole g anomalies' to freeze, when there was a loud banging on the front door.

Who could that be . . . maybe Ian, she thought, glancing at the clock.

She pushed the cat from her lap and tightened her dressing gown around her to quickly cross the room. She peeped through the small square window in the door, surprised to see that the person now walking away from the cottage was much shorter than Lineker. The man stopped just before the gate and turned abruptly, hurrying back toward her front door. It was Grafton. He looked agitated, too agitated to keep still. She opened the door quickly, 'Dr Grafton . . .'

'Can we talk – inside. Please.'

By now Chris was worried. This was not the self-important windbag of the committee room, but a man who looked much older, and was clearly distressed.

'What's wrong, what's happened? It's not . . .?' her voice faltered, remembering that Ian had been intending to meet with Grafton, and at the sudden premonition of the awful. 'It's not Ian is it?'

'Yes, I'm afraid it is. The Russians have got him. They want us to retract his work - your work. If we don't . . . they'll hurt him.' Grafton's lower lip was trembling

'What in God's name . . . what on earth are you talking about?' hissed Chris, the colour draining from her face.

'I've just met them. They threatened me again. We mustn't tell anyone or they'll hurt him.'

'So where is Ian?' demanded Chris.

'I don't know. Emelienko - that's the man who offered me money - the man who said he was from the Society for Responsibility in Science - he was with the other man, the one who assaulted me on the hills.' Grafton gave a strange involuntary yelp that Chris realized was the sound of a man choking back tears. 'I've already told the police, they know about that,' Grafton concluded.

'They know Ian's missing?' asked Chris, confused.

'No, I've not told anybody that Lineker's missing . . . no . . . the police know about me being assaulted . . . from before. Emelienko warned me not to tell the police about Lineker – they say they'll hurt him – I believe them. I've come straight here. This is all so . . . it's madness. I can't believe this is happening . . .what can we do . . .?' Grafton, was babbling, he seemed to be losing control, and Chris noted with concern, he smelt of urine.

She reached for her phone, dialling quickly, her lips pressed together tightly as if trying to contain her emotion. Grafton fell silent, looking across at her intently, neither of them daring to breathe, the only sound the metronomic hum of an unanswered ring playing through the receiver pressed to her ear.

'No reply on his mobile,' she said, dialling frantically again.

The same sequence played out, the lack of response creating the almost tangible presence of a creature defined by absence, like the empty outline of a cartoon ghost.

'Shit, he's not at home either . . .' Chris was trembling, in shudders. Her eyes moistened as she looked at Grafton, a final plea in the interval of disbelief before hope is extinguished by despair.

'His satellite phone . . . where's the number.' It was a rhetorical question; she was guiding herself by the spoken word, scrabbling for anything that might avoid the unthinkable. Chris pounded at the keyboard of her computer, searching emails for the message where Lineker had first told her excitedly of the recently acquired satellite phone, and a new project to test the new physics by calibrating a GPS with a correction derived from Process Physics, rather than the standard method using Relativity.

'Here it is . . . here it is . . . this is it.' she said, simultaneously banging the numbers into the touchpad. They listened for the ringing, staring into each other's eyes, with the peculiar intensity of those so distracted by thought that they look without seeing.

Someone answered the phone. It was a stranger's voice, the guttural rasp crushing her hope as completely as a footfall extinguishes an insect on the pavement.

'Wait,' it said.

Chapter 49: help this hurt

(3.05 pm)

'Dr Lineker has message. He will read you.' The deep voice was Russian and mannered, as inauthentic as only a bad actor or the real thing would risk. The sound of clunking suggested the phone was being handed over.

'Is that you Chris?' Lineker sounded anxious. It frightened her, it was a tone she could not imagine him using.

'Yes, it's me, are you alright . . .?' she was asking, when again there was a muffled sound in the distance, and Lineker gasped as if in pain.

''But help this hurt,' he said.

She heard it clearly in the background, a man shouting: 'Only read note, only read note.'

'Of course Ian . . . tell me what I must do?'

'I grown intense,' said Lineker, 'but help this hurt.'

'I'm not understanding you,' she said, the sound of her distress sticking like a jagged wedge in her throat. 'I'm sorry . .
'

'Time for angry speech,' Lineker said, again there was a swishing sound and a yelp of pain. 'Angry speech,' he repeated.

The scuffling sounds intensified, the agonizing thumping of someone being beaten, before the voice started again.

'I am Dr Ian Lineker.'

Chris listened in shock, horrified that she could only recognize the Australian accent to confirm this must be him, his speech halting with the harsh rasp of laboured breathing. 'You have seven days to publish a retraction of my work. If you do not, I will be killed. If you go to the police, one of you will be killed.'

The phone went dead, and Chris sank to the floor, tears pouring down her face as she sobbed, almost silently. Grafton looked away, embarrassed, unable to offer comfort except to offer her a tissue retrieved from a box on the computer desk, which she used to dab at her makeup that had left flecks of black around red-rimmed and puffy eyes.

'What can we do Dr Reynolds?' asked Grafton

'They were beating him. Badly. I've not heard anyone whimper like that before. And he was talking in a strange way,' Chris was distraught.

'Shouldn't we go to the police?' added Grafton.

'I don't think we can go to the police . . . they said someone would be killed if we did,' she whispered, barely audibly.

'I was told the same but the police are trained for this . . .' Grafton began, before she cut him off.

'No, what we'll do is have a cup of tea,' she said, already moving toward the kitchen. 'We'll work things through calmly and make some decisions.' Her upper body was straight with a rigid self-control and her progression unnaturally smooth, as if she was gliding on rails.

An instant after she had left the room, Grafton heard a strange muffled sound like a swallowed choke. He started toward the sound, certain she was crying but unsure if he should follow to try to offer comfort. The noise suddenly changed, an eerie keening that grew in volume and pitch, to reach a howl that was more unnatural than human. Grafton felt the hairs on his neck stand out, his bowels turning to jelly. There was a huge crash, the sound of breaking glass and ceramics, then a stillness, complete except for the residual humming in Grafton's ears.

Oh my God, thought Grafton. 'Dr Reynolds. are you alright?' he called out.

Chapter 50: gobbledygook

(3.10 pm)

To Grafton, too afraid to follow her and confront what might have happened, it felt like minutes before Chris spoke.

'I'm fine now thank you, Dr Grafton.'

Her voice was measured, even and studiedly calm as she came back into the living room, moving with an exaggerated purposefulness, like a robot. 'It's okay,' she said quietly. 'I have an idea.'

Concerned at how strange she seemed, Grafton watched her intently as she rummaged in the drawer of a side-cupboard and retrieved a large notepad and pen. "Time for angry speech' Ian said. What do you think he meant by that?' she asked, staring before her almost vacantly, the question posed as if it didn't anticipate a response.

'I can't . . .' Grafton let his reply die away, realising she was not listening, and he had nothing to say. He noted the promised cup of tea had not materialised, and he noticed the trembling of her hand. Apart from her ashen complexion and the puffiness around her eyes, Chris looked composed.

'I just don't get it. Ian was talking so differently, almost in code. Chris repeated the words, her head tilted as if listening to the sounds. 'Angry speech, angry speech . . .' *Yes, it must be a clue of some sort - he's trying to tell me something.*

The realization expanded into an image - Ian, locked in a room, fearful, desperate to communicate something to her - and all she could hear was the question looping in her mind. *Why? Why is this happening?*

She thought back to Llanthony and their conversation. *Just this morning . . . a lifetime ago.* And with a wrench of guilt, she remembered her indifference, her lack of feeling for him.

Think, she urged herself, *think.* She started to hum quietly, an unconscious mannerism that when stressed would often happen as she tried to relax her mind, hoping for some clue and the sort of inspiration that in her mathematics had rescued her before from a seemingly impossible conundrum.

Time for 'angry speech'. 'Angry speech.' It came to her, at first half-imagined and faltering as in a dream, then delivered in an instant. *'Cross Word' – is that it?* 'He may have meant 'Cross Word,'' she announced. *Yes, he would have remembered.*

Chris had been only the second woman to win the Times Crossword championship, and had done so at a speed that was still a record five years later, and she had retained the habit of churning anagrams in her head to keep herself amused. She scribbled the phrases down on the paper, while Grafton watched, bemused.

'But help this hurt,' she repeated aloud, feeling the trembling inside, the creative energy poised to receive its gift.

'But help this hurt,' - 'Publish the truth.' Bingo!

"Publish the truth," she said out loud. 'He's saying "Publish the truth". It's an anagram.'

'Good work Dr Reynolds,' said Grafton, impressed. 'How did you . . .?' he asked, but Chris did not hear him.

'The other phrase he used . . . 'I groan intense,' 'I groan intense,' . . .what's going on there?' she repeated the words slowly. *Am I spelling it right? How about 'I grown intense.' Bingo 'Einstein wrong' – yes, that's it - 'Einstein wrong.'*

'He's saying 'Einstein wrong,'' she announced, the excitement bubbling in her voice. 'He doesn't want us to refute Process Physics - he wants us to fight on. 'Einstein wrong - publish the truth.' He's saying 'Einstein wrong - publish the truth.'

'Jesus,' Grafton shook his head as he breathed out with the faintest trace of a whistle. 'He's got courage – I'll give him that.'

'He's an exceptional man . . .' Chris began, as the tears started again - tears of relief, admiration and fear – tears that stopped as quickly as they had begun.

'We will publish the truth. Somehow, we will,' Chris insisted, her face suddenly transformed by her resolve.

And don't worry Ian; I'll get you out of there. Whatever it takes.

Chapter 51: of course

(3.20 pm)

'Okay! The sooner we start; the sooner we get Ian back. Tell me what you know, everything - in detail,' asked Chris, drying her eyes with another tissue.

'Of course Dr Reynolds, of course. But first, can you think why anyone would be interested in your research?' Grafton's habit of control was reasserting itself.

'Dr Grafton, you need to understand something here,' she said through gritted teeth. 'I intend to find out who has got Ian and where they are holding him. Then I will free him. That is a grave responsibility and I am not entrusting it to anyone other than myself. Do you understand Dr Grafton?'

'Why . . . um . . . I . . . well,' Grafton's reflex was to be angry at the impudence of an employee two rungs beneath him on the management ladder speaking to him as if he were an idiot, but the memory of Shirov quickly dissolved any objection, to be replaced by relief that someone else was assuming responsibility. There was something about her demeanour too, a forcefulness he had not seen before. It required his obedience.

'Yes . . . yes of course, Dr Reynolds, of course. But you must be careful, these are very dangerous people.'

'Thank you for your warning Dr Grafton. I don't have time for niceties so it is important you understand that I require you to do exactly as you are told. Is that clear Dr Grafton?'

'Why yes, yes of course Dr Reynolds.'

'Okay. Why don't we start by calling each other 'Chris' and 'Bill'? Is that alright with you . . . Bill?'

'Why of course Dr sorry, err, Chris. Of course.'

'Now before we consider what someone may want from our research, I want to know who that someone is. That will make it easier to assess their interest. It's possible this isn't Russians at all - but an American Internet Church. They may have a connection with SRS.'

'It sounded more like the Russian Mafia to me,' insisted Grafton.

'Well, let's not prejudge anything. When we know who we're dealing with, it may become more obvious how to recover Ian. You have a phone number for Emelienko?'

'He left me a number yes, from before, but I would imagine he's not using it anymore, they're too easy to trace. I assume they won't be using that satellite phone again either.'

'You're probably right. The email he sent - do you have the email address handy?' asked Chris.

'I don't think that will help us,' replied Grafton anxiously. 'I did reply to it a couple of times but the last time I tried I got a message back saying the address was 'unknown.'

'Could you let me have a copy of it anyway? Maybe there is information in it that will help.'

'Of course Dr . . . Sorry, of course - Chris. But according to Emelienko someone else is behind all this. Emelienko refers to them as his 'client' - he says even he doesn't know who they are.'

'Okay - send the email and we'll take it from there, and let me have his phone number. Though as you say that probably won't be working either.'

'How is the email going to help if it isn't active anymore?' asked Grafton. The cat let itself in via a flap in the door and purring, rubbed herself against Chris' leg. Without looking Chris reached down to scoop it onto her lap where before long it curled up, the rasping purr audible but unnoticed by the anxious humans.

'Computer networks work on addresses, as you know,' Chris explained. 'Everything sent has an originating address, and an address where it should go,'

'And you can find that out from the email header?' asked Grafton

'I don't know yet, but it seems a good place to start.'

'There's the Head of IT chap at MRI - Ray Cheung - he'd know all this stuff,' said Grafton, his voice suddenly optimistic.

'Yes, we're lucky to have him as a resource, but until we know the limits of this problem it's best not to involve anyone else. They have been quite clear - if it gets to the police, someone will be harmed. The fewer who know, the better,' said Chris sternly. 'For the moment anyway.'

'You're right of course, I wasn't thinking. Somehow they knew I reported the assault,' said Grafton dejectedly. 'Well, I'll be off now, and forward the mail as soon as I'm back at the office.'

Grafton stopped on his way to the door. 'But . . . how do we research this Chris - if we can't ask anyone?'

'We google it of course.'

Chapter 52: cache withdrawal

(4.00 pm)

Aziz parked the car outside Beaky's farmhouse, its geometry slightly crumpled as if the present was losing its claim to a part of history that the past was determined to retain. The house was two stories high, with tall redbrick chimneys rising from a steeply pitched roof. Smoke from one of the stacks curled upwards in a tight spiral, before gathering parallel to the ground like the puffs from a steam train, mimicking in miniature the cumulus clouds assembling high above. With its walls clad in ivy and paint peeling from the window frames, the building had a comfortable look, the sort of country style which offers vindication for the idle by confirming that sometimes appearance can be improved more by neglect than by duty.

Aziz knocked on the door. The house smelt and felt occupied, but there was no reply except for a yelping bark from inside, the high-pitched wheezy yap of a rickety dog.

'It's just me Shep,' Aziz shouted, the sound of scratching on the door indicating the old-timer wanted to come out to greet him. Aziz turned away from the house and wandered back toward the car, stopping to lean over the stone wall of an orchard and watch a huge Welsh boar roaming loose as it snuffled toward him, its snout raised to savour human scent. Framed by albino lashes, the boar's eyes peered intently past ears of heavy-leather which obscured his view like the blinkers on a dray horse, as if the huge creature was trying to identify whether the uninvited visitor was friend or foe.

'See no evil, my old mate,' said Aziz affectionately to the boar, who grunted a welcome in response and flashed his yellowed tusks, then chomped lazily on the remnants of a cider apple while offering his great neck for a scratch to Aziz, in casual trusting intimacy with his latest human visitor.

The intense pressure on his neck was immediate, sudden and overwhelming. Aziz fought against panic, grabbing up to secure the arm that was throttling him and wrenching down on it to save his windpipe as he felt the first wave of nausea and the swirling onset of collapse, like a crow beating inside his head, whose wings threatened to obliterate the light as they closed in to cover him with darkness.

He was operating on training alone, without margin for fear, his strength ebbing as he clung desperately to the powerful forearm inching inexorably to rob him of life. He stamped down with his good leg, feeling the shock as it hit the ground and stamped again, reaching further back. This time he felt the raised contour of his assailant's foot and heard the sharp cry of pain almost into his ear, as honest and personal as a lover's gasp but muffled and distant, an echo down a narrowing tunnel as dizziness engulfed him.

The vicelike grip loosened slightly, and the change inspired a final surge to break free, as with all his adrenaline-fuelled strength, Aziz twisted, lashing out with an elbow that cracked into the ribs of his attacker. Aziz rolled forward and away, bobbing up again to face his enemy, his arms raised in readiness as he prepared to defend or attack.

Deep laughter rolled up from the massive man, as he crouched holding his ribs in pain. 'You little fucker Aziz - you little fucker.'

'For Christ's sake Beaky! You're a fucking arsehole you know that...'

'Crept up on you while you were ogling my pig. You always did like pigs didn't you?' chuckled Beaky.

'Maybe why I've always got on with you,' replied Aziz grimly.

'Lovely to see you too, you nasty little shit. Come on in.' Shaking his head in an imitation of exasperation, Beaky beamed affectionately at his friend, before sighing deeply and laughing again.

'I was about to have a couple of tofu burgers and then a nice fat joint followed by my normal little twenty winks. That was 'winks' not 'wanks' in case you're wondering.' Beaky laughed again. 'Have you eaten?'

'I am kind of hungry Beaky, but I've got enough on my mind without any enhancement thanks so I'll pass on the drugs. Don't let me disturb your beauty sleep though.'

'Shut the fuck up . . . you little fucker . . .' said Beaky 'and come on in.' He crouched to enter the kitchen through the low doorway, and digging through the fridge retrieved ingredients and started to prepare a salad.

'Well, to what do I owe the pleasure? It must be over a year, yes?'

Aziz peeled carrots on one side of the island bench, and methodically recounted his story, describing PORTAL, the threats to his daughter and himself. On the other side of the bench Phil Jones listened patiently, asking the occasional question as he prepared a dressing and glanced up to stare intently at his old comrade as if the reading of the inner-man was of more relevance than any of the incidental details of his recent troubled encounters.

'So how can I help you Mike?' asked Beaky.

'Do you know where I can get kitted out Beaky – but maybe now you've gone all 'vegetarian' that's not your interest anymore.'

'So you can't stop bad guys unless you eat dead cow, is that it?' replied Beaky with a smile on his face.

'I don't know, we've all changed that's for sure,' said Aziz. 'I've got a Glock I took from the Yanks at Llanthony - it's too traceable to me - can you use it?'

'Sure, I can remove its ID, have it recycled. You were saying they were US government types. Who precisely are you up against here?' asked Beaky.

'They seem to be CIA agents working as a security detail attached to the internet Church. I don't know exactly, it's too early to tell what's going on,' replied Aziz. 'I may need back up Beaky?'

'Mike, if you ask - I'm there, you know that. But I've got a nice little business here selling herbs and teas and I'm not looking for trouble these days. So don't ask until you're sure, okay?'

'Sure Beaky, I understand,' replied Aziz.

'And how secure are you?' asked Beaky.

'What do you mean?'

Beaky was laying the table, carrying condiments, plates and cutlery as he traversed the uneven slate floor, occasionally peering out of a small window to check the driveway outside.

'Let's step outside. We can eat later,' said Beaky, scooping up his jacket. 'It's okay Shep. No need to come too,' he reassured the old Border Collie, who had struggled to his feet to join them. The dog ignoring his advice, wandered outside with them as the big man resumed. 'Were you followed? Do they have a device on your car? Are they listening to us now for instance?'

'Shit - I hadn't thought of that ..' replied Aziz. 'Actually it's their car. I'm going to get rid of it when I get back to London.'

'I think you should assume they at least know where you are. Things have changed since we saw service, it's just too easy these days.' The dog headed back inside as Beaky led Aziz to the battered Land Rover Defender that was parked at the back of the house. They drove straight up a steep hummock away from the road, in silence. Each negotiated privately whether to broach the memories they shared, both fearful of reviving the ghosts of a troubled past. The spell was broken as the diesel sighed into silence and Beaky swung from the wagon.

'I've got a good stash - some of it stored locally - ACR assault rifle, flash-bangs, sawn-off Remington 870 magnum with Hatton rounds - very naughty and very nice. How do you fancy a 9 mm Sig Sauer P226, magazine extended to 20 rounds, no numbers, no history and as good as new?'

'What . . . you're unbelievable, are you starting a war?' Mike laughed, 'If they catch you with that arsenal you'll be inside for a while longer than last time I reckon.'

'So where do you think I got the contacts for this lot?' asked Beaky. He was clearing some vegetation away - the shiny glint of a rivet was the first indicator of a steel trapdoor that in under a minute he had thrown open for their inspection.

'I'll take a piece of that explosive too if you don't mind?' asked Aziz peering inside. 'This stuff isn't service issue by any horrible chance is it?'

'Best not to know, Mike.'

'You couldn't organise a couple of passports for me too could you, Beaky. One in my name and a Joe Doe too. They took my passport when I . . . you know, got into trouble. I never asked for it back.' He looked awkward. 'And I have the feeling I'll need to go abroad in a hurry. Maybe go knocking on some doors.'

'I can look into it, we'll take a mug shot of you back at the farmhouse,' the trap closed with a groaning yawn, 'and by the way, you need a bit of a refresher with your technique,' added Beaky 'I could have had you if I wanted . . .'

Chapter 53: oh shit

(4.05 pm)

It was only forty minutes since Chris had asked Grafton for a copy of Emelienko's email, but she had already found most of the tools she needed to start tracking Lineker's captors, either on websites offering services for free, or downloaded 'shrink-wrapped' from the web for a small fee of ten or twenty pounds. She was staring at the computer screen when the email arrived, the metallic resonance of its receipt notification sending a quiver through her arms, as far as the long fingers capped with the bright red nail polish that she noted vacantly, was starting to chip.

It took her just twenty seconds studying the email header to identify the Internet Protocol (IP) address, the unique number assigned to every computer on the internet. Using a free utility, a further fifteen seconds was all the time needed to discover that Emelienko, or his computer at least, was in London, his locality given as Hampstead Heath, give or take five miles. Ten seconds later another free website had identified his ISP, or Internet Service Provider as SmileyNet.org, based in Andover.

For the next forty minutes Chris acquainted herself as best she could with the hacker's world of covert control, unauthorised access and forbidden entry, surprised at how easy it seemed and how open these enthusiasts were about their techniques and generous with the tools they had devised. A world of anarchic and harmless innocents, or so they seemed to her, eager to showcase their skills to fellow enthusiasts and redress their social isolation with the cool condescension of the initiated.

Well there's a sister here who's damn grateful to you nerds wherever you are, she said to herself. Doing something had raised her spirits. *'Hang in there Ian, I'm on my way.'*

A few years previously, Chris had been disturbed by an article she had read about the intrusion of the nanny-state into everyone's lives and the possibilities of 'homeland security' computer surveillance and now she realized the time she spent had been useful research.

Cloaking software . . . that was it, she remembered. Within ten minutes, she had downloaded and installed Hyde-IP on her computer, enabling her to access the internet anonymously by bouncing communications around a network of servers at many locations around the world, leaving the originating computer's identity untraceable. This was to be her smokescreen.

From the web, she bought software called SpyBoy that gave remote control over someone else's computer, and hid the program in an email she sent to Emelienko's Internet Service Provider, SmileyNet. She used her Hyde-IP smokescreen browser to send the email to ensure it remained anonymous. When the ISP clicked to open the document, they triggered a small front-end routine that she had written, and activated the spy program. Chris was able to access files on the ISP computer. Just 30 minutes later, in the ISP's customer record files, Chris had found Emelienko's street address in Mayfair, and another active email address. She remotely uninstalled her spy software from the ISP's machine, and deleted the document she had sent them.

With this link in the chain disposed of she turned her attention to Emelienko's computer. She composed a fake email, appearing to come from SmileyNet, his internet service provider, using one of their genuine templates she had taken from their system. Her email offered to upgrade Emelienko's internet connection speed if he clicked on the button, with the same SpyBoy software hidden behind it. Again it was sent via the cloaking software to conceal the true origin of the email. When Emelienko clicked on the button to accept, unknown to him she would be able to access his computer too. The same thing would happen if he clicked on the button to reject the offer.

If people had any idea just how insecure their privacy is . . . she thought, as exhausted and anxious, she decided to make a cup of herbal mix 'cleansing tea', bought from the health food store. The squeaking of the garden gate and a cheerful humming warned of someone approaching up the garden path.

The 'rat-a-tat' on the door concerned her, it seemed too urgent, too demanding. She ran quickly to the living room to look from a side window and saw it was the Courier service, the man holding a flat envelope and a device to record her signature.

'Small packet delivery,' he shouted when he glimpsed her peeking out. She answered the door, signing for the little parcel.

'I tried this morning. Got no answer so I thought I'd catch you on my way home,' he said cheerfully.

'Err . . . thanks, appreciate it,' Chris thanked him. She felt conspicuous, and awkward, unprepared for any form of social contact and concerned that the turmoil in her life would be apparent to the man.

'You alright love?' he asked, with the sensitivity for the abnormal that is a hallmark of both the affable, and the busybody.

'Fine . . . yes . . . just fine. Thanks. Lot on at work,' she replied, further discomforted by the realization of a tic in her left eye.

'Sun spot activity, love. Everyone's mad for a day or two, don't you worry,' reassured the man, doffing his hat in a cheerful cameo of respectful service, as he headed back to his parked van.

She carried the parcel inside, checking the 'from' address as Pasadena in the USA. 'Who do I know in the States?' she asked herself, ripping off the cover. Inside was a DVD, unmarked, with no note or explanation of who might have sent it or for what purpose. With trepidation, she slipped the disc into the DVD player of her computer, and sat to watch.

The image was fuzzy at the start, then focused on the white limbs of a woman, her arms stretched out above her, a man's head buried between her legs. She was moaning gently. The man raised himself, moving clumsily up her body, his erect penis bobbing awkwardly.

'*What in God's name!*' thought Chris, appalled and alarmed that anyone would send pornography to her, and for what conceivable purpose. The camera zoomed in, focusing on the woman's face, gradually clearing beyond the heaving buttocks of the man. To her horror, Chris realized: the face was hers.

Chapter 54: think first

(4.30 pm)

After Grafton had forwarded Emelienko's email to Chris he sat fidgeting at his desk, trying to think calmly, and staring occasionally at a clock which appeared to be running at half speed. It was 4:30 in the afternoon. A senior member of his staff had gone missing only a few hours before, and was being held to ransom - or so he had been told by the Russian thugs outside the Winter Gardens. The kidnappers, or their agents, were demanding the retraction of research that he was responsible for. He had delegated responsibility for sorting all this out to a junior at a time when she was evidently, and understandably, very distressed. The whole thing was totally surreal, a bad B-movie, but it was happening. He had been assaulted - he knew that was real, too real. How would all this look when it was investigated, or, heaven forbid, at an inquest?

Not good, Grafton decided.

He had to act. If only he could work out what was best, how he could help Chris, save Lineker, and save himself? How could he recreate the hero he had become during that terrible cow disease crisis, the heady days of youth and risk, when the future held only promise and he could run upstairs two at a time, inviting breathlessness as a chance to rejoice in the miracle of being alive.

'*One step at a time, William, one step at a time,*' said Grafton to himself.

He reached for the phone, simultaneously retrieving the Emelienko email on his computer screen. He could taste the fear and his heart was beating as he dialled the number shown in the email. His nerve failed him, so he put the phone down to steel his resolve, drew some deep breaths, and tried again. Number unobtainable.

'*Thank God,*' he thought, immediately disowning the reaction as out of character, the shivering in his limbs gradually subsiding and a taste of metal intruding into his mouth.

'Okay, that does it,' he said out loud. 'Can't get hold of this gangster myself. Wouldn't be right to ask a junior assistant to solve it on her own. Leaves me no option.'

Grafton put his jacket on, tidied his desk for a couple of minutes and set off to look for Stanley Warner, Head of Security in his office downstairs. His step felt lightened.

Despite what Chris had said, he had made a decision and he was sure it was the right one. *Must let the authorities know that Lineker is being held hostage*, he said to himself. *This could get serious. Someone could get killed.*

Chapter 55: far far away

(Australia)

Loathe to abandon the wilderness that for many months had slumbered in its icy embrace, winter had revisited. After so long living outdoors, the girl was used to it, her body recalibrated to a different version of the ordinary. She pulled the sleeping bag tighter around her ears for a few more minutes of cosy comfort. Pete was still asleep next to her, though the tree was swaying more than usual, and it was this that had awoken her. For six weeks they had maintained their vigil, high above the forest floor, perched on the little platform that Pete and Arjuna had built forty-five metres in the air, nesting in the canopy of the mighty trees of the Australian Tarkine.

Sometimes the contractors showed up shouting abuse, their bellies soft and their hearts hardened to the wanton destruction of the pristine and the defenceless, that she and her dishevelled crew were intent on hindering. To start with she had shouted back, a strange experience for a girl so shy and so naturally quiet. But she had not recognized her voice, it had lacked conviction, and she had soon succumbed to her natural role, the sylph, the silent witness, a human being content to allow the forest simply to be. Pete was stirring.

'I'll be off soon,' she said.

'No worries girl, I'll help you down. Just give me a minute. Bridie not here yet?'

'No, I'm meeting her at the drop off.'

The girl picked her way carefully through the forest, its silence reaching deep within her. During the long drive to the south of Tasmania with the radio playing, Bridie's cheerful chattiness drew her slowly back from the dream of a different world to deliver her in Huonville, where she shared a house with other like-minded people, a group the local paper and news crews dismissively tagged as 'activists'.

She threw her backpack down on the carpet and sat awkwardly on the settee, readjusting to the warmth and stuffiness of being indoors and discomforted by the buzzing whine of the fan in the old computer that the household shared. She got up to check her emails and her Facebook account.

One entry caught her attention amongst the usual chaff of gossip: 'Isabel Aziz - PORTAL.com, the Internet Church, wants to be your friend.'

'Tea's ready,' shouted Bridie, distracting Isabel from the computer, as she turned toward the kitchen.

Chapter 56: sick

(5:15 pm)

Chris made it to the toilet just in time, retching on empty, the whole despairing mess that life had become expressed through an involuntary reflex, a gurgling spitting expulsion of mucus and bile. Straightening up, she wiped her mouth clean and returned to the computer.

It was her and Lineker - there was no doubt in her mind. They had been filmed at Llanthony. She dug in her purse for the card that Clinton, Baedeker's secretary had given her, and phoned the number.

A man replied. 'Clinton Schwartz is not available. Who should I say called?'

'Tell him Dr Reynolds phoned.'

'And what shall I tell him it's about, Dr Reynolds?'

'Just tell him it's . . .' for a moment she was at a loss, 'just tell him it's urgent.'

A chirruping sound from the computer distracted her. She put the phone down, fascinated by the message on the screen. Emelienko had activated the program. She had access to his files, and to his emails.

'Yes,' she shouted, a fist clenched in the air to mimic the cliché of competition, the 'fuck-you' gesture of self-congratulation from the tennis court to the football field.

Find out who gives the orders, who pays the bills, and I'm nearer to you Ian, she whispered, excited at the illicit power and the prospect of real progress.

She had sifted through forty or so of Emelienko's emails when the phone rang.

'Dr Reynolds. Clinton Schwartz of PORTAL.com.'

'You people are beneath contempt. How dare you. How can you possibly . . .?' she was shouting into the phone.

'Dr Reynolds, I can assure you whatever has upset you, it has nothing to do with the Church.'

'You absolute bastards . . .' she began, 'how can you live with yourselves, filming someone like that?'

'Dr Reynolds,' Clinton interrupted, 'I can guess what has distressed you . . . it may be our agency friends have overstepped the mark. I know they were very annoyed with Mr Aziz.'

'I . . . well . . . what the . . . what in God's name have your issues with Aziz got to do with Dr Lineker or me?' Exasperation mingled with her anger, but did nothing to dilute it. 'We have absolutely no connection with Mr. Aziz.'

'I understand both of you declined our offer of employment, and you left with him even though he had brutally assaulted American citizens?'

'This is madness. I don't know anything about an assault. How does our declining to work with you link us in any way to Mr Aziz? It was you who arranged for him to drive us back. Our privacy was illegally violated before we left with him, and in any case, all this is absolutely irrelevant to a gross and unspeakable invasion.'

'Ah yes. We at the Church believe respect for privacy is absolutely paramount. We of course do everything we can to safeguard our own privacy. The CIAO agents whose actions have annoyed you, they share our concerns - and our objectives.'

She slumped onto the sofa, suddenly dizzy with fatigue.

'So you admit you are behind it. But you don't have the guts to take responsibility for it.'

'I am sure if our privacy is respected, yours will be safe too, Dr Reynolds. Just a word of caution to you. Mr Aziz is not to be trusted. We know whilst at Llanthony he recorded a private conversation. He then told you and Dr Lineker he had made the recording. You must understand with Mr Aziz we are dealing with a psychotic and deeply troubled man with a history of mental instability.'

'What on earth!' she protested. 'How dare you . . .' but Clinton persisted, overriding her interruption. 'My advice is to have nothing at all to do with him or you will place yourself in harm's way too.' Clinton hung up, his final remark tearing another rent in the fast unravelling fabric of her life.

Her mind raced with unanswered questions. How did they know that Aziz had a recording? How did they know that Aziz had told her about the recording when he had only informed her and Ian of its existence in the car on the drive back? The car must have been bugged, in which case they must also know she had proposed using the internet against them? But they had filmed her with Ian the evening after she and Ian had refused their offer, the day before their return from Llanthony. So Clinton's suggestion they had been filmed because his agents were annoyed with Aziz was a fabrication. The Church must have planned blackmail from the outset to ensure their silence, or perhaps, to coerce them into doing as the Church wanted. Somehow Aziz had riled them even more than they had - that was very clear.

'Good on him,' she said out loud, remembering the quality of forceful directness and his lack of pretension, qualities she found appealing. Suddenly she remembered that Aziz had said he would try to kill Baedeker. *'Oh my God that's it. At least we argued against it,'* she thought, initially concerned about herself and Ian. *Aziz may be in trouble. I should warn him* was her second thought, *He said he and his daughter were threatened, even before this.*

But why would the Church want to snatch Ian? They wanted Lineker's Physics research to succeed. It was Emelienko who was demanding it be discredited. Unless the Church was involved in some sort of complicated double bluff, Chris was sure they were not holding Ian. She would warn Aziz, then forget the video, at least for the time being - recovering Ian must remain her sole focus.

She rifled through the rest of Emelienko's emails, finding nothing that suggested contact with a 'client' who might have commissioned Emelienko to contact Grafton. She downloaded a password breaking program, and set it to run overnight so as with a bit of luck, she could access Emelienko's bank account in the morning, in the hope it might disclose some clue.

The world still looked grim. Dispirited by her lack of success, Chris decided she might as well go to bed, and was turning to switch the laptop off when something stopped her.

Of course, why didn't I think of that earlier?

Chapter 57: tosser

(9.00 pm)

For twenty minutes Chris hammered away at her computer keyboard until, unnoticed by him, the little blue light of Emelienko's web cam flickered on, and Emelienko's life was no longer private. From two hundred miles away Chris could see into Emelienko's living room, or part of it, finding herself both fascinated and disappointed by the mundane ordinariness that the muffled sounds of a TV set in the distance did nothing to relieve. She stared at her screen for a further ten minutes, embracing the role of 'voyeur' as willingly as the other misdemeanours she had already accumulated in the previous few hours.

Nothing. As fruitless as the emails she had trawled through. Exhausted and upset, she decided for a second time to abandon her pursuit but her progress toward the bathroom was halted when the phone rang.

It was a strange strangulated tone, a warbling, unfamiliar sound that initially distressed her. *Even the phone is stuffed up now,* she thought until suddenly wide awake, she realized it was not her phone. It was Emelienko's. She rushed to the computer screen in time to see Emelienko reaching across the desk.

'Yes,' Emelienko said, followed by a burst of communication in a language she could not understand until the one word 'Spaseebo,' that she recognized.

'Shit,' thought Chris, scrabbling to configure the recorder that had been included with the web-cam software. Emelienko was finishing his conversation in what Chris assumed was also Russian. His final words were in English. 'Yes. 2:00 afternoon . . . tomorrow . . . da.'

Emelienko replaced the receiver and Chris watched mesmerised, hardly daring to breathe while Emelienko typed with his eyes slightly lowered as if he were staring at her chin, his face life-sized and close-up, blotchy and pasty. The surreal intimacy repelled her. She quickly flipped away from the webcam to review what he had typed with her remote control software relaying his screen onto her laptop. Emelienko had sent an email. She scrabbled to check its contents.

'Six days left.'

My God . . . it's to Grafton . . . he's warning Grafton.

Now the portly Russian was dialling a number. Almost immediately, he seemed to be answering questions:

'Yah. Mayfair. 7105 - AMEX. Indian maybe Chinese. Nyet - not dark - I want light . . . 1:65 maybe 1:75. Now is good. Third bell from top. Is good. Is good.'

What's he up to? A takeaway maybe? Chris wondered.

'Slim, must be big tits, teens . . . must be young,' added Emelienko.

'I don't believe this . . . he's ordering a girl,' said Chris out loud. 'The odious shit.'

Emelienko lifted himself slowly from his chair, disappearing into the gloom of the room behind to return quickly with a bottle of whisky. He poured himself a drink, before hammering at the keyboard, staring intently at the screen. His sweaty face was reddening as flecks of spittle formed on his lips until flicked away by his tongue that protruded slightly from a mouth that was open and gasping for air. The veins on his forehead were straining like strands of spaghetti lodged under the skin.

What . . . what's going on now? wondered Chris, tapping instructions into her keyboard to see what had so affected Emelienko. On his screen two young woman were engaged in gymnastic oral sex.

Is he . . .? Is he having a goddam wank? she wondered, a suspicion almost immediately confirmed by the sound in her speakers of a pig-like grunting that gathered in pace, and by Emelienko's brilliant blue eyes now bulging in their sockets with the frightened glare of a sentinel frog.

How dare he . . . and a prostitute too. I'll show the pervert, thought Chris, fury obliterating even the clarity of her vision as she hammered at the keyboard. *He even thinks I'm too old . . . as if anyone would go near the disgusting creep unless they had to,* she raged as she typed:

'Your name is Emelienko and your address has been forwarded to the vice squad Marylebone police station.'

She was about to press 'send' but paused to add 'You sick fuck' to the message designed to flash up on Emelienko's screen. The delay fragmented her anger.

No, too risky. She turned off her computer. *I'll get the bastard when I catch up with him in London.*

Fatigued by the ugliness of it all, she lay on the bed.

Men are just Grade A sickos, she sighed, and after searching briefly in her bag for the card that Aziz had given her when he'd dropped her off in Malvern, she reached for the phone.

Chapter 58: from little things

Aziz was sitting in a pub on Shepherds Bush Green, occasionally sipping from a pint of Fullers when he got the call.

'Dr Christine Reynolds here. Is that Mr Aziz?'

Whoa. Aziz felt his heart surge.

'Yes Dr Reynolds, it's me. What can I do for you?' he asked, his voice sounding slightly higher than normal. Oddly so, he thought.

'I don't mind telling you that I haven't got a lot of time for men just at the moment. But I believe in doing the right thing, and I have information that I think it's important you know.'

'Oh . . .' replied Aziz, completely confused and unsure how to respond. 'Sorry about . . . that.' Chris heard the uncertainty in his voice.

'Look nothing personal okay.' Suddenly Chris too was unsure where the conversation was headed and decided to start again. 'PORTAL know you recorded your conversation with them.' There was a pause.

'Did you tell them?' asked Aziz, his spirits sinking. He had wanted to think the best of someone, at least for longer than this.

'Good heavens no - no. I think your car had a device in it. I would put it in the GPS if I was doing it, most of the technology would already be waiting for you.'

'Right, oh well.' There was another pause 'That changes things a bit.'

'Yes, I was thinking the same thing. It means they know you said you would try to umm,' she paused. 'Umm . . . you know . . .' terminate' Mr. Baedeker.'

'Right, that's a bit tricky. Funny thing is - I'd actually decided to forget about that - for the time being.'

'I think you should look out for yourself. I think they wish you harm.'

'Yeah, they probably do. Looks as if my quarrel isn't just with their CIA types. If they know about the recording, I reckon it just got more 'official." Aziz was still intrigued by Chris's opening remark – it had seemed to refer to an issue of great interest to him - her attitude to men. 'How are you by the way?' he asked.

'Actually it's a difficult time.'

'Oh, I'm sorry to hear that. What's the problem?'

'They've got . . .' was as far as Chris got. The tears flowed uncontrollably. She was surprised at her outburst, but there was something about Aziz that seemed to make it okay for her to cry. She tried again, '. . . they've taken Ian.'

Aziz felt his heart melt. He wanted to say 'There, there . . .' hold her, smell her hair, comfort her. This time, he recognized the tenderness in his heart for what it was. But a part of him he could not disown, was also pleased to hear that misfortune had befallen his rival.

'Bastards. That fucking Church,' was all he risked. 'Fuckers,' he added, as he thought about it again.

'No, I don't think it's the Church. It's the same Russians who assaulted Dr Grafton, our boss.' She was recovering quickly. 'I'm going to London. I've tracked down a man, the Russian who is acting as a go-between. He is meeting another man tomorrow at two in the afternoon.' There was a forlorn remoteness in her voice but beneath it Aziz detected something he found reassuring. As a military man he knew it was a quality no-one could be taught, but was the most important of any attribute. Her 'fighting spirit,' the inner resolution not to yield to adversity, was still intact.

'I'm in London. We must meet.' Again Aziz was surprised at his tone, its urgency and its sincerity. He remembered his decision to avoid her until the threat from the church was neutralised but discarded it in the instant - this was a greater need. And it suited him.

Chris had recovered her composure completely. 'Yes, good idea,' she said without hesitation. It was her turn to be surprised, at how right that felt.

'But I might have given a wrong impression with the Baedeker problem. I'm not into killing people in case you were thinking . . .'

'Good God no . . . this man is the only link we have to Ian – the last thing I want is him dead. One o'clock - Speakers Corner - is that good for you?'

'Yes – 13.00 hours – Hyde Park - I'll see you there. Take care of yourself, Dr Reynolds.'

'Call me Chris.'

'Okay Chris, I'm Mike; remember?'

'Of course . . . goodnight Mike.'

'Goodnight Chris.'

They hung up. Aziz clenched his fist beneath the table, a muted version of the same gesture of satisfaction that Chris had employed just twenty minutes before. He downed the beer in one go, and ordered another.

Chapter 59: who can you trust

(10.00 pm)

She was almost asleep when the knocking came on her door. It was quiet, but insistent. Chris got wearily out of bed.

'Who is it?' Her voice was high-pitched, a seam of fear scratching at its normal texture.

'Dr Reynolds. It's me Dr Grafton. Sorry to trouble you. It's not urgent . . . it's just I need to speak with you if that's okay.'

She checked from the side window to confirm Grafton was on his own and opened the door.

'I know you said not to contact anyone but I have. I thought you should know. I've told Janbir Chatterjee that Ian is being held.'

'I wish you hadn't done that Bill.' There was a coldness, and an irritation in her voice.

'Janbir knows the editor at New Scientist - they were at Imperial together - it will make it easier to get the retraction published that Emelienko wanted. Of course like me, Janbir isn't a fan of Process Physics, so I think he's quite keen to see it dis . . .' Grafton stopped as he realized what he was saying. 'He's one of us Chris - he wants to help. I told him not to tell anyone else about what's going on.'

'Alright Bill. I know Janbir. Not very well, but I'm good friends with his wife. I'm sure it will be okay.' Chris yawned, digesting the situation and annoyed at Grafton but deciding that what was done, was done. 'You didn't come round to tell me that did you?'

'I couldn't sleep. I went for a walk on the hills - your light was on.'

'The light, oh . . .' she relented, remembering his ordeal and understanding that he might need company. 'Sure Bill, that's okay. Come on in, we'll have a cup of tea. I've been too busy tracking him down to think about anything else. I know where he is. I'm going down to London tomorrow to see if I can find anything more.'

'You've found Ian?' asked Grafton, astonished.

'No,' replied Chris, suddenly crestfallen, Grafton's question reminding her just how much more there was to accomplish. 'Emelienko.'

'Excellent work, Dr . . . Chris. Can I ask how?'

She ignored the question. 'Emelienko is not the problem. It's whoever's got Ian that we need to find.'

When Grafton had been to the police to report the kidnapping, the detective had insisted Grafton not tell Chris that the police were now involved, but had declined to tell him why. There was a pause while Grafton worked out what that allowed him to say whilst following the police instructions.

'I really think you should let the police handle this. It's a very serious matter, they're trained in dealing with this sort of thing.'

'Yes, yes, you're right. If I can't find out anything tomorrow, we'll go to the police.'

Grafton looked relieved. 'I don't mind telling you I'm really pleased to hear that - you can't do all of this on your own.'

'Actually there's someone who can help me. Someone in London.' The remark popped out, a strange mix of little-girl boasting and adolescent flirtation. She felt a slight warmth on her cheeks.

'And who's that?' asked Grafton.

'He's just a chap . . .' She stopped, listening to the resonance of her own comment and realising she was looking forward to seeing Aziz. There was something slightly nutty about him, an irrationality that she found amusing, and a combination of diffidence and authority that intrigued her.

'He's a guy I met in Wales, an ex-soldier, tough seeming.' She wanted to say more, and find the right words, not for Grafton's sake, but for her own.

'He's . . . I suppose you'd have to say . . . manly.' The word had appeared. She had never used it to describe anyone before, and for a reason she didn't understand, it made her uncomfortable.

'Well . . . okay. But be careful Chris - we don't know how dangerous these people are.'

'And they don't know how pissed off I am,' she replied.

September 23rd

Chapter 60: what a drag

(1.00 pm)

Chris was waiting, leaning against the railings. Unable to relax after Grafton's late-evening visit and anxious at the uncertain prospects of the following day, she had endured a restless night and an edgy drive from Malvern to London, but in the unseasonable warmth of an Indian summer, she finally started to unwind as she watched the office workers eating their lunches, and the tourists venturing onto the Hyde Park deck chairs.

The scene reminded her of when as a teenager she used to photograph the crowds at Speakers Corner where the bubbling energy and good-natured banter had made an appealing oasis from the mayhem around Marble Arch. She remembered too how eager she had been to escape the bustle of London and begin life as an undergraduate in Brighton. But it seemed different now. The city's sclerosis had eased, and its lifeblood flowed more freely with the honk of horns and the pall of exhaust fumes replaced by the occasional cavalier cyclist weaving between an orderly succession of black cabs and red buses.

A tall man was leaning against the railings too, watching her from a distance of twenty-five metres, his line of sight occasionally interrupted by the thronging crowds. He was thickset, carrying a briefcase, and wearing a black pinstripe overcoat, a crutch incongruously tucked under one arm. His blonde hair framed thick sunglasses.

By five minutes past one o'clock, Chris was becoming anxious - she had agreed to meet with Aziz on the hour. She noticed the man too late. He was striding towards her, covering the distance between them in a few moments, before his powerful hand gripped her firmly on the upper arm, thrusting her forward then pulling her quickly down the subway towards the tube, the whole manoeuvre accomplished in just a few seconds. Her panic exploded in a flash of fear.

'Help . . . help me. . .' Chris was shouting until the sound was muffled by a gloved hand over her mouth. She kicked out as best she could, the scuffle attracting the attention of two passers-by, late-teen Afro-Caribbean men, with the easy swagger and powerful build that nature and narcissism had moulded in the gym.

'You alright love?' one asked, as they stopped and turned in a clear challenge to Chris' attacker. The man released her too late to stop her flailing hand from finding its target, gripping his hair and yanking at it viciously.

'It's me . . . Aziz. It's me . . . Mike,' he was hissing into her ear as his wig sailed off in one direction and his sunglasses curved through the air the other way, to clatter flimsily on the concrete.

'What the fuck . . .!' sniggered one of the black men.

'What on earth are you playing at Aziz?' Chris was saying, the anger lending a high pitched cracking tone to her voice.

'They may be watching you. I was trying to get us out of sight quickly,' said Aziz, exasperated. 'Fuck off fellas. Can't you see we're friends?'

'Takes all sorts mate.' snorted one of the young men.

'It's okay, thanks . . . just a misunderstanding,' Chris confirmed.

'Get yourself some counselling, guys,' shouted the other youth as they ambled off, smirking and laughing. 'You're disturbing the peace.'

Chris and Aziz stood in silence looking in opposite directions, listening to the youth's hoots of merriment clattering down the tile-lined tunnels until they had receded to nothing.

'Well you're feisty. . .' Aziz began, pleased at how she had defended herself.

'And why on earth are you dressed like that?' demanded Chris, cutting him off.

'I think I was followed. I lost them in the public toilets with this disguise.'

'You're taller than I remember,' she accused him, as if challenging him, her hands on her hips, the feeling of incipient laughter bubbling onto her face.

'Platform shoes I'm afraid.'

'Very eighties,' she smiled, watching him.

Aziz had retrieved his sunglasses and was struggling to refit the wig on his head.

'Here, let me. We wouldn't want to be conspicuous or anything would we?' she offered, reaching up to adjust the headpiece, the smirk formed across her lips disappearing as they stood face to face.

It was the first time they had touched and the first time they had stared into each other's eyes without the distraction of speech. Each, in their own way, recognized it was a moment they would remember. Chris was the first to look away, embarrassed by the raw intimacy of the exchange.

'We need to be out of here,' ordered Aziz.

'I would never have picked you as a disguise sort of a chap,' she said more quietly, as side by side, they started to walk briskly toward the tube.

'A friend of mine kitted me out. Hard to tell with Beaky whether he's taking the piss these days.'

There was a lightness to Aziz, as if excitement and the future were acting on gravity. She could sense the change in him, and its origin. It pleased her to have an effect on this unusual man; a man who made her feel unusually safe.

'Why the crutch?' she asked.

'Hides the limp, and the shotgun too. Where are we going?'

Chapter 61: hedonista

(1.15 pm)

While they walked, Chris quickly summarized for Aziz everything that had happened in her tracking down of Emelienko.

'So you know he's meeting someone at 1400 hours, but you don't know who it is?' asked Aziz.

'That's right,' admitted Chris. 'They spoke mainly in Russian – at least, I assume it was Russian - I didn't have time to get it translated.'

'Well it's a start. We'll watch his place, follow whoever shows up and talk to them if that's appropriate.'

'Okay,' she said. 'We're a bit early, fancy a bite to eat?'

They found a Greek restaurant, 'Hedonistas', opposite Emelienko's address. After checking out the menu, Aziz suggested they look elsewhere.

'I'll buy,' offered Chris, remembering Aziz no longer had paid work and understanding his reluctance. 'I insist.'

They asked for a window seat, with a clear view of the entrance door of Emelienko's apartment block, and ordered lunch. Chris declined alcohol, Aziz ordered a whisky. His mood changed, becoming more serious and purposeful.

'Look . . . umm . . . err . . . Chris. Forgive me for being blunt, but kidnap is a serious offence. Whoever has got Ian won't want to be caught. On the drive back from Llanthony you told me the people who assaulted your boss want to stop your research and discredit it. Is that still right?' asked Aziz.

'Yes, that's what they're saying.'

'I don't want to distress you but . . . are you certain Ian is still alive?'

'Well no . . . I'm not . . . I've just assumed.' She looked alarmed, sipping from a glass of water to clear her throat.

'Well . . . this is how I see it. We have to make it clear to them that he is essential to your giving them what they want. If he is alive, that will keep him alive until they get what they want. At that point we snatch him - or before if we can,' concluded Aziz, relieved that he had come up with something that sounded at least like the start of a plan.

'Yes I see. Supposing he is . . .' her voice faltered.

'If he's already dead. . .' Aziz picked up her thread, the soldier's need for common purpose overriding any thought of sensitivity, 'then . . . well . . . then it doesn't really matter what we do, I imagine.'

Aziz looked at her, seeing how shocked she was at the stark nature of the predicament they faced, laid bare by his assessment.

She's not trained for this Mike, go easy, he reminded himself, before pressing on. 'So I want you to work out how we can prove your science is shit . . . and a convincing argument that the only person who can do that is Dr Lineker.'

'That's an argument that makes itself really,' said Chris wistfully. 'Search on Process Physics and Ian's name will come up. His name is virtually synonymous with the Theory.'

'I thought you were a part of it too?'

'I'm very much in the background. I'm a technician to Ian's inspiration. The man is a genius, though for God knows what reason, people are blind to it at the moment.'

'Okay - that's kind of not good. If he is the 'man', then they have to - sorry to have to say this – if he is still alive, then they will kill him as soon as they can, presumably as soon as he renounces all this new science malarkey.'

'It's not 'malarkey'' Chris winced and fell silent.

'Sorry, I didn't mean . . .'

Aziz was the first to break the silence. 'Don't worry, when we know more about Emelienko's setup, I'll work out how to get him back.'

She smiled at him without conviction then looked away, knowing neither of them was convinced by his bravado.

Aziz stole glances at her as she toyed with her meal. Her stress was evident. Blackening rings were starting under her eyes and her face had taken on an almost translucent whiteness with the skin drawn tight across her cheeks. To Aziz she looked like an alabaster statue, the epitome of wronged humanity - sad, stoic and enduring.

For Chris, thought had ended. She had decided the situation was hopeless, and realized with a flurry of anger directed at herself, and at Aziz, that she had pinned her hopes on him, and he was as powerless and confused as she was. The vacancy in her mind was almost restful. Acceptance of despair had dissipated her anxiety, and for the moment its struggle was replaced by calm, a condition she recognized from when in mathematics she encountered a problem that seemed insuperable.

Preoccupied with her beauty, Aziz was speechless, feeling the awfulness of the situation for her, and his failure to imagine how to set it right.

'I've got an idea,' Chris said suddenly, brightening, the gift of inspiration arising unheralded in an instant.

'Yes . . .' Aziz responded, almost involuntarily, her mood lifting his spirits like a ray of sunshine on a rain-soaked sky.

'They want the science renounced in public - well - why don't we make it as public as you can get,' she said. 'There's a show 'TruthSayers' on American TV. They take old wives' tales or common sayings, and by running scientific-type tests establish whether they're right or wrong.'

'I know that show,' confirmed Aziz. 'The last one I saw was whether fire can travel along spilled petrol quicker than a car can drive.'

'Yes . . . that sort of thing - they have a huge audience – it's incredibly popular. If we get Ian on the show . . .'

'Then we can grab him once he is in a public place.' Aziz finished her sentence. 'Yep, that makes sense. . .' beamed Aziz, keen to seize whatever was on offer, 'if we haven't already managed to get him before then,' he added quickly.

'And instead of proving our science is wrong on the TV show, which is what we tell them he is there to do, we arrange for an experiment to prove Process Physics is right!'

The words were delivered quickly, urgently, as if driven by her gathering excitement and the prospect of success.

'Is that good?' asked Aziz doubtfully, wondering if he was missing the point.

'Yes. That's what Ian wants us to do. 'Publish the truth'. Because if we've got him safe and sound, and the truth is broadcast across the world, then they've lost, he's no use to them anymore.'

'Hang on,' said Aziz 'If the experiment is going to prove your stuff is true, why would they show up for it with Ian?'

'That's the interesting thing. Modern designs of this experiment suggest Einstein was right and we're wrong. That's what they will be using - a modern version - they can even provide the equipment themselves. But then we surprise them after we've made Ian safe by explaining the errors implicit in the modern equipment and repeating the experiment with a different design that proves we're right.'

'If you think it would work that sounds good.' Aziz called to the waiter for another whisky. Chris declined a second coffee.

'The experiment I'm talking about is one of the most famous in science history. It's called the Michelson-Morley. First run in 1887,' she explained.

'I may be losing the plot here,' said Aziz, 'This experiment proves you're wrong or right?'

'Well oddly enough the original one proved we're right, but it was misinterpreted by Michelson – ironically they gave him a Nobel prize for it. I know that sounds incredible but back then they just didn't have a theory to properly calibrate the equipment. The design of modern equipment uses a vacuum to shine light through. That produces an effect that exactly cancels out the difference we're trying to detect, so it fails to reveal crucial data. Hard to believe I know, but the modern one gives a false reading,' said Chris, undeterred.

'But the old-fashioned type, your version - the same as the first Michelson-Morley – that does give the true result, and proves you're right?' asked Aziz.

'Absolutely . . . but there's a slight problem.'

Aziz was thanking the waiter for his whisky. 'Sorry, you were saying there's a problem,' prompted Aziz.

'Yup . . . we haven't built one before. We'd have to devise a new setup. I'm sure Ian could . . .' She stopped, embarrassed. 'I'm sure I can work it out, but we've only got six days and an awful lot to do.'

'And why would they risk putting Ian on TV where he could say what he wants. How would they know he will renounce the science?' asked Aziz.

'They will believe we've only agreed to it to get him back, not that we can prove our argument. Remember they will be putting up their own equipment. Their best advice, or so they'll believe, is that we will be proved wrong whatever Ian says. They have a century of conventional wisdom on their side. This will be their chance to blow us out of the water.'

Chris suddenly looking crestfallen. 'Though, now you mention it, why would they risk putting him on TV where he could just say he's been kidnapped?'

'That's more my area,' Aziz boasted. 'I can think of a number of ways to stop him from saying anything they might not like. For instance, they could tell him they'd kill him first and then you if he upsets them.'

Aziz didn't allow her the time to think about it. 'Why are they doing all this Chris? What is it about your science?

'I wish I knew, but I haven't got a clue, it's a total mystery to me too.' She was silent, again weighed down by a sense of the awfulness of the situation.

Aziz looked sympathetic. 'Well obstacles are there to be overcome, right?' It was his turn to lift the atmosphere. 'And while all this is happening with the experiments, I snatch him. Should be easier in a studio or wherever they do these shows.

Sounds good.' He looked thoughtful for a moment. So did Chris.

'Bizarre isn't it?' she said breaking the silence that had descended again. 'I never thought I would be trying to convince the science establishment of the value of Process Physics on a popular TV show of all places – but if it gets Ian into the open, then it could be perfect for us.'

'Except for one other big nasty,' replied Aziz.

'What's that?' she asked.

'No offence, but how do you get a popular TV show interested in a hundred-year-old science experiment that proves what everybody believes anyway, except you and Lineker of course?'

'Ah right.' She had been wondering if there were any alternative but had decided there wasn't. 'PORTAL want our Process Physics proved, right? They are also very obviously interested in reaching the masses. That's what we were talking about in Llanthony. Well . . . we tell them we can do both if they make it possible. We tell PORTAL they must put up the money to persuade the TruthSayers show to take on a re-run of the Michelson-Morley.'

'Oh shit,' said Aziz 'Do we have to?'

Chapter 62: follow up

(1.30 pm)

'You know PORTAL have threatened my daughter don't you?' asked Aziz. 'And their CIA goons are after me as well.'

She cupped his hand with hers. The gesture seemed to emphasize the ornate ring on her finger, and the heavy bracelet on her wrist that Nandini had given her when she saw her last. Embarrassed, Chris gently withdrew her hand.

'I know how hard it must be for you to work with the Church. I can't imagine how awful it is to have your daughter threatened.' Aziz was looking at her intently.

'Believe me Mike,' continued Chris, 'the Church aren't flavour of the month with me either. You may as well know,' she added, blushing, 'they filmed me and Ian together.'

'What? As in . . . 'together'?'

'Yeah. In Llanthony.'

'Shit . . . unbelievable.'

She could see that Aziz was uncomfortable.

'We don't . . . we're not . . . together . . . anymore,' she added, knowing he would care.

Aziz tried not to react, though his heart skipped a beat, somewhere just the other side of relief.

'You can't work with scum like that Chris, surely?' asked Aziz.

'I can to save Ian, and if I could think of any other way, I would. The Church has got the money and the manpower to push this really hard. We haven't.'

'Well if they're in, then I'll have to sit out, at least from the TV show. Anyways, I decided a while back I would have to forget about the Church until Isabel is safe.' He didn't mention that concern for Chris had been the other factor in his decision. 'I'll see if Beaky will stand in for me.'

'That would be the 'Beaky' you told me about before, the one who gave you the disguise right? He's ex SAS too?'

She was worried, anxious that Aziz wouldn't be there to rescue Ian. Aziz understood.

'Absolutely. Phil 'Beaky' Jones - served with me in the regiment, plays it by the book – well he used to before he became a hippy - but Jesus, he's tough as buggery. There's only one man I'd rely on more than me - and that's Beaky.'

'Thanks Mike . . . we don't have much time before they . . .' Chris was unable to finish the sentence, an appreciation of the risk to Ian overwhelming her with a fleeting sense of panic. This time Aziz placed his hand over hers.

She looked up through moistened eyes and saw how attractive Aziz seemed. The toughness of a rough-hewn ex-soldier mingling with an unexpected tenderness.

Will you be my hero Mr Aziz? The idea amused her - and it didn't frighten her. *My knight in battered armour.'*

There was something appealing about the thought of trusting Aziz, of having him at her side, something visceral and primitive that conscious description would only sully. *Funny . . . I never imagined it would be someone like you.*

'What are you thinking?' Aziz asked, curious, responding to her smile.

'Just wondering how things will turn out,' she replied, *and how all this came about? Can it really only be yesterday that they took Ian?*

She looked at her jewellery again, thinking how far removed she felt from the self-centred maths major sharing tea with her friend Nandini, as they watched the ducks, listened to the doves and shuffled thoughts like a pack of cards. That had been theoretic, a debate about the answers to questions.

This is not a question of answers, she thought, *this is real.*

Chapter 63: face facts

(1.35 pm)

Too damn real.

It was a watershed moment for Chris. The realization of how pivotal she had become to mapping safe passage through the chaos that threatened them gave her a different energy, enthralling her with the promise of its potential but chilling her with the weight of new-found responsibility. Her day-dreaming suddenly felt like an indulgence; and a luxury that time could not afford.

'Have you warned your daughter?' Her tone was clipped, efficient. Aziz found it reassuring.

'I spent yesterday trying to track her down, from one address to the next. The last person I spoke to thought she'd gone to Tanzania, a couple of years ago.'

'Have you tried Facebook?'

'No, should I?'

'How old is she?'

'She'd be seventeen now, I think.'

'Absolutely you should - here let me.' Chris took her iPad from her bag and tapped at the screen.

'How do you spell her first name?'

'I.S.A.B.E.L.'

'Is this her?' asked Chris.

'No . . . she's a redhead.' Aziz was peering at the screen.

'How about this girl?' said Chris showing him another picture.

'No she hasn't got dreadlocks.'

'When did you last see her?'

'Three years ago. For an hour or so.'

'What's Isabel's middle name and her birthday?'

'Caitlin. 14th July.'

'This is her then definite - she's in Tasmania, not Africa.'

'So her mum took her back to Australia – I never knew,' Aziz said. 'They were living over here when I last saw her.' He seemed affected by the idea. 'I wonder if Isabel was in Oz same time as me.'

Chris could understand why physical proximity, without knowledge of it, would add poignancy to the sorrow of an estranged father, whether by the hand of fate or by the will of the child. She felt the trickle of sympathy, like the melt water from a block of ice.

'And she's got dreadlocks!' Aziz seemed shocked. 'So what now?' he asked.

'Ask to be her friend and send her a message.'

'How do I do that?' he frowned, bemused.

Chris sighed, 'Here, I'll open an account for you - just fill in these details - I'll show you how - and write a message to her.' She tapped again at the screen, then offered him the device.

Aziz took it, and reaching into an inner pocket of his jacket, removed a small dog-eared notebook. He carefully opened it to a particular page and lining up the iPad, started to type, pressing the screen slowly, one finger at a time. Occasionally, he would stop and delete an entry, painstakingly resuming where he had left off.

Chris was growing increasingly frustrated at the rate of progress. 'Here, let me.' she said, gripping the iPad and turning it to her.

'No . . .' he started in protest, but she was already looking at the few lines he had written.

He was blushing, fiercely. 'My counsellor . . . my advisor . . . he told me to write stuff down about what I feel . . . I thought this would be okay . . .' He stopped in mid-sentence, a glum resignation had replaced the embarrassment.

'It's fine . . .' She was less rushed, more circumspect this time, almost gentle as she turned his notebook toward her and started to type in the words from the page.

I fought with men
I conquered pain
and I told the tales that soldiers tell
but I left behind my Isabel

'It's beautiful Mike,' she said, turning the screen back for him to see.

He sighed with the weariness of guilt. 'I was only eighteen when we married. It just didn't work out, what with joining the army too, being away so much . . . then I was injured, got sick . . . inside.' She saw he was blushing again.

'I understand,' she said, as he pushed the machine back to her. In the same instant she pressed 'send', Chris recognized that her feeling for Aziz had changed. The difference bemused her. She brushed her hair back from her face, and smiled at him.

Chapter 64: you must be joking

(1.45 pm)

'Look,' said Aziz.

A young man was walking jauntily down the pavement. He stopped at the entrance to Emelienko's block and rang one of the array of bells, appearing to have a brief conversation over the intercom before pushing on the heavy door to go inside.

'It's only 13.45, so it's still 15 minutes before our man is due. This guy could be visiting anyone,' said Aziz. They waited impatiently, until Chris suddenly started: 'I should have thought of this earlier.' She was pulling at her bag.

'If I'm quick we can see what Emelienko's up to. She hammered furiously at her iPad, activating the web-cam on Emelienko's computer. 'He's just thanking someone inside the flat, saying goodbye - it could be the guy we saw going in - timing is right. If the same man comes down in a minute, then I reckon its him.'

'Yep, here he is,' said Aziz. The young man was opening the front entrance of Emelienko's apartment block, looking to left and right before slipping through into the open.

'Okay I'll follow him, see where he leads us. Here's a spare phone, my number is already in it. Don't use your regular phone.'

'Don't you need it?' asked Chris.

'No I've got another. I borrowed them back there at Speakers Corner. Only use it once, then wipe it with a cloth and throw it away.' Aziz rose quickly to leave the restaurant, and moved off along the opposite pavement in the same direction as the young man had taken down the street.

Aziz's sudden departure had attracted the attention of the waiter, who was now looking across at Chris. She gestured to him to bring the bill, and was gathering her jacket and looking for her purse when she noticed Aziz had left his crutch behind. She remembered Aziz had said there was a shotgun concealed in it. *Was that just a joke?*

Across the road, another man had stopped at the door of the apartment block and was speaking into the entry-phone. Chris checked her watch. The time was 1:57. The man was waiting at the entrance. Shortly after, a second man exited the front door of the apartment block to join him. With a slight gasp, she recognized it was Emelienko. Deciding quickly that she had to follow them, she rose from her seat to go to the bar and encourage the waiter to hurry, so she could settle the bill as quickly as possible.

'My friend has left his crutch behind,' she said. 'He'll be back soon to collect it. Would you mind looking after it for a while?'

She glanced behind her to check on Emelienko's progress. Emelienko and a lean-looking man with a brutal scar across his face were walking across the road. They were heading directly toward the restaurant.

Chapter 65: to the cleaners

(1.58 pm)

As he followed him, Aziz weighed up the young man, assessing what sort of threat he represented, what type of person he was. When the man stopped briefly in front of a newsagent to look at the silicon enhanced breasts of a magazine cover girl, Aziz had a good look at his face. It was open, clear-skinned and worry-free.

Typical psycho, thought Aziz, *doesn't give a fuck.*

The young man was light on his feet, slimly built, new trainers, clean jeans and hooded top.

Knife man, Jujitsu type, need to restrain him quick, need to stop the arms.

The man caught the tube heading west. So did Aziz. Aziz followed the man as he got off at Ladbroke Grove tube station, and then down Oxford Gardens through the infill between the dreary discontent of White City to the west, and the oozing smugness of Notting Hill receding to the east. Aziz hailed a cab, telling the driver, to the driver's annoyance, to take him to the end of Oxford Gardens just 400 metres down the road to overtake his target. By the time the young man reached him, Aziz was stooped down, his back to the road, pretending to weed one of the tiny front gardens.

Sell your life and end up on your knees, Aziz thought. *That'd be right.*

There was an angry banging and an old man's fist shook at Aziz through the window.

'Fuck off yourself,' shouted Aziz, rising to head away from the young man who was turning to witness the altercation.

Bugger, thought Aziz, heading left at the next junction, his plan to round the block and catch sight of the man as he progressed up Latimer Road. Aziz broke into a jog, his awkward lopsided motion more evident with increased speed until rounding the second corner, he looked to the left and right. The street was empty. As if on cue, a door opposite opened, the young man exited carrying a black plastic bag and emptied it into the wheelie bin outside.

Gotcha, thought Aziz, crossing the road quickly and standing in front of the dark green front door that the man had just closed behind him. Aziz knocked and the door opened quickly, the man still in the hallway.

'Yes?' he asked, his eyes widening in recognition of Aziz as the quarrelsome gardener he had seen a few minutes before. Aziz had planted his foot firmly over the threshold, so as the door could not be closed.

'You know a man called Emelienko,' stated Aziz.

'Who the fuck . . .?' began the man. Aziz lunged forward, a vicious chopping blow striking the man on his temple. As he fell against the wall, Aziz grabbed his arm, twisting it behind him and used the momentum to bang his head on the faded wallpaper. The man crumpled to the floor. Aziz fastened plasticuffs to his outstretched wrists, frisking his clothes for the concealed weapon he was sure would be a spike, or a stiletto knife.

'Ah, here it is, you sneaky little fuck,' he said out loud, feeling inside the inner pocket to withdraw the weapon whose sharp point Aziz had identified through his clothes. It was a ballpoint pen.

You nasty little shit, thought Aziz, well trained in the science of converting the everyday into lethal killing tools. *You don't fool me,* now feeling along his shirt collar for a hidden shaving-blade, a bodkin or wire.

'What is it Danny, what's the rumpus?' came the call, a woman's voice weak and anxious. Aziz rushed down the corridor and burst into the room that the voice had come from. A very small frail woman was seated in an armchair, next to a bar heater standing in the fireplace. She was wrapped in a blanket, that in surprise at his sudden intrusion she let fall to reveal an acrylic nightie, as she stared up at Aziz in surprise. Opposite her, slumped in another chair was a man, barely conscious. On a small table, a near-empty bottle of whisky lay close to his outstretched hand, next to an ashtray overflowing with cigarette butts and used matches.

'What in God's name?' started the woman, her eyes bulging and her skin ashen white. Aziz was almost as surprised. He spun on his heel and strode out of the room to retrieve the young man, now groaning as he lay on the floor of the narrow hallway. Aziz dragged him back into the room. The old woman, her veins standing out from her skinny arms, her silver hair shaped in a brittle bun, gestured up to Aziz with a claw-like hand.

'For God's sake spare us. Spare us.'

The old man barely registered any reaction, his rheumy eyes flickering open like a bloodhound roused from a deep siesta, before his head lolled back against the unfashionably prominent wing of the threadbare armchair. His flies were undone, an orange stain on his grey underpants confirming his helplessness and dissolution.

'Do you know Emelienko?'

'Of course I do. I'm his cleaner,' shrieked the old woman, recovering her natural animation. 'A proper gentleman - unlike you, come bargin' in like this, you heartless bastard.'

'And what does Danny boy do for the Russian prick?' continued Aziz, taking his cue from her line in insults.

'Danny was taking his ironing back for me. Pat is sick again – can't you see? I couldn't leave him.' Her anger flared again, 'And what business is any of this to you?' before faltering to add more quietly, 'Who are you anyway? Are you with the welfare?'

There was silence for a few moments, each appraising the other.

'Look, there's been a misunderstanding here.' Aziz was contrite, realizing the extent of his mistake and suddenly fatigued. He breathed deeply, a feeling of panic welling over from the back of his head.

Pull it together Aziz, he said to himself, *pull it together.*

'I'm leaving now - case of mistaken identity.'

Aziz stepped over the still prone body of the old woman's son, stooping to quickly cut the ties around his wrists, then headed for the garden. He heard the wailing start from inside the house as he jumped over the garden fence into the street behind and set off down the road.

The first drops of a drizzly rain pattered a sibilant hiss on the hardness of the grey paving stones, gentle mood music to soften the thump-scrape of his footfall, as Aziz hurried away from the house. He covered his face with his hand as a mother pushing a pram, crossed the road, some instinct warning her to avoid passing him too closely.

'What a fuck up,' he said under his breath, 'fucking civilians.'

Chapter 66: under down under

(Australia)

It had been a couple of days since Isabel Aziz had got back from the forest before she thought of checking the computer again and found the still unanswered Friend request from PORTAL.

This time she looked more closely at the accompanying message. *God is in the trees that whisper his name, in the stars that shine his light, and in a heart that shares his love.* She accepted the request.

But when she saw her father's name on a second request, she shook her head slowly from side to side, in exasperation and in sadness. *I knew this would happen . . . now I've grown up, he wants me to look after him.*

Isabel was only fourteen when she had first dabbled with the Tarot but had quickly abandoned what she felt was its fussy theatre, to rely more directly on her own gifts for a glimpse of a future that sometimes she was certain could be seen. She had enjoyed some success, at least enough to establish a reputation amongst her friends as 'sensitive'. They would joke with her, asking if a future event was auspicious, or what would be the likelihood of a relationship prospering. Her advice had proved useful, though she recognized she was less clear in matters of her own heart where the heat of emotion could easily conceal the flickers of intuition.

But now she felt a tremor in her fingers, a forefeeling that this was one of those moments that would act as a fulcrum in the seesaw of life and that the good times she had enjoyed in Tasmania, might be coming to an end.

Without reading his message, she deleted the request from Aziz.

Chapter 67: sprung

(2.00 pm)

'Look, I've changed my mind. I'll wait for my friend and look after the crutch myself thanks,' said Chris. 'And another coffee please.'

The waiter looked relieved to get rid of it, handing the crutch back over the counter to Chris. It felt suspiciously heavy. She resumed her seat at the window just as Emelienko entered from the street. Emelienko appeared to notice her immediately, smiling leeringly in her direction, and nudging his companion very slightly. The one-eyed man looked toward Chris, his expression quickly settling into a sneer of dismissive contempt.

It was an odd sensation. Chris was familiar with Emelienko's podgy face. It was as if the computer screen that had acted as a one-way mirror had now dissolved, projecting her into his company, unprepared and defenceless. As if she had fallen through the looking glass.

He doesn't know me - just a sick old lech staring, she reassured herself, taking some papers out of her briefcase with the intention of appearing occupied, then replacing them quickly fearing Emelienko might see them and in some way identify her.

Don't be silly, she thought before the chilling realization that her picture was on the MRI staff list website, and Emelienko could very easily know what she looked like.

'May I join you Dr Reynolds?' called out Emelienko.

Chris ignored him, and the goose bumps on her arms.

Emelienko and the other man were approaching Chris' table.

'Have you made a mistake?' she asked. 'I don't think I know you.'

'No mistake. You don't know me Dr Reynolds. You know of me. My name Vladamir Emelienko. We have mutual acquaintance - Dr Lineker. I sit down - you very lonely here.'

As he lowered himself into the seat recently occupied by Aziz, Emelienko waved a hand at the other man, a signal confirming he should remain standing.

'I am here for eating lunch with Mr Shirov,' Emelienko smiled. 'And why you here Dr Reynolds . . . so near my places . . . you live and work in sunny Malvern, yes?'

'I don't know what you're talking about,' said Chris, the fear tangible on her lips.

'Dr Reynolds. My colleague watch you long-time in Malvern. We know where you live, colour of funny little car, where you jogging, where you shopping, where fat friends live - and colour of bra and sexy little panties.' Emelienko licked his lips, as if he were savouring her fear, mixing it with the fantasies his monologue had provoked. 'If we want hurt you - you already hurt. I ask again. Why you here? Call it professional interest. So I do better next time.'

Chris felt a surge of repulsion overlaying her fear.

'It's a pure coincidence - I'm meeting a friend in a few minutes,' she said.

'To deliver walking stick. Is that right?' he asked, his eyes flicking to the crutch. 'Dr Reynolds - I eager to see the end of this - make everyone happy. I contact Dr Grafton to ask how progress. It is very . . .' He searched for the right words, 'good thing . . . we meet. The sooner we . . .' again there was an agonizing delay while Emelienko sifted through his vocabulary, 'facilitate . . . Dr Lineker's, how I best say, 'returnings', the sooner we all get on with lifes. Please, just tell me. How you find me?'

'Okay Mr Emelienko, I'll tell you,' said Chris. She paused, playing for time as her mind raced over the conversation with Aziz, fearful for her own safety and fearing the worst for Lineker.

'But first, how do I know that Ian is still . . . alive?' The words were almost gasped, as if giving expression to an unthinkable possibility might curse it into fact.

Emelienko spoke quickly to Shirov in Russian. Shirov nodded his assent then strode to the door, exited the restaurant and turned left down the street. 'My driver go to get car. He fetch proof for you. Now answer me, or things get bad for you Dr Reynolds.'

'I tracked you through your phone conversation with Dr Grafton,' she replied.

'Really? I not know you do that. How was possible?'

Chris was thinking on her feet. 'I pretended I was your daughter trying to find you because my mother had died and the telephone company gave me your address.'

'I see,' reflected Emelienko. 'Police not involved Dr Reynolds? Would make many difficulties.'

'No, absolutely not.'

'Then why you here?'

'I wanted to meet with you to tell you that I will go ahead and discredit Ian's work publicly.'

'Good Dr Reynolds. Very pleased. But why not ring bell to flat?'

'I was going to but I saw someone was there, outside, when I arrived - he went in so I came across here to wait.'

'Why pretend not you when I speak to you?'

'I'm used to being bothered by strange men, I have to be very careful', she said.

Emelienko seemed to be weighing up the plausibility of this comment. Chris was relieved when he continued.

'Why not get Dr Grafton speak to me?'

'Dr Grafton said he wasn't able to reach you. I wanted to tell you I'm arranging for a TV show to run an experiment that will disprove Ian's work.'

'Excellent Dr Reynolds. Please client very much.'

'Ian must be there. No-one will believe it unless he is there.'

'Science is science Dr Reynolds. If experiment fails your work fails - then my work finished.'

'No - it's not that simple. The experiment has shown that the speed of light is a constant which is what Einstein based his theory on. Ian argues that the calibration of the equipment is wrong. It is the existence of space as something real that this experiment sets out to establish, but it only shows that if you accept Ian's recalibration of the data. He has to renounce that personally.'

'Very good . . .' Emelienko snorted with derision. 'Very nice to let him go, very nice for you,' said Emelienko beaming affably. 'You write note for Dr Lineker - tell him plans. I will send note to client.'

A black Mercedes had pulled up outside, and was manoeuvring to park on a double yellow line.

A phone rang in Chris' pocket. It was Aziz.

'Don't look up. I'm outside. I can see you. Who are you with?' he said.

'Later today,' she replied breezily

'A friend?' asked Aziz

'Not at all.'

'Do you need help?'

'Really well, thanks for asking,' said Chris.

'Well do you or not?' Aziz was irritable.

'That's not necessary thanks,' replied Chris.

'Okay. I'll follow him when he leaves - bring my crutch with you.'

'See you then, bye,' said Chris.

She turned to Emelienko 'Just my friend confirming he will be here in a minute.'

Shirov was entering the door. He handed a small package to Emelienko.

'Then you must hurry.' said Emelienko. 'Write message for Lineker, quick,' his voice had transformed from its earlier cheeriness.

She scribbled a note. 'We'll do Michelson-Morley, on TV. You must be at show to renounce P.P Trust me. Chris xxx.' Emelienko accepted the note.

'Dr Reynolds, I like easy life but I not fool – I know people .
. . I know women . . . how they think . . . women say anything to
get own way . . . little voice tells me you talk much bullshit.
This not game. Six days - you have six days.'

He threw the package onto the table and turning abruptly,
strode out into the street. Chris watched Shirov opening the
door of the Mercedes and Emelienko getting in. She breathed a
sigh of relief, the tension almost overwhelming her, and the
smell of fear wafting up from her clothes.

As she opened the package a bloody tissue fell out. The
misgiving of something awful had barely formed before it
disintegrated in the horror of what was revealed. In the folds
of the tissue was the end of a finger, neatly severed at the first
joint, bubbles of blood not yet congealing on the soft meat and
bone that was exposed by the cut.

Chapter 68: turn of the wheel

(2.05 pm)

The Mercedes pulled away, merging into the line of traffic along Charles St. Peddling energetically in its wake was a powerful looking ruggedly-handsome man, his face set with determination and his blonde wig slightly askew toward his left eye. The car drew clear of Aziz in Berkeley Square but stopped for traffic lights in Bruton Street. Aziz was close again by the time the car had halted waiting to enter Regent Street, and he watched impassively as the driver swung the limousine into a private parking lot behind Hamleys. Aziz threw the bike aside, part of its broken lock still dangling from the cross bar.

When Shirov and Emelienko entered a block of offices, Aziz was just one floor away on the stairs below, but his progress was stopped when he came to a glass security door, through which they had entered only a few seconds before. *Fuck – what now?*

Aziz took out his phone and photographed the name plates of the several businesses the other side of the door.

At least it's intel, he thought, *maybe Chris can use it.*

Aziz tried to phone Chris, but her phone was engaged, and he was about to leave when Shirov appeared the other side of the door. His stance and attitude suggested he was immediately suspicious of the dishevelled and overheated Aziz, still recovering from his exertions on the bike.

'Can I help you?' asked Shirov, in his heavily accented guttural rasp as he opened the security door and stepped through.

The two eyed each other in silence, the stalemate of mutual respect in fighting men, who sensing they have much in common, also know that history and circumstance have conspired to see them implacably opposed.

'Just leaving actually,' replied Aziz, readjusting the Sig handgun concealed in his jacket pocket so as it was no longer pointing at Shirov's belly, before he turned and hobbled his way down the stairs to the busy street below.

Chapter 69: the good life

(California)

'Clinton,' Baedeker greeted his assistant with genuine warmth, 'and how are we today?'

'Very well sir, thank you.'

'Another day in Paradise awaits.'

Baedeker strolled to the French windows and onto the balcony overlooking crew-cut lawns and a sea of deep blue. He leant casually against the tall Corinthian marble pillars that framed the portico, accepting without comment the sunglasses that Clinton handed him before he slipped off his robe-de-chambre and allowed it to unfurl in generous coils on the floor. Now naked, he bent forward clasping his hands behind him and extending them high above his head, his backside displayed without shame or second-thought to his ever-attentive companion. Baedeker straightened up standing tall, and breathed deeply, savouring the fragrance of bay laurel that wafting in on the gentlest of sea breezes added a trace of ozone to the scintillating clarity of the morning light. Baedeker' body was tanned, supple and finely muscled. The body as a work of art.

As he moved gracefully back into the room his penis, weighty and long, lolled from thigh to thigh, challenging, insolent, casual. Clinton ran his tongue along the underside of his upper lip, pinching it briefly between his teeth, as he exhaled slowly to release the breath that he had held slightly too long after the first tiny gasp that was his involuntary homage to Baedeker's physical presence.

The subtle reaction had been noticed by Baedeker and the communication between them, though unspoken, was now explicit. That knowledge, and the implicit cruelty of Baedeker's indifference to any desire other than his own, sent a shiver of anticipation through Clinton, his body stirring as he imagined himself, abject and helpless, abandoned to Baedeker's complete control.

'Would sir like . . .?' began Clinton.

'Not this morning Clinton,' Baedeker interrupted harshly. 'What do we have planned for today?'

'A busy day sir,' Clinton cleared his throat. 'Here is a list of appointments. And you're dining with the governor this evening.'.

'Is he coming here?'

'Yes, sir. We're sending PC5 for him.'

'Which one is five?' asked Baedeker.

'That's the baby jet-powered chopper commissioned a couple of weeks ago.'

'Good, I haven't seen that one yet. Roy tells me it's a blast. Arrange an afternoon for me to take it out myself, with Roy on board of course to talk me through it.'

'Yes sir. Where would you like breakfast this morning?'

'The conservatory would be fine, and I'll be dining with Cindy. She's taking a shower.'

'Cindy sir?'

'Yes, beautiful young thing, so pure, so spiritual. Joined Paula's team recently.' Baedeker started, as if suddenly remembering something. 'Oh yes . . . she needs a lift to Berkeley in an hour from now.'

'I'll take care of it sir,' said Clinton. 'You'll see in the notes sir. I received a call just now from Dr Reynolds.'

'Dr Reynolds?' asked Baedeker, slipping back into his robe.

'The physicist you met in Wales, in Llanthony.'

'Ah yes the pretty one who lacks confidence - I remember she saw herself as more of a mathematician. I was always good at math Clinton, at school, you understand. What did she want?'

'She wants the Church to help her prove the new science is right by conducting an experiment on TV, for maximum publicity she says.'

'That's wonderful news Clinton. I thought she and her boss Dr . . . I forget the name.'

Clinton presented a shirt to Baedeker, who shook his head impatiently.

'Dr Lindacre, sir,' called out Clinton, looking for an alternative.

'Ah yes Dr Lindacre. I thought they were opposed to our mission.'

'Yes, that was the case sir.'

'Why the change of mind, Clinton?'

'Well I do know the new CIAO team . . .'

'I never asked you if you liked that name, Clinton?' interrupted Baedeker.

'I can think of nothing more appropriate for a joint security detail with the State Department. Very clever, sir.'

'Thank you Clinton. I interrupted you. You were saying?'

Baedeker, still naked from the waist down, had accepted the shirt and was allowing Clinton to do up the buttons.

'Well, they did gather material on her relationship with Dr Linacre, perhaps that had an influence,' explained Clinton.

'Lindacre Clinton. Well, that's all good. Get them over here and we can chat about her idea. No, hang on . . . invite just her, Lindacre seemed a bit simple-minded. Yes, that would be better, get her over on her own. I'd like to meet her again.'

'I'll take care of it sir,' said Clinton.

Chapter 70: nadir

(4.00 pm)

After a troubled drive back from London, by the time Chris finally reached Victoria Cottage, she was exhausted, with the deep fatigue of someone stranded in despair. Every shred of optimism had been obliterated by the awfulness of the sawn-off finger; and how casually it had been tossed toward her. Normally, in times of stress, she could gather strength from solitude. This time, on her own, it was different.

She fed the cat and made tea, watching with irritation as the milk curdled then rose in rancid blobs and swirled in a playful whirlpool around the surface. She threw the tea into the sink, and checked the fridge, feeling the reproach of the yellowing leaves of the lettuce, and regretting the unnatural smoothness of a Bolognese sauce in a small bowl that bore witness to her neglect.

Was she being punished; paying the price that Catholic school had cautioned her would be extracted from sinners? Was she in some awful way responsible for Ian's fate - an Eve to his Adam – their night together the forbidden fruit that she had offered and he had accepted, propelling them both to inevitable tragedy?

She had not allowed herself to feel too much until then, recognizing it was not emotion that would free Lineker, but action. But now she cried - for him, for herself, for all misfortune and as her tears dried, she realized she was crying too for the unborn, for the future.

There was a sharp rap on the door. A stern authoritative voice shouted, cutting into her like a knife.

'Dr Reynolds. Open up please. It's the police.'

Chapter 71: dial e for entry

(4:04 pm)

Aziz had received no reply from Chris's phone in his several attempts to contact her, and his disquiet that he had assaulted an innocent man left him confused about what he should do next, so he decided he should regroup in his bed-sit in Barons Court rather than return immediately to Hedonista, the restaurant where he had left Chris. At home, he discarded his disguise, showered, and after an hour sitting about, walked to the local library, where he hired thirty minutes of internet time, and checked to see if he had received any reply from his daughter.

Frustrated by inaction, Aziz caught another cab back to the restaurant, and again waited opposite Emelienko's flat. He hung around for half an hour, taking the occasional cup of coffee and walking round the block. Finally, prompted by boredom and the chill that was a distant outrider of evening's approach, Aziz sauntered across to the panel of entry phones and pressed the buzzer to Emelienko's flat. There was no reply. Aziz tried another buzzer but again received no response. The third buzzer he tried was answered in the high pitched croak of an old lady, her vowel sounds so modulated by poshness that she was almost unintelligible.

'My keys. I left them in my flat,' he stated.

'Which flat?'

'No 6.'

'Is that the apartment with the Russians?' she asked.

'That's the one,' said Aziz, pleased at how easily common knowledge had established his authenticity.

'Then go back to where you bloody well belong,' came the response. She hung up.

Jeeze, thought Aziz. *Nice . . .* He tried another bell. A young man answered.

'Yeah.' A flat monotone, vocal infill for distraction, the sound that nothing would make if it had a voice.

'This is no 6, I've left all my keys in the apartment. I can't get into my car and I'm late for a business meeting. Can you let me in please?'

The buzzer sounded. Before Aziz could thank him the man had already hung up.

Aziz knocked on the door of Number 6 and receiving no reply, picked the lock quickly. He remembered the name of the two-week training course which he had attended in Hereford - 'ENTER' or the 'Easy No Tamper Entry Resource', and how he had chosen it rather than the rival 'SAS', 'Safe and Secure' course across town, whose trivializing appropriation of a key component of his identity had irritated him.

The apartment was furnished with a rococo clutter that Aziz found repellent. Not only because its kitsch was so at odds with his natural austerity but also because as a trained soldier, he was offended by anything impractical including the dysfunction of confusing excess with luxury. Aziz sat briefly in one of the gilded chairs in front of the matching large desk and sneered up at the alabaster cherubs which beamed coyly back in apparent myopic seizure either side of the huge over mantle mirror. He stood, discovering the mirror was positioned so high that it only included his head, then he strode to splash his face with water from the gold taps glinting in the bathroom before returning to pull back the heavy quilted curtains from across the windows. It was obvious the place was no longer occupied and Emelienko had left, though the ashtrays were full and the garbage overflowing.

Aziz picked up the phone from the desk and pressed Redial.

'Indian embassy, trade desk,' came the reply.

'Oh - I may have misdialled - what number are you there?'

'This is the Indian embassy sir. How can I help you?'

'I'm trying to contact a man called Emelienko?' asked Aziz.

'I see'.

'It's about Dr Lineker,' said Aziz

'Sorry, I can't help you - I've never heard of either of those gentlemen,' said the woman. 'And who did you say you are?'

'Dave Brubeck. I've got a packet to deliver to Emelienko.'

'Okay I see. Have you tried phoning him?'

'No answer. Do you have a number for him?'

'Sorry. Does he know where to find you?'

'Tell him to phone me on 07899 781 776.'

'Thank you Mr Brubeck.' She hung up.

Knowing it was less than a plan but more than simple vandalism, Aziz tore the phone from its socket, and tucking it under his arm, left for the street below.

Chapter 72: please explain

(4.05 pm)

Chris opened the door to the cottage and let the policeman in.

'I'm here, Dr Reynolds, because Stan Warner the Security Chief at your place of work, was found this morning with a paperback book stuffed down his throat,' said Detective Inspector Cullen, wasting no time in getting to the point, as he strolled through the door.

'My God,' Chris was shocked, reaching out as she steadied herself to sit in a chair. 'Is he . . .?'

'Actually, he didn't look too chipper. He was a retired cop you know - a good man. Would you know anything about this?' asked Cullen.

'Nothing, nothing . . .' she replied, her mind racing, trying to understand, trying to keep up.

They said someone would be killed if . . . Bill Grafton told Chatterjee . . . did he go to the police?

'Poor Stan. He was a good friend of Dr Grafton,' she continued.

'You see Dr Reynolds, I have a problem understanding exactly what's going on here.'

'Right . . . I see,' lied Chris.

'Thing is,' continued Cullen, 'it doesn't look good for you.'

'In what way inspector?' Chris asked, trying hard to quell the sense of rising panic and the dizziness that was blurring her vision.

Cullen didn't bother to reply, but strolled around the room, moving objects slightly, peering out the window, in the way a cat toying with a mouse extends the agony simply because it can.

'Well, let me see.' Cullen suddenly announced. 'They tell me you have enjoyed a meteoric career, then you got a job working for a maverick scientist.'

So this is about Ian.

'Dr Lineker is a man of extraordinary ability - it's just a question of time . . .'

'If I may continue Dr Reynolds. Dr Grafton doesn't seem to share your opinion,' Cullen cut through Chris' protest.

So it was Grafton . . . what else has he told them . . . does he realize he's got Stan killed. Chris felt her energy drain, her mind chattering to make sense of it.

'Dr Grafton makes it clear to you and Lineker that your career prospects are at risk. A Russian man contacts Grafton offering inducements for the research to be dropped. Dr Lineker isn't interested. Then Lineker goes missing and the Russian contacts your boss again to say Lineker is being held by a third party and he will be harmed unless your research is discredited. Next thing we know, you're off to meet the Russian, illicitly, in a London restaurant. From a photograph we showed him, taken while you were in the restaurant, Dr Grafton has confirmed the man goes by the name of a Mr Emelienko.'

How the hell did they get onto that? Chris felt a slight shivering in her arms, and a feeling of mild nausea starting in her stomach. *They must have been following me.*

Cullen had stopped his circuit of the room, at the computer, before continuing.

'You were accompanied by a tall blonde man. Who was he Dr Reynolds?'

'Mike Aziz,' she replied. 'I can explain all of this.' She regretted immediately she had been so forthcoming. *Aziz thought the Americans would be after him, would the British police be helping them?*

'I'll be asking you to do precisely that Dr Reynolds. And how do you know this Mr Aziz?'

'I met him two days ago in Llanthony, at a work conference there. He was our driver - that's Dr Lineker and me. He drove us back to Malvern.'

'Interesting. Ben check out Mike Aziz for me. Pronto please.'

Detective Ben Simmons was in his early twenties, with rounded features and oily hair in what might have been a mullet hair cut had the barber found the courage of Ben's convictions. As instructed, Simmons left for the car outside, fiddling with the stud in his ear in an unconscious mannerism. When he passed Chris he fired a schoolboy's snigger at her, adding a further twist of ugliness to his fishlike face.

'So this driver, your Mr Aziz,' continued Cullen. 'He arrived with you at the restaurant with a crutch but, strangely, left without it.'

Cullen resumed his circuit of the room.

'While you were chatting with Mr Emelienko and his sidekick, who by the way is a man called Shirov wanted for questioning on an assault of Dr Grafton, your Mr Aziz brutally attacked an associate of Emelienko. It happens that the man Mr Aziz beat up is also a dodgy character. Chap called Danny Spillane. He has form for Grievous Bodily Harm and Wounding with a Knife.'

'Is Mike Aziz alright inspector?' she blurted out, her concern for him overcoming thought at what she should or should not say.

'We don't know what happened to Aziz. It would appear he left by the rear garden fence.' He paused. 'You seem to be keeping some very bad company Dr Reynolds.'

'I was trying to find out who is holding Ian.'

Cullen ignored her and continued. 'I can see to save your career you might wish to distance yourself from Lineker - gain brownie points as the one who discredits him. But there is something I don't understand. Emelienko is a known rogue and 'fixit' man. It appears his normal line is arms deals, brokering big business stuff rather than nasty little kidnaps. So it's intriguing how you'd manage to get him involved in something like this. Perhaps your Mr Aziz exerted some influence on Emelienko by beating up his man.'

'This is all preposterous inspector!' Chris stood up from the chair to remonstrate more effectively.

'Sit down please,' Cullen's voice was raised in anger. 'You are on thin ice Dr Reynolds - you have a lot of explaining to do, not least of which is where is Dr Lineker. We'd also like to know why you didn't come to the police in the first place.'

'I didn't go to the police because I was fearful for Ian's safely. And I don't know where he is. But I can explain all of this.'

For five minutes Chris took the inspector through the sequence of events that had culminated in the restaurant including how she had traced Emelienko. She omitted though to mention the webcam link and a strong intuition told her it was best not to tell Cullen of the plan for the TV program TruthSayers that she had suggested to PORTAL they sponsor. When she got to the end of the narrative, she went to the freezer and took out a sealed plastic bag.

'This is the end of a finger that Emelienko threw on the table - how can you imagine I'd be part of this?'

'My, this is interesting.' Cullen was peering at the finger in the bag. 'You didn't think to mention any of this to the police?

'I've already explained . . .' began Chris.

'I'll want to take your computer away to verify some of this techno-speak you've been giving me - if you don't mind,' continued Cullen.

'Take what you want,' replied Chris.

Cullen had reached her computer desk again. The front door of the cottage creaked open and Cullen again was joined by his assistant, who handed him a piece of paper.

'Ben, have a quick look over the computer please,' Cullen asked, as he absentmindedly read the notes he had been handed.

'Mr Aziz seems rather unlike the man you had lunch with yesterday in London, Dr Reynolds. According to this description Mr Aziz is only 5' 9" inches tall and has dark hair. He was arrested for disorderly conduct and resisting arrest a few years ago - described here as potentially dangerous, with a known history of psychiatric disorders. Ex-military type -

they can be very nasty if they go bad. Not a good match with the man who went with you to the restaurant, is it Dr Reynolds?'

By now, Cullen was standing in front of Aziz's crutch.

'The crutch saga intrigues me if I can put it that way. This wouldn't be the item in question would it by any chance, Dr Reynolds?'

Chris swallowed hard, a thump of dread hitting her in the chest as she remembered Aziz had said there was a shotgun in the crutch. Flustered, she was about to explain that Aziz had been in disguise when the obvious occurred to her that it would help Aziz if the police thought someone else had assaulted Danny Spillane in West London. Cullen was reaching out for the crutch.

'Of course. How silly of me . . .' she had begun, when she was interrupted by Ben, his voice excited and urgent.

'Boss quick. Check this out.' Cullen crossed the room quickly to look over the shoulder of his colleague.

For the second time Chris watched in horror as her face appeared on the computer screen partly shrouded by a man's naked buttocks.

'Oh Christ,' she sighed.

'Oh my, oh my.' Cullen was chuckling. 'Now what do we have here Dr Reynolds? You have been a busy girl haven't you? Looks like you've still got a bit more to explain. That wouldn't be the real Mr Aziz in your porno movie would it by any extraordinary coincidence?'

'Inspector Cullen, your tone is completely inappropriate. This video was illegally recorded without my knowledge and consent. If I thought this had any bearing on Ian's abduction I would explain - but it doesn't.'

'I see, tell you what – let's just pop down to the local station for a nice cup of tea and a bit more of a friendly chat shall we.'

'Are you arresting me Inspector?'

'Just detaining you for further questioning.'

'On what grounds?'

'Well . . . I would like to see if further criminal activity has occurred here. Let me summarize it for you,' Cullen replied in a matter-of-fact voice. 'You have already confessed to several infringements of the Computer Misuse Act. You have lied to an investigating officer. You have conspired with a person unknown to commit an assault. You have obstructed a police investigation. You were the last person to see Dr Lineker before he was abducted. We have you on film meeting individuals we believe are implicated in his kidnapping and you have the motive to benefit from his disappearance. Oh and keeping human body parts in your fridge - I'm sure we have a law in our noble and civilized society that discourages that too.' Cullen sounded bored, the sort of bored that was intended not to be mistaken for genuine. 'There's the small matter of a murder investigation you may be able to assist us with as well. Of course you do not have to say anything, but it may harm your defence if you do not mention when questioned something which you later rely on in court. Anything you do say may be given in evidence.'

He brightened a little as he continued. 'Looks to me like you're distributing pornographic material, or perhaps using it for blackmail too.' His face was set in an expression of contempt as he finished. 'Or even, given your tendency to regard yourself as completely above the law, maybe your car outside isn't taxed - I haven't checked yet.' His face was now only a few inches away from her face. She could smell cigarettes.

'Should I bring the crutch, boss?' asked Ben.

'Why would you bring the fucking crutch, Ben? Jesus give me strength. We'll get forensics to look at the crutch when they go through this place. Bring the fucking computer.'

'I'll just go to the loo,' said Chris, grabbing her bag from the table before slipping quickly through the door and ignoring the shout of 'Wait', and the thump of feet hurrying to follow her.

Chapter 73: flushed with success

(4.10 pm)

Chris slammed the door behind her and sat for a moment on the toilet seat. The tears from before the police visit had flushed away the fear, and she had gathered her strength. She felt unexpectedly calm, but perplexed.

Why is this happening to us?

'As quick as you can Dr Reynolds,' came the shout from the other side of the door. 'We haven't got all day.'

'I'd be a lot quicker if I knew there wasn't someone hanging around outside,' she shouted back.

But what does 'why' really mean?

Chris had always adopted a pragmatic outlook on life, but she knew from her research that however useful science can be, there are always more truths to be revealed than can be deduced merely from a set of assumptions and the application of logic.

Just like Ian said when we looked at that old book.

She felt a wave of affection as she thought of the open-minded curiosity that made Lineker so special to her, and how they had discussed logic's 'blind spots', comparing the mathematical rigor that Gödel had given to understanding the limitations of science with quotations from the second-hand book she had bought from a shop near the Abbey in Malvern.

'Thought can never be more than a play of light on the surface ripples of life's mysteries even if an occasional brilliance has shone through to the waters below.'

'We need to get going real soon Dr Reynolds,' came the shout.

'The greatest truth lies in the still and silent depths where the mystic and the poet occasionally venture, and the unfathomable is the source of being.'

'Just a moment,' she shouted back.

Come to think of it, she mused, *it's sort of appropriate in our Physics with a 'now' moment represented by a result only partly dependent on the previous moment, that there isn't the implication of a direct causal connection with the past.*

She could hear the muttering of the policemen outside, and knew her time alone was nearly over.

Maybe the 'random' element in our Iterator equation means it's a mistake to assume everything has to have a 'reason'. Things can . . . just happen.

'If you don't open the door I'm afraid we will have to open it for you.'

'Two seconds,' she shouted, grimacing as she took the stolen phone that Aziz had given her. 'Girl's business.'

I like that . . . new car sticker material . . . 'Self-referential-noise component of stochastic iterations invalidates mechanistic determinism'. Not quite as punchy as 'SHIT HAPPENS' but . . .

'Bugger' she whispered as she found the phone battery was flat. 'Shit does happen.'

She swopped Aziz's SIM card into a new prepaid phone she had bought in London, and texted Aziz.

'Couldn't use secure mobile due to flat battery - phone me on new number - 07889 751 788 - crutch in Malvern my place - I'm arrested - police looking for you. Security chief MRI murdered. Emelienko ID known. Your ID known. Take care.'

The banging started on the door as she removed the SIM card, and after wrapping it in toilet paper, flushed it down the toilet before slipping the phone with a dead battery into the back of a packet of tissues in the cupboard beneath the wash basin.

'Time's up Dr Reynolds.'

Chapter 74: truth

(California)

Cindy Lopez rubbed her eyes with tiredness. She decided a juice break was a good idea before her yoga class, and she could justify the time away from her desk as a chance to let the ideas that were not quite congealing into an expressible form, simmer in her unconscious.

She stood up to lean on one of the partitions that defined her work area. 'Hey Mark, fancy a chat?' she asked the young man in the booth next to her.

They were both ex-Harvard, early twenties. He spoke with a 'West Wing' monotone that had no time for melody, a common affectation amongst the self-consciously bright American freshmen whose words were fired in bursts of speech, a machine gun rat-a-tat-tat of syllables; as if only a staccato delivery could keep pace with the hyperactivity of the mind.

'Sure doll.' He raised himself from his chair, stretching his arms above him as he turned to face her. 'If you promise to tell me the latest from the cutting edge of your new science?' His voice was sarcastic, but friendly.

'I'm working on something called 'Gebits' - it's for Paula.' She spoke with the endless drawl of the southern states, her voice almost 'hokey' in its lethargy, easily filling the intervals that he had so adroitly created.

"Gebits' - isn't that a sub-Saharan rat?' he fired at her.

'Very funny ha-ha,' she said as they sauntered between white walls, the Californian sun streaming horizontally through tinted windows, as the corridor wound around a pool, where swans pavaned between the lilies, and carp flashed their white bellies as they chased minnows through the roots.

'No - actually 'Gebits' stands for 'geometric bits of information'. Anyways, these guys in the UK started with an equation from quantum chromodynamics. That's a theory describing how forces operate within an atom. If you strip out space references from the equation, and simplify it, you get an equation they call an 'Iterator' that maps connection patterns between nodes.'

"What do you mean by 'nodes'?'

"Nodes' are just notional 'points' - where connections interact. They have no particular reality in this way of looking at it - not yet, anyways. They're like traffic circles are to roads. The information is in the pattern, how stuff joins up, not in the 'objects' that are joined - think of a subway map - you know the underground railway. It's a different way of looking at it. Almost a different way of thinking. It's called 'Process Physics'. If you want to drive from here to Atlanta you're interested in the route, not the traffic circles, right?'

'Okay,' he replied, slowly this time, considering the implication of what she had said. 'So where are you going with this?'

'You add in a random variable to this equation, then take that result as the start point to compute it again, but this time add in different random input, and repeat this, again and again and again, representing the progression of time. Adding more roads if you like.'

'By computer I assume?' he asked.

'Of course by computer,' Cindy replied, making a cheeky 'isn't it obvious' face at him in imitation of exasperation, before she resumed. 'Well, if you plot the sequence of values that emerges from these computations, what you find is a pattern of connections like a map. Turns out, and this is the interesting bit, this pattern looks very like a neural network, or the pattern of the brain.'

By now they had reached the café, an Edward Hopper pastiche in greens and creams with a long wooden bar and rows of shiny stainless steel bottles behind clunky fifties style glasses. A juke box, that played real vinyl records, added colour and pinball-active animation to the far wall. She ordered a Cinderella juice cocktail.

'These 'gebits' arise where certain connections re-establish themselves so as they have continuity in time, they linger in the now.'

'And the others just fade way?'

'Yes. But the ones that persist develop characteristics that behave in a way that corresponds to the three-dimensional space we all know and love. That is, the further you get from a node, the more connections you have. The guys who did this work say this is like 'space' emerging from their Iterator equation.'

'So space isn't just emptiness - its stuff too. It's filled with goddam rabbits.'

''Gebits', Mark – 'Gebits'. Freaky eh? But there's more. Different 'Gebits' with stronger, and different connections, start to act like 'matter'. They call them 'defects' in 'space.''

Mark studied the drinks menu and ordered a diet Coke. 'So space and matter are the same stuff, differently connected,' he said.

'And' she replied, pleased he was up to speed with the implications, 'they affect each other too - think gravity and so on,' she added.

'That's incredible.'

'It's all in their papers - very innovative,' said Cindy.

'So what do you think?'

'Well, I think that if one or more of these connections disappears but then reforms at a different time, that could account for a lot of paranormal type effects. Do you want to walk with me?' she asked.

Taking their drinks, they strolled into the sunlight, headed toward the ornamental Japanese gardens with its little wooden bridge toward the Acer trees in differing configurations and colours, artfully arranged so as the colours splashed across each other, merging and separating like a Monet or a Bomberg painting. A discreet meditation area was set amongst great river-stone boulders and burbling water features that coloured the silence with a tinkling lullaby. When they were installed on a cedar bench they sat for a moment absorbing the peacefulness.

'You were saying about the supernatural?' asked Mark. 'Are you thinking about a connection established to the past or the future in some way?'

'Sort of, but maybe more like a connection re-established,' she said with emphasis.

'A recreation 'now' of what was the 'past' - a 'ghost' of the 'past' if you like.' Again she lent emphasis to the word 'now' before completing her sentence, 'or a set of connections 'now', that will re-emerge in what we call the 'future' when that too becomes the 'now'. That would explain how you might see into the future.'

'So there is only a 'now' in their theory.'

'Yes. That sort of appeals to me - doesn't it to you?'

She turned and looked at him directly her bright blue eyes shining with animation and vitality. She slipped her sandals off and raised her legs onto the bench to half recline, her thick blonde hair falling heavily away from her shoulders.

'A 'now' that potentially is linked to everything that ever was or everything that ever will be,' she added, stretching her arms in relaxation. A suppressed yawn fleetingly distorted her handsome face.

'Cosmic. Nice work. One problem - why doesn't everyone see these ghosts or premonitions if they're really there?'

'People are more or less sensitive to the subtle. Not everyone gets 'atmosphere'. Not everyone thinks the same thoughts.'

'Well that's good work doll, and you've only been in PORTAL a couple of months?'

'Yeah, I'm really lucky, I know that. I met with Saul. He's really sweet. He wants me to move from 'Truth' to 'Word."

'I spoke with him once . . .' Mark's account tailed off rapidly, realising his initial enthusiasm was misjudged since his connection with the great man was so clearly less than hers. 'Well make sure Paula knows about all your work before you move - it's kinda interesting. I must be getting back. I'm half way through an ancient geek translation, whoops, I meant Greek.'

'Another thing,' said Cindy, dreamily, as she curled her toes on the finely cropped lawn on the way back. 'You know you meet someone and you just know you've met before?'

'Sort of,' replied Mark, judging it expedient to pretend he knew what she was talking about.

'Well. This means maybe you have. You're just re-establishing a connection, not with them materially, but something finer, more esoteric, more ephemeral.'

'What, like their soul or something?'

'Absolutely. With their inner goodness. Their eternal spirit. Well that's how I feel about me and Mr Baedeker.'

Chapter 75: he who would dream

(7.00 pm)

It was just getting dark when Aziz got to Malvern. He had read the text message that Chris had sent him and concluded the need to retrieve his crutch and shotgun would double up as a convenient excuse to see Chris again. He drove the little Fiat which he had stolen in London, past the car-parks that catered for the hill walkers and into Gullet Quarry, where trees would conceal it from anyone passing on the road. He then walked up and over the hills to look down on Victoria Cottage from a distance. An hour later he skirted the cottage, working slowly and methodically round it, before he was satisfied that no-one was watching, and no-one was at home. Aziz let himself in through the picket gate to the kitchen garden at the rear of the house and picked the lock of the door that was so low that even he had to stoop slightly to enter.

The cottage had an abandoned feel; devoid of warmth, and missing the blended scent of human occupation, it seemed forlorn. It reminded him of Emelienko's abandoned flat, though the two residences were alike in no other way. A tangle of wires beneath the desk, and the dusty residue where the computer screen had been, reinforced a sense that the space itself was grieving, its melancholy triggered by injustice, impassively witnessed. Or so it seemed to Aziz, whose denial of nuance for so many years in his career as a soldier was now developing into a preternatural sensitivity, as if the unused potential issued at birth had reappeared later in life, distilled and concentrated.

His senses were further heightened by a fierce protective anger for the woman he had met just two days previously, but who he sensed had already become a lightning rod for his emotions. He imagined her at his side, strong and capable but tender and yielding, a companion who could help him through the mutable world of feeling, and perhaps, recognize his awkwardness without reproach. *But a woman has needs like a man . . .* he thought, the brief respite returning him to a barren reality; and the thought of her with Lineker.

The anger hit him suddenly. It was the wrath of the frustrated lover, and of the hunter, returning to the cave to find his mate had been snatched by a pack of craven curs. He felt the same thrill he recognized from battle, the liberation of discovering that the law is not written in old men's books, but forged in the inferno of the moment from the molten slurry of what is possible and what is not.

'Fuck you; you fuckers,' bellowed Aziz, a barking battle cry of triumphant fury that would not be denied. He would save her whatever the cost, and recover her from the police station by whatever means were necessary.

Not far away, unknown to Aziz, another man shouted at the night, and though Dr Grafton did so for different reasons, their inspiration was from a common source and their goal had a common purpose.

Aziz strode to seize the crutch, expertly dismantling it and reassembling the Remington shotgun concealed inside.

The phone rang - prosaic, regular, humble - summonsing him down from the Valhalla he had exultantly occupied, back to a small room somewhere in the English Midlands.

'Hello,' said Aziz. 'Who is this?'

Chapter 76: freedom's just another world
(7.00 pm)

Grafton sat with his back against the squat metre-tall obelisk that formed the trig point on the Worcestershire Beacon, marking the highest point on the Malvern Hills. It was the first time he had ventured onto the Hills since he had been assaulted, a humiliation heightened by the constant anxiety that of late had troubled his days and disturbed his nights. He hoped that exercise and fresh air would bring him the opportunity to gather his thoughts, thrown into further turmoil by the call from Detective Ben Simmons asking him to visit the station and telling him that Dr Christine Reynolds had been detained, a development that had shocked him profoundly.

It was obvious the police had made a mistake and he felt a harrowing guilt that his contribution had worsened an already desperate state of affairs. He could justify his actions in going to the police but he could not be proud of them. It seemed so long since he had felt anything like the inner glow of personal satisfaction that he wondered if his memory of former integrity had been no more than a young man's self-delusion.

The evening wind was strong and cold behind him, the occasional rain squall hurrying from the west to briefly lash his uncovered head before gambolling down the steep slope for an easy rush across the Worcestershire plain and on towards the distant Cotswolds. Grafton looked down on the street lights that sputtered into life, shaping a cobweb pattern in the fading greens of the trees and the red-brown of countless roofs; and realized he was at a turning point.

Starting as a small boy when he was taught to read, the dead hand of conformity had gripped Grafton with its primary tool - fear. With self-expression only permitted if it accorded with the prescription of others, his creative vitality had shrunk to hide in a refuge of drabness and he had forsaken even mischief in his bid to find approval. On some mornings before school, when his dread was particularly acute, his tearful pleas to be rescued from the daily ordeal had been dismissed with a cheery jauntiness by his allies of last resort, his parents. Sometimes they had taken the time to explain that his reaction was unavoidable and that his discomfort was temporary, each assurance further dousing his ebbing spirit until charred embers were all that remained of the once bright innocence of childhood play.

The departing sun shot a ray through the clouds, a finger of light pointing to spotlight a distant house surrounded by fields, the effect as if space itself had dissolved, so suddenly had the obscure been made visible. A similar revelation occurred inside Grafton. He knew that he had envied Lineker the sort of freedom that Grafton had never known, and was forced to admit that his cankerous ill-will had secretly delighted in Lineker's abduction. Part of him had even gloated in Chris Reynolds's detention. In the debris of his guilt a glimmer of humanity flickered, the disgust at what he had become cauterizing the fear from his spirit. Grafton leapt to his feet, determined to break free from the shackles of the past, and the respectability that still imprisoned him. 'Aaargh,' he shouted at the plains below.

Unknown to him, little more than a kilometre away, another man released from the bonds of convention also shouted at the night, and though in their private epiphany one found self-release and the other self-realization, neither imagined their lives would soon converge in common purpose.

Encouraged that the wind had dispersed his outburst without trace, Grafton risked a full throated scream, rising to a crescendo till his eyes bulged and his ears popped. Reaching even deeper into his lungs he revived the sound, until gasping and elated, a sudden foreboding had encouraged him to turn and nervously peep behind him where two chubby teenage girls were looking in his direction, open-mouthed with horror. They turned to scamper back down the path from which they had approached unseen.

Shit, Grafton thought, before he strode off in the same direction, after waiting a considerate interval so as not to distress them any further.

225

Chapter 77: banned band

(7.05 pm)

'Dr Reynolds please?' asked the voice on the phone.

'Who is this?' replied Aziz.

'This is Clinton Schwartz from PORTAL.com, the Church for a Better World. Who am I addressing please?'

Aziz felt the hairs on the back of his neck rise. He steeled himself to reply in as neutral a voice as he could manage, remembering that Chris wanted to use the Church for publicity.

'This is Miles Davis. I'm afraid Dr Reynolds isn't in, I can give her a message if that would help,' answered Aziz.

'Okay,' said Clinton cheerfully. 'I got no answer on her cell phone. Can you tell her we want her to come to the US to discuss her proposal to publish her work on TV?'

'That may be a problem for her. I'm afraid Dr Reynolds has been arrested for kidnapping Dr Lineker. I was on my way to negotiate her release.'

'Kidnapping Dr Lineker . . .' There was the sound of chugging laughter through the receiver, the sound of a man performing amusement.

'You've got to be kidding me man. That is seriously unreal. Are you her solicitor?' continued Schwartz.

'Her solicitor?' repeated Aziz, wondering briefly whether to accept Clinton's suggestion before he decided it was as good as any. 'Indeed I am.'

'So you're telling me Dr Lineker has been kidnapped?'

'Yes he has,' said Aziz 'but not by Dr Reynolds.' Aziz, too, imitated someone laughing, knowing it sounded synthesized and hoping Clinton would understand the rebuke.

'No, that doesn't sound like her style. Why would they think Dr Reynolds of all people would do a thing like that?'

'I think her attempts to trace him have worked so well the police assume she must be part of it.'

'Ah yes, Sherlock Holmes, Agatha Christie . . . We know how you Limeys go about things,' chuckled Clinton. 'And what's the word on Dr Lineker?'

'I can't help you there,' replied Aziz.

'I understand. Sorry your name again was . . .?'

'Herbie Hancock' replied Aziz.

'What, as in . . .?'

'That's right.' Aziz stopped him short.

'Thank you, Mr Hancock. Tell Dr Reynolds we'll be in touch.'

Chapter 78: visiting time

(7.30 pm)

Grafton parked outside the police station, walked inside and rang the desk bell. The young officer who attended him noted his details and rang up to tell Inspector Cullen that Grafton had arrived. There was a delay of some ten minutes before the Inspector came down, as if he were making a point that his time, and how he filled it, deserved priority over anyone else's.

'Thanks for coming in Dr Grafton.'

'You've made a terrible mistake arresting Dr Reynolds - surely that must be obvious to anyone who . . .' began Grafton.

'Actually it isn't,' replied Cullen coolly. 'Can I ask when you last saw Stan Warner?'

'Stan . . . I don't remember . . . I spoke to him yesterday on the phone about two o'clock. I asked him if he knew anything more about the assault on me. Why do you ask?'

Cullen ignored his question. 'Any further contact or news since then?

'None . . . nothing . . . no. Is there a problem?' asked Grafton.

Cullen raised a supercilious eyebrow and continued, 'Dr Reynolds contribution to this mess may be even more than we had first suspected. We did a trawl on a certain Mr Aziz, an associate that Dr Reynolds freely admitted to knowing. He's an ex-soldier she said she first met in Wales.' Cullen paused, thinking he had discerned a flicker of recognition in Grafton's face.

'We've had intelligence from our US colleagues about Aziz. It turns out they would very much like to interview him too. They're telling us he's a lot nastier than our own records suggest. He has a history of paranoid schizophrenia and is a violent psychotic.'

'What on earth does this have to do with Dr Reynolds?'

'Well according to her she was with Aziz when she met the man you reported - Emelienko.'

'She met with Emelienko. Where, how did that happen?' asked Grafton, surprised.

'As I was saying,' continued Cullen. 'We saw her companion and he didn't match the description of Aziz. This man subsequently carries out a vicious assault. Thing is, he had a crutch, and we now know Aziz walks with a limp.'

'So?' demanded Grafton.

'So we have found CCTV footage from a subway near Marble Arch that confirms the man with a crutch was wearing a wig. We are open to the possibility that indeed it was Mr Aziz in disguise. We also think that Reynolds and Aziz were blackmailing Lineker. When that didn't work, they had him removed.'

'Why in God's name would Dr Reynolds do that? She worshipped the man! And why would she say she was with Aziz in the first place if they were involved in a kidnapping, and how would arresting her help free Dr Lineker?' spluttered Grafton.

'That's why I've asked you to come in Dr Grafton. What can you tell me about this science she was doing that might make Dr Reynolds want to silence Dr Lineker?'

'Hang on - slow down here. You really are barking up the wrong tree. We are all respectable scientists. There is nothing in their science that is not in the public domain.'

Grafton paused. For him this was a second moment of truth. His customary reflex was to condemn Lineker's Process Physics but he realized any criticism would not help free his colleagues, and that his assessment of the worth of Process Physics had already been formed before his cursory perusal of its content. His mind had been closed - the suggestion that Einstein was wrong had been enough for him to dismiss it. He had to admit to himself he had never bothered to seriously appraise the new theory and he was halted in his shame.

'What is it Dr Grafton?' asked Cullen, responding to the delay.

'I was reviewing the science in my mind,' replied the old Grafton, but it was the new Grafton, the Grafton who no longer inhabited a world of only black or white, who continued: 'Absolutely first class. Ground-breaking work of the highest order. Brilliant stuff! It will revolutionize physics.'

'Okay Doc,' said Cullen contemptuously. His cynicism had not impaired the sensitivity to human lies that had on occasion made him such an effective detective. 'You want to play hardball. Things have moved on in the last few hours. I was planning to release Dr Reynolds but the Yanks are pressing me on this. They want Aziz. He attacked their agents in Wales, as it happens. As well as that, it seems he has been telling serious porkies about a US internet-type Church. I can tell you, some very important people are not at all amused.'

'Surely the Americans' desire to catch . . .' began Grafton.

'If I may continue.' barked Cullen harshly. 'Dr Reynolds has involvement with Aziz. There is an image from a video I want to show you. The woman is Dr Reynolds and I have to say she is one nice piece of . . .' his voice trailed off as he smirked lasciviously, 'it's quite - how shall I put it - saucy. We want to know the identity of the man. Is she indulging Mr Lineker or Mr Aziz?'

'I'm not sure what you're suggesting officer but I'm not looking at private pictures while one of my team is held by terrorists and the other is wrongfully imprisoned.'

'Stop right there, Grafton. I've been pussyfooting around with you and your pompous bullshit long enough. The key to all this crap is 'How-I-suffered-in-Iraq-fuckwit-piece of shit, Aziz.'

Cullen was warming to his tantrum. 'We've mobilized the bloody MET and half the fuckin' CIA as far as I can tell - this is not tea at the vicarage. You will do exactly what I tell you to do. If I'm telling you to look at a fuckin' picture of some slut fuckin' you will look at the fuckin' picture.'

Grafton stared in horror at the outburst, made worse by the suspicion that Cullen's apparent enjoyment of his own crude theatrics mirrored a tendency in Grafton that he had until very recently been only too happy to indulge. Cullen had stopped briefly to draw breath. 'I'm after this psycho. Our 'foreign' friend, Mr Aziz is shaping up as the key to both the Lineker abduction and the Stan Warner case.'

Grafton was shocked, uncertain what to say, uncertain what was going on. 'What Stan Warner case? What's happened to Stan?' he asked. An intercom buzzer sounded, distracting Cullen from a response.

'This better be important Ben . . .' threatened Cullen, his voice with the hectoring tone of a man confident no-one dare oppose him.

'Chap here to see you, sir.' Ben's voice rose then tapered off - unusual, almost antipodean.

'Not now Ben.'

'Chap is very insistent sir.'

This time Ben Simmons' voice was unnaturally low, as if he was a singer warming up with a routine of vocal acrobatics. In the next short sentence, the upbeat soared, insouciant, flying free, then plunged back down to a melodramatic halt.

'Says he's come for Dr Reynolds.'

Flat and deep, the final delivery was so mannered, almost confiding, that a chill ran through Cullen's spine as his assistant whispered the words, lingering on the zzz's like a hissing snake.

'Says his name is Aziz.'

Chapter 79: forty south

(Australia)

Gestated in the unknown vastness of the Southern Ocean, a spring wind had gathered in Storm Bay, its icy fingers gripping the port of Hobart before dancing up Criterion Street to strum on the plate glass that sheltered the pavement cafe patrons from the worst of its numbing cold.

Isabel rolled a cigarette, smiling, and lent back. She was tanned, a glow of well-being suffusing her face; body and mind in harmony. Bridie fidgeted opposite her, uncomfortable even near to a cafe, and resentful of the cost.

'Enjoy,' Isabel said mockingly, 'best coffee in Hobart, and a latte every six months isn't going to hurt anyone.'

On her feet were thongs, showing beneath baggy silk pants, the colours long since faded to a dull purple by countless washes. Her ochre-orange pullover had leather elbows, a crude shell necklace hung round her neck and the vast collection of spirals and whirls of red-hued hair fell like Medusa's snakes in cascading dreadlocks down her back or were secured firmly to the top of her head with a stout wooden pin. Isabel was a striking sight, perfect teeth and clear complexion, the clarity of youth augmented by the radiance of vigorous good health.

She, at least, was mercifully unaware that they were not welcomed by the regular assembly of the dutiful that crowded into the little cafe every morning for their daily fix. Her appearance rebuked the office harpies in their designer sets and clustered jewels, offended the jump-suited health nuts with their immaculate trainers and chain-saw voices, and challenged the men in suits to measure their worth against her wildness, a task for which their conformity would leave them uncomfortably disadvantaged.

There was one man who was different. He approached their table with an easy affability, gesturing to the empty chair. 'Is this free?' he asked in the roller coaster tones of Nordic

Europe. Isabel was intrigued. He was young, shamelessly blond, with sand-white eyelashes and patchy fluffs of beard.

'No worries,' said Bridie to the newcomer, 'make yourself at home.'

Hearing the man's accent, Isabel asked him where he was from, and what brought him to Tasmania. He explained he had just arrived to see its great Gondwanan forests and how in his native Iceland nothing comparable existed. He had heard of the Tasmanian destruction of its majestic trees for wood-chips, an obscenity that had brought him here to help put a stop to it if he could. The Tasmanians shared their knowledge with him, and their sense of outrage, pleased to find a willing audience for opinions that they explained were perversely unwelcome by the majority in their homeland. Throughout their homily, the visitor smiled cheerfully, and nodded enthusiastically at every proposition expressed and concurred with every opinion ventured.

Her initial warmth to the newcomer cooled somewhat. Something about his manner made Isabel uncomfortable, but she could not place it, unsure if the shadow that she sensed was because after too long in the forests with only friends to speak to or bitter enemies to fear, she was unpractised at meeting strangers. Bridie took to him though, and invited the man home to sleep on the floor until he was established with a place of his own, describing their meeting as fortuitous, as they were ideally placed to assist him with his intentions, and his goals they too held dear to their hearts. But Isabel was unsure.

The man suddenly asked if they believed in God, and the initial surprise at his broaching the topic was rapidly replaced by satisfaction when he agreed completely with their replies. Bridie explained they were inspired by the majesty of nature, which to her was as near God as they needed to be. He recounted how in his own case, such an appreciation of the 'miracle of being' had brought him to what he described as

'PORTAL.com, the Church for a New Way and a living witness to the Glory of God.'

'I've just made them a friend on Facebook - Synchronous or what!' exclaimed Isabel, forgetting her initial discomfort with the stranger and too captivated by the coincidence to profit from her gift of clairvoyance.

'It's the fastest growing Church ever,' the young man said. 'It meets the needs of the times.'

'Are you a missionary?' Isabel asked, some vestige of premonition reasserting itself.

'I am,' he replied, enjoying the mischief of engineered misunderstanding.

As they rose from their table the caffeine-junkies pointedly ignored them, and after they had gone, refrained from any reference to them, critical or otherwise, as if a mere mention of the intruders would validate their differences.

That evening, installed on his sleeping mat behind the sofa in the Huonville share-house, Magnus texted his handler in California: 'Contact.'

Chapter 80: thanks but no thanks

(7.35 pm)

The door burst open with a cracking sound, one of the hinges ripping from the wall where Aziz had kicked it, the other twisted and pulled loose with its bent screws clinging to the splintered woodwork. Detective Ben Simmons was thrust through the door, a plastic wire pulled tight round his throat and lifted, so as it dug deep into the underside of his chin. Holding the wire behind the policeman was Aziz, a Remington shotgun hanging loose from his side supported by a shoulder sling.

'I've come for Dr Reynolds - take me to her,' demanded Aziz.

'Calm down matey - you're on camera . . .' began Cullen.

Aziz raised the shotgun and blasted the camera high on the walls. Grafton and Cullen ducked, instinctively shielding their heads with their arms, as the dust and debris settled and the blast reverberated and died, the silence complete except for the humming of deafened eardrums.

'So you'd be the prick in charge,' said Aziz, 'and who the fuck are you, arse-wipe?' he continued, looking at the other man.

'Dr Grafton - I'm Dr Lineker and Dr Reynolds's manager at MRI,' replied Grafton, '. . . thank you very much I'm sure,' he added quietly under his breath, the resistance of respectability asserting itself.

'Were you the one attacked by Emelienko's goon?' Aziz asked.

'Yes, that's me . . .' Grafton's shame at the memory of his ordeal was worsened by the realization he now had a public identity as a victim.

'I'm Mike Aziz. Chris's friend . . .' It was the first time Aziz had referred to himself this way. He paused briefly to consider the novelty, and found it pleased him. 'So what are you doing here?'

'I've come to get Dr Reynolds released,' answered Grafton.

Inspector Cullen tried again. It was brave, but futile.

'This is your last chance. If you leave now I can't promise this won't go any further but ...'

'That's not how it goes ...' Aziz stopped him. 'Put your cuffs on and ...' Before he had completed the sentence Cullen lunged at Aziz, who easily countered the blow and lashed out, striking Cullen full in the chest with his fist in the same motion he used to throw Ben Simmons sideways against the wall. The inspector deflated like a balloon, immobile on the floor.

'Please, no - in God's name, no,' shouted Grafton, deeply disturbed by the ferocity of the punch.

'Don't worry doc, he's just winded.' Aziz was stooping to tie the policeman's hands behind him with plasticuffs as he lay on the ground.

'Quick we don't have long.' He hauled Ben to his feet. 'Take us to Dr Reynolds, shit face. And fucking hurry.'

They were taken down a short flight of stairs, on every corner a camera dutifully recording their progress and displaying it on an array of screens on the first floor in an office marked 'Administration' with one of its windows swinging open where Aziz had first gained access to the building. The seat opposite the screens had a jacket arranged over the back of it, but the seat itself was unoccupied. Its usual tenant was sitting where Aziz had left him, bound and gagged, on another seat at the end of a corridor in a room with 'Gents' written on the door.

In the basement, on one side of a wide corridor, were three cells. Only one was occupied. Chris had a wad of papers in front of her, and was scribbling vigorously. She stopped writing to look up at the disturbance as Aziz, Grafton and Detective Simmons entered.

'Gentlemen - I heard some banging about ...' she beamed at them. 'Why am I not surprised to see you Mike? But Bill, I didn't know the two of you had been introduced,' she said, looking from Aziz to Grafton and back.

'I'm so sorry Chris - this is all my fault - it never occurred to me the police would arrest you,' Grafton started.

'Let's just assume you are way too trusting shall we . . .'

'I've learnt my lesson; I can tell you . . . this has all been so distressing . . .' Grafton continued.

'Yes, it has,' replied Chris, more quietly. 'And so sad to hear of Stan Warner's murder.'

'Murder . . . my God.' Grafton held his hand to his forehead, and seemed almost to collapse, catching himself by leaning against the wall for support. 'Murder . . . I didn't know. How terrible . . . how . . .' Grafton seemed in shock. 'I'm so sorry. Believe me I had no idea . . . no idea.'

'No time for confessional Doc,' said Aziz, 'we've got to get out of here.'

Grafton ignored him. 'The Russians must have a contact in the police . . . poor Stan. I'm so sorry . . . I shouldn't have told them.'

Aziz turned to Ben Simmons. 'I want you in that toilet and lock the door behind you,' Aziz demanded, indicating a room off the corridor. 'After you've freed Dr Reynolds.'

'Just a minute fellas,' Chris's statement rang out, strident and clear. 'I'm not going anywhere.'

Chapter 81: joyous is when sung as one

(7.40 pm)

'What the . . .' started Aziz. 'You're kidding right?'

'When I leave here it will be as a free woman,' she replied. 'Not as a fugitive.'

'Jesus girl. I've come in here to get you out. I wasn't invited in you know, there's a trail of cops out there . . .' The disappointment was evident in Aziz's voice.

'Girl?' She frowned at him briefly, before continuing. 'And I certainly appreciate the gesture Mike, but this is not a war zone. You can't just charge around getting what you want with brute force.'

Aziz hung his shoulders, embarrassed and despondent, like a schoolboy caught stealing sweets. She paused for a moment, seeing the effect of her harsh words and relented, looking at him fondly: 'I really appreciate your concern Mike.'

With no time to waste, the look vanished quickly, as she communicated instructions to the two very different men who were now in her eyes, informally at least, her 'troops'.

'Bill, here are a series of notes on an Interferometer design. You will have to get up to speed and refine the details yourself.' Her delivery was quick, no nonsense, efficient. She handed him the notes she had been working on. 'And I want you to draw up a list of all the magazines, journals and newspapers who can report the results after the TruthSayers program, or publicize it in the run up. Send it all to PORTAL.com, send it to Clinton Schwartz. We've only got six days to get all this together before they kill Ian. Are you okay with that?'

'My God Chris . . . kill Dr Lineker. Of course,' bumbled Grafton confused and distressed at the mention of killing, a threat made too real with the news of the murder of his friend, Stan Warner.

Chris turned to Aziz. 'Mike we need to ramp up looking for Ian. If we can get to him before the show that would be a whole lot safer.'

'I've got a lead but I need help with Emelienko's phone,' Aziz replied.

'I'm not sure I understand what you're talking about but whatever it is, I'll sort it out as soon as I'm out of here, all right? Bill, I've been too busy on the Interferometer to worry about contacting a lawyer. They said I was just being held for questioning but it's been several hours now. Can you recommend anyone?'

'I'll get Lawson round before you can blink, Chris, don't worry about that. He's a personal friend from Oxford. You seem to have upset just about everybody Mr Aziz, you may need a lawyer yourself,' added Grafton.

'It's a talent I acquired when I started to express an opinion,' replied Aziz wryly, noting with a slight incline of his head the distant sound of approaching sirens.

'Okay, so Chris ain't coming. Come on Grafton, let's get the fuck out of this shit hole before the cavalry get here.'

Grafton shook his head to refuse the invitation and in disapproval at the language.

'Do you have to conduct yourself so coarsely Mr Aziz?' he frowned. 'I understand this is a difficult situation but . . .'

'You'll be pleased I won't be at the TV show then, though I'm not sure my SAS buddy is going to be any more polite than me,' Aziz chuckled, already heading for the door. *That's if he agrees to help,* he reminded himself.

'Mike,' said Chris sharply to his retreating back. Aziz stopped and returned her gaze, suddenly conscious her image would be fixed in his memory like a frame in a movie, frozen in time.

'Look after yourself . . .' she said, her voice faltering briefly with emotion, 'and thanks.'

'I . . .' Aziz could get no further. Unable to express the complexity of his feeling and confused by the significance of the moment, Aziz risked only a dismissive: 'I'll see you,' as he slipped through the doorway to quickly ascend the stairs, and out into the cloaking shadows of a Malvern night.

Chris understood the awkwardness that called out to her, and his courage. Tenderness surged through her, an unfamiliar feeling, like a pulsing wave from her heart to her fingertips.

'See you babe,' she whispered, so quietly that Grafton asked her what she had said.

She paused. 'Oh,' she replied, 'it's nothing.'

Chapter 82: now we have your attention

(California)

Baedeker sipped his coffee and cast his eyes down the briefing notes he had received from section leaders. Dr Paula Valence's Truth Division report into new research on the possible background to paranormal phenomena caught his eye, and the note attributing the work to Cindy Lopez. Baedeker had recently sent word to her via Clinton that he had no desire to continue seeing her; and it irritated him to be reminded of her. He drew a line with his yellow marker pen to indicate the reference to Cindy should be deleted and added the comment 'Humility is its own reward,' in the margin, before turning to the next page.

Baedeker perused the progress report on the TruthSayers TV program that PORTAL had agreed to sponsor and came to the item that recorded that Dr Lineker had been kidnapped, and Dr Reynolds had been taken into custody. The entry was short and succinct, and so was Baedeker's response.

'Clinton, my office - now,' he barked into the phone. Clinton was knocking on the door just two minutes later.

Baedeker didn't wait for Clinton to speak. 'This is good news Clinton. I take this as a sign. We don't know who has got Dr Lindacre right?'

Clinton's mind raced to guess what had attracted his boss' interest. 'Lineker, sir. I spoke with Dr Reynolds's solicitor, it was a very brief chat. He was on his way to try to secure her release.'

'That's not good enough - we need to short circuit all this. It seems we have just six days to set up the show. Tell the security people we need her out now. Tell them to find out who has Lindacre too. Any problems get me Barry Haswell.'

'Sorry sir, Mr Haswell . . .?'

'Deputy director, based in Langley. Come on Clinton, keep up.'

'We have a liaison meeting with the CIA chaired by Deputy Director Haswell scheduled next Monday, sir.'

Baedeker rose from his chair and paced around the table to approach Clinton. It was one of Baedeker's several talents that he could emit menace, in a way that no-one could pinpoint, but no-one would mistake.

'Too slow Clinton. I want you to mobilize all of our resources in the UK - I want her released within the hour. When you face the opposition that I believe we are facing, you have to act without equivocation. Do you understand?'

'Absolutely sir. Within the hour.'

'Any news on that lunatic who wants to kill me?'

'He calls himself 'Mike Aziz' sir. We've made contact with his daughter.'

"Aziz' - yes I remember. Good Clinton. Then it's time to bring him in,' said Baedeker.

'I guess it's not surprising a man with a history of mental problems would turn on his own?' Clinton commented.

'How do you mean?' asked Baedeker.

'Originally he was trying to recruit the scientists Lineker and Reynolds, to help him work against PORTAL. Now he's taken Dr Lineker and he's trying to frame Dr Reynolds,' replied Clinton, realizing too late from his expression, that Baedeker was not pleased with Clinton's contribution.

'No, no - don't misunderstand what's happening here.' Baedeker looked serious. 'This is not the work of some deranged soldier, Clinton. It's quite clear to me. Look at the facts.' He leant back on the desk, enumerating the points of his argument on his fingers. 'We have emerging research on the paranormal from the Process Physics papers and a notion of God to support the New Covenant - very interesting work. We have a plan using a TV show to prove the truth of this new Process Physics. We are about to show that Einstein's physics has been a confidence trick. Lo and behold - both our scientists suddenly go missing. Are you getting it Clinton?'

'Sorry sir, no.'

'Einstein was a Jew, Clinton. Einstein was a Jew.'

'Of course, the Jews again. Sorry sir, that should have been obvious to me.'

'Don't worry. You look after the details - I'll do the big picture. And get Aziz into a jail and Dr Reynolds out of one - can we get on with it Clinton - pronto - do you understand? I want solutions - and I want them now.'

Chapter 83: up close

(Australia)

Isabel languished under the shower. After months at the protest it still felt like a guilty luxury. She shampooed with a sodium bicarbonate mix she had prepared herself, rinsing in diluted cider vinegar. Her hair washed she reached for the soap, lathered herself generously, acknowledging with a slight gasp the stinging urgency of the spray jet that sent cascading bubbles scudding down her stomach and thighs. Her limbs were powerful, the muscles toned and heavy but though she moved with feline precision, her proportions suggested she would rarely achieve elegance.

She pulled on a tight top leaving her midriff exposed with its elaborate tattoo of a small snake rising up her stomach. She didn't bother with a bra, her breasts were small and tight, and she was pleased with the attention or disquiet that her prominent nipples attracted, confirming what seemed either the silliness of society, or its misogyny, depending on her mood.

Tonight was open night at the Republican bar in North Hobart. She would play guitar and sing if she got the chance, and her eyes were bright at the prospect. Her spirits were lifted too by the chance to be sociable, the urban bustle so different from the place of her lonely vigil where the majesty of the trees that should have brought peace, was defiled by the agents of greed, who routinely imported their violence and mechanized destruction.

Isabel had invited Magnus to come along with her, and she thought with satisfaction of their growing friendship. He seemed unusual, different from most men. He had explained he was, like her, a vegan, and he cycled everywhere he could. They had talked for hours that afternoon - she captivated by his eloquence and intelligence. He had explained the workings of the Church and how they were determined not just to worship but to act on the problems of the world through charitable and educational programs. He had outlined concepts and possibilities that to her were a revelation, drawing parallels between science and religion, illustrating their convergence. He showed her the latest discussion paper that had gone out to Aleph members of the Church on the new Process Physics and explained its implication for a modern interpretation of God, drawing parallels with what he had learnt in his Masters degree in theology at the University of Iceland where he had specialized in Ancient Chinese Philosophy.

She listened enthralled as he described how the new science proposed the building blocks of reality as connectivity patterns, and how the nature and persistence of these patterns determined a gradation from a dynamic space which we mistake for nothingness, through ephemera like thoughts and emotions to solids and materiality.

'That's so cool,' she had said, clapping her hands together in excitement, when he explained how the Confucians a thousand years ago had believed something very similar, describing emptiness not as a void but as a substance or 'breath' from which everything is derived with differing degrees of density.

She had borrowed the Process Physics papers, promising to study them later and she had laughed like a young lover when they hurried for the bus, oblivious to the disapproval of those who scarred by disappointment, saw her vitality not as an inspiration but as a reproach.

That evening Isabel played and sang exquisitely, the simple directness of 'Throw your arms around me,' pleasing Magnus who was confident that she was singing for him, and that when he chose, he would have sex with her and consolidate his control - she would belong to him, and the Church. When the bar called closing time and Isabel gestured she was going out back for a moment, Magnus, pleased with himself, sent a second message - 'Secured' - to his controller.

Unknown to him, in the gardens at the back of the pub two young people were locked in a shared passion, a hungry tongue probing Isabel's mouth and insistent fingers easing into her. Isabel was moaning gently as she lowered her head to accept the breast offered her by the other girl, who pressing hard on Isabel's shoulders pushed her to her knees so as she could suck, nibble and penetrate the welcoming flesh. When the fat girl cried out, Isabel, masturbating frantically, joined her in orgasm.

The dog next door sensing the excitement gave a dutiful bark that decayed into a grumpy rumble, a tacit comment on this intrusion, and a reminder to the world that ownership of territory should take precedence over any activity however frenzied, even if human strangers might dare to behave otherwise.

September 24th

Chapter 84: keep on moving

(8.00 am)

Far below in the soft early morning light, Great Malvern Priory rose imperiously from the reddening plumage of trees jostled by a freshening breeze. One of its gusts reached out to give a playful nudge to the Citroen Deux Chevaux as it jolted and purred its way down Wyche Road. Just a mile from the town centre, the little car stopped at the bottom of the hill for the junction with Wells Road, where the oncoming traffic was obscured by a dangerous blind bend. Chris strummed the steering wheel, impatient to get to work for the early start she had promised herself, and eager to make up for the time her arrest had wasted.

An old man, stooped and slow, was hobbling across the road, a clothbound bundle tucked under one arm and the other hand holding a handkerchief that he used to periodically wipe his nose which protruded from the line of a woollen beanie pulled low around his face, as if to catch the dribbles provoked by the chill of the autumn morning.

The man paused in front of the car and turned to look intently through the windscreen. Chris sensed immediately something was not right, but before she could react, the figure had moved to the side with suddenly acquired agility and was groping at the swing window of the passenger door, scrabbling to find the latch. Chris, terrified, swivelled in her seat kicking out at the hand. With a loud bang the window smashed as an elbow cracked into it and the door suddenly swung open.

'Drive, drive . . . it's me . . . they were watching your house, they'll be close - drive.' The voice was immediately recognizable.

'Jesus Mike . . . you frightened me, you've smashed the bloody window for Christ's sake,' Chris protested, as the car lurched forward, slowly gaining speed.

'You can tell them I forced you - downhill, here turn right - we'll go quicker downhill.'

'We can't - it's a one-way street. Mike!'

Her shouted protest was ignored. Aziz grabbed the wheel to direct the car now rapidly gaining momentum, down the side street, steering the bucking Citroen half onto the pavement to avoid an oncoming car, its shocked driver pressing the horn in furious condemnation of their recklessness, long after they were out of sight.

Aziz craned to look behind them. 'Yeah, we're being followed all right - a car turned down after us - pull up here, we'll be better off in the gardens.'

As the car slewed to a halt, Aziz dived out of the door shouting 'Follow me,' as he hurled himself through a gated entrance to disappear in a thicket of rhododendron shrubs. The urgency in his voice left Chris deciding it was simpler to obey. She crawled after him, feeling the snags pinching at her tights and the dirt colonizing her clothes and hands until she found Aziz waiting in the dense cover of the bushes.

'Good – the Gents, come on.' Aziz sprinted the short distance and banged his way into the Men's toilets. He popped out again to guide her.

'Quick - in here.'

Inside Aziz broke a window at the back, smashing out the glass and throwing his coat over the remaining splinters.

'Hurry - through you go,' he entreated.

'Mike . . . who's after us . . .?' asked Chris exasperated.

'They were tailing you to get to me - the police - they've been after me since I visited you in gaol,' he said, 'I need to give you a couple of things . . . and they were watching your house.'

'Mike, wait - listen . . . PORTAL sent me a message saying they've got your daughter. Just that - 'Tell Aziz we have his daughter' - that's all it said.'

'Shit,' said Aziz. There was a silence. Aziz cradled his head in his hands, his normal resilience seeming to collapse. For an instant, she squeezed his hand in hers. This time he didn't withdraw it.

'I'm sorry Mike.'

'Right.' Aziz drew a deep breath, gathering himself, and his resolve, then held out the bundle he had been carrying. 'This is the only lead I've managed to get on Dr Lineker. In the basket is the phone I told you about. It's got a number in its 'redial' memory that is the last one Emelienko phoned from his Mayfair flat. There's also the mobile that I used to photograph the doorway Emelienko's bodyguard visited. There were several nameplates on the wall. I'm reckoning he must have visited one of them. Maybe we can use it.'

'How so?' she asked.

'I was hoping you'd tell me,' he replied.

'I'll see what I can do.'

The distant thwack of a helicopter could be heard high above.

'So, they're up there too. Look - it's safer if I leave you here. It's me they're after, not you.' Aziz climbed onto the top of the water cistern, reaching up to haul himself through the toilet window.

'Mike.'

He looked back at her, halting in surprise at what he saw. 'What the . . .?'

'Quick, swap clothes,' she ordered, already down to her bra and panties.

'No . . . bad idea . . . it's too dangerous. If they think you're me, you could be shot.'

'Just do it Mike,' said Chris irritably. 'You're not going to fit in my clothes but I will yours. I'll be your decoy and I need you out there - looking for Ian,' insisted Chris.

Aziz was stealing glimpses at her. It made her feel good to see the admiration in his eyes, to be recognized as strong, and to be so exposed to him physically - it made her feel sexy.

'Okay. But make yourself known to them at the earliest opportunity,' cautioned Aziz, as he stripped off the old man's clothes to leave him in a vest that Chris noted appreciatively accentuated the faceted shapes of his heavily muscled arms.

A minute later she was dressed in his clothes.

'Do you find this apparel appealing, kind sir?' she flirted with a mock curtsey, wanting his approval, the bagginess hinting at her shape and adding mystery to the promise of perfection.

It was a tease that Aziz was only too willing to indulge as he surveyed what to him appeared no less than a supermodel in grunge.

'Yes I do,' he replied. 'You look gorgeous.'

Chapter 85: skin deep

The swap completed, Chris and Aziz squeezed through the window at the back of the toilet block and walked briskly to the nearby taxi rank outside the Post Office.

'Gloucester,' said Aziz, as they hopped in the back.

The driver was hesitant, clearly uncomfortable with their bizarre appearance and breathless urgency.

'We're going to a fancy dress rehearsal for the Police Pension charity fund raiser, I'm going as a poofter and this is my dad, okay?' said Aziz.

He stared at the man, a look of male to male aggression as threatening as a meat cleaver in the hands of a madman. The driver looked away, defeated and compliant.

'And turn the radio up,' commanded Aziz. 'We don't want to be listened to by any Tom Prick or Harry – get it?

The driver smiled weakly and nodded, unable to trust his voice with a reply. As the taxi moved off, Aziz told Chris how he had watched her house and hidden from the police scouring the great ridgeback of the hills after his invasion of the police station. The line of police had passed within six feet of his hideaway, but he had survived undetected. Later, when they came back with dogs, he had hidden in the pond beneath St. Anne's Well, then broken into a house to steal a change of clothes.

'I could use the name of that solicitor who got you out so quickly,' commented Aziz ruefully, 'they're really after me this time.'

'Actually I never saw a solicitor,' Chris explained. 'A Superintendent arrived - he said he was from Cheltenham - he told me I was free to go. He said I must have friends in high places, 'the APC no less' was his comment.'

'That's the Association of Police Chiefs. We did bits and pieces for those fuckers when I served. We were told they're not just 'above the law' - they are the law. It must be PORTAL who got you out - Clinton Schwartz mentioned they had a tame top cop when I first met them at the airport,' Aziz grimaced. 'Pull over driver.' They were still in the outskirts of Malvern, in a tree-lined avenue.

'I thought you said Gloucester,' the man protested, his reflex to challenge a short-changed fare overcoming his fear of Aziz.

'Yep, carry on driving to Gloucester after we've got out, okay. Now pull over - here's your money and keep the change.'

When they were out, the cab roared out of sight, the driver relieved to be stopped by a police road block just two minutes later, his story bubbling excitedly from him as he recounted his lucky escape from 'the madman' and 'his bitch'.

Aziz broke into a parked BMW on the other side of the road from where the cab had put them off. After just a minute the engine roared into life.

'Hop in,' he invited her.

The car hurtled down the road, travelling at speed through the Worcestershire countryside, each of its occupants thinking of the other – he, acutely aware his companion was a beautiful woman cross-dressed in seductive castoffs – she, wondering whether to be amused or distressed that beside her was a burly man with a skirt wrapped part-way round him and a woman's top over his shoulders in a parody of pantomime.

Bad pantomime, she decided.

'Isabel never replied to my Facebook request.' Aziz said, his mood changing with the respite of the drive. 'I don't know what to do.'

She noticed it was the first time he had sought her advice. 'I'll send her a message, maybe she'll talk to me.'

'If she can,' said Aziz, totally despondent. 'Maybe she can't talk to anyone.'

This time Chris could find no words to reassure him, as the weight of her own worries bore down on her. 'Just five days left to rescue Ian before they . . . I'm really afraid for him.'

'I'll tab over to Beaky's,' Aziz replied, 'see what we can set up - don't worry, I'll sort it.'

She smiled briefly at him, grateful that he would try, but unconvinced by his attempt at optimism.

'How can I get in touch?'

'Leave a message for me on the comments section of the Guardian on-line, the first arts story - and let me know how it goes,' she said. 'Sign off as 'SASSY' and I'll know it's you. If you need to meet, we'll meet at Shepherds Bush Market tube station okay? Just let me know when.' They were pulling into the railway station in Worcester.

'Okay, you'd better hop out for a moment,' he told her, 'They need to get a good look at your version of Mike Aziz. But remember - as long as they think you're me - you're in danger. Make yourself known to them as soon as they get near you, and tell them I threatened you,' he said, getting out the other side of the car as he opened an umbrella he had retrieved from the bundle he had carried with him.

'See you later.' Aziz shuffled off toward the train station, an unlikely drag-queen, emanating defeat and misery.

Chris watched him walk away, believing he was thinking of his daughter and of her. She was right, but unaware Aziz was also reflecting that Beaky had already refused to help.

'Keep it together soldier, you're not on bloody holiday,' she bawled on impulse. Aziz immediately stiffened, standing upright as if to attention, before turning to flash her a toothy grin and shouting back. 'Yes sir ma'am, sir.'

Aziz saluted extravagantly before striding off, his limp with the uneven falling gait that was his hallmark almost absent as he swept past the ogling faces and into the station. She watched him go before crossing the tarmac to the cab rank.

'Malvern,' she barked at the taxi-driver.

The cab eased into the flow of traffic as the helicopter high above with a distant chop/chop beat and a leisurely sweep through a broad semicircle, turned to follow it.

Aziz bought a ticket to London, boarded the train and in the toilets changed into the clothes that he'd carried in the bundle under his arm. He lowered himself out of the window on the side away from the platform, crossed the tracks and slipping unseen from a goods yard behind the station, steeled himself for the thirty-mile cross-country march to Hereford.

Chapter 86: cold fish

(Australia)

Isabel had told Magnus she was staying in town with a friend after the concert, and she had not invited him along. It had annoyed him, but after stopping for a double beef burger at a Hungry Jacks behind the service station on the southern exit from Hobart, he had called a taxi for the forty kilometre drive back to Huonville.

The Church had treated him well, transferring him quickly into its Clean Team, but he felt no gratitude, seeing it as no more than just recognition of his already remarkable achievements. He still smiled when he remembered how the prosecutor had tried to present him as a psychopath in his trial in Reykjavik for the arson attack on a university hall of residence that had killed five students. The reports to the court had recommended Magnus receive psychiatric treatment, but the case against him was never proven, failing through contamination of the evidence for arson by one of the fireman at the scene. His defence had also cited his brilliance, and the high expectation of his outstanding contribution to academic life.

Study had come easily to Magnus. He never wasted energy on conjecture, and his degree course had quickly provided him with an effective camouflage. With its limited vocabulary, he had found the language of the numinous less challenging than the Chinese he had also learnt at college, though neither was a vehicle for the expression of anything that was meaningful to him. He watched unmoved as others were comforted by exchanging their notions of the 'spiritual', and despised them for their gullibility and needy anxieties. So different from when he had watched the fires burn; and heard the screaming. That had been real. Those people had discovered what living really was - they had no delusions of 'the other' when they had died.

Magnus' father, a senior official in the Ministry of Finance, always suspected Magnus was guilty. Eager to see Magnus leave Iceland and escape the publicity that the arson case had attracted, he had managed to secure Magnus psychiatric treatment in the US to coincide with his placement with PORTAL. The Church had been told of Magnus' medical history but were happy to take him, assuring his father that they had a proud record of 'integrating special-need individuals back into society and ensuring they realized their full potential.'

Magnus was settling for bed in the living room in the Huonville house when a blip announced the receipt of a message on the house-share computer. It was Isabel's Facebook account, that she had left open on the screen. Magnus read the message, from someone called 'Chris Reynolds', warning Isabel she might be in danger and urging her to contact her father.

'Minn ó minn . . . what fun miss piggy, what fun.' He smiled as he deleted the message. Magnus was not worried; such warnings were to be expected, but it reminded him that time was running out and he needed to act quickly. He sent a message to his controller in California. 'Completion imminent. Further contact only after return.'

After his routine exercise of sixty sit-ups Manus went to bed, savouring the thought of tomorrow, and the prospect of excitement.

Chapter 87: the long way home

(8:20 am)

It took just three minutes before the unmarked police car fell in behind Chris's taxi, its flashing light suddenly illuminated to indicate to the driver to pull over. Nothing happened for a further three minutes, at least nothing external to the taxi.

The taxi driver grew increasingly anxious, fidgeting and looking round, shooting questions at Chris, until his panicked attempt to understand what was going on was overtaken by a babble of surfacing anxieties, released while his mind was distracted by the smell and taste of actual fear. 'Kamal . . . and auntie no better . . . how will we . . . who will . . . the rent . . . already . . . why my cab? Why did you choose me?'

The man's outpouring was abruptly interrupted when a second police vehicle, a van, screeched to a halt in front of the isolated cab. Four policemen jumped from the van carrying handguns. A fifth brandished a Heckler/Koch MP5SFA3 semi-automatic carbine. 'Step out of the car, hands above your head,' the megaphone voice intoned, 'and kneel on the ground.'

Chris remembered the urgency of Aziz's warning. *If they think you are me, you may be shot.*

'Jeez . . . what a mess,' said Chris to no-one in particular. *So how do I convince them?*

Show them of course. Yes – that's it. Show them. She quickly stripped off the jacket, and hid the phones that Aziz had given her in its sleeves. Then she took off her shirt, considering for a moment whether to remove the bra that offered minimal cover to her breasts. She glanced down at her nipples engorged by the cold, prominent through the thin material and decided it was unnecessary.

Your lucky day boys, she thought as she stepped from the car, knowing she was afraid, trusting in fate and the power of the primal. As she raised her hands to clasp them behind her neck, a slight uplift presented her at her most sexual, challenging the men with her vulnerability, as different from their armoured aggression as skin is to steel. At first the police lowered their guns before training reasserted itself, though now their fear had gone.

Suddenly remembering the name of the unknown benefactor who under instructions from PORTAL had ordered her release from jail, she shouted: 'I am Dr Christine Reynolds and I want to speak to Assistant Commissioner Lawson.'

She took a step forward and started to repeat herself to ensure she had been properly heard. 'I am Dr Chris Reynolds and I want to speak to . . .'

'Don't move or you will be shot,' was the megaphoned reply, but somehow even through the electro-static, this time the voice lacked conviction. She heard the sounds of laughter bubbling amongst the policemen and knew that the mood had changed, and so had the risks - she was now a near-naked woman surrounded by a pack of hostile men.

After four interminable minutes, the sergeant approached her carrying a blanket. He apologized profusely, explaining the delay and commiserating with the awfulness of being held hostage by a fugitive terrorist. Assisted by her carefully chosen half-truths, it took another ten minutes to dispose of further phone calls and identity checks - 'Just to fill in the paperwork, Doctor Reynolds you understand' - before Chris was being driven at speed in a police car back to Malvern.

'Can you drop me off at my Deux Chevaux outside the Winter Gardens?' she asked.

'Sorry ma'am,' the policeman replied, 'the vehicle is with forensics - but I can take you home.'

Chapter 88: countdown

(8.40 am)

Chris watched the police car race off down the hill, leaving the tingle of acrid exhaust and the faintest trace of oil in the freshness of the morning air, even after the stillness had returned. She found she was thinking of when Aziz had driven away just two days before, with a similarly masculine roar of purpose and efficiency. The memory was reassuring - she had a man to protect her from other men.

Pushing the cat away, Chris gathered up the small parcel that the postman had left on the doorstep of Victoria Cottage. She swung the front door open and went upstairs to change into a warm jumper and training pants before phoning the police station to ask when she could recover the Deux Chevaux.

'Forensics won't be finished until four this afternoon,' they had told her so she made herself a cup of tea and finally seated at the kitchen table, opened the parcel.

The sight of a rusty stain on the tissue, and the sudden thumping of her heart were the first indications of inexorable and imminent horror. As she held the tissue, the finger suddenly fell out, its yellowing nail contrasting with the whiteness of the waxy flesh as it lay upturned on the surface of the table. She shouted out loud, a gasping exhalation of revulsion and outrage and she pushed backwards from the table, the involuntary action spilling the tea in a single wave as the cup crashed and shattered on the ground.

Gasping, she rushed to the sink, a dry retch from her stomach robbing her of breath as completely as a sudden wave of dizziness robbed her of vision. Recovering, she returned to the table slowly, as if the finger might harm her, and found the note. It said 'Every day - another.'

Five more days - no, please, God no.

Chris slumped on the floor without moving, except for the occasional spasm of trembling that wracked her body as the tears started to flow. The minute hand had described an arc across a quarter of the clock face before the numbness lifted, and her crying eased. She rose unsteadily from the floor and crossed to the kitchen cupboard, fumbling amongst the cartons, then she carefully wrapped the finger in cling-film and after covering it in ice in a polystyrene party cup, placed it in the freezer.

By the time she had showered and changed, her mind was made up.

Okay, you bastards. The gloves are off.

Chapter 89: falling in love

(Australia)

Clouds had descended to cloak the hills in a mantle of grey. Suddenly the shroud parted to reveal Mt. Eliza, the lower flat-topped peak en-route to the ascent of the mighty pyramid of Mt. Anne, now visible behind it.

Shit, thought Isabel, looking at the angle of access up the mountain, is *that even possible for Angie?* The mist swirled teasingly for a few brief seconds in the lateral morning light then once more the view was lost from sight.

Isabel shouted encouragement to her friend, 'That's where we're headed.' Angie replied with a thumbs up gesture to indicate she was ready for the challenge, and as a gesture of affection for the lover with whom she had shared the night.

When Angie had drawn level with her, Isabel rose to her feet and pressed on up the steepening track with Angie following close behind. Before long, both women stopped to take off their packs and hand them through the narrower sections where the dolerite columns soared from a common base and constricted the way up, while Magnus continued in front of them, his face set and truculent.

'It's so wild, and beautiful,' said Isabel smiling at Angie, as they huddled together on a rock to share dried cranberries. 'Have you ever thought how we are created by what we see?'

'And we share it,' said Angie, reaching over to kiss her lightly.

'Exactly - we share it with each other, a common consciousness, and we share it with itself - you could say with the Spirit - yes, it's our vision of the Spirit, as nature is revealed to us.' It was a special moment for the two, their own union mirroring the subtler sense of an appreciation of oneness with their surroundings.

Magnus glanced down and saw them holding hands, twisting his resolution into an even tighter skein of malice, the desire to humiliate Isabel sexually now abandoned in his overriding intent to do more focused harm, and by the limiting discomfort of the cold. 'Slut bitches,' he muttered under his breath. 'Come on, it's easier up here,' he shouted down to them.

They turned to signal each other a look of good-natured exasperation, before hurrying forward to catch him.

'I didn't realize he'd be such a pain. I'm sorry,' said Isabel quietly to Angie.

'He's just jealous,' replied Angie, pinching her on the bum ostentatiously, certain that Magnus would see the gesture and confident in the security of her newly consolidated romance.

The walk across the exposed plateau to the base of Anne took ninety minutes, the lower slopes another thirty minutes. After a late lunch, they negotiated the rock shelf before reaching the base of a ledge that sloping away from the mountain above a fifty-metre drop presented a hazard in the rain or ice, and a frightening prospect in any conditions to those blessed, or cursed, with an active imagination.

'Angie and me will rope up, do you want to be tied on as well?' shouted Isabel.

'No - I'll be fine on this. I'll go up first and help Angie,' Magnus shouted back, a plan already formulating in his mind.

In a few minutes Magnus was out of sight, reappearing to shout down: 'Okay, I'm ready. Come on Angie. I'll grab your hand when you're over this rock. The next section is a bit exposed.'

In a moment he was gone again and as Isabel secured her back against a boulder, Angie tentatively eased her way up the slanting rock. It took five minutes of climbing before Angie's head drew level with Magnus's feet as he waited for her on the flatter rock above. He held his hand out to help her. She accepted the offer and Magnus eased her up, smiling a rictus of simulated welcome, until almost level with him, she tentatively stood up, loosening the grip her fingers had on his wrist, as she turned to review the rock face she had just climbed.

Magnus did not release his grip. Instead he pulled violently at the same time lowering his body backwards and down to fall on his back, in a graceful wrestler's throw, the whole fluid movement accomplished in an instant. Angie, despite her weight, was propelled over him toward the sloping rock surface behind, her eyes popping with fear and astonishment. Her flailing other hand scrabbled for an indefinite instant at the rock, the nails chipping and breaking in a desperate attempt to halt her slide, staring at him incredulously with a look of horror and despair as she slid toward the edge. Magnus grinned back.

As she slid by him, with an inspired reflex she suddenly whipped her other hand to clamp onto the waist belt of his backpack, bringing her to a frantic slithering halt poised on the knife edge between the more horizontal ledge and the sheer fall beyond it, most of her body now hanging helplessly down the wall. Her abrupt halt had carried Magnus skidding to the same edge, his fist beating at her hand to release her grip, as he screamed at her, the noise whisked away by the mountain wind.

Far beneath them, Isabel felt the rope tighten, pulling her to her feet. She fell back to counter the lift, wrapping an arm round a waist-high shrub, desperately afraid something awful had happened but unable to see or hear what it might be.

As Angie's other hand locked onto the belt, Magnus started kicking her in the face, breaking her nose in a spurt of blood and raising ugly welts across her cheek. Her resolve was so fixed it seemed other than human as she clung to his waist belt, edging Magnus inexorably toward the drop as more of her body inched over. The shift in equilibrium, when it came, was instantaneous.

Suddenly they were both over the edge, their roles reversed as Magnus clung for his life to Angie. The combined weight of the two on the rope yanked on Isabel, who losing her grip on the shrub, was whisked skyward to leave her suspended in mid-air, breathless, terrified and winded, slowly rotating as she shouted to be told what was happening.

Magnus was trapped in a death embrace with a formidable opponent. One of his arms was dedicated to holding onto the rope around Angie, but she was tied to the rope with two hands free to beat him off. She smashed her elbow into his face, gouged at his eyes with her fingers and pummelled him on the head repeatedly with a fist. When that didn't work she bit his hand, spat at him and clubbed him, until his face was a twisted bloody mess, like the innards of the road-kill they had lamented on the drive south.

Finally, almost with resignation, Magnus let go. It was as if he recognized that his adversary not only had a greater commitment to life than he did, but also a moral entitlement to outlive him, a perverse conclusion for someone who had always dismissed the notion of virtue as no more than a self-serving fantasy.

Angie heard Magnus screaming something as he hurtled to the ground, but she couldn't tell what. Magnus himself had no knowledge that this last word had also been his first - 'Freyja' - the name of the nanny who had cared for him from when he was born until he was twelve. He had only recently found out from a newspaper archive that Freyja had not been 'called away' as his parents had always told him, but in fact had died in a car crash. Discovering their deception had gone some way to healing the hurt Magnus had always felt that Freyja had left him without saying goodbye, but had provided further ammunition for the anger he already felt for his parents.

Magnus fell just twenty metres. Not much compared with the thirteen hundred they had ascended, but Angie knew his cartwheeling drop was enough to shatter his head like a watermelon as it bashed into the granite outcrop below. She imagined the film of viscous red, and the flecks of white and rejoiced in the cruel indifference of nature that with the wind and the rain would quickly scour the surface back to the glinty grey of naked rock.

As Magnus fell, Isabel jolted down a meter, until the rope wedged into a crack above her, leaving her dangling three metres above the ground. She sensed through her anxiety that something was resolved; and somehow irretrievable.

Angie lacked the strength to climb the rope and had no knife with which to cut it. She watched helpless as the sun lowered beneath the horizon and the wind strengthened from the south west, carrying the scent of the arctic wasteland in its bitter eddies. When the storm arrived she was hanging with no shelter from its fury or defence from the gusts that repeatedly swung her into the rock face, adding fresh injuries to her already battered face.

Protected from the brunt of the weather, Isabel made it to the underside of the rock above her, but in many attempts could not scale the horizontal ceiling that obstructed her ascent. Unable to know if it would jeopardize Angie's safety, Isabel made no attempt to cut the rope. They cried out to each other, but even this comfort was denied them by the roar of the wind.

Angie clung to life for about seven hours after her fall, until she fell asleep for the last time, lulled into oblivion by the thought of Magnus' brains splattered across the rocks, somewhere unreachable beneath her. But it was meagre consolation. Angie died with her heart full of longing and hate, and a sense of bitter loss.

Chapter 90: housekeeping

The horrific image of the second amputated finger still seared in her mind, and with no car, Chris decided the prospect of going to work was out of the question. She checked the time. *Not even nine - can it really be less than an hour since I was swapping clothes with Mike . . . in a public toilet?*

She retrieved the phones Aziz had given her, arranging Emelienko's landline telephone and Aziz's mobile on the desk vacated by her computer, which had not yet been returned by the police. She thought for a while, then took out her laptop. She bought a Phone dialler program over the internet, downloaded it, plugged in Emelienko's phone and hit redial. When a man replied from the Indian Embassy trade desk she simply said 'Sorry wrong number', and then checked the log file on the dialler program to retrieve the telephone number. Stage one accomplished she turned her attention to Aziz's mobile.

That was quick thinking Mike, she thought, browsing through the nameplates Aziz had photographed outside the door that had prevented him following Shirov. There were several names, 'Harmony Massage', 'Shepherdson and Wright – Accountants', 'PBL Design Studio', 'SOS(IS) Ltd', 'NRZ Holdings' and 'Stonewall Construction'. Chris looked up the websites of each organization and noted their contact details, except for Harmony Massage who weren't online. She raided the Westminster City council website for a pro-forma page that she adapted, and sent a tailored email to each of the companies on her list, masquerading as a letter from the Council. The fake email would offer an amnesty for non-payment of Rates, and no charge for the next quarter if current occupancy details were forwarded to enable records to be rebuilt following a computer crash. Cheekily, it threatened court action if no reply were received in twelve hours.

That'll get 'em . . . is there anything more irritating than a council bureaucracy? she shrugged, the thought evaporating into the void of rhetoric as she ran through the logic sequence in her mind, checking her reasoning for errors as she tapped at the keyboard to construct her one-off spy program. When completed, she broadcast the email and its embedded Trojan, to the companies whose nameplates Aziz had photographed on the mobile he had given her in the public toilets.

As soon as the attached pro-forma was opened her mole program would begin burrowing, deleting its own log files to limit its traceability as it crawled progressively through every part of the unsuspecting company's computer system. By grafting itself to their outgoing emails, it would infect other companies too so as the enquiry grew exponentially.

Her virus program was designed to delete itself after twelve hours, and to remove all incriminating emails. The code had one object in mind - to find a match on the computer system for the Indian Embassy telephone number that Emelienko had phoned immediately before he had hurriedly vacated his Mayfair flat, and report back to Chris the name of the company using that number.

Tired from the effort of writing the program and the emotional battering from an already overloaded day, she lay down for a few minutes until realizing there was no escape from the constant churning in her mind, she decided to take a stroll through the hills. Even if it would not bring peace – it would at least be somewhere different.

Chapter 91: the first cut is the deepest

(Australia)

Isabel was helicoptered to hospital in the early morning. The bushwalking couple who found her had summonsed help by activating their Personal Locator Beacon, and were pleased to share the horrors of their discovery with the local TV station. Seduced into callousness by the unfamiliar attention, they told how the girl had been suffering from hypothermia and seemed to experience hallucinations, mistaking her rescuers for her mother and father who had come to bring her home.

Isabel took the news of her lover's death badly. After only a few hours and before the police arrived to interview her, she discharged herself from hospital, deciding she would abandon forest activism and its inevitable confrontations. Within half an hour of messaging PORTAL to ask how she could become more involved with their work, she had received an invitation to visit the Church headquarters, and a transfer of funds to purchase an air-ticket.

Just fourteen hours after she had been rescued, Isabel took the first flight out from Hobart. She felt it as a form of penance for her contribution to the death of her friends; a tribute to the lover with whom for such a short time she had stolen an interlude of happiness, and as a way of honouring the young man who had shown her the way to the ministry of God.

Chapter 92: the hills are alive

(10.45 am)

It was as it often is. The birds greeted Chris with scolding chirrups and the trees confided in hushed whispers as billowing clouds scudded across the celestial stage, dissolving and reforming in endless permutations of shape and shade. But for once, the magic was not enough.

No longer preoccupied with technical matters, the image of the amputated finger again filled Chris's mind with a tangle of horror. She felt her belly, wondering once more if she was pregnant and knowing more clearly than ever that this was not a good time for a baby.

She thought about Aziz, admitting to herself the strength of her feeling for him, and confused by its components. On the surface, she and Aziz appeared to have so little in common, she was surprised at how important he had become, and how quickly.

Is it because neither of us . . . really belongs, she mused, acknowledging in herself what was so evident in him – the status of the perennial outsider.

His regard for her seemed so old-fashioned, she wondered if that was part of the attraction, and whether her interest in him would last, or suddenly seem inappropriate, as had happened so often before when her desire to lose herself in intimacy had collided with her anger at the prospect of being controlled.

There was something different, almost primitive about Aziz. *Animal even,* she smiled. Or was it his unpredictability that contrasted with her own self-discipline, a work ethic that had brought her professional success and independence, but at a price. *Mike seems lonely. Is that it? Is that what we have in common?* She had always avoided naming her isolation, but now she could see its outline, in the shadow of another.

Chris realized she was missing this unpredictable man. *Have I fallen in love with you Mr Aziz?* she wondered, sensing the ache. *Whatever the reason.*

As she walked, the feeling of being followed accompanied her, and with it the sudden urge to spin round and catch the darting figure as it leapt for cover behind a tree. She sighed, resigned to the nervousness of the prey in a land of predators and admitting how damaged she was by the turmoil of the previous forty-eight hours.

She felt guilty about Ian, intensifying the need to make amends in the only way that seemed possible – ensuring his physical well-being. They had shared a night of intimacy just hours before he had been abducted, and however much she rationalized it, somehow that added to her sense of responsibility.

Awful timing. Nandini will crucify me when I tell her about Mike.

She turned homewards for a fidgety return, clarifying in her mind the many challenges she faced. The list was daunting. *Must buy a new outfit. Something a bit more girly - to please Nandini,* she thought, *and Mike . . .* The thought had invented itself, uninvited, colouring her cheeks with a flush of excitement, and embarrassment at the priority of vanity at a time when so much more was at risk. The realization refocused her mind.

She needed to formulate with Aziz how they planned to snatch Lineker from the show. She had to speak to Grafton and check his progress on the Interferometer that would form the centrepiece of the TruthSayers TV program. Emelienko was still waiting for information about the detail of the show, and so were PORTAL who she was relying on to ensure it got off the ground. She should take a pregnancy test, retrieve her car and take the second finger, the one still in the freezer, to the police. The memory of the morning package shocked her with the realization that the five days that remained were not too few, but excruciatingly too many.

Something else was nagging at the back of her mind - the flash of pleasure at tracing its origin immediately dispelled by her reaction to the content - a small matter of a porn video with her in a starring role that required some sort of strategy to deal with, whatever that might be and if such a thing were even possible.

By the time she entered the little garden at the front of her home, she had decided on her priorities. When overworked, the important thing was to delegate. As she retrieved her keys, Chris assessed the help available to her.

Not sure about Grafton. PORTAL can get things done however disgusting they are - if they can help free Ian, everything else is secondary. Mike certainly seems to be able to handle himself – though you wouldn't think so if you didn't know him. Mike's friend Beaky too – he could be very useful. Two SAS blokes might be a bit much though . . . must phone Nandini again . . . see what she thinks.

She entered the cottage and hurried to her laptop to scan the several messages on the screen. The one she opened first was from her mole program. It simply said 'Konkreton t/a Stonewall Construction.'

Chapter 93: anne

(Australia)

'Why are you so interested in my dad, anyway?' asked Isabel. 'I really don't know very much about my father. And don't want to either.'

The uncharacteristic anger in Isabel's voice showed Magnus he had overstepped the mark.

'I've always found things difficult at home; just wondering how other folk deal with it . . .' Magnus replied, 'that's all.'

She eyed him coolly, unconvinced. 'Okay . . . no worries.'

The fat girl was a slower walker than either Isabel or Magnus, so had started five minutes in front of them up the steep ascent toward the mountain top, where the dancing clouds encircled the crags and breathed tendrils of frosted mist across the plateau.

'Let's see if we can catch up with Angie,' Isabel suggested, jumping up to shoulder her pack.

Magnus felt the bile rise, a reflexive reaction to her wholesomeness. He despised Isabel's lack of sophistication, her simplistic morality and her hippie scent of musk and pepper, and he watched her leave without comment. As Magnus studied the curves of her backside, he thought again of the pleasure he would take in fucking her. Sex with her would confirm how easy she was to manipulate and afterwards, it would be easy to get her to return with him to the States.

'I'll have you up the fucking arse, you mindless bitch,' he said quietly to himself as he too heaved his heavy pack on his back, and started off up the slope, 'and your fat friend.'

Angie's presence was a source of great annoyance to Magnus and aggravated by the difficulty of the ascent, his petulance had become hard to conceal. It was he who had first suggested the walk up Mount Anne in Tasmania's South West, a walk he had read was difficult but spectacularly beautiful. He had been surprised at Isabel's reluctance to join him and frustrated when Isabel had said she would only consider it if her friend came too. He had decided to go ahead with the trip anyway but Isabel's eagerness to include Angie in everything was an impediment he had not anticipated.

Almost, as if she knows something, Magnus thought to himself.

Seated on a rock, Isabel and Angie were admiring the view and laughing together when he drew up to them. They stopped when he arrived – a coincidence that prompted further doubt.

Are they laughing at me because I was slower than them up the slope?

It was late when they reached the hut at High Camp, the sun already reddening and the shadows merging into black. Like a fortress built by giants, Mount Solitary rose huge and inconsolable from Lake Pedder, its vast moat carving an intricate jigsaw of bays and tributaries into the desolation of wilderness. In the distance, jagged mountains reached their sawtooth profiles to claw at a tumultuous sky of blue, black, and grey, as if the conflict with the gods had left the heavens themselves battered and bruised. It was dark, gothic, magnificent and cruel. They watched in silence, human preoccupation stilled by the grandeur of nature.

Magnus was least in its spell. 'Stunning' he said, knowing his charm.

Isabel looked at him, noticing the dimple, the twinkle in his eyes and the wide welcoming openness of his face and for a moment the building resentment she felt toward him relented.

'Awesome,' she replied, as the fat girl laughed.

'We'll share a tent in one of the sites just down the way,' said Isabel cheerily. 'Then you can have the hut to yourself.'

The fat girl laughed again, the raucous agitation of the sound out of place in the placid serenity of the mountainside. Magnus didn't protest though by now he had no doubt something had gone wrong, but he was unsure what.

Much later when he went to the toilet, he saw light from the little tent half hidden in the stunted trees and shrubs. Silhouetted against the wall of the tent, as graphic as an early silent movie, the profile of the fat girl was clearly visible. She was on her hands and knees, her pendulous breasts swinging freely as she lowered her head, its outline suddenly obscured in an inverted 'v' shape that Magnus realized must be Isabel's knee as she lay on her back. The gentle moaning began almost immediately. Magnus felt the fury surge into his throat.

He had not received authorization, but on a remote mountain, this had to be the perfect opportunity. On the last job he had received praise for his initiative, and thinking on his feet. *Why not do something similar here?*

Magnus had made up his mind. He would fuck Isabel, whether she wanted to or not - then he would kill her. But first he would kill the fat girl.

Won't be long, Miss Piggy, won't be long.

Chapter 94: beaky

(12.30 pm)

'Mate,' called Aziz.

'Err . . . yes,' replied Beaky. Some half a mile from his Herefordshire farmhouse, Beaky was sitting next to a rivulet that flowed across a meadow, a fishing rod in one hand with a line stretching downstream in the current.

'It's me - Aziz. Don't react. I'm under the bush to your left.'

'Where? I can't see you.'

'I'm in the water. It's bloody freezing. I've just legged it all the way from fuckin' Worcester.'

'Really . . . what the fuck for? I was looking at the wrong bush. I see you now . . . good work Mike, I'd never have guessed you were there.' Beaky shook his head with a tired smile on his face. 'But why precisely you're hiding in a stream is probably best overlooked for the moment eh? I'll get the Landie - won't be long.'

Ten minutes later the 4WD was backed up to the river's edge. With the rear door swung open, visibility was obscured except from a narrow angle across the river. When Aziz was inside, concealed on the floor, Beaky stashed his fishing gear and his supply of beers.

As they drove slowly back to the farmhouse, Beaky shouted back to Aziz, still crouched out of sight in the back of the Land Rover. 'And to what do I owe the privilege Mike? You're not after more armaments I hope. You left with enough to start a war, or should I say to end one.'

'I'm in deep shit, Beaky. Remember the Church who threatened my daughter. Last time I saw Chris - that's Dr Chris Reynolds - she'd been contacted by the Church with a message for me. 'Tell Aziz we have his daughter.' They've got her. I don't even know where she is. The cops are helping them too.'

'So why can't you just convert and make everyone happy?'

'They're sickos Beaky . . . but Chris wants to work with them to release her boss, Dr Lineker. He's been taken hostage. He used to be her boyfriend by the way,' Aziz added.

'Is that right?' Beaky wondered why Aziz had mentioned their relationship. 'So the Church people have kidnapped this Lineker chap too?'

'No, we think it's the Russians.'

'The Russians!' said Beaky, his eyebrows raised.

'Look, I hate asking, but I need your help to spring this guy when they do a TV show. I'm trying to find out where my daughter is, so I may not be around to do it myself.'

'Look mate. I don't want to overstep the mark here. But you were in a bad state after we got back from duty and to be honest, you look like shit now.' Beaky stopped the car, swivelling in the seat to look behind him. Beaky looked at Aziz intently. 'Are you all right?'

'Not really Beaky, no. Half the fuckin' world is after me.'

'I understand that. What I meant was - didn't they put you on medication for a while?'

'Don't go there. Beaky . . .' said Aziz, anger rising in him. 'Goddam pills . . . every bloody day. So what are you saying - you think I'm dreaming all this?'

'It's tough for all of us, but if you think too much you'll only make it worse. We're not responsible . . . don't forget that.'

'Maybe we are,' replied Aziz quietly.

The remark surprised Beaky into silence, but he resumed after a while.

'Jesus, I'm as paranoid as the next man. You know that.' Beaky's tone was more conciliatory. 'I had a visit from the police, asking if I'd seen you, so obviously you're in some sort of shite,' continued Beaky. 'Why are the cops looking for you as well as this Church, and last time didn't you say it was the CIA?'

'I busted into a Malvern police station to free Chris Reynolds,' said Aziz.

'Did you?' Beaky frowned, looking serious. He continued, 'Mike - don't take this wrong but why don't you come with me to Hereford? There's a counsellor woman they've got there. Big tits, huge arse, she's magic. I've seen her a few times, always feel better afterwards, she smells fantastic.'

'There's no time for that sort of . . . but look . . . I've met someone . . . it's . . . different,' he shot his friend an anxious glance, not wishing to reveal too much, before continuing. 'You think I'm paranoid. I'll prove it you. They're probably listening to your house. You thought they were following me yourself, remember?'

'Yeah someone sure. But not a Church, the CIA, the Russians, the police, a jealous ex-lover and a girlfriend,' Beaky smiled.

'I'll prove it to you. When we're inside the house, use my name. We'll have a fight, I'll give you a thump, tie you up and then I'll be off. See how long it takes them to visit.'

'What, like they do in the films?' asked Beaky.

'Exactly, then you can't be accused of helping me.'

'Oh dear . . . calm down you sad fucker. We are not having a pretend fight. If anyone comes around - and I have to say I think it is extremely unlikely - I'll just tell them I was about to contact them, okay? Speaking of which, how do I get in touch with you afterwards?' asked Beaky

'Use this phone. My number is on it.' Aziz tossed a phone forward and Beaky caught it deftly.

'You said you want the scientist grabbed from a TV show. When is that exactly?'

'Five days from now. I reckon it'll be in London.' Beaky considered what he'd been told for a moment, then shook his head.

'I'm sorry Mike. If I thought I was helping you I'd be in, but my advice is - have nothing to do with any of it. It isn't your war - just look after your daughter.'

With no interest in the whinger's talent for making someone else responsible for his own misfortune, Aziz didn't explain that his daughter wanted nothing to do with him and in any case he didn't know how to help her, or that he now regarded Chris Reynolds's concerns as his own.

'Okay Beaky, I understand.' Aziz turned away to hide his disappointment. Beaky saw it, choosing to change the subject quickly. 'Let's eat . . . there's a couple of little fishies in my basket. We'll be super quiet eh? And test your theory about all these bad guys out to get you?'

Before they arrived at the farmhouse, Aziz hopped out of the Land Rover and slipped in through a side window as Beaky unloaded the car at the front, giving Shep a friendly pat as the collie wandered out to see what was going on. Aziz and Beaky prepared and ate the meal, cooperating easily with sign language as they had done many times before in combat.

When they were ready Beaky said loudly,

'Aziz, what a surprise. I wondered where you were,' in a pantomime voice. 'You know I have to hand you in to the police don't you?' The enunciation was too clear, its tone teetering on amused.

'Better be off then,' said Aziz, his voice strained and robotic, like a bad actor auditioning badly.

'I'll get you for that you fucker,' Beaky said aloud, pushing his fist to his mouth to suppress the laughter that threatened to overtake his composure.

'Take this for the journey,' he whispered, pushing a homemade muesli bar into Aziz's hand. 'Good luck mate,' he mouthed, this time heartfelt, as Aziz left the way he had arrived.

Fifteen minutes later, as he finished the washing up Beaky had decided the experiment confirmed his worst fears for his long-time companion.

'You need more help than I can give you Mike,' he said out loud, saddened that his proud warrior friend had found no rest, even when the battle had long since ended.

Suddenly Beaky froze, craning his head to one side to better identify the trace of sound scratching at the outermost limit of his hearing.

Shit, the mad little fucker's right after all, he thought to himself *. . . so there is a goddam bug in here. They must have been in here when I was in Hereford . . . bastards.*

The pulsing thrum of a distant helicopter rapidly grew to a deafening clatter overhead contested by its bellowing loudspeaker that broadcast echoing threats at the grey-tiled roof beneath it.

Good on you Mike . . . who'd have thought it. Raided a cop station. You champion little sod.

Beaky thrust an arm from the window, raising a finger in the universal gesture of contempt, and turned back to the kitchen. This was the second helicopter to have visited in the last two days. The first had called to collect an emergency order of hibiscus tea for a hotel on the Welsh border. Beaky brewed himself another cup of hibiscus tea from the small amount he had left, then sat back to await his uninvited guests.

Chapter 95: autumn fall

(3:00 pm)

'Konkreton t/a Stonewall Construction.' Chris read the words slowly, savouring her success.

Her mole program had trawled through the companies whose name plaques Aziz had photographed, looking for the number retrieved from the phone he ripped from the wall of Emelienko's Mayfair flat. The mole had found the number, a phone extension in the Indian Embassy, in Konkreton's computer records.

So . . . Emelienko's thug, Shirov, visits a building with Konkreton's nameplate on the wall; someone in this Konkreton outfit has the number of the Indian Embassy on file; Emelienko speaks to the Embassy just before he leaves his flat. Good . . . but . . .

Her satisfaction at her progress was short-lived, the emerging pattern immediately prompting further crucial questions.

Who are Konkreton? Why would they be involved in Ian's disappearance? And what do the Indian Embassy have to do with any of this?

A google search on Konkreton revealed nothing useful, and her attempt to find distraction in work proved equally futile so after ten minutes Chris phoned Nandini to suggest they meet in an hour, planning in the interim to make a long overdue trip to the supermarket. Returning from the shopping, Chris had also included a detour to the small designer clothes shop in an alley near the Abbey, run by a friendly French woman, so that by the time the taxi had dropped her off at home, it was already 3:30 pm. She was unpacking the shopping bags when the phone rang.

'I need to talk to you. Your mobile isn't working.' Grafton sounded petulant. 'I thought you said you were going to be at work today.'

'Sorry Bill - I did plan on an early start but I got kind of hijacked on the way in.'

'Well, can I come round?'

'I'm not sure that's convenient,' she replied, trying to disguise the feeling of free fall and its accompanying panic from her voice

'There's a lot I need to tell you.' he insisted.

'Well, okay . . . if you can get here quickly - we'll have a bit of time before a friend gets here at four.'

'I'll be there in five minutes.' Grafton sounded excited, and more youthful than she remembered.

When he arrived, she noted he was starting a light beard, concealing the weak chin that had been one of the less attractive features of his face, and he was no longer wearing glasses. She noted too that his head was shaved, celebrating his bald patch with the assertiveness of an advertising executive, rather than the previous attempt at concealment which had simply branded him as a loser.

'Come on in,' she smiled, slightly bemused at the transformation and noting the spring in Grafton's step as he strode into the living room.

'This is my design for our Interferometer - the fibre optic one - based on your notes of course. I've sent it to PORTAL and discussed the format of the show with them. Also, I got a message from Emelienko asking for details of the show. He wanted the information dropped off at the desk of the Lyceum Theatre of all places. I did it yesterday,' continued Grafton. 'I confirmed we agree to them using their own design for the Interferometer. Presumably that will be the vacuum based version.'

'You have been busy - I appreciate this - I really do. I was wondering how I could cope,' she smiled. 'Here, take a seat.' They sat opposite each other at the kitchen table.

'I was contacted again by the Special Branch guy that Stan,' Grafton's voice faltered, '. . . that Stan knew in London.' He looked up briefly, pausing for a moment. 'He told me that

Shirov, the man who assaulted me on the Hills, has been sighted. They got him on camera in West Acton. They're following him apparently. It sounds like it could be a good lead on Ian.'

'Do they have an address?' asked Chris.

'I don't think they would tell me if they did. I think I was just being reassured that my assault case hasn't been forgotten. This chap was a personal friend of Stan. I reckon he was making his own mind up about me.' Grafton stopped, interrupting his own breathless delivery to look closely at Chris. 'You look tired.'

'Yes, I am a bit. I've had better days to be honest.' She sighed and forced a smile, trying to hide from him that her sleep was now routinely reduced to a few fitful hours a night.

'We've only got five days,' she said, feeling the dead weight of despair somewhere near her heart as she pictured again the finger which had arrived that morning in the post.

'But anyway . . . you seem to be enjoying yourself. The beard suits you. And the contact lenses.' She smiled at him again, and he smiled back.

'Thanks Chris. Funny thing is I do seem to have a new lease of life at the moment. I've read Ian's work several times - I have to admit I may be a convert. I especially like his argument that the role of actual measurement in science is often conveniently overlooked, especially on the quantum level.' Grafton was unfolding his drawings across the kitchen table. Chris picked up the cat which had jumped onto the table, and gently dropped her onto the floor, where, purring loudly, she wound herself around Chris' legs.

Grafton was continuing. 'The work on this Interferometer has reminded me you often need a theory to interpret observations on your instruments, before you can use the data to support a theory.'

'Couldn't agree more. Hence the importance of 'paradigm', and a credible interpretation of the mathematics. We take a lot for granted with every deduction we make,' Chris replied. 'You said the drop-off for Emelienko was at the Lyceum Theatre - isn't that just down the road from the Indian Embassy?'

'I wouldn't know. Why do you ask?' Grafton wondered.

'Oh it's probably nothing. Do you want to leave your design for me to look at?' she suggested tactfully, reluctant to consider it just then. 'It's not my field - never have been too good with practical stuff - but I am interested.'

'Yes, love to. I'm very proud of it actually. Janbir has helped too.' Grafton was digging inside his briefcase to find a document. 'It's portable, uses very accessible parts and instead of combining the beams for display on a screen I've used an optical beam-joiner to avoid any fuzziness in the projected image, and I use a photodiode to measure the light intensity. Ah, this is what we need,' He pulled out a thin folder of specifications. 'To tell you the truth, I'm quite handy at building things, years of model aircraft you see.'

'I'm surprised to hear Dr Chatterjee helped you. I thought he was sceptical of Process Physics?'

'I'm not so sure. Janbir can seem fairly conventional in his approach but we've had some good discussions about the concepts and he's a first class man, he really is. He's assured me he's open to any experimental evidence - wherever it leads.'

'Well . . . I think that's all we've ever asked of anyone.' She was looking at him levelly. 'Can you operate the machine on the night? I'm going to be busy . . . trying to make Ian safe.'

'Didn't that Mike Aziz chap say his friend would be there? An ex SAS man?' asked Grafton.

'That's right. 'Beaky' Jones was in Mike's regiment,' she replied. 'Haven't heard yet if he's agreed to help.' She sighed, a plaintive sound, the sound of a deep fatigue.

'But . . . we soldier on eh? I'll make us a cup of tea?' She got up to put the kettle on, as Grafton stood too, pacing over to the window to look outside.

'There's some good news,' she said, stopping at the kitchen door as it occurred to her Grafton might know something about the Konkreton connection. 'I may have a lead on Ian myself.'

'Fantastic Chris, what've you found?' Grafton turned from the window to sit again at the table.

'It's really too early to say.' She changed her mind, some intuition making her reluctant to share the information with him, or tell him about the finger in the fridge. Grafton sensed it.

'Look I hope you haven't lost faith in me because of that police thing. A lot of my thinking has changed. It really has. The last week has been awful . . . and sort of liberating at the same time. I don't regard authority in quite the same way as I did before, that's for sure.'

'I think we've all been changed in the last few days,' she agreed. 'God knows how all this is going to end. Milk and sugar?'

'Just milk please,' Grafton confirmed. She went over to the fridge to retrieve a carton of milk. The cat, deprived of Chris' legs crossed under the table to try her luck with Grafton, who, feeling the contact, reached down absent-mindedly to stroke her head.

'Friendly moggy, you've got here,' said Grafton as Chris re-emerged from the kitchen.

'Yes . . . Erwin's all bark and no fight,' she replied.

'Erwin?' Grafton looked confused. 'Unusual name. Rings a bell somewhere . . . ah of course - Erwin Schrodinger - 'Schrodinger's Cat' . . . very funny!' Grafton pushed the cat away firmly with his foot as he tried to sound casual. 'By the way, I'm separating from my wife.'

'Oh. I'm sorry to hear that,' said Chris.

'No it's okay . . . it really is . . . actually it's long overdue,' he explained. 'Mary and I have hardly spoken in years. Setting up this thing with PORTAL I've been having long chats with a highly intelligent young woman - she's really quite wonderful - she works for them . . . I mean PORTAL.'

Grafton gave another light kick at the cat, who gave up on him and hopped gracefully into an armchair to start methodically cleaning herself, occasionally glancing disdainfully at Grafton as she licked her butt, one leg thrown high into the air over her shoulder.

'We've been talking . . . over Skype you understand,' continued Grafton. 'We've discussed science, religion, philosophy, God, self-fulfilment, everything. It's like being a student again. She's reminded me of the potential in life, especially for the young of course - the energy, the enthusiasm -but they say it's never too late.'

'Don't forget the Church has a dark side too, Bill. I wouldn't get too involved with them if I were you.' Chris was suddenly anxious, fearful that Grafton was making another serious error of judgment. She poured the tea.

'Don't worry about me, Chris. I'm an irretrievable atheist. No, it's not the Church. It's her. She's a lovely young thing. You'll have to meet her when she comes over for the TV show. She'll be part of the PORTAL team. She's just been dumped by her boyfriend and was quite hurt by it.'

'I see. Do be careful, won't you? People on the rebound can seem very unfeeling,' Chris was even more worried for Grafton, this time on a different level. 'Just remember a young woman has options, even if she seems quite vulnerable at the moment.'

'She's really sweet Chris, and it's not like that. Anyway, her ex was an older man too.'

The word 'too' confirmed to Chris that her concerns were justified.

Grafton continued unfazed. 'Her name is Cindy.'

Chapter 96: skype's the limit

(3.45 pm)

'Let's talk to her now.' Grafton suddenly appeared animated.

'What? This PORTAL girl? Isn't she in the States?'

'Sure, but she's an early riser, I often talk to her early and it's nearly eight o'clock over there.'

'Not a good idea. Nandini will be round soon.' Chris objected, but Grafton was already opening his laptop on the kitchen table.

'Just for a minute. . .?' Grafton sounded plaintive.

'Well okay.' Chris shrugged. 'Give me a shout when you're ready,' she added as she went upstairs to change. After a couple of minutes, Grafton called up to her and by the time she had descended, he was talking excitedly to the figure on his screen.

'Dr Reynolds - I was so excited when Bill - I mean, Dr Grafton - said I could talk with you. I'm a great admirer of your work,' said Cindy, as Chris leant over Grafton's shoulder into the camera's field of view.

'Ian Lineker's work. I just do the maths,' said Chris, without too much goodwill, preoccupied with the thought of what the conversation was keeping her from.

'Of course . . . yes . . . I'm so sorry Dr Reynolds,' said Cindy. The remark was clearly genuine.

'Call me Chris.'

'Thanks Chris. I find some of the implications amazing. I'd like to look at how this approach to Process Physics can be seen as a way to approach complex systems more generally,' said Cindy.

'There's huge scope there I'm sure I looked at something similar,' replied Chris, warming to the outgoing American. 'My current thing is the effect of Modular Forms on the flow of time - that's an area you might be interested to investigate too,' continued Chris.

'Look sorry - I'm a philosophy major, my math has got serious gaps. What's a Modular Form?' asked Cindy.

Grafton was beaming with pleasure, the sort of relieved enthusiasm when two introduced favourites seem like they're going to get on.

'Modular Forms are equations that describe symmetric transformations so as you end up exactly where you came from. Rotating a square or a circle are the most familiar examples. You can flip them or rotate them but they still look just like they did when you began.' Chris was indicating with her hands what she meant. 'But Modular Forms can be much more complicated. If changes over time can be represented by a Modular Form - would you end up where you started, that's the intriguing question?'

'Maybe, but isn't there a problem with that Chris?' Grafton looked sceptical, trying to intrude back into the conversation. 'In your equations what drives the process representing time is randomly generated input. How likely is that to recur in any pattern, never mind one that takes you back to where you were before?' he asked.

Cindy seemed interested in the idea. 'How likely is the evolution of life and consciousness - which is the ultimate in 'patterning', from the random interaction of a stew of hot gas - yet evolutionary theory depends on that and has become part of the scientific bible,' she said.

'Absolutely right,' agreed Chris. 'I reckon it's enough to establish there is a mathematical possibility - then the seeming infinity of time can do the rest by generating every option as an actual event.'

'Do you mean if you give something enough time then however unlikely it will happen eventually?' asked Grafton.

'Yes, that's exactly what I mean,' agreed Chris, impatient to move on. 'But could you also say this 'time loop' that brings you back to where you started, represents a different dimension hidden 'in time,'' Chris was musing out loud. 'The string theorists postulate many dimensions hidden 'in space' because they have a geometric model of time. This becomes the Process Physics time-based equivalent - multiple dimensions in time as unknowable loops.'

'Wow Dr Reynolds - great idea,' said Cindy.

'It's all just a bit of fun,' replied Chris. 'Lovely talking to you Cindy – but I'm afraid I have to go - and so does Bill,' she added sternly.

Chapter 97: fair's fair

(California)

'There's something I want you all to know.'

Baedeker leant back in his leather chair and surveyed the small group assembled either side of the great walnut table in the conference room at the Joy Centre, headquarters of PORTAL's North American operation in Pasadena.

'This is a priority project for us.'

He rose from his chair, and strolled down one side of the table until he was standing at the other end, before continuing his sentence. No-one interrupted. 'We want to get it right, but there are forces of evil aligning against us.'

Baedeker began pacing again, like a nineteen thirties Godfather, relaxed, unpredictable, somehow threatening. 'Knowing what we are up against inspires me to greater effort, something I believe you will see reflected in progress to date. Clinton, could you just run us through the details?'

'Of course sir,' replied Clinton reasonably. 'Well . . . to start with we've established a number of specialist teams under the banner 'God Speed'. God Speed Publicity are contacting newspapers, magazines, specialist publications and so on. They have an advertising campaign ready to go with Brownhill and Adler on the theme of 'New beginnings - The Battle for The Future.'

'No. I don't like that,' Baedeker interrupted. 'Try Fassbinder and Volkman. Tell them we want 'Present Perfect - The Time for Truth is Now.'

'Yes sir, I'll get onto it right away,' Clinton, flustered at first, quickly resumed his report.

'We have invited Dr Williams from the jet propulsion lab at NASA just down the road, to act as moderator for the show. He's here today as Devil's Advocate if you like, on behalf of the old science,' he gestured to the man seated opposite him.

'Not an enviable position Doctor - not in this building,' laughed Baedeker. A restrained and nervous titter swept through the assembly.

'We have received input from a Dr Grafton of Malvern Research Institute on the new Process Physics science,' Clinton was continuing. 'We had hoped to get the mathematician in the team, Dr Reynolds, to come over to further her case but she was unable to join us.'

'I thought the good doctor had resolved her misunderstandings with the British authorities, Clinton. I understood we had arranged for her release with the contacts we have within the British police?'

'Pardon me sir, yes, that's correct. She is no longer detained, but she is very preoccupied with Dr Lineker's disappearance. Should I ask Dr Grafton to come instead?'

'No, I can't see that would help, Clinton. I would like to meet Dr Reynolds again when some of this excitement has died down, you understand. She had a transcendent quality about her. I recall she was quite charming.' Baedeker had stopped to look out of a window. There was a preoccupied peacefulness about him.

'I'll make sure to arrange that sir,' replied Clinton.

'You were summarizing progress, Clinton.' Baedeker had resumed his leisurely stroll, the slightest slowing indicating when he was directly behind one of the seated delegates, before gliding on to the next.

'We have a 'fix-it' group - God Speed Logistics,' Clinton resumed where he had left off, 'and of course this committee meeting today - God Speed Steering.'

'Thank you Clinton,' Baedeker picked up the narration. 'So you see gentlemen, PORTAL is investing considerable effort and expense in ensuring this show becomes the media event of the decade, unless there is another royal wedding . . . or death.'

Another polite chuckle went round the room.

'We have already put six million dollars into this project because - and I make no apology - we want it to decide the outcome in our favour,' he stared impassively at the small bearded man shuffling through his notes at the other end of the table.

Benny Wiseman looked up, like a schoolboy registering a teacher's question a moment too late to avoid criticism.

'You do understand our position Mr Wiseman I'm sure?'

'Yes, we certainly do sir,' Wiseman replied, 'but as executive producer of the show I have to say we pride ourselves at TruthSayers in not prejudging the outcome of our investigations.'

'No-one is asking you to cook the books.' Baedeker's voice was raised in sudden irritation before his frown dissolved in apparent boredom and he glanced at his watch.

'Clinton, can you supply Mr Wiseman . . .' Baedeker paused again as if lingering on the name, 'with his answer.'

'Of course sir. If I can just explain the set up,' Clinton replied. 'The other side will be putting up their Interferometer experiment which we are told by Dr Grafton will be the standard design. This will indicate that Einstein and conventional physics is right. We have invited Dr Williams to speak a little more on that. Dr Williams if you will.'

Dr Williams began his explanation. 'Okay, put simply they will be rerunning the Michelson-Morley experiment. If you throw a ball along a moving train in the direction of the train and bounce it back, it will take longer to return than if you throw it at right angles away from the train and it bounces back to you, right?'

'Is that obvious?' asked Wiseman.

'Maybe not, but it is what happens,' replied Dr Williams. 'We will effectively be doing the same thing with light. We will split a beam, sending it in line with the direction of planetary orbit of the earth and at a 90-degree angle to that. These beams will be reflected back by mirrors placed the same distance away from the source. If light has travelled at the same speed in both beams, we won't see anything. If light has travelled at different speeds, we will see interference patterns, like the ripples of two passing boats that 'interfere' with each other on a lake. You get calm areas where they cancel out, and bigger waves where the ripples reinforce each other. We use a machine called an Interferometer to look for these effects which in the case of light interference are shown as dark bands across a screen. The experiment has been done countless times. It has found nothing. I can tell you now it will prove Einstein was right, light has the same speed whatever direction it travels.'

'But the Church wants to show the opposite of that right?' asked Wiseman perplexed. 'That's right Mr Wiseman. Our interest is not particularly in the speed of light itself,' Clinton intervened. 'If Einstein is shown to have made a mistake and Process Physics is confirmed as right, then that will enable us to use its implication of a mind-like network underlying reality to develop a more modern notion of God. We have people working on that already.'

Benny Wiseman nodded, then turned to say something to his personal assistant seated next to him. Lucy was an enthusiastic young woman in her early twenties, wearing heavy spectacles and a plain brown jumper. Her light-brown hair was short and curly and she had a big mouth with tombstone teeth but it was the near-braying laugh with which she responded to Wiseman that most reinforced the equine flavour of her straightforward friendliness.

Baedeker was looking at Lucy with an expression of fascinated horror on his face as after her humorous exchange with Wiseman, she once more scribbled notes on the paper in front of her. Baedeker beckoned to Clinton with a finger. When Clinton had joined him some distance from the seated group, Baedeker spoke very quietly and firmly. 'Don't ever let anything like that happen again.'

'Sorry sir, what do you have in mind?'

'That woman of course - the one next to Wiseman. The laugh Clinton; the laugh is simply unacceptable. I can't remember when I last saw someone so dreadful.'

'Of course sir, I'll attend to it right away,' replied Clinton reaching for his phone.

Dr Williams had resumed his summary of the science. 'The Church's position notwithstanding, there is something that needs clarification. Dr Grafton from the Malvern Research Institute has submitted a modified design. He is arguing that there are effects associated with sending the light beam through a vacuum, which is what we do in a modern Interferometer. He says the change in distance that light has to travel in the Interferometer due to movement of the earth is exactly cancelled by a contraction in the length of one of the arms of the device. He is suggesting using an optic fibre to carry the light signal to replace the vacuum. Refraction in the optic cable will slow the speed of light so these effects he refers to won't exactly cancel. The arm will contract the same amount, but the light will travel slower and you'll see a difference. Or so he says.'

'Well, is he right?' said Wiseman.

A young man had entered the room, and was tapping Lucy on the shoulder, suggesting she accompany him for a background briefing in the nearby Word library. She seemed surprised, and flattered.

'No, what he is missing,' continued Dr Williams, 'is that although there can be a contraction effect in physical objects as we know from Special Relativity, you only find it if the object and the measuring location are moving relative to each other. From a fixed point, you won't find that.'

Baedeker had returned to his end of the table as Dr Williams continued. 'Dr Grafton says the contraction is not relativistic but physically derived . . . an absolute effect. Of course that's nonsense.'

'Gentlemen, we are about to have some peace,' Baedeker announced loudly. 'Enough of this toing and froing.' They all looked round, puzzled. Baedeker waited pointedly while Lucy gathered her papers. She whispered something to Benny Wiseman who nodded his assent, and then she headed for the door.

'There now . . . that's better,' said Baedeker when she had gone. 'As I was saying . . . Lineker will be arguing the case for his new Physics and I expect him to do a better job than Williams has just managed.'

Baedeker looked disdainfully at the scientist seated near him before resuming. 'You may already have heard, Dr Lineker is being held by the forces of evil - kidnapped. We are assured he will be at the show but if there is a problem, Dr Reynolds is on standby. To make this possible for her and to facilitate the recovery of Lineker, the show must be held in the UK.'

Baedeker looked around, like a bar-room bully daring someone to challenge him. 'I want maximum publicity - we only have five days. We'll tell the media Lineker is on a walking trip in Australia, and will be out of reach until the screening. We don't want to worsen Lineker's relations with his abductors by advertising the real cause of his disappearance,' he paused. 'When he is recovered, then our contribution to that success can be fully acknowledged at the proper time. If he is not, then at least we can show we tried to free him. Understood everybody?'

'Sir, I must caution you, this definitely won't work - this is not science - this is wishful thinking by crackpots,' Dr Williams insisted. 'This will not help your cause.'

'Enough Doctor.' Baedeker's voice was uncompromising as he held up his hand to silence Williams. 'I am well aware of the opposition of the scientific establishment to any form of unorthodoxy, just as I am only too conscious of the prejudice our Church experienced when it first started to spread The Word in the new era.' His voice was lapsing toward the singing cadence of the messianic preacher. 'Indeed many of our proposed reforms in social policy are still finding resistance by backward thinkers. I am used to following the path untrodden.'

Mr Wiseman had been fretting with his pen while Baedeker spoke, now he ventured an objection. 'I just don't see that we can make the show work commercially if we have to take our people to the UK - we have twelve staff, we have forward schedules, months of planning goes into these things. We can't possibly do a show in just five days.'

'For Christ's sake,' Baedeker exploded, seemingly losing control. 'You must have your thirty pieces of silver . . . right? It's always money with you people.'

There was a shocked silence in the room, as each dared to imagine which 'people' Baedeker had in mind.

'Will another million pay for your goddam' airfares and a further million get you out of bed in the morning to actually make this happen?' demanded Baedeker, as he swept towards the exit of the room. 'Extend our fullest hospitality to Wiseman won't you Clinton? Baedeker turned with a flourish, framed in the doorway, leering back into the room, 'And make sure we give him something to remember us by.'

Baedeker was gone, but somehow his atmosphere lingered on, as if the ghost of his hostility remained to oversee the subsequent conversations and subdue any loose talk, simply by the possibility of its presence.

Chapter 98: light relief

(California)

That evening Benny Wiseman was going through his program schedules and, interrupted by a tap on the door, answered the sound to find an attractive woman in her mid-thirties, wearing black stockings and a tight white nurse's uniform exposing a generous cleavage. She offered Benny a manicure and foot massage, assuring him it was a normal part of PORTAL hospitality.

Benny was tense after a hard day but though tempted, he declined, explaining that he was tired and preferred to spend the evening alone.

Some five minutes later a second knock introduced an extravagantly handsome young man, in a close-fitting T-shirt who offered Benny a full body massage, indicating it would help Benny find relief from any stress accumulated throughout the day. Again Benny declined, after thanking the young man for the considerate offer.

Using the internal phone, Benny spoke to his assistant, Lucy, to wish her goodnight, and then phoned his wife to tell her about the day he had endured. He described how he had misinterpreted PORTAL at first, how considerate they had been, and of the generous offers for personal grooming he had refused. His wife agreed that it was easy to think the worst of people, especially followers of another religion, and tolerance was always the best policy.

Benny and his wife said goodnight to each other, and Benny went to bed. Quickly asleep, he never heard the almost imperceptible click of the remote camera control that activated by movement had turned itself off, to share his night of tranquillity in the Joy Building, headquarters of the North American operation of PORTAL.com.

Chapter 99: friend indeed

Shortly after Bill Grafton's departure, the creaking of the garden gate preceded a light tapping on the kitchen door to announce Nandini Chatterjee's arrival. As Chris opened the door, Nandini's arms were thrown open to hug her.

'My dearest friend, what a pretty blouse . . . that's more like it dear.' Nandini held Chris at arm's length, studying her intently. 'My . . . you look tired. Sit - I will make the tea - you put your feet up, you need your rest.' Nandini kissed her enthusiastically on the cheek.

'I'm fine Nandini, but there's a lot going on. Could you run me down to pick the car up after we've had a cuppa - it's at the police station - there's something I need to drop off there too.'

'The police station . . . oh dear nothing serious I hope . . . of course I can drive you down, no trouble at all. First, get comfortable and tell me all about yourself.'

Chris felt the surge of self-pity that Nandini's sympathy always provoked in her. But this time sensing she had no margin of emotion to waste, she resisted.

'Lots of bad stuff going on I'm afraid, - but I'm okay . . . really.'

There was a steel in Chris' voice as she gestured to Nandini to sit on the settee. 'They're cutting Ian's fingers off, and mailing them to me, one every morning.'

'Oh my . . . how awful!' Nandini exclaimed, pressing her clenched fist to her mouth in horror at the thought of what she had heard.

For the next ten minutes Chris summarized the recent events that had disrupted her world, culminating in her suspicion that there was some connection between Emelienko, the Indian embassy and Konkreton. Nandini seemed surprised, and confused.

'Konkreton,' she said, hesitantly. 'Do you mean the construction people?'

'Yes, that's right,' said Chris, spelling the name out. 'Have you heard of them?'

'Absolutely, when Sampatti took them over, Janbir bought their shares.'

'Sorry Nandini, who are Sampatti?'

'Sampatti Pl is one of the biggest companies in India. They started in construction many years ago. They're a blue-chip - cars, shipping, oil, gas, finance, Bollywood - you name it. Lots of people have their shares. We became interested in them when Janbir heard they were bidding for the contract to build the next generation Hadron Collider. Janbir is always interested to invest in hi-tech, especially related to his own research field you follow.'

'The bloody Hadron Collider!' said Chris. 'So where does Konkreton fit in?'

'They have a track record for pouring concrete for huge projects - dams and so on. Janbir thinks that's why Sampatti bought them, a strategic symbiosis - the latest hadron collider is going to be one of the biggest engineering builds ever.'

'God what a waste of money,' said Chris wistfully. 'Talk about 'the Emperor's Clothes' - looking for dark matter and whatever they need after the 'gosh how surprising we've found what we were looking for' Higgs Boson.'

'You don't think they'll find the new particles then?' asked Nandini.

'They'll find something all right – every time their funding is up for review.'

'Do you think they will be telling untruths dear?' asked Nandini, concerned that her friend would think such thoughts.

'No, it doesn't work like that. An experiment produces data, in the case of the Hadron Collider, from the measurement of levels of electromagnetic energy. The scientist has a theory of how things work - an 'ontology' or a 'view of the world' - in this case, as you know, the so-called 'Classical Theory'. When they measure a fluctuation, or find what appears to be a statistical correlation, they have to account for it within the theory - in the case of the Hadron Collider they do that by calling it a 'particle', as if it's a 'thing' whereas it's no more than a 'frequency'. This is why the more their theory is in trouble, the more particles they will find. It looks like progress - but it isn't. It's a crisis - like plugging a leaking dam and calling each of the plugs by a different name. But who will pull the plug on a multi-billion investment. If we had a fraction of that . . .'

'Ah, yes. Your Dr Lineker's physics doesn't need all that to balance the equations does it?'

'Cook the books more like,' replied Chris cynically, as she stood up to fetch the kettle that again was whistling on the stove.

'Speaking of cooking . . . how is the bun in the oven as they say, if you don't mind me asking dear?' enquired Nandini, sensing anything personal was for the time being a secondary issue for Chris.

'Oh, I still haven't had . . .' Chris suddenly stopped. 'My God, could it be . . . Why didn't I think of this before?' she said.

'What dear, could what be?'

'Well Ian has a theory that doesn't require all these add-ons that classical physics needs to get the maths to work. Do you remember an article that appeared in the New Scientist giving Ian's point of view?'

'I do remember . . . Janbir got very excited about it. It was called 'Time to throw some light on dark matter'. Dr Lineker was putting your case that a lot of research was a waste of money,' replied Nandini.

'That's right' replied Chris. 'Ian was very pleased to have someone publish him. So, let's think this through. There is a tender invitation to build a new Hadron Collider - I believe they're calling it the Huge Hadron Collider. The claim is it's needed to find Dark Matter and Anti-Bosons, because the previous two weren't big enough - or so they say. Shortly after the New Scientist piece, Bill Grafton was approached by a Russian offering us money to silence our work. We refuse to give up the research. The company that wants to pour the concrete for this monster Hadron Collider is Russian. Then, Ian is kidnapped by people with some sort of Russian connection. Sampatti, the company that is bidding for the overall contract is Indian, and owns the Russian company, Konkreton. We know for a fact that the Russian go-between for the kidnappers has made at least one call to the Indian embassy.'

'It is a cascade of coincidence' agreed Nandini, enjoying the alliterative potential of her adopted language. Chris hurried to the computer. A couple of minutes later, she announced excitedly,

'The contract for the Huge Hadron Collider is not signed off yet. It's worth seventeen billion dollars US. Its due for decision in two months.'

She looked elated, and exhausted. 'I think it could be Ian has been kidnapped by the people who want to build the HHC. He's being held to shut him up and discredit his research in case it threatens investment in their stupid machine. Just so they can make money.' She paused, before adding: 'Is there any limit to the greed, or immorality, of these people?'

Nandini was the first to break the silence. 'Maybe once they get the contract they'll let him go, they won't care whether the physics is right or wrong,' she suggested, trying to cheer her friend up.

'I agree they won't care about the physics. My concern is they're only keeping him alive to take part in the TV show, and they plan to kill him whichever way things turn out. God knows what they'll do to make him say what they want - and he's so stubborn.' Her voice was cracking and hoarse. 'They're already cutting his fingers off. We've got to find him before the show . . .the involvement with the next Hadron Collider makes that even clearer in my mind.'

'And why is it you are thinking that?' asked Nandini.

'If they let him live he can provide evidence against them. If I wanted to dispose of a body . . .' Chris paused, temporarily overcome by emotion, 'I know what business I'd like to be in.'

'Do you mean . . .?'

'Yes,' said Chris grimly: 'Concrete.'

Chapter 100: beaut

(5.00 pm)

Aziz was studying a computer terminal in Brixton library, chewing on the homemade muesli bar that Beaky had given him. It had taken him a detour all the way to Aldwych to lose the two men he was sure had been following him, and he was already in a bad mood when the attendant had told him it was only fifteen minutes from closing time. He called up the online Guardian website, as Chris had suggested to him when they had driven from the Malvern toilets to Worcester Railway Station, and left her a coded message in the comments section of the first story. The message specified a meeting for the following day at the prearranged place - Shepherds Bush Market tube station.

A rotating banner on the screen flashed up the day's minor stories. One picture showed a spectacular looking mountain, and a word that in the heading had subliminally caught his eye. Aziz waited, poised to click on the image when the story came round again, even though he was uncertain of the content that had attracted his attention.

Seconds later, he read the headline - 'Tragedy in Tasmania, lone hero survives wilderness horror.' Aziz's eyes rushed forward to consume the story, impatient with his own rate of reading till he came to the words that he hadn't dared anticipate, yet knew the universe had somehow conspired to place before him - 'Isabel Aziz'. He went back and read again, fascinated, totally absorbed, until he got to the part that reported that one of the dead killed in the tragedy was described as a missionary from PORTAL.com, the internet Church, and that Isabel alone had survived the ordeal.

Aziz leapt to his feet, punching at the air in triumph, 'You beauty - that's my girl,' he shouted. 'Fuck you Church - suck on that Church!'

Furious faces jolted up to frown and hiss at him, a chorus of 'Shh', 'quiet', and 'outrageous' intermingled in a seething wave across the room as a large black security guard hauled himself from his chair and trundled toward Aziz.

'Excuse me sir - that is completely unacceptable - you'll have to leave if you can't restrain yourself,' he said, sizing up Aziz to test whether he should risk a more physical eviction.

'Sorry . . . good news from Australia - that's all.' Aziz was smiling. 'Someone got wasted. My little girl survived . . . she made it look like a climbing accident.'

The guard backed off, talking quickly into his radio to demand back-up, his voice cracking with urgency as he explained he was dealing with a trouble maker who was clearly very disturbed.

'It's a long story . . .' said Aziz, still sharing the experience with the guard, as he packed his bag and set off jauntily toward the exit. He suddenly gave another loud whooping cry, a spontaneous explosion of satisfaction as he slowed at the door to gather his collar high around his face. Hunching lower to disguise his uneven gait, he stepped into the busy street.

Two men were waiting for him, each holding a gun pointed at his head.

'On your knees cocksuck. Hands behind your head. Slowly.'

Aziz appeared unaware of the instruction. His face crumpled in agony, as he stared with wild-eyed concentration at the space between the two me, like a mannequin left stricken and immobile, while the window stylist is preoccupied elsewhere. His hands came up to clutch at his chest, a hoarse panting gasp whistled from his mouth, as spinning round, he fell to the floor. Frightened and confused by his bizarre behaviour, the gunmen started shouting, bellowing warnings at the body in front of them.

Aziz was lying face down on his bag, immobile, when one of the policemen shot him in the back. Overtaken by a reflex of adrenaline, the other man fired two more shots into the prone Aziz, before a crashing silence descended on the desperate scene.

Emerging from the doorway, the security guard, appalled at what he had witnessed, bellowed his rage at the policemen as he rushed to help Aziz.

'He was having a heart attack . . . he's just a nutter . . .'

A policeman was shouting back, his voice charged with a mix of fear, excitement, and the intoxicating thrill of sanctioned violence:

'Step away sir, do not approach the body.'

To no avail. The man was over Aziz, sobbing breathlessly:

'For Christ's sake, you killed a man for making a noise in a library.'

Chapter 101: peekaboo

(5.05 pm)

The guard rolled Aziz over. Aziz's hands rested on his chest clutching short black tubes. Aziz gave the guard a melodramatic wink and a cheery smile. At first the man smiled back involuntarily, Aziz's goodwill summonsing a reflex that was faster than the brain, until the guard's reasoning mind caught up, and he sprang away in alarm.

As a man of action, Aziz knew that time is measured by event, and in every frozen instant is the potential to stamp a different narrative over the stories that others would tell. By the time the stun grenades had rolled under the policemen, Aziz had somersaulted to his feet and dived into the library porch, his hands pressed to his ears, kneeling in the foetal position. One of the policeman got off a shot, grazing Aziz's thigh before the first flash-bang detonated, followed in an instant by the second. The policeman fell to his knees holding his head, the other policeman staggering forward in a daze.

The man still standing was recovering rapidly. Aziz leapt to close the distance with him, reaching out to seize his gun with one hand as he prepared to chop him down with the other.

The blow was never delivered. Aziz looked at the disoriented man, unable to defend himself, and for Aziz the frenzy of conflict suddenly calmed, as if the compassion which his training had taught him is the Achilles heel of every professional soldier, had somehow refused to relinquish its claim on his soul.

'We're all just working for the man, eh mate?' Aziz said, surprised at his own reaction.

I reckon I'm just not suited to this line of work anymore, he thought, as he hobbled off, the pain in his back where the bullets had smashed into his ballistic vest now excruciating, and the blood starting to flow freely from the gash in his bad leg.

Chapter 102: bad timing

(California)

Cindy's normally generous disposition had been progressively eroded while she waited for Baedeker to summons her to his apartment for 'private discussions', as he had done every day for a fortnight, until the calls had stopped the day after her return from Berkeley. She had never been in love with anyone until she met Baedeker, so her disappointment had been absolute when he had ignored her after the church service the day before. Cindy didn't understand what she had done wrong, or why Baedeker had suddenly lost interest in her.

So when her work colleague, Mark, had lent over the partition to the adjacent office cubicle and asked Cindy if she wanted to have lunch with him, though she nodded her acceptance, her lack of enthusiasm was poorly disguised.

'Well . . . how are you going?' asked Mark as they strolled toward the garden, his normal cool monotone replaced with a teasing buoyancy designed to compensate for her heaviness of spirit.

'Fine' she replied, without conviction. She looked tired, and though it was only a few days since the problems with Baedeker had begun, she had already lost weight. Mark lingered over the signs of leanness that had given her a more feline immediacy, as if the stripping off of the layer of puppy fat with its 'girlie' connotation had projected her into womanhood. He knew from PORTAL gossip that she was 'available' and Mark sensed an opportunity. He imagined her face down on the pillow, and his cock deep within her.

'It's just his way - don't worry about it,' he said, knowing she would understand only too well he was referring to Baedeker. She didn't reply. Mark was staring at the top of Cindy's breasts and forced himself to look up earlier than he wanted, in the hope she had not noticed.

'Tragic about Magnus being killed like that . . .' he said, making conversation, knowing that little remained of the topic that had not already been discussed to exhaustion around PORTAL.

'Yeah, apparently the girl who survived – Isabel 'somebody' - is coming out to visit us soon. That's something I suppose,' Cindy said flatly. 'It must be God's will.'

Joined only in wanting, they sat in silence on the cedar bench - he consumed by the future and what he did not have; she tortured by the past and what she knew she had lost.

'I'm thinking of asking for a transfer to Africa. There's a water project there. I'd like to do something practical, something useful,' she said.

'Oh, I thought you were off to the UK - some TV show or something,' Mark was trying to keep things normal-seeming, to be the friend that their relationship had hitherto assumed.

'Yeah, but only for a few days,' she replied, distracted.

'Interesting?' he asked.

'Yeah' she brightened briefly. 'Science-y . . . you know, stuff I told you about already,' she said, the cadence dropping to dampen further inquiry.

He summonsed his courage. 'Why don't I take you out for dinner this evening?' He reached for her, clumsily covering her hand with his, feeling the hum in his fingertips as they rested on her thigh.

'What, like on a date?' she asked, turning wide-eyed to look at him, pulling her hand away.

'Well . . . yeah,' he answered.

She leapt to her feet, transformed, shocked. 'First Saul, then some old man in England, now my best friend is coming on to me.'

There was the first hint of a sob. 'Why don't you men just let me be . . .?' she asked, bewildered.

Suddenly she burst into tears, skewering Mark with her distress, open-mouthed, mortified. By the time she turned a few moments later, for a stumbling run past the water feature and back to the office, her anger had clarified, 'Why can't you all just fuck off and leave me alone!'

September 25th

Chapter 103: stood up

(8.30 am)

Chris had seen the message that Aziz had left for her on the comments section of the online Guardian story. Her initial enthusiasm at the prospect of meeting him had been dampened by the realization that she would have to leave Malvern by 5 am, to make the rendezvous at 8:30 am that Aziz suggested. It had been a long drive, at least half of it in the dark.

This better be worthwhile, she thought, as she waited outside Shepherds Bush Market tube station, feeling the lifeless breath on her tights of the early morning breeze that sent a chill through her legs and lower body. The strap from a soft leather bag draped over her shoulder occasionally pressed her corduroy jacket against the fullness of her breasts as she gathered her arms more tightly around herself and stamped her feet to clear the burn of cold in her toes, for a moment regretting the new miniskirt and light shoes and irritated she had taken only the most basic precautions against an approaching winter.

She wore a loose knit scarf, burgundy beret and a similarly shaded lipstick with emerald earrings that matched her eyes, so that the overall effect straddled the subtle boundary between urban smart and Parisian bohemian in an artful simulation of the unstudied. In spite of the cold, Chris was excited by how it made her feel, and the prospect of meeting Aziz.

Where is he? She checked her watch for the third time in five minutes, trying to appear casual as another wave of London commuters leaving the tube station swept past her with the urban defence of preoccupation expertly maintained by the women who pretended not to see her, but abandoned by the men who chanced a second glance or a curious stare. A lumbering moron, too crude to appreciate that the game had rules, reacted to her with a grunted obscenity as nuanced as a burp relieving gas before continuing on his way.

Go fuck yourself arsehole, thought Chris, initially surprised at the vehemence of her reaction, then realising it was because she was scared.

'Here - this is for you.' The boy was about twelve, with curly black hair and a wide-mouthed grin. He shoved a piece of paper toward her, which she took hesitantly. By the time she had unfolded the paper he was running back to join his mates, kicking a ball against a graffiti spattered wall in a disused building site, where oily puddles collected between the tilted slabs of concrete and saturated the litter of a summer's neglect.

'Can't make it. Sorry,' the note said.

A tall handsome man was striding toward her, quickly covering the ground to close the distance before she realized she was his target.

'If you don't mind miss,' he said, with a strong American accent, prizing the crumple of paper from her fingers, and reading its contents into a microphone hidden on his sleeve. 'Sorry to disturb ma'am,' he said, pushing a card into her hand, his face set in a supercilious sneer. 'Let us know if he attempts further contact.' He strode off again toward the boy playing soccer. The card simply said, 'CIAO - security through integrity' above two phone numbers marked as 'UK' and 'International'.

Chris felt assaulted, disappointed and elated at the same time. *How do you do it, Mike?* she asked herself, as she left to retrieve her car in the multi-storied carpark half a mile away.

Threading through the heavy traffic, she drove north from Shepherds Bush past the clinical enormity of the Westfield Shopping Centre, intending to join the A40 and the procession westward to Oxford, and then home. The fake growl of the Deux Chevaux's little engine rose to a hoarse crescendo, then during a change to a higher gear dropped to a sudden silence as if stalled, only to stutter miraculously back to life, still struggling but slightly calmer, like an asthmatic fighting to breathe who stops on every staircase step for temporary relief.

'Chris . . .'

The shock hit her like a blow, lifting her from the seat as the little car slewed to the left, then over to the right before steadying.

'Easy girl. It's me . . . I'm back here . . . just keep driving.'

'For Christ's sake Mike. That's just so not funny, you frightened the . . .'

'I just wanted to say 'Hi.'' With his head pressed to the floor of the car, only her legs were visible to Aziz. 'You look great if you don't mind me saying.'

'Thanks . . . but . . . I'm a bit on edge.' She was glancing anxiously in the mirror. 'There was a man back there looking for you . . . thank God you're alright.' She spoke quickly, as if from the inertia of panic. 'I saw the news on TV . . . about Isabel . . . what a relief.'

'Fantastic news yeah. . .' Aziz began, but she interrupted, knowing that time was precious, and it was not the good that required attention, it was the bad news.

'They're cutting Ian's fingers off.' She wanted to tell him urgently, as if sharing the information would relieve her anguish and in the hope that, somehow, Aziz could wake them from the nightmare. '. . . and mailing them to me.'

'Jesus. That's not good . . . how many?' he asked.

'Two - so far . . . one a day . . .' Her voice choked, with the horror of it. 'We've got to get to him, Mike. As soon as we can. We can't wait until the show, it's another four days.' She was looking anxiously in the mirror again, to see if they were being followed.

'Any progress with Emelienko's phone – the one I gave you?' he asked.

'Yes. It showed he was phoning the Indian embassy. It's looking as if a company called Konkreton is behind this. They're owned by an Indian multinational called Sampatti. I don't know for sure, but maybe that's a connection with the Embassy. Sampatti want the contract to build the next Hadron collider. Our work shows it's a waste of money. I think that's why they want to discredit us . . . oh yes, and Shirov has been seen on a camera in West Acton.'

'Okay.' He sounded weary. 'Drop me off at the next tube. I'll get straight over to Acton, and see what I can find.'

Chapter 104: pay time

(9.00 am)

Aziz was riding a pushbike he had stolen from outside the tube station and had pulled out to overtake the early morning refuse truck stop-starting its way along Westbourne Avenue when he felt the vibrations against his chest. He grabbed the phone before its third ring, pressing the speaker 'on' button.

'Aziz?'

'Yeah Beaky – how you going?'

'Been better.' The pause alerted Aziz to the prospect of something wrong. 'Mike - I'm in.'

'You're in - great. Thanks mate,' replied Aziz. 'The show's in four days.'

'Now. I'm in now. Where do you need me?'

'Can you make West Acton tube - noon?'

'I'm leaving now. I'll be there - 12 o'clock - West Acton.'

There was a tone; Aziz knew something was wrong. 'What's happened Beaky?'

Aziz slowed to allow a taxi in front of him to thread its way down the narrow street through the lines of parked cars, their cloned uniformity mirroring the featureless houses on either side.

'It's Shep. They cut his paws off,' said Beaky. 'There was a note - pinned into him - it said 'Mind own business.''

'Shit - I'm so sorry Beaky. This Russian guy - Shirov - it could be him. But how do they know?'

'My place was bugged, like you said. Maybe they've got a cop who's feeding them. I had to shoot him. Fourteen years old, kindest creature I ever knew. Who would do a thing like that?'

Aziz had never heard Beaky cry before. He thought he heard it now.

'Someone's gonna pay Mike.'

'That's for sure - someone will pay alright.'

Chapter 105: the hornet's nest

(California)

'Welcome to LA dear' said the hawkish woman. She was tall and thin, in her fifties, her coiffured grey hair matching an efficient business suit in grey linen, with a subtle pink piping on the lapels and cuffs. She stood next to a stout man who lowered the sign with 'ISABEL' scribbled on it as she leant forward to give Isabel a perfunctory hug. The smell of mimosa scent and morning coffee that followed her like a cloud did little to soften her aura of aloof superiority.

'My name is Dr Paula Valence - I'm head of the New Science section of the Truth Division at PORTAL, and a medical doctor too. I've been told to . . . take care of you.' She flashed a grimaced smile at Isabel. 'Let Arthur help you with your bag - the car is outside. It will take about thirty minutes to get to our headquarters in Pasadena. There's a room prepared for you - you can rest on the way.'

Staring out of the window, Isabel felt no need to speak – just numbness - as if the capital of her resilience had been expended on the mountain in one agonising session of torment and suffering that had left her detached from anything real, like a robot in a dream.

The tiredness was catching up with her. She thought back on her journey - leaving Hobart over 24 hours ago and the short flight to Melbourne where she had been stuck for three hours waiting for the long-haul connection through to Los Angeles. But her fatigue seemed insufficient to explain the feeling of unreality that was interfering with her attempt at relaxation, nor could it account for the increasingly insistent suspicion that somehow the future was leeching into the present.

At first she tried to explain it away, the brilliance of the sun was disorienting, American culture was so pervasive and its built environment so homogenous that it was not surprising that everything would seem familiar. But this was more than that.

She set herself tests. *What would be the next building around the corner? What was Paula about to say?*

The results were inconclusive, so she sat in silence as the car turned onto the Foothill Freeway, heading south at a leisurely 50 mph.

'How long are you with us honey?' asked Paula, half turning to look at Isabel slumped in the rear seat.

I knew it, thought Isabel, a stir of excitement in her veins that her gift of presentiment might be crystallizing into something more specific, more detailed, than she had experienced before. *I knew that's what she was going to say.*

'Just till the inquest date is finalised,' replied Isabel out loud.

'Of course, yes. A terrible thing - we were very upset to lose Magnus. Such an awful accident too. He did some terrific work when he was with me, before he transferred to the Outreach section. Such a waste, so much promise.' The words were delivered quickly - like an accusation.

It left Isabel uneasy. She could not know that the incessant activity of Paula's finely-honed intellect was in large measure a strategy to distract her from the sexual frustration that Paula herself no longer recognized as the primary source of her restlessness. Nor could Isabel know that the same tension was the reason for a prejudice against anyone who by virtue of gender might be considered a rival; Dr Valence was a woman who disliked women.

The silence returned. *So what's your particular interest?* she'll say next, thought Isabel.

'I understand you're interested in the work on the paranormal some of our younger people are looking at?' said Paula.

Close, very close, but she would say that wouldn't she? thought Isabel. Out loud she replied, 'Yes, that's right. I'm interested in the possibility of connections made across time.

Magnus explained that you are looking at a new science that might have an explanation for how such a thing is a real possibility.'

'Maybe,' replied Dr Valence. 'Cindy Lopez, one of my assistants here, has done some good work on the notion of space being the connectivity pattern between events.' Something about her voice suggested Paula didn't approve of Cindy.

'Yes, Magnus discussed connections across time too,' added Isabel. 'I like the bit about how if connections can give rise to matter and space, then why can't a connection linger from the past, or some trace appear now of something in the future?'

'You did get into this didn't you,' said Paula, combining the language of admiration with a tone of scepticism, leaving Isabel, for a moment, unsure what she really thought. 'I must introduce you to Cindy.' The now open contempt in her tone surprised Isabel, and discomforted her. 'I reckon you and she would get on really well.'

'The thing is . . .' Paula continued, as if she was reciting something of mundane overfamiliarity, 'this Process Physics assumes that it's only time that doesn't need expression in terms of something else. Time is more real than 'stuff' if you like - it doesn't have a 'time line' like classical physics that you can travel on. So you may have let wishful thinking get in the way of proper understanding if you think you can time travel.' Her voice was flat as she concluded: 'In Process Physics only the 'now', is real.' The emphasis suggested there was no room for debate, she had delivered a conclusive truth and had no wish to discuss it further. 'Have you been to LA before, dear?' Paula asked, the abrupt change of subject somehow dismissive.

Isabel mumbled a reply, feeling her self-confidence draining away in the atmosphere of disengagement that her new acquaintance was projecting. They were heading down a wide boulevard, the sun reflecting off the tops of skyscrapers of geometric glass and glinty steel in kitsch contrast with the scrofulous palm trees that lined the road.

'That's why we at PORTAL are interested in Process Physics - the status it accords to the 'now." began Paula. Isabel was surprised at the resumption of Paula's monologue, wondering if, aware of her own abruptness, Paula had relented. 'We see it as potentially a vehicle to fuse eastern mysticism and Christianity - the basis of a world religion - that is the real value of this - not so much another take on 'Dr Who."

Of course everything happens in the now, thought Isabel, *that doesn't mean it hasn't happened before or won't happen again.* She judged it best to say nothing that would appear to directly contradict Paula.

Suddenly Isabel was sure. *She's going to say 'though mystics, seers, witches and prophets have never been . . . by such a rigid view*, she thought.

'Though mystics, seers, witches and prophets have never been hidebound by such a rational view,' continued Paula.

Yes, Isabel felt her heart leap. *I knew it, just a couple of words missing.*

'I know this sounds strange but I think that may be happening to me, at the moment,' said Isabel, her enthusiasm to share her excitement overcoming her assessment of the cynicism of her host.

'Excuse me . . . you can see the future or the past?' Paula sounded amused, not 'with' Isabel, but 'at' her.

'Well, I have the sense I recognize things yes,' said Isabel excitedly.

'Do you mean a sort of Deja vu?'

'Sort of - but forward to,' replied Isabel. 'For instance, I knew what you were going to say just now.'

'Okay.' Paula sucked air into her lungs: 'What am I going to say next dear?' she said, her condescension blatant and shameless.

'I don't know,' replied Isabel, wounded by the hostility of the challenge.

'Okay.' It was obvious Paula was unimpressed. 'You may have temporal lobe epilepsy to some degree dear, don't worry about it. One would expect the condition to be exacerbated by tiredness. You are tired aren't you?'

'Yes,' said Isabel flustered, surprised at the reaction. 'But I'm not so relaxed as I was . . .' she began, intending to explain why the ability might have forsaken her.

'And of course you've been through a traumatic time haven't you,' interrupted Paula. It was not a question; it was another dismissal. 'We'll give you a thorough evaluation when we get you back to the centre. There are a lot of questions we want to ask you.' There was something too stern about Paula's manner.

Isabel felt tension developing in her shoulders, and realized she had no idea any more what the future had in store, or what plans the Church had made for her.

Suddenly she felt very alone - and very afraid.

Chapter 106: the good guys

(12.30 pm)

'And what makes you think this sicko is holding your scientist chappie near here?' asked Beaky, as he and Aziz peered out from the bay window of a first floor terraced flat, its walls covered in ivy that sent outrider tendrils to etch into the mortar then upwards, to entwine around the chimney stack high above the sloping roof.

'The police told Chris Reynolds's boss that Shirov had been seen in Acton. I left a tracker on his car some time ago when he and a guy called Emelienko ambushed Chris in a cafe. I cycled around until I got a signal from the device, then I followed him. He went over there,' Aziz was pointing to a flat in a council block across the street, its geometric conformity designed in a different era from the terraced houses, but for the same class of tenants.

'This place had a pile of letters on the doormat,' said Aziz waving his hand as an invitation to Beaky to appreciate the crowded little living room, with its settee and bright red chairs arranged around a small old-fashioned TV. 'So, I came in here, maybe half an hour before I left to meet you at the tube.'

'The police are watching these fuckheads from where exactly?' continued Beaky.

'See that window,' Aziz pointed across the street and down the road, 'next to the orange awning - they're in there for sure.'

'So if we get the chance we'll recover this Lineker guy right?' asked Beaky.

'That's the mission. They're promising a finger a day. He's already lost a couple and maybe another today, and there's another four days till the show. And, we think they'll kill him as soon as they've got what they want - so the sooner we can get him out of there, the better.'

'Why not leave all this to the police?'

'Would you trust the police to recover someone you cared about?'

'But we don't care about this scientist do we?' asked Beaky.

'Not personally no, but Chris Reynolds does.'

There was another pause, while Beaky considered what he'd been told. Both digested the obvious, neither wishing to overplay their understanding.

'You're in love mate,' said Beaky finally.

Aziz savoured his new status. It gave him an identity, a legitimacy that his life had lacked for some time - it pleased him - though the pleasure was quickly infused with uncertainty. He did not deny Beaky's accusation and the silence caught them both by surprise.

'And your daughter is safe too. Maybe things are looking up,' commented Beaky.

'For now at least . . . yeah. I reckon they are. I'd like to have a pop at the internet Church crazies, but I promised Chris that can wait till we've extracted this Lineker guy.'

They sat next to each other staring out of the window - Aziz buoyed by the possibilities of a happier future, Beaky weighed down with unfinished business.

'I'm a bit cross about all this,' said Beaky. Aziz recognized the understatement.

'Of course . . . I understand.'

'I reckon it's time we took control . . . you know . . . made a difference,' declared Beaky.

Aziz reflected on the transition, sensing that from now on the competing priorities of staying alive and the need to prevail would be determined not just by themselves, but by each other.

'Like the bad old days,' agreed Aziz.

'Not really, no,' replied Beaky. 'This is personal.'

As a storm cloud passed overhead, the greyness of the street deepened and the wind gusted to gently tweak a single yellowing leaf from the plane tree outside and lower it sliding and twirling in the gloom toward the rustling anonymity of the pile below.

Suddenly Beaky turned. 'Did you hear that?' There was the scratching sound of a key at the door.

Chapter 107: all on board

(12.32 pm)

Chris tapped on the door to Grafton's office, and entered when the sound was returned by a shout of welcome.

'Ah Chris, how convenient, I was just thinking it's time for lunch,' Grafton greeted her cheerfully.

She looked around at Grafton's office where the tidy organisation of the previous week had been replaced by a chaotic jumble of papers, books, overflowing bins and electrical gadgets, strewn across the floor.

'What's new?' continued Grafton.

'When I got back from London this morning, there was a parcel waiting on the doorstep . . .'

A sudden choking sound at the back of her throat interrupted her as if suddenly ambushed by grief. She coughed, glancing up at Grafton hoping he might not have noticed, and continued. 'It contained the medical notes of a friend; and another finger - and still four days to go.'

'How awful, how dreadful.' Grafton shook his head slowly from side to side and looked at her anxiously, noticing the lines etched across her forehead and the darkened indent of her hollowed cheeks.

'Are you eating properly - you're a bit green around the gills,' he said, uncomfortable with the unfamiliar role of carer. 'Here sit down,' he invited, starting to clear the chair of papers, shuffling one pile with the next and occasionally throwing a wad toward the bin.

'I'm fine – you know - in the circumstances - but I'm not hungry,' she smiled at him reassuringly. 'Just returning your Interferometer plans. They look good.'

'Oh . . . thanks for that,' replied Grafton, the excitement returning to his voice. 'Janbir was a big help - I think he's seen the light so to speak - says he wants to be part of the new science, now he's looked at the papers.'

'Well . . . that's good news. I'm very close to Nandini, you know - Janbir's wife – maybe she's persuaded him. She's convinced we're on the right track and I know they've discussed it. Have you heard anything more from Emelienko?'

'Not since I sent him the last lot of the background material, no.'

'I wonder what's going on,' Chris replied. 'I spoke with Benny Wiseman - the producer at the TruthSayers show. He says now some Indian man is issuing instructions - they don't know his identity. He seems to have taken over from Emelienko.'

'I haven't heard anything more about the search for that thug that works for Emelienko either,' added Grafton.

'Well, I have some news there, Bill. I dropped Mike Aziz off in Acton a couple of hours ago - he's trying to trace Shirov.' Chris wondered for a moment how much to tell Grafton, but decided quickly that anyone who had experienced the trauma of Grafton's assault could only be an ally against whoever held Ian. And anyway, this was a very different Bill Grafton from just a week ago.

'Did I tell you we believe it's a company called Konkreton behind all this - they're owned by an Indian multinational called Sampatti?' she asked. 'They're bidding for the next Hadron Collider contract and I believe they regard our research as a threat to the project going ahead. They're putting up a guy called Dr Ranjeesh Puri Patel to represent the case against us - he's a prominent string theory advocate - have you heard of him?'

'No, can't say I have,' replied Grafton.

'Well Dr Patel just happens to be a big-shot on the liaison committee for the next Hadron Collider - his specialty is dark energy.' Chris resumed. 'Why am I not surprised by that?'

'Where there's muck there's brass,' said Grafton, imitating a heavy Yorkshire accent. 'I've seen some of the TV ads for the show. You can't pick up a magazine without an insert falling out or a special edition going on about 'Showdown for the new frontier'. 'Space-time or Time for Space' is another one I saw today in the *Physics Journal* of all places,' said Grafton, in his normal voice.

'PORTAL don't do things by halves,' she commented. Grafton had continued sorting papers even after Chris was seated, and was now stuffing them into different boxes on the shelves against the far wall of the room.

'The article said that Ian is hiking in Australia,' continued Grafton.

'PORTAL wanted to keep everything about the show upbeat. They also wanted to account for Ian's absence without provoking his kidnappers. Remember . . .' She was going to say 'Stan,' but decided not to distress Grafton by reminding him of the murder of his friend, so quickly changed the subject instead.

'PORTAL want me to appear on the show,' Chris said, peering at Grafton to check if he was okay.

'Great Chris,' observed Grafton, without any real enthusiasm.

'The show's going out live - the other side are insisting on that - hence the four am start to catch primetime TV in the US.'

'Four am – God – that will be hard. Where's it being filmed?' Grafton sounded interested again.

'At a studio belonging to Channel Twelve in Acton.'

'Acton - where Shirov was seen,' noted Grafton, his face reddening in apparent distress.

'I have to go there tomorrow for a wardrobe fitting.' Chris wondered why she was confiding in Grafton, then realized glumly it was because there was no-one else. 'They want me to look 'sexy',' she added ruefully.

'I'm sure they know best.' Grafton appeared uneasy at the prospect he might be consulted to offer an opinion on a woman's appearance, especially a woman that until recently had been the subject of his own fantasies. He picked up a wafer of electronics and inspecting it closely, hoped his appearance of preoccupation would encourage the whole subject to go away.

'There's something I think you should know.' She drew a deep breath. 'PORTAL have a video of me and Ian.'

'Actually I already know that Chris - they told me at the police station – you know, when you were locked up.' He put the board down, fidgeting, as if he were uncomfortable.

'Oh really,' she was surprised. 'Well, the thing is . . . PORTAL are using it to pressure me - or so they think. The content is sort of . . .' She stumbled for the right expression, 'compromising.'

'I understand,' replied Grafton quickly. 'Is there anything you can do about that?' he asked, his tone stern to hide his disapproval and embarrassment. He reached for the device again, as if the distraction might save him from whatever was coming.

'Well actually I've already done something,' she replied. 'I posted it on YouTube half an hour ago.'

Chapter 108: home visits

(12.35 pm)

'All clear ma'am, false alarm - safe to go in now,' declared Aziz as he pushed past the middle-aged lady standing open-mouthed in the doorway.

'Gone on holiday . . . my arse. Well done Aziz – so where next?' asked Beaky, as they hurried down the stairs from the first floor flat.

'I'm not sure . . . I didn't know the owner would come back early. It said the 13th on her calendar,' replied Aziz defensively.

'She'll report us you can be sure of that. Bit of a fuck up Mike, if you don't mind me saying, and we still need to find out the layout of Shirov's place, how many are in there; how they're armed. Standard operating procedure is there for a reason you know.' Beaky sounded irritated.

A few strides and they were through the garden, out of the front gate and heading past the uniform row of terraced houses with their bay-windows and bins. On the other side of the street was the forbidding concrete and grime wasteland of a West London Council housing estate, spilling across the road like a canker.

It was another hundred yards before Aziz broke the silence. 'We could try getting intel from the police in the flat opposite.'

'What . . . just go in and ask them to tell us what's going on?' sneered Beaky.

'Yes, something like that is what I had in mind. They'll be watching us now anyway, so we don't have time to sod about, whatever we decide,' said Aziz. 'So let's just knock on the door and request politely if we can share their information.'

They had stopped and were facing each other, the mutual resentment now undisguised.

'Nice one Mike. I'm sure they'll be very helpful,' Beaky snorted, looking down at Aziz.

Aziz ignored the rebuke. 'We'll say we're working for PORTAL. We'll say if they've got any questions suggest they phone for Assistant Commissioner Lawson.'

'And who is Lawson?' asked Beaky.

'He's a high ranking cop who does favours for PORTAL. He belongs to the Church. He arranged for Chris to be released from jail when the Church decided it wanted her out.'

'And if they phone this guy what then?'

'We'll persuade them to be reasonable.'

'And if they don't phone this guy?'

'We'll still persuade them to be reasonable.'

'So basically, we have to persuade them to be reasonable,' said Beaky looking perplexed for an instant. 'Okay, I get it.' A broad smile illuminated his face. 'Nothing ventured . . . I've got just the right tool for the job.' Beaky smiled as he patted the hold-all bag slung over his massive shoulder.

They crossed the road and ascended the stairway to the second floor of the drab sixties block, the graffiti-lined walls adding a gesture of colour to the expanses of grey. A young black kid whistled as he skateboarded along the deck access toward them.

'How you going, junior?' asked Beaky cheerfully.

'Fuck off asshole,' the youth replied, his progress barely faltering as he dismissed the intrusion, clattering down the stairs and out of sight within seconds.

'What's it coming to Mike? Kid just needs a damn good thumping and instead he's running wild.'

'Maybe he needs not to live in a shit house like this,' replied Aziz. Beaky had produced a weapon, 'And what the fuck is that?'

'I forget sometimes you're a bit out of touch mate. It's an AA-12 gas operated fully automatic shotgun, 300 round per minute, 20 round magazine, internal mechanism for minimal recoil, stainless steel, virtually no maintenance,' explained Beaky, holding the gun out so Aziz could admire it, 'and there's a whole choice of different rounds for it too. I've just got standard pellets. Nothing else like it to clear a room.'

'Nice one Beaky, but you won't need it, shove it back in the bag for now.'

'I thought we were going to persuade them to be reasonable?' asked Beaky.

'It's an offence to threaten an officer of the law with a gun, not to mention a cannon like that. I'm already in deep shiite but you're not. It's all about psychology - we just convince them they've got more to lose than we have. No call for fisticuffs.'

'Well you always were the lateral thinker . . .' said Beaky, 'but if the shit hits the fan then I'm gonna fan the shit with this mother okay?'

'Trust me,' replied Aziz, his fist rat-a-tatting on the green door in front of them. 'We won't need artillery.'

'Who is it?' came a shout from inside.

Chapter 109: just calling

(12.40 pm)

'Back up from PORTAL - Assistant Commissioner Lawson authorized attendance,' replied Aziz, rapping once more on the door of the flat.

'Never heard of you or him - you've got the wrong place - just fuck off before you get into trouble,' the policeman shouted in reply from the other side of the door.

'Jeez,' said Beaky. 'This place has a really bad effect on people.'

Aziz ignored him. 'Open the door mate, or we'll have to open it for you,' he shouted evenly.

There was a scuffling noise from inside and the door swung open suddenly with a crash - a big man was standing there, solid and defiant.

'Thanks mate,' said Aziz coolly, strolling in as if he had been invited to a dinner party. The man began shouting, his voice cracking with fear and fury as he grabbed a pistol from his side-holster and pointed it at Aziz. A second policeman rushed into view, saw the intrusion and took aim at Aziz too.

'Calm down guys, no need for any of that.' Aziz was smiling at the two policemen. 'Let me just explain some things here.' Something in his tone of voice and his calmness demanded their attention. This was a different script, challenging the source of their reaction. Aziz continued, like a teacher might explain a new word to a ten-year-old - part recitation, part sympathy.

'My name is Mike Aziz. I am trying to free a Dr Ian Lineker who we believe is being held by a man called Shirov in the flat you've been watching.' Aziz looked around him at the room they had just entered. Binoculars on a tripod were half hidden behind the net curtains across an expanse of carpet that, greasy and damp looking, displayed its twirls and twists of elaborate orange like cat sick between the threadbare patches of brown and beige.

'You must understand that both me and my colleague here are highly trained,' continued Aziz. More to relieve his own tension than gain any advantage, the big policeman readjusted his position, backing off slightly, tightening his grip on the gun.

'Now, if you shoot me and I accept you can - my friend will kill you both - you can be sure of that.'

'Reckon I will,' said Beaky, his deep voice deliberately modulated to convey authority and resolve, as part-concerned and part-amused, he played his part in the drama that Aziz was directing.

'It's a terrible thing to rob someone of their future, and everything they might have been,' continued Aziz.

'Did you get that from a Clint Eastwood movie?' interjected Beaky.

'Shut up Beaky . . .' The policemen were darting glances at each other, suspecting their antagonists were not completely sane.

'If you shoot my friend here, I will kill you both. I won't need a gun to do it - I'm sure you understand.'

'The *Outlaw Josie Wales* . . . that was it,'

'For Christ sake shut up Beaky . . . this is serious.'

The much younger policeman, sweat standing from his forehead, was shaking slightly. 'What do you want?' he blurted, the sound of adrenalin cracking in his voice.

'We want to know who is in the room you're watching, how many, how they are armed, and who they're holding - just a bit of information - and then we're on our way.'

'Who the fuck are you guys working for anyway?' the bigger man barked.

'Freelance,' said Beaky. He shot a mischievous glance across at Aziz. 'Doing it for love.'

Assuming he was dealing with hit men from a rival gang, the big policeman was growing increasingly anxious as he assessed the competing claims of honour, complicity in a massacre, and preservation of his own life. Did Aziz's air of complete confidence mean he and Beaky were supremely competent, indifferent to their own safety, or both? Whatever the case, the cop didn't fancy his chances.

'Okay,' decided the big policeman. 'I can tell you this. It's a gang of Russians and an Indian man - but they're just sitting about, killing time - there's been nothing since we got here - there's no hostage.'

'Couple of people entering the flat just now, sir,' said the younger policeman looking at the monitor. His words were corroborated by the tinny relay from the cheap speakers as the sounds of a muffled greeting were suddenly replaced by shouting in a building crescendo of agitated voices.

"Nothing happening' . . . well what the fuck is that then?' demanded Beaky staring at the screen.

The big policeman lowered his gun, and hurried to look. The screen showed a man being tied to a chair, a bag concealing his face while another man - Shirov - stood over him. Shirov was waving an Uzi machine gun in the air and bellowing in Russian, his broadcast voice sounding strangely disembodied so that the thinness of its delivery added to the surreality of the drama unfolding on the screen. Suddenly the sounds stopped. Shirov had smashed the barrel of the weapon onto the concealed head, and the man was slumping forward in the chair.

'Jesus – it's Lineker!' Aziz was heading for the door. 'Come on mate.'

'Wait . . . there are six of them,' the policeman yelled, deciding whoever Beaky and Aziz worked for they should at least know something of the odds stacked against them.

Beaky and Aziz hurled themselves down the stairs, the metallic clatter of their boots reverberating up the stairwell. Near the bottom, Aziz jumped the final steps to the corridor below, pushing off the concrete wall to propel himself sideways round the corner. For a moment he faltered from the impact, clutching his side in agony at the stabbing pain in his ribs from the green/black bruising - a memento left by the lead that had smashed into his bulletproof vest outside the library in Brixton. He waited, recovering his breath as Beaky lumbered up behind, then launched himself again down the next flight of stairs.

As they burst into the street the two were close together. 'We'll go in hard - to the max,' Aziz shouted, swinging the shotgun suspended from a sling under his arm clear of the coat where it had been concealed from view. 'Me first - you back me up.'

'Shit . . . this is more like it . . . I thought you'd gone weird on me in there,' wheezed Beaky, his breath gasping as he struggled to sustain the pace.

The youthful skateboarder had frozen, terrified, as the two hurtled toward him. 'Hey prick,' Beaky shouted, slowing for a moment to bellow at the wide-eyed boy, his face red and gasping just a foot away from the cowering youngster. 'Fuck you too.'

The young policeman was watching from the balcony as Beaky and Aziz scurried into view.

'What the . . .? Quick . . . look - they've got shotguns', he shouted, summonsing his colleague who having rushed to join him, gabbled frantically into the radio.

'Back up needed. Armed riot in progress. Flat 17 Poplar Buildings Armitage Close, Acton. And for Christ's sake . . . hurry.'

Chapter 110: here's the thing

(California)

'Hi, pleased to meet you. I'm Cindy Lopez - Research Assistant in the Truth Division.'

'Isabel Aziz. Dr Valence told me I should look you up. Hope you don't mind me bothering you at home?' Isabel wore baggy shorts and a light T shirt. She felt excited by the newness of it all, content to enjoy the warmth of a Californian afternoon, and the heady smell of the exotic.

'Not at all. Paula said to expect you.' Cindy smiled warmly. 'She told me you're interested in our work. Come on in.' Cindy stepped back to allow Isabel into the room. 'I'm really sorry to hear about Magnus - we were all so shocked - and the loss of your friend, how terrible for you.'

'Yes, it was . . . awful,' replied Isabel, feeling tears forming in her eyes and realizing that Cindy was the first person she had met for a long time that seemed genuinely sympathetic.

It was a small modern room, bright and functional, without luxury. The bed, chairs and table in the angular light brown softwoods had robbed the room of slightly too much space so that it teetered near cluttered, but was saved from uncomfortable by its immaculate tidiness. A small picture of Jesus above the bed, and a calendar, were the only decorations on the walls.

Isabel sat on the bed, and Cindy sat opposite her on a chair. 'So what aspect of our work is it that interests you?' asked Cindy.

'I suppose you could say I'm interested in magic,' Isabel replied.

'Magic!' Cindy laughed appreciatively. 'My thing is philosophy - I did Philosophy of Science and got a Masters in Theology at Harvard - that's why they took me on. Maybe the distinction between magic and science means less and less these days anyway. What do you mean by 'magic?'' asked Cindy.

'The mysteries. The things you can't see or touch. The connections we have with different times and other creatures. Dr Valence said that was your area.'

'Well Paula was right - I am interested in the paranormal - you could call it that anyway. I'm working on something called Process Physics. Its equations describe a brain type network that seems to underpin everything - we like it as a sort of 'mind of God' at the deepest level of reality – it's very exciting work.'

'Seems to me the mind of God would be connected to the past and the future,' said Isabel, her eyes sparkling again as she let her imagination travel. 'I find that fascinating, the idea that we can know the future.'

'An all pervasive Mind, yes. I've seen a computer model of the universe, building on the observations of the space telescopes. It's amazing how the galaxies seem strung out like a network too,' explained Cindy. 'It's as if the same patterns repeat from the unimaginably small to the inconceivably vast. That's what a fractal process gives you, the 'small' is a microcosm of the 'large', like a cauliflower floret is a mini cauliflower,'

'Extending not just in space but in time too,' said Isabel, 'I believe sometimes I can foretell the future.'

'Well, that's interesting, but this work has a crucially different conception of time from classical physics. There isn't a notion that the 'past' and the 'future' have a 'reality'. Everything happens in the 'now.''

'Paula was explaining something like that to me,' said Isabel.

''Space' and 'matter' emerge from this process. So if you can get degrees of materiality ranging from what seems to be nothing all the way to say, something as hard as a diamond, then I don't see a difficulty with ghosts, thoughts and other ephemera in between too,' added Cindy.

'That's what I wanted to discuss with Paula,' said Isabel, a defensive satisfaction in her voice.

'If the connections that are the underlying processes linger into a 'later now' or persist from a 'previous now', then we might recognize the past or the future I suppose. I'm not sure that's the same as foretelling the future,' said Cindy, her voice full of caution.

'But what about when I'm sure something is going to happen and then it does, or that when I meet someone, it's as if I already know them.'

Something about the remark seemed to trigger a reaction in Cindy. Her good mood suddenly collapsed. 'I used to feel that way about too,' said Cindy wistfully. 'But now I think I was just fooling myself.'

Chapter 111: perfectly frank

(California)

'A long iron,' called Baedeker to the black-suited caddy, inscrutable behind dark sunglasses. The man reached for the club.

'The 16th at Cyprus Point has got to be the most beautiful green in the world, don't you think Frank?' Baedeker's outstretched arm swept across the vista, as if he was personally summonsing the waves that sighed onto the rocks far beneath them, and somehow controlling the ocean that cast its mantle of white-flecked blue from the cliffs below to the far reach of the distant horizon.

The senator laughed. 'It was certainly worth the wait to join. I'm very grateful to you.'

'Caddie, some space please.' For Baedeker there was no distinction between an order and a request. The man strolled off. 'So before I show you how not to play golf - what's the concern, Frank?' Baedeker's charm was just the right side of unctuous.

'It's the Jews, Saul. You know a lot of us support your initiatives on limiting population growth. We have to slow the runaway train. It's just I've heard that the PORTAL program is targeting Jewish interests too. There could be a problem there.'

'What's the problem?' Baedeker barely registered his interest, as he shimmied his backside to prepare for his drive down the green.

'We don't want to make enemies, Saul. We could lose the impetus of goodwill. Word from my committee is that a team at the FBI are thinking of investigating PORTAL, a guy called Bernstein is heading it up. It would help if some of your team were to cut back on the rhetoric.'

'I understand Frank . . . Clinton.' Baedeker waved at his assistant, who was sitting in the motorized golf caddie fifty metres away. Baedeker waited until Clinton had joined them.

'There's been a misunderstanding that Frank has kindly brought to my attention. I want $5 million donated to a Jewish charity by the end of the week. I want the donation to be anonymous. And I want Costigan on the phone now. Costigan heads up our Word division,' confided Baedeker in an elaborate aside to the senator, 'obviously something has gone very wrong with our communications, I'll see he . . .' Baedeker paused as if reflecting on the best course of action. 'I'll fire him immediately.'

The senator was accustomed to a world of reports, recommendations, and reviews. He was alarmed at this development, the weight of his own role in affecting the world so immediately and irrevocably was an uncomfortable responsibility.

'I really appreciate your response, Saul,' he blustered. 'You must understand it is more a question of timing than content - many of us appreciate the sincerity of what you're doing here.'

'Yes of course, Frank, and I appreciate your . . . how shall I say . . . frankness.' They chuckled briefly, without humour. There was something elusive, and unidentifiable about his manner that nevertheless suggested that Saul Baedeker, not a man to trifle with the distinction between messenger and message, was annoyed with the senator. The senator sensed it, and regretted it.

'Ah there's Chun Li on the next green,' said Baedeker. 'If you'll excuse me I've been meaning to chat with him for some time. By the way did the Lakeside Project get its funds on time? I know you take an interest,' asked Baedeker.

'Absolutely Saul, we're very grateful to PORTAL.'

'Not at all. Any time Frank. Till next time.' Baedeker turned, gesturing over his shoulder for Clinton to follow. The abrupt abandonment left his adversary without opportunity for reconciliation, unsure whether to blame his discomfort on Baedeker's dismissive arrogance or some fault of his own.

Baedeker was already many metres away, calm, confident, in the moment.

'Here is Costigan on the phone sir.' Clinton held out the receiver to his boss.

'Costigan. The Jewish lobby is onto us - we have to back off for the time being - I'm moving you to Manna for a while, same salary and so on - and review all of the comms security.' There was a delay while Baedeker listened to the response.

'Appreciate it, Liam,' he said. 'Of course . . . yes . . . all of them - encryption . . . everything. Appreciate it, bye.' Baedeker turned his attention to Clinton.

'There was something on my mind,' he mused. 'Ah yes . . . on the way over here . . . did I hear you right? Didn't you say the Reynolds video is on YouTube?'

'It's massive sir, massive. We've pushed it along of course and it's gone completely viral. Apparently the interest in the TV show is the largest ever; assisted by the YouTube video. We're pitching the show around her as the centrepiece to leverage that. The actual experiment is unlikely to be very theatrical so for the show itself we'll be using a lot of computer graphics, and other effects – so they tell me anyway.'

'So, the shares in . . . what's the name of the parent company of this TV show? What was it . . . TruthSayers?'

'That's the name of the show, sir, yes. The production company is TwiceRight sir. The shares have trebled.' Clinton had anticipated the question. 'Very astute purchase by you, sir,' he concluded.

'Not me Clinton. The shares were bought by PORTAL.'

'Of course sir, yes, by PORTAL.'

'She is a looker I must say - very smart too, very smart. Have you seen the video yourself, Clinton?' asked Baedeker, lining up for his next swing and ignoring the Chinese man, Mr Li, who had provided Baedeker with his excuse to leave the senator and who was gesturing a greeting to them from his buggy.

'No sir, not my thing really.'

'And Dr Lindacre will be at the show?'

'So we are assured, sir, yes.' Clinton assured him.

'I see,' replied Baedeker calmly. 'Ah, Mr Li, how are you,' he suddenly shouted, starting to stroll toward the buggy that had stopped thirty metres away.

'By the way Clinton - this girl from Australia - the Aziz girl. Was she responsible in some way for the Magnus tragedy?'

'We think not sir. She seems completely innocent.'

'Best to limit her movements just in case, eh Clinton?'

'Yes of course sir.'

'Perhaps you could have her sent up to my suite so as I can assess her more personally.'

'Yes sir, of course. I'll have her sent up this evening.'

Chapter 112: a physical process

Prompted by the quivering of Cindy's lips, Isabel reached out to touch her arm, and comfort her.

'Sorry, I still get upset.' Cindy cleared her throat, recovering quickly. 'I had something going with someone for a while, I got it wrong that's all.'

Cindy inhaled deeply, then seeing Isabel's still anxious expression added, 'A new breath for a new beginning.' She smiled, the brave smile of someone wanting to move on.

'What was I saying?'

'Something about whether we can see the future,' offered Isabel. 'With some people, when I meet them, it's almost as if I already know them.'

"Yes, of course. Well, in Process Physics the progression from one moment to the next is worked out by an input that is random. It gives a direction to time. The random is entirely unknowable - that's what random means - so the future is unknowable. It has interesting implications for free will, fate and so on.'

'I don't really get it. Why bother with 'random' at all?' asked Isabel.

'You need it to properly represent time. For this physics, time is the absolute - nothing else is like it - so that's where it starts. The old systems started with a few assumptions about matter and laws of motion and so on. They pretended time was a geometric line, but of course you can travel a line in either direction. So they spent forever arguing about why time only went one way. But many of time's properties aren't like a line at all.'

'What about history, one thing comes after another,' asked Isabel.

'That's the one property of a line that is really useful - sequencing. Problem is that because of that we've ended up thinking that's what time really is. If I measure your height with a tape measure, I wouldn't end up thinking you were a tape measure would I?'

'Okay,' said Isabel, suspicious of where she was being led. 'But I've watched a puppy grow to be a dog. I've seen a baby grow into a child and a seed into a plant. I'm sure there have been times when I have foreseen the future. I believe we are as much pulled into the future as we are propelled in the present or pushed from the past. Maybe your random input is only random from our perspective, or the nearest we can get to representing something we don't understand. Maybe there's another perspective from which it isn't random at all.'

'I'll buy that one - but that would be God's perspective,' said Cindy, impressed by the vehemence of the young Tasmanian. 'But who knows where we're headed? We're looking here at a very radical new theory. It's another step to abandoning the old mechanistic world view that has dominated thinking for the last couple of hundred years, in favour of something more organic, alive. You don't understand everything about a flower by pulling it to pieces, do you? It might even give us a scientific understanding of consciousness instead of mistaking the things that accompany it with the thing itself.'

Cindy's imagination was feeding on her excitement, and it suited her to have such an interested audience. 'Of course everything has to fit all of the data we establish empirically - this is still science - but that's not my department.'

'So how do you explain that sometimes I feel I can recognize things into the future if the random makes them unknowable,' Isabel persisted, eager to get back to what she regarded as the point of interest.

'Well I can see the possibility for snapshots if you like - something in the moment that remains connected to another moment from the past. Or a 'now' connection that will re-emerge in a future 'now'. But I don't see how you'd get a preview of a whole future 'movie'. That would require a whole bunch of 'randoms' to reoccur in exactly the same sequence. Ghosts I can believe in, Groundhog Day, I can't.'

Chapter 113: born free

(12.45 pm)

The young man with a fleshless face and a foppish wave of bleach-blond hair, sensed a disturbance outside. Following his intuition, he moved to the window to check.

A single burst from Beaky's ACR assault rifle bored three precise holes through the window glass in the near same instant they also drilled three circular holes in the Latvian's forehead, mincing his brains to mush as the copper sheathed bullets each fanned into a deadly cone of pulping shards. He slid, almost gracefully, to the floor, the look of affected indifference that had shaped his boyish good looks in life, unchanged, though now more cruelly appropriate in death.

By the time his companion, a heavily bearded Indian man had crawled across the floor to find out exactly what had happened, Aziz was already at the top of the stairs on the first floor, and moving quickly down the corridor toward the peeling paint of the flat at the end, his 9 mm Sig Sauer P226 pistol, grabbed from a belly-band holster, now appearing as if glued to his hand.

When he saw the Latvian die, a survivor's imagination and the reflex of training prompted Shirov to immediately position himself behind the entrance door, shouting orders in Russian for his men to face the unknown, outside. Goaded by his cursing, two men bundled out, pistols held in readiness, the glint in their eyes of animal fear and its bastard offspring, fury. The whip crack of two shots, the second so immediate it seemed to echo the first, filled the length of the concrete passage, as one man fell backwards awkwardly into the room, the other staggering confused and shocked for two steps down the corridor before he fell face forward, a pool of blood puddling gently around him. Aziz was hobbling quickly nearer when the body lying across the doorway was kicked out into the corridor and the door banged shut.

The deafening crash of his shotgun round tore the door from its hinges before Aziz quickly hit the ground in a forward tumble to lob two stun grenades through the swirling dust and into the room, propelling himself after them with a judo roll across the floor. Aziz released his next shot, killing the bearded man.

In the same instant, Aziz saw an explosion of light, heard the sound of his gun clattering across the floor and registered the dim and distant realization he had been struck with considerable force on the side of his head.

The unspeakable agony slowly subsided, shuffling away behind a curtain of black that lowered over his eyes as Aziz recognized with a sense of inevitable detachment, the conscious world was slipping away. Resisting the pull, he forced his eyes open to see Shirov standing above him, a twisted grin revealing a gold tipped tooth, his gun pointing at Aziz's face. He saw Shirov's trigger finger tightening, and without any sense of drama, or even regret, resigned himself to his imminent death.

Chapter 114: fuck up

(12.48 pm)

Through a mist, Aziz saw Chris Reynolds reaching out to him, her face radiant with concern, inviting him to get up. Like a familiar landscape transformed by an approaching storm, her troubled expression revealed a different aspect to a beauty he had assumed was complete. The image was calling him back to life; the energy rushing to refill his lifeless limbs.

Aziz twisted violently, projecting all his strength and resolve into movement - desperate, pleading and furious. A bullet skimmed his face, cutting a groove like a knife through steak and exposing tiny spheres of crimson which gathering together, flowed down his cheek to smear his tongue and lips with the bright taste of blood.

Aziz's legs circled Shirov's shin, finding a heel lock to bring him crashing down, the gun thrown from Shirov's hand curving as if in slow motion through the air. From the corner of his eye Aziz saw that another man had rushed into the room, a man carrying a commando knife, a man that Aziz knew he'd seen somewhere before.

Shirov rolled as he hit the ground, breaking the lock, and jumped to straddle Aziz, a small knife in Shirov's hand whistling down toward his chest. Aziz caught the wrist a nanosecond before impact, deflecting the blow so as the knife stuck with a quivering thwack into the floor, inches from his left shoulder.

Before Shirov could free himself, Aziz stabbed with his outstretched finger, hard, hurting Shirov, feeling the sickening pop and splatter, realising too late he had chosen the already sightless eye. Aziz sprang to his feet, his boot whistling toward Shirov's head. To his surprise Shirov caught his foot, and yanking back on it threw Aziz backward, rushing after him to throttle him from behind, his forearm locking onto Aziz's throat.

Russian Samba, thought Aziz, identifying the combat style even as he struggled for his life and remembering Beaky's reproach that Aziz had lost his edge when Beaky had ambushed him at the farmhouse with a similar choke. Aziz seized the knife still impaled in the boards and drove it hard toward Shirov's foot. Shirov avoided the blow, flipping over him and aimed a high kick that connected, sending Aziz crashing backwards.

Like a mantra of doom in the recesses of his mind the words *as good as I was,* taunted Aziz, feeling the blood now flowing freely down his face. Shirov was rushing forward to engage him, stopping in an instant, as Aziz's retrieved his second pistol from an ankle holster and aligned it with Shirov's head.

'Wait . . .' came the shout, the Irish lilt reminding Aziz this was the man he had clubbed to the ground in the dingy flat of Emelienko's cleaner, as Beaky crashed through the door gasping for air, his machine gun poised to spray the room with death.

'Or I'll slit the fucker's throat.' The knifeman, Danny Spillane, had a dagger around the neck of the man whose face was hidden in the bag.

'Stop, Beaky. No,' shouted Aziz. Beaky froze, his physical discomfort immediately swamped by the deadly urgency of their predicament.

'Drop your weapons,' barked Shirov. Retrieving his own gun, Shirov backed behind the seated figure, who had ceased struggling and was listening intently, as if trying to understand what was happening.

The instant Beaky's machine gun hit the ground, Shirov shot the seated man at point blank in the head, then immediately fired at Beaky and Aziz, both now diving for cover as they scrambled to recover their weapons. Beaky's machine gun burst killed Spillane, and peppered the door through which Shirov had lunged, as Aziz drove himself up and after him.

'Check Lineker, for fuck's sake,' he shouted, as he crashed through the door in time to see Shirov sliding at speed down the fire escape at the back of the flats before the wailing of rapidly approaching police sirens rewrote the game plan in Aziz's mind. Abandoning the pursuit, Aziz bounded back into the flat and over to the window.

'Cops are coming,' he shouted at Beaky.

'I'm hit Mike . . . the shoulder,' said Beaky, moving awkwardly toward the chair with the slumped man, crimson beginning to saturate the hessian cover. 'Hurts like buggery.'

'Shit . . . they're here', said Aziz looking down on the road beneath them. 'Come on – we're out of here.'

Eight men were jumping from two vans, cyborgs in black body armour carrying assault weapons and sniper rifles. Their faces were concealed by helmets with dropped visors, their knees and elbows covered by padded protectors and their big boots thudded as they ran to rehearsed positions, crouching, kneeling or sheltering behind their vehicles.

'Get out Mike - now - I'll tidy up,' said Beaky joining Mike at the window. 'Abseil out the window onto that back roof and into the garden, there's rope in my bag.'

'Enough rope for two of us or do we go one after the other?'

'I can't make it with my shoulder messed up - you're on your own.'

'Don't be daft - I can lower you down – quick.'

'Bullshit Mike. You've got 30 seconds before they're here .. . I'll get off with a year or two. If they get you - you'll do ten,' said Beaky, grimacing with the pain. 'Here, take the ACR - that way they can't pin the shooting on me.'

'Shit Beaky, this is a complete fuck up.' Desolation suffused Aziz, knowing he had failed Chris, and was about to fail Beaky too. It flushed the adrenalin from his body in a wave of sudden exhaustion, as much of spirit as of body.

They touched hands briefly, a token handshake designed to bypass emotion. 'If you make it I'll be at the Bellevue, Shepherds Bush. Take care . . .'

Aziz turned to whip the sack from the man's head, its cloth now a gaudy flag of death. A large hole had splattered his brains on the inside of the bag, the distorted features set in the twisted agony of pure terror. Even so, the face was unmistakable.

'Jesus Beaky, it's Emelienko - they've killed Emelienko.'

September 26th

Chapter 115: hard times

(California)

'Ah . . . Our little philosopher. Do come in,' said Baedeker, 'Paula tells me you've made quite a name for yourself already.'

Isabel looked at him, fascinated, unsure whether to be appalled or amused. Baedeker was reclining on a white leather sofa, wearing a voluminous dressing gown of burgundy velvet with a fake fur collar, like a drag queen on a day off or the head of a porn empire whose sartorial taste has failed to keep pace with their commercial success.

Or is it me that's naive and he understands exactly what he's doing? she thought, suddenly disquieted that this man might not be so easily dismissed, and that his inappropriate appearance was evidence of arrogance rather than insensitivity.

'I don't think of myself as a philosopher but I am fascinated by anything that suggests the divine.' Isabel was still excited to be able to use such language without ridicule.

'Wonderful to hear my child. If only there were more like you,' he beamed at her, the thick mat of hair on his chest throwing off occasional glints of silver that sparkled against his heavily tanned skin like the sudden flashes from a shoal of fish as they dart for an instant in the sun

'Does he oil his chest?' she wondered to herself, her concern increasing as the gown slipped to reveal a matching muscled thigh, this time the depilated skin smooth beneath its improbable tan.

'I'm forgetting myself,' Baedeker rose elegantly and approached her. 'Can I get you a drink?'

'Thank you, a juice would be wonderful.'

'A juice? We have stronger beverages. I'm a great believer in the improving power of Absinthe or the 'Green Fairy' as the French termed it. Do you know it was illegal here until 2007, and now it's made just down the road, well a couple of hundred miles away, that's all. I drink it with champagne - I believe it's called 'Death in the Afternoon', after the Hemingway novel'.

Baedeker suddenly gave an unexpected twirl, quick enough to raise the hem of his gown, before finishing the rotation exactly where he had started, head upright, with the self-assured precision of a ballet dancer.

'Voila,' he declared, in triumphant appreciation of his own display. 'Yes, Hemingway - a favourite author of mine - so ironic - so very masculine - so tragic.' He laughed, a chortling inclusive fusion of paternal reliability and naughty insouciance.

Isabel found that despite her initial reaction she was attracted to this peculiar man, who seemed so at home with himself. She approved of his evident indifference to the opinion of others, in contrast to the vulnerability she had endured for most of her adult life and that scarred her with constant doubt. However unusual he seemed, she was starting to like him, comforted by his effusive goodwill, and conspiratorial mischief making.

She started to relax, looking round at the exotic layering of marble and leather, the lush abundance of house plants, and the plunge pool bubbling down steps some forty feet away. A grand piano stood in one corner, a thirty-six string Sylvan harp standing next to it. Sunlight formed an oval of brilliance on the adjacent floor beneath a blue period Picasso, the only painting on any of the whitewashed walls.

'Oh, go on then,' she said, surprised at the irresponsible music-hall tone of her voice as if she was being drawn ineluctably into silliness. She was buoyed by the sense a 'one-off' would not threaten her values or lifestyle, and keen to avoid the self-reproach that had often ensued when she had bowed to caution in the face of adventure. 'Just this once,' she confirmed.

Baedeker went to the drinks cabinet, and mixed her a drink. He turned to look at her, his small sturdy frame standing upright, a bull fighter's posture, proud, capable, theatrical. He handed her the drink, then crossed to the sofa, and flicking his gown extravagantly to either side, seated himself regally on the shiny leather.

'Come and sit,' he invited, patting the space next to him. 'I understand you're interested in our work with the new physics. It offers scientific support to our sense of God as immanent, in everything, universal.'

'Yes I've been fascinated by that,' Isabel replied, her enthusiasm edging out her residual discomfort, as she sat well away from Baedeker at the end of the couch. 'I read about morphic resonance when I was thirteen. It . . . well . . . it just seemed so magical to me.'

'Morphic resonance?' queried Baedeker.

'Yes . . . it's the idea that a skill can be transmitted throughout a species once enough members of the species have acquired it. There's no scientific explanation, not yet anyway,' she added.

'Is that why kids can work computers and their parents can't?' interrupted Baedeker, seeming to be enjoying himself immensely.

'And I have felt sometimes that I have a pre-knowledge of the future - as if an outline is arriving before the actual event, a fore-feeling,' Isabel continued, distantly aware she was being brave.

'I see, my dear, fascinating, fascinating. 'Fore-feeling', yes, love it, love it.'

Baedeker held his drink aloft. 'I sometimes drink these with Viagra,' he said, flashing his white teeth at her.

The remark hit her like a sledgehammer.

Oh shit, she thought.

'Not that I need to, you understand.' Baedeker was unaware of her reaction. "Peter' is quite capable of looking out for himself.' As if to illustrate his point, Baedeker's gown was showing an increased heaviness in the groin area.

'Come my dear,' he said, his hand patting the sofa next to him, motioning her to sit closer.

'Look I must be going. Paula is expecting me,' Isabel protested.

'I can square things with Paula, don't worry about that. Sit.'

The tone was subtly different, the sort of shift a woman in that situation is acutely attuned to. Isabel was now very concerned but unsure if her reaction was from an excess of imagination, or the urgency of justified panic. She remained seated at the end of the sofa, out of arm's reach of Baedeker, who ignoring the rebuff, slid enthusiastically down to her, his thigh touching hers. He suddenly gripped the hem of his gown, and pulling it decisively to one side, exposed his erect penis.

It was standing upright, a pulsing missile of purple veins and straining skin, the glans shiny and tight like a snare drum, nodding slightly with every beat of his heart. Baedeker made no attempt to disguise its condition. 'You can touch, don't be shy,' he suggested, reaching out to grip her arm tightly, his head inching toward her.

Chapter 116: bellevue

(6.00 pm)

It had been a tiring drive from Malvern to the chaos of a London rush-hour, where the hordes sat patiently in traffic jams before their evening ritual of domestic barter and the sterile choices that served as a substitute for individuality. Or so it had always seemed to Chris. But this time, wearied by the agony of conflict, she found she envied the commuters their routines, and the luxury of boredom. She parked her little French car in the back streets of Shepherds Bush and walked a couple of hundred metres to the short flight of steps outside the entrance lobby of the Bellevue Guest House. A couple of old men sat on benches in the front garden, smoking rollups and sucking on cans of Carlsberg lager.

Chris pushed the front door open, entering gingerly into the hallway, its dankness and threadbare carpet confirming the neglect that the poverty of the neighbourhood had increasingly forewarned was likely. The place was in miserable retreat from vitality, a home of sorts for those who had been abandoned to navigate the dead ends of life in solitary anonymity and who purposefully ignored each other, not from indifference, but to avoid adding the humiliation of public recognition to the weight of private failure.

'You'll be wanting room five,' said the woman behind the counter. 'Mr Smith is expecting you.'

Chris didn't enquire how she might have known, or who Mr Smith was. She rapped on the door, too loudly, looking to left and right, preparing to apologize, as you might if you spilled a little wine on a carpet and hoping that the hostess had not noticed, nevertheless prepared yourself to be challenged. The door opened and Aziz beckoned her inside. 'Thanks for coming.'

'I left Malvern as soon as I got your message . . .' she started, but gasped when she saw his cheek, the crusted blood thickening around a makeshift bandage of gauze taped across his chin.

'Not as bad as it looks,' he assured her. 'Any news of Lineker?'

'Nothing,' she replied, 'apart from another finger this morning.'

She saw how awkwardly Aziz moved, how battered and tired he seemed, not just physically, but in spirit too, dangerously resembling the shuffling dossers she had passed on the steps outside.

'Mike, what's happened?' She was emptying a bag as she looked at the livid tear across his cheek. The first aid dressings he had asked her to bring tumbled out onto the bed.

He told her of the carnage in the flat and how Beaky had been left behind, an account bare and clinical delivered in the succinct language of a military report. She dabbed gently at his cheek and he flinched as the iodine swab cauterized the wound with its stain of orange.

'Sorry babe,' she said, 'it's for the best.'

Early in life, Aziz had chosen the world of men where toughness is honed to follow a well-defined path. This discipline had been reinforced by his military training which warned that the mirages of emotion can sap strength and weaken resolve. But Chris' concern touched something within him that though stunted through neglect, was not yet dead; to Aziz, the jolting inside felt dangerously close to self-pity.

'Let's take your things off,' she said, tugging at his shirt to help it over his head.

She looked at him, an involuntary intake of breath acknowledging the masculine power of muscles faceted into distinct planes across his stomach and along his arms with the definition of idealized soviet-era statues, or cut diamond. She gave a second gasp, this time from horror, when she saw the scars across his withered thigh and the bruising, huge and livid across his side and back, where the lead had smashed into the bullet proof vest.

'Jesus H,' she muttered, her body responding to his masculine strength even in its dereliction, and her heart to his frailty. He looked back at her, appreciation in his eyes and the hint of an apology in his smile.

Chris reached forward, kissing him hesitantly on the lips. Curious, Aziz responded slowly at first, then more greedily as he felt her tongue flicker inside his mouth, inviting him with increasing urgency to join her in desire until, without warning, his demon sauntered into the void that a myriad sensations were leaving in their wake. *This won't work,* it whispered. Confused, Aziz faltered, and the magic was gone.

He remembered how she had comforted him. *Sorry babe, it's for the best.* The word 'babe' resonated through him. Who would describe him, a gnarly wreck of a soldier, as a mewling brat? It was outrageous, risky. But it also suggested some other world of unknown rules, a world of transgression and a doorway to experiment. The kiss thrilled him with the giddiness of possibility. Unlike ever before, this was an invitation to make love with a woman who emanated sexual allure as naturally as summer honeysuckle will waft its scent in the still of the evening to suffuse it with the edgy promise of another dimension. *But not with you,* the demon reminded him.

Chris could feel his frustration, and knew it matched her own. She took his hand to lead him to the bed.

'I have problems Chris . . .' he began, her beauty suddenly powerless against the stigma of doubt that the psychiatrists had branded into his self-image as indelibly as the Chinaman had etched a tattoo of an eagle into his shoulder.

'Shh,' she said, 'there are no problems, just us - come with me.' She undressed and they lay together in silence, naked under the covers of the single bed, his arm around her, until the dark descended outside and she fell asleep.

Something woke her in the night. A solitary tear had tapped her on the back, a speck of salt from the river of sorrow that engulfed him. She lay awake too and, sensing the wisdom of the dispossessed imbued throughout this temple of gloom, she did not react, though her heart called out to him as the rain strummed in bursts on the window, and the wind moaned its sympathy to the trees outside.

Chapter 117: hard as nails

(California)

Against her better judgment, Isabel reached out to grip Baedeker's erection. There were several reasons that prompted an action that for her was so out of character. Partly she was curious. She had never before experienced such a grandstand view of a mature male organ, boasting its engorgement so shamelessly. She was impressed by its dimensions, astonished at its stature rather than by any sexual potential, though its purpose was so clearly unambiguous that it provoked a flash of imagery, with attendant memories of arousal and regret. Being of a kindly disposition, she was willing if she could, to relieve the evident distress it was causing Baedeker, rather as someone might offer to share the load under which a fellow traveller was struggling. But mainly she was afraid. Chillingly aware of her own vulnerability, she hoped to avoid antagonizing Baedeker, by agreeing to his request.

She felt its hardness, and its heat, squeezing slightly to test its velvet elasticity.

Baedeker gasped 'There's my girl - now suck it.' He was pressing gently but firmly on the back of her head.

'No I can't,' she replied, horrified and repelled at the thought.

'Yes you can,' he breathed, gripping her hair resolutely to force her down. She knew she was in serious trouble, and feared that Baedeker's demands would escalate as his sexual excitement now obviously overrode any consideration for her, as if she was threatened not by a man with an erection, but by an erection with a man, both she and Baedeker incidental to the imperatives of lust.

Isabel felt panic rising to overwhelm her as she pleaded through her tears, 'Please let me go, please . . .' whilst struggling to break free. Baedeker didn't seem even to hear her, forcing her inexorably down. By now, she was certain he would try to rape her.

Isabel had studied Aikido for three years in Hobart, the only girl attending the classes, leaving when the sweaty proximity of the male instructor had become too uncomfortable. She struggled to remember her training, reaching above her and whimpering with fear, as she scrabbled to find Baedeker's hand with hers.

The two were locked in a fidgety embrace, like statues from antiquity suddenly infused with life but unable to free themselves from their original cast, the movement of either impeded by the obstructive presence of the other. But their near-motionless shuffle did little to disguise how desperate each was to win control; he for transitory relief, she to avoid a life-time trauma. Suddenly, she had his wrist and the mold was broken. Falling away from him, she applied a twist, simultaneously bending his hand back toward his forearm in a classic move of self-defence.

Baedeker screeched with pain, releasing her as he leapt up. Now on her feet, she took a flying kick at him, the upper curve of her foot impacting on his balls. Baedeker fell immediately to his knees, moaning and holding himself, his face contorted with pain. Pointing defiantly at the ceiling, his cock still strained, its chemical-fuelled demands undeterred even by the collapse of its host.

Isabel ran, terrified not just at the threat to her but at what she had done. In total confusion, unsure where to go or what to do, she was sobbing uncontrollably as she rushed outside, banging the door open as she fled across the lawn. Terrified even of being seen, she suddenly remembered that Cindy lived in the residential wing across the courtyard from Baedeker's villa. The change of surface unsettled her, she slipped and fell, the white gravel tearing at her knees before she staggered across the yard and into the corridor that accessed the tidy units where the junior staff lived, to round a corner at the end and bang loudly on Cindy's door.

The door opened and Isabel pushed through, fighting for breath as she sobbed. 'He tried to rape me, he tried to rape me,' her chest heaving from fear and exhaustion. Cindy didn't need to ask who.

She put an arm round Isabel, comforting her, 'Come and sit. You'll be safe here.' There was an icy determination in Cindy's voice. 'We'll get the pervert, don't you worry. This time he won't get away with it.'

Chapter 118: ouch

(California)

When Clinton found Baedeker, he was slumped on the couch, a handkerchief crudely gathered to contain ice cubes held to his groin.

'You called sir,' asked Clinton, viewing him anxiously.

'You know I am a very physical man, Clinton?'

'Of course sir.'

'But I am not a beast - I am not an animal.'

'Of course not sir. Can I ask what is wrong?'

'I have been assaulted by that Aziz girl - I thought she wanted me, Clinton.'

'I'll alert security to find her immediately . . . I should have mentioned it sir - she's a lesbian.'

'Ah, thank goodness,' sighed Baedeker, his vanity stronger than his venality, and the blow to his pride more hurtful even than the physical pain. 'That explains everything. I wished you had told me earlier Clinton - it would have avoided this misunderstanding.'

'I'm sorry sir. How can I help?'

'Phone medical please Clinton - tell them to hurry.

Chapter 119: he had it coming

(California)

Cindy fetched a blanket, wrapped it round Isabel's shoulders, and put some Brian Eno music on the player, its faltering melody dicing the atmosphere into isolates of time, as the two young women shared their fear and anger in an unspoken sisterhood of regret.

'I thought I could see into the future,' said Isabel forlornly. 'Looks like I was wrong.'

'The 'future' can only be a manifestation in the 'now' like everything else.' There was the ring of conviction in Cindy's voice. 'Even if the future is an 'open book', it's not enough just to be 'sensitive'. Not if some of the pages are missing. And anyway, maybe you were expecting a human and you got ambushed by a worm.'

'Maybe that's it,' began Isabel.

'He raped me too,' Cindy added tentatively, testing the idea, wondering if she would be safe in such unfamiliar territory, even supported by a sympathetic companion.

'What?' Isabel paused, astonished. 'I didn't know. He never actually raped me - I got away before he could - did you report him?'

'No, I didn't. Well . . . he didn't 'physically' rape me either.' Cindy's anger at Baedeker was still tempered by regret, denying her the consistency that comforts those who simply hate. 'It seemed okay at the start . . . but now I can see he was taking advantage of me all along. To me that's rape by a different name.' She was looking out of the window, nervous at what was going to happen and daring to formulate such an accusation.

The police will be here soon, it's been five minutes since I phoned them,' said Cindy. 'How did you get away from him, from Saul?' she asked.

'I kicked him in the balls,' replied Isabel.

'Wow - go girl!' Cindy exclaimed, her voice tailing off as her ill will against Baedeker was replaced by the thought of what might be permanent damage to him. She looked at Isabel suspiciously, re-assessing her, shocked that she could be so violent. Isabel saw the change in Cindy and shrugged, the shrug that acknowledges lack of choice in the teeth of the inevitable. The forlorn humanity of the gesture dissolved Cindy's brief hostility, reminding her where her loyalties lay.

'He had it coming that's what I think,' Cindy said, relaxing somewhat, though they sat again in awkward silence.

There was a loud knocking on the door.

'Who's there?' shouted Cindy.

'Security. Open up please,' came the reply.

'Just a moment,' Cindy shouted back.

'Quick, hide . . . I know how to get rid of him,' Cindy whispered to Isabel, immediately pulling off her jeans then directing a transfixed Isabel by a flicking motion of her wrist toward the bathroom. Cindy opened the entrance door slightly, wide enough for the man to see she was only partly dressed.

'I'm about to shower,' she said, peering round the door.

'Sorry miss. I'm looking for Isabel Aziz, five foot six inches, dreadlocks, Australian?' The guard was clearly embarrassed.

'No, sorry, can't help you there,' replied Cindy, 'I haven't seen anyone like that,' shutting the door firmly in his face.

Cindy fetched Isabel, inviting her to sit once more on the bed. Isabel couldn't stop herself from registering that Cindy had attractive legs, and she stole a glimpse at the darkened recess beneath the flimsy fabric of her panties with a guilty flutter of excitement.

'Hey - look - I'm sorry,' began Cindy, prompted by the excuse she had manufactured for the guard, 'I should have offered earlier.' She was crossing to check the window. 'Do you need a shower?'

'I would, please . . .' Isabel began, but was stopped by Cindy's excited interruption.

'Look they're carrying the bastard away,' a half-smile sat awkwardly on Cindy's handsome face. Isabel joined her and they looked out together, peering around the curtains as Baedeker strapped to a stretcher was being carried across the precinct toward the medical wing. Clinton, walking by his side, was holding Baedeker's hand.

Chapter 120: a tree falls

(California)

Isabel showered with the door left partly open.

'So what did he do to you?' asked Cindy.

'He tried to get me to suck his thingy,' shouted Isabel from the shower.

'And did you . . .?' asked Cindy, suddenly alarmed, the sexual imagery of another woman with Baedeker stirring the jealousy from her subconscious.

'God no, that's when I kicked him,' Isabel said.

'Bastard,' said Cindy, 'the fucking bastard.' She felt but never identified the relief that hid behind the fury. 'You just can't trust men . . . if ever there was living proof that nothing is real.'

'What do you mean nothing is real?' Isabel stuck her head out from behind the door.

'I mean things aren't necessarily what they seem.'

'Love is real.' Isabel was emerging from the shower, a towel draped around her.

'Yes, love is real. God's love anyway - no - I'm talking about our perceptions,' said Cindy, more as if she were talking to reassure herself than engaging with Isabel.

'Sorry . . . I don't get you at all?' asked Isabel.

'You know the saying - if the tree falls in the forest and no one is there to see it, does it really fall?' Cindy was still thinking of Isabel sucking Baedeker's cock.

'I know the forests and I believe it does,' said Isabel.

'Well . . . it does, and it doesn't. You see something happen, there's a series of events, molecules on the move. But an ant might see it as something else, a series of colours, who knows? There are countless different versions of consciousness looking at the same event in completely different ways - they won't draw the lines where we draw them. They won't necessarily see anything we might recognize as a tree.'

Isabel plonked herself down on the bed next to Cindy, looking into her eyes intensely. 'If nothing is there to construct a sense of it as a 'tree falling' then it's just a molecular dance - a pattern, amongst other patterns,' concluded Cindy.

'Great idea,' said Isabel cheerfully, the towel dropping briefly from her shoulder.

'Remember the idea of molecular dance is just another representation too - all this talk of science as truth has to be handled with care.' Cindy was excited now. 'We're just looking for something that works and gives us a bit more insight at a deeper level.'

Almost inadvertently, Cindy disclosed the agitation that her thinking was designed to calm. 'If you love someone you create love – doesn't mean it wasn't there if something goes wrong.'

Isabel was looking at her new American friend, wide-eyed in admiration. 'So no perception is completely real, but every perception has its own legitimacy?' she suggested.

'Well put,' said Cindy, 'that's why we must never forsake a trust in God. Only God is not 'created.'' They stared at each other and laughed, the rush of communication subsiding.

'Shall I dry your hair?' asked Cindy, rising to get another towel.

The sudden blaring whoop of a siren stopped her, and she ran to the window. A police car sped up the drive with its orange light flashing and halted abruptly at the reception block. Two policemen bundled out of the car. The brilliance of the light outlined their uniform in a rim of gold and their boots scrunched on the gravel before they clattered their way inside.

'Hurry, the police are here,' said Cindy. 'We need to speak to them.'

September 27th

Chapter 121: a little death

(5.00 am)

It was dark outside when Aziz was awoken by the sound of vehicles, each still with its own individual signature, before the morning rush hour swallowed them into an amorphous hum. Chris Reynolds, her face serene and attentive, was looking at him. 'Ah you're awake – welcome to the morning.' She reached out to him. 'Sit up – here – like this,' guiding him, arranging his limbs with a matter-of-fact preoccupation, like a nurse preparing a patient. He was naked, on his knees, unsure what to expect.

She smiled, kissed him briefly on the lips then knelt before him. For Aziz, it was a new feeling - not what she did, but the way she did it. At first the sensations were diffuse and manageable, then grouped to create an entity with its own life, separate from the Mike Aziz he knew, as if he was watching himself from a distance.

The equilibrium of pleasure was short-lived. A flicking tongue sent shocks from his cock through his belly and thighs, the stabbing feeling extinguishing his mind as he gasped and buckled over her, gripping her hair in both hands for support, and hearing a distant shout from someone he did not recognize. He felt the pressure growing, the crescendo building on a pervasive rhythm, a tsunami of his senses carrying him ineluctably to a rapidly approaching oblivion.

For an instant, curious, he wondered how he was responding, and in the distraction, the spell was broken.

Chris sensed the change but was now indifferent to its effect, acting only as her own arousal demanded, she resumed the rhythm of squeeze and suck at a higher intensity, again shutting off the commentary in both their minds and rekindling the fire that Aziz had resigned himself to never knowing again.

His external world began to blur to increasing irrelevance as his awareness was reduced to the sensation that he was in her grip, directed by her, and that she was summonsing an equal energy, a force greater than his sense of self, that was not 'his' to control – it was the real Aziz, elemental, uncaring and urgent, that was surging to find life.

As he came, she watched him, feeling his helplessness, his body wracked with convulsive waves that grew slower and further spaced. She squeezed his cock again, exulting in her power. He moaned and pushed her hand away as if in pain, then fell back on the bed exhausted.

They lay silent for a while, cocooned in the scent and shimmer of intimacy. She watched his smile start, a smile of self-congratulation at readmission to the world of manhood, and the cruelly exclusive club of normality.

'I was told I could never . . .'

'I know, I got a letter - from PORTAL - it said a lot of bad things about you. It had copies of your case notes.'

Suddenly, the mood was fractured. For Aziz, it was as if life had resumed from where it left off, though now they were lovers, he knew it was no longer the same.

'It took a few lines to realize what it was. I'm sorry Mike . . . I didn't read on . . . I burnt it,' she added, haltingly.

'How did they get hold of my goddam case notes . . . so much for confidential . . . Jesus Christ. People with 'right on their side' will do anything, won't they?' He looked concerned. 'Is that why you . . .?'

'Absolutely, soldier. I don't want my man firing blanks when all he needed was a little TLC.'

He laughed, her gamble had paid off.

He took her in his arms again, they kissed and made love leisurely, he pleasuring her until she climaxed, urgent and vocal so that he covered her mouth with his hand, anxious lest anyone in the room next door should hear.

'Mike you know I'm a porn star don't you - PORTAL filmed me with Ian.'

'Yeah, you mentioned that.'

'And I put it on YouTube.'

'Yeah I know - it's plastered across all the headlines - I haven't watched it,' he said.

'Thanks,' she said. 'You need to know I may be pregnant.'

'Yes, you told me in that cafe in Mayfair.'

'Ah,' she said. 'Does that worry you?'

Her phone rang, and she picked it up before he had time to reply.

'Thanks, I'm fine,' she said. 'Actually no, I'm in London . . .'

'It's Bill Grafton,' she mouthed to Aziz.

'What, who told you that? 'No it can't be . . . he's alright . . . doesn't matter how, but I know.' She was silent for some time, listening intently, her anxiety increasing. 'Thanks Bill - yeah, come round this evening. My place . . . thanks. Bye.'

She drew a deep breath, as if preparing for something difficult.

'Grafton says the police raided a flat in Acton yesterday. They found four bodies. They're saying there was a terrorist - he resisted arrest - so they killed him.'

'Usual disinformation I imagine . . .' Aziz started.

Again she pressed on, her face white with concern for him.

'They say it was you that they killed.'

Aziz seemed shocked as the realisation overtook him. 'Oh fuck . . .' he said, 'they've killed Beaky.'

Chapter 122: who cries last

(California)

There was a splintering sound at the door lock. The girls looked up, just before the door burst open and Clinton entered, a big man standing behind him in the corridor.

'So . . . why am I not surprised,' Clinton said glaring first at Isabel, and then at Cindy. 'Do you have any idea of what you've done - you silly, silly, girls.' He delivered the word 'girls' as if there were no more offensive form of address.

'How dare you make these accusations to the police. Did it give you pleasure to see Mr Baedeker dragged from a hospital bed and led away in handcuffs - is that what you want? Do you understand that your puny tantrums may impede the solution to the greatest threats facing mankind today?'

'We will not . . .' began Cindy, but Clinton shouted her down.

'Be quiet. You have said more than enough, believe me. Now I will tell you what is going to happen.' He paused, as if daring them to interrupt again.

'Isabel - you will retract your allegation of sexual assault. Perhaps you don't realize, because you are a minor, Mr Baedeker could go to jail for five years on a felony charge. You are not schoolchildren - this is not fun and games and hurt feelings. I can assure you Mr Baedeker is not going to jail to satisfy the ego of some immature lesbian bitch?'

'What . . .' Isabel tried to protest.

'Shut the fuck up,' Clinton shrieked. 'You do remember you're a suspect in an unlawful killing investigation in Australia, don't you? You may be interested to learn that Magnus filed extensive reports detailing his concerns for his own safety.'

'I don't believe you,' protested Isabel.

'The court most assuredly will. We will be attending that inquest and the evidence we give will be influenced by your behaviour in the next 24 hours. Paula clearly failed to properly assess your vulnerability - we know your father has a history of mental illness and your mother died when you were still a child. You are a deeply disturbed individual – but Mr Baedeker wants to help you. He is prepared to enrol you in our Harmony program. We are hoping that the company of devout believers of a similar age will give you some bedrock of certainty to rescue you from the devils that are plaguing you.'

'And if I do not agree?' asked Isabel.

'You will be acting in a way that will cause great hardship to yourself,' Clinton spoke through gritted teeth, 'and for your friend Cindy.' The threat was unambiguous. Clinton switched his attention to Cindy.

'Cindy. You will withdraw your hysterical allegation that you were raped by Mr Baedeker. We have film that will confirm you most certainly were not. Do I make myself clear?'

Cindy gasped at the implication of what Clinton was saying.

'You will be withdrawn from the Truth Division. Clearly you lack the maturity to deal with theoretic reflection without succumbing to neurosis. You too will be enrolled in the Harmony program. If this goes well, you will be allowed to re-join Paula's division, in some capacity at least. If you do not do as I indicate, you will be released from the Church. In that event I cannot speak for the integrity of the video. Of course, your actions will have a direct bearing on the well-being of your friend Isabel, who will be trying throughout that time to achieve her own recovery. I am told you have a little brother, Timmy, who is just eleven. Apparently he wants to come here to visit his big sister.'

'You hate-filled bastard . . .' spat Cindy.

'I understand why you are upset. This has been a traumatic time. Any questions?'

Cindy's face was flushed with fury, her fists locked together. Isabel looked vacant, distracted, almost care-free.

'Good. Three more things. You will be confined to campus. For your protection you will wear electronic tags. And you are forbidden to contact each other. Okay?' He rapped on the door. The blonde agent with the bulging muscles entered the room, one of the three men who had accosted Aziz in Llanthony.

'Miss Aziz, please come with me,' he held out his hand in a beckoning gesture.

Isabel stood and turned to face Cindy. 'Cindy,' she said 'there are people you can't talk to - there's no point. They only understand the language of power. This will all end okay - trust me - my father will come; I can see it - he rescues us.' Isabel pretended to a certainty that belied her inner doubt, for on this occasion, she saw nothing but darkness, and fear.

Cindy reached out and squeezed Isabel's wrist, but whether it was to offer comfort or to acknowledge its receipt, neither girl was sure.

Chapter 123: a woman knows

(10.00 am)

The sun was still low in the morning sky when after her night with Aziz in London, Chris parked the little Citroen in the car park in Grange Road next to the Malvern Theatre. She fed the meter, then hurried to the chemist on the corner of Church St. and Graham Rd.

Can't go back . . . not yet. The home that had been a refuge had become a place of torture, when she thought of what might await her on the doorstep.

She walked quickly to the toilets that she had last visited with Aziz, wondering if the association with the dramatic that some places acquire is a random effect, or some determinism was operating that she had yet to understand. Inside the 'Ladies' she occupied a cubicle and unwrapped the pregnancy test. She read the instructions and waved the wafer like stick through a tinkling flow of urine as instructed, then waited for a second line to appear next to the control line, and confirm she was pregnant.

The Michelson-Morley for mums, she joked to herself, her attempt to remain cheerful feeling increasingly futile during the seemingly interminable wait. After ten minutes, the test result was negative. *Thank God, thank God . . . and I was so certain.*

She approached Victoria Cottage with trepidation. As she feared, another small parcel was waiting for her on the doormat. She picked it up grimly, and went inside, steeling herself for the ghastly horror of what had already become her morning ritual.

Chapter 124: art resurrection

(11.05 am)

It was a few hours since Chris had left to drive back to Malvern before Aziz decided he needed escape from the melancholic claustrophobia of his room. He went outside to sit on a bench with his back to the wall in the paved front garden of the Bellevue Guest House and was staring without focus at the weeds emerging from the gaps between the tiles when he heard his name called.

'Mike.' Beaky was smiling up at him from the road below. 'You sad little fucker.'

'Beaky, what a pleasure.' Aziz reached down to offer his hand to the massive man. 'Great to see you - come on up.' Beaky ascended the steps, and Aziz gestured to him to take his place on the bench.

'So how the fuck did you make it out?'

'It's a long story. I had a fentanyl for the pain . . .'

'Fentanyl?'

'New stuff - quicker than morphine shots,' Beaky explained. 'Then I sort of half-climbed out the window supporting one of the dead guys in front of me, like he was still standing in front of the window, in the room, you follow? I was holding my sidearm so it looked like the bad guy was pointing a weapon.' Beaky stopped, curious. Aziz had seemed almost casual in his greeting.

'Not surprised to see me then?'

'Not really mate,' said Aziz.

'Okay,' said Beaky, disappointed at the economy of the response. 'Well . . . when they came in, I fired a few rounds. They blasted away for a bit then they hid round the corner. I let go of the dead guy and abseiled down the rope same way as you. It was a close run. I reckon they didn't go near him for a little while, gave me the chance to leg it.'

'You were covering for me Beaky, appreciate it.'

'I owed you, Mike.'

'You didn't, but either way . . . it's quits now,' smiled Aziz. He reached over to pat Beaky appreciatively on the shoulder.

Beaky winced. 'The shoulder hurt though, I can tell you - still fuckin' does.'

'Shit . . . sorry mate. And why did they say it was me who got clipped?' asked Aziz.

'I left your passport on the guy. I figured you needed the break. I've still got the other one you asked for - the one with you wearing the blonde rug. It's in the name of Ivor Wigan.'

'Ivor Wigan?'

'Yep - apparently his name was all they could get in a hurry.'

'I wonder why that is, Beaky?'

'Dunno - life's mysterious ways I would think. So . . . how come you're not surprised to see me then?' Beaky had reflected on it while he was talking.

'When I heard they'd slotted someone they said was me, at first I thought they'd got you, but then I remembered they said there were four bodies and a terrorist, but we left five of them - if you were still in there it would have been six.'

'You always were the thinker, Mike,' said Beaky. Aziz stood up and leaned wearily on the post with the shabby sign on it that boasted the name 'Bellevue', though the only 'view' was of a dilapidated pub across the road.

'Are you still on for grabbing Lineker at this TV show . . . with your shoulder injured like that . . . it's just two days to go.'

'Sure. I'll be fine. Let me know exactly where and when?' asked Beaky.

'Will do.' said Aziz. His tone and demeanour had suddenly become distant, suggesting he was preoccupied with something else, as if the drizzle of the grey London morning had moistened not just his jacket, but reached inside to dampen his spirits too.

Beaky looked at his friend, wondering at his mood. Aziz sensed it. 'Sorry I'm not more cheerful mate - it's just I've had some news that's got me worried.'

'Which is . . .?' asked Beaky.

'The sick fuck who heads up the internet Church has been arrested for sexual assault of a minor. It said the girl he assaulted was from Tasmania.'

'Shit, is she okay?' asked Beaky.

'Well that's the worry. The news report said PORTAL is concerned about her mental health and they've issued a request for any family to join her over there as quickly as possible.'

'And that's just you, right?' asked Beaky.

'It's me they're after - no doubt - they threatened Isabel even before they heard me say I wanted to kill their chief. Now they've got her - they want me too.'

'What'll you do Mike?'

'I think 'Ivor Wigan' has to hop on a plane to California.'

'Shit Mike - 'Ivor Wigan' - sorry mate - never noticed.' He gave a hearty chuckle, controlling it quickly when Aziz glared across at him.

'You've got to laugh mate - what a fuckin' show. C'mon, let's go inside and you can get me a brew,' said Beaky, wrapping his good arm around Aziz as they turned back to the boarding house, its peeling paint suddenly given texture by a lateral sun, leaden and faint, that was leaking through a jagged tear in the featureless sky.

September 28th

Chapter 125: stateside

(USA)

Understanding that there are other ways to express resolve than through action, Aziz was versed in the art of apparent acquiescence - and biding his time. Now the bustle had subsided Aziz thought back to his childhood, as he often did when seeking sanctuary from the present, remembering the beauty of the countryside and the purity of a childhood optimism uncluttered by regret.

He remembered too the pig who when he approached would throw herself on the ground in front of him, offering her bristling belly to the stick he used to scratch her, her parallel rows of teats quickly attracting a line of pink miniatures, jostling for a feed. He pictured again the myriad tiny crab-like insects who lived on her vastness, redistributing themselves amongst the stacked terraces of her skin, as he poked and itched at her dirt-spattered neck. He smiled at the memory, savouring the honesty of mud and mothering, beyond artifice, beyond the hollow ring of speech.

'Mr Wigan, or should I be addressing you as Mr Aziz?' A different man, a man in a suit, richer, smoother than the first official was talking to him, his face animated with a blandness that suggested even the vestige of irony had forsaken him.

Wanker, thought Aziz.

'Yes, that's my name,' Aziz replied, for a moment relishing the straightforward ease of confessing common knowledge, bypassing the first line of defence his training had taught him was essential. The man turned and left the room.

Aziz . . . a four letter word . . . is that why people find it so offensive. Aziz smiled to himself. *At least he left me that, more than he left mum.*

Already fatherless, Aziz had found himself without a mother too, if a mother's love is judged not just by physical care, but by her valuing the qualities of her child.

Did you ever really know me? he wondered. *After I started to remind you of him?*

He thought back to the elaborate theorizing of his shrink. The man had suggested that his mother's animosity had given Aziz an outer resilience, but had left the boy guarding his true nature, fearful that something about his inner self was repugnant and the closer he became to others, the more likely they were to betray him. Aziz had found it plausible but had not anticipated his feelings for Chris Reynolds would unlock this turmoil and replace the bravado of the unloved with the diffident vulnerability of the lover. Aziz could sense the change and was exhilarated by it, though he knew enough to recognize that both were rooted in fear.

The first immigration official re-entered the room; this time he stayed. 'Today must be your lucky day - apparently you're expected at a place called PORTAL. They're sending a helicopter over to pick you up. Would you like a cup of coffee while we wait?'

'One sugar, thank you,' said Aziz, pleased that so far, everything was going to plan.

Chapter 126: tired of waiting

(California)

Aziz estimated it was only a few hours since they had cuffed his wrists and, even before the helicopter was airborne, slipped a bag over his head. He had felt the warmth of the afternoon and smelt the jacarandas when the machine landed, a brief respite of comfort before he had been bundled inside, the bite of the air-conditioning adding a chemical note to the atmosphere, like the chlorine of an indoor swimming pool.

They had beaten him and demanded to be told where he had left the watch on which he had recorded the conversation with Baedeker. They had threatened him with what they would do to Isabel if he did not tell them what they wanted to know. Then they beat him again. When he said nothing, they had dragged him to the room where the music played.

Cheerful heartfelt singing was accompanied by the rhythms of happy clapping. Rising from the music, the poised quasi-melodious singsong voice of a preacher started calmly, reassuringly itemizing the stresses and pitfalls of modern living, and slowly built to a climax of frenzied evangelical zeal. Aziz listened to bits, but rapidly tuned out from the content, judging from the tone that its purpose was not for him. The volume was cleverly maintained loud enough to reveal its intention to irritate, a fact which on its own succeeded in annoying him. When mercifully a pause suggested the sermon had ended, it began again from the beginning.

After several repeats, Aziz finally managed to ignore the sound but the loop stopped, breaking into an intermittent sequence, as if the tape was slipping. He wondered if somehow they had linked it to his biorhythms and he knew without much reflection, that the intent was to stop him from sleeping, and that the interference was working.

He got up to bang on the door and shout, as much from a sense that he should play his part, as in any real expectation that his actions would have effect.

'*Don't resist* . . .' he thought, '*resist nothing.*' He knew his condition was deteriorating, but with nothing against which to measure time other than the beating of his heart, he did not know how quickly. He had no plan, no inkling of what he intended and he denied himself even images of his newfound lover, choosing to ration memory of her for leaner times, and not reduce their effectiveness by overuse.

Instead he chose a line from an Eric Burdon song as a mantra to encourage a shut-down of his mind and imagination. 'Old cop, young cop, feel alright - on a warm San Franciscan night.'

Again, and again and again.

Chapter 127: even the good times are bad

(10.00 am)

When Chris tapped on the front door of the cottage in White Leaved Oak, it was Janbir Chatterjee who answered the door.

'Dr Reynolds, so pleased to see you.'

'Good day Dr Chatterjee. Is Nandini in?'

'She is expecting you, yes. I'd like you to know how thrilled I am to be working with Dr Grafton - we've documented the design of the Interferometer and now we're doing a lot of testing,' continued Chatterjee. 'We would appreciate your input into the calibration calculations. I understand the show is tomorrow very early in the morning, so time is of the essence.'

Initially surprised at Chatterjee's burst of enthusiasm, Chris replied wearily. 'Yes, a four o'clock start for me I'm afraid. I'm meeting with Bill - Dr Grafton - at one o'clock this afternoon - perhaps you should join us.'

'Sadly, I cannot Dr Reynolds – I am afraid I have a meeting already arranged at that time,' Chatterjee replied, the animation in his voice producing a squeaking emphasis on the higher tones. 'But I can speak with Dr Grafton after you have met with him alone . . . ah here is Nandini.'

'Dear girl - how lovely you look - I told you henna would work on you,' cried Nandini as she approached. 'Let the poor woman in Janbir. Tea dear? Come through to the kitchen, and we will have a chin-wag,' she said.

Nandini led Chris through to the kitchen of terra cotta tiles and oiled oak cabinets, its rustic atmosphere enhanced by miniature Indian paintings on the walls and a subtle aroma of spice wafted by the warmth of the Aga. The pastel blend of lilac/purple and green light that suffused the room was filtered through jasmine climbers clinging to the windows as if eager to peer in and share the aura of domestic welcome that seemed to surround its mistress.

'I took a test, Nandini. I'm not pregnant.'

'Oh . . .' began Nandini.

'I'm so relieved. This might sound crazy, but I believe the baby knew this wasn't the right time, and decided not to come after all,' Chris sighed, surprised that she found the thought so depressing.

'Probably wanted a bit more clarity on the father, I wouldn't wonder dear,' said Nandini.

Chris looked at her levelly, deciding not to pursue the subject. 'But I am in love,' she announced, unsure whether to be embarrassed by an assertion she had never made so emphatically before, to herself or anyone else.

'Joy, joy, joy . . . how wonderful!' Nandini started spinning. Her braided hair rose elegantly from her back as she clapped her hands together, before she stopped, sank to her knees in front of Chris, and taking Chris' hands in hers, kissed them lightly on the fingertips.

'I'm so happy for you. Sometimes one must simply wait for the shadows of self-doubt to lift and reveal the sunshine of happiness,' she paused. 'So they have found the good Dr Lineker?'

'No Nandini - no,' Chris faltered, her cheerful sharing of good news suddenly seeming more like a scandalous heartlessness. 'No - that's still a nightmare. They've cut off six of his fingers. They post them to me. Every morning . . . it's . . . well . . . it's . . .' She could hear the hoarseness starting in her voice.

'How wicked. How can people be so cruel?' exclaimed Nandini. She gave Chris a brief hug. 'But you are in love you were saying?' There was a frosty seriousness about her. 'Again.'

'Yes, he's called Mike Aziz.' Chris was hesitant, the earlier mood shattered by the thought of the nightmare that was Lineker's waking reality, and by the disapproval that Nandini's expression did little to disguise.

'That is the Italian boy right?' asked Nandini sternly.

'French, Nandini - French. But no, not Kim - this is someone else.' *I knew Nandini wouldn't approve . . . am I behaving badly?* Chris wondered anxiously. 'Mike's in his thirties - he's an ex-soldier - he's half English and half Lebanese - he's just adorable - so hunky and sweet. He loves me too.' Again, she seemed surprised by the words that had tumbled from her mouth.

'A soldier - what do you have in common with a soldier?' Nandini demanded.

'He's not crude and violent or anything like that, in fact he's quite shy seeming.'

'Maybe it's because neither of you really belongs anywhere.'

The remark shocked Chris, and the possibility that Nandini had stumbled on an unfamiliar truth.

'Does he know you were in a sex film?' Nandini continued.

'Oh . . . you know about that?'

'Who doesn't? Janbir told me everyone at work is talking about it. Of course, Janbir hasn't watched it, he's assured me.'

'I was filmed by that awful Church group - unknown to me of course – trying to blackmail me. So I figured I'd just go ahead and publish it. Take the wind out of their sails so to speak - I've had to pay a price,' Chris finished ruefully.

'You should sue them, dear, sue them.'

'I can't just yet. They're helping to get Ian back - they've paid for the TV show and everything . . .'

'So the soldier knows you were in this film?'

'Mike,' Chris reminded her.

'Yes, this Mr Mike - you say he loves you.'

'Yes Nandini. We just seem . . . 'connected' to each other . . . it's hard to explain . . . he seems to need me too.'

'For cooking, cleaning, and rumpy-pumpy, and for mummy to kiss it better. They're all the same - and we fall for it - even educated women like us.'

The bile in Nandini's voice disturbed Chris, the more so because it was unexpected. 'Nandini - you sound unhappy.'

'I'm sorry dear,' said Nandini. 'It's just Janbir - he's so secretive these days - spends all his time at home on the computer - playing with his 'share portfolio,' he says.'

Chris looked out of the window and for a moment the beauty of the garden was tainted. She saw the exuberance of the honeysuckle, and wondered if it too had denied the sun to its companions, until even the brightest amongst them had withered in its shadows, just as something seemed to have robbed Nandini of her zest for life.

'Says he'll be able to retire soon. Then he's always off for meetings in London - never offers to take me - and he seems so worried all the time, at least when we're alone,' Nandini concluded forlornly 'Where once was light, is only darkness.'

They sat in silence, Chris reflecting that the people she had relied on most were now reliant upon her, and what that might imply. Suddenly the way ahead seemed clear and with her resolve, came defiance.

For starters I'll decide myself what's right and wrong. And I'm not apologizing to anyone for falling in love. It was exhilarating, and a little scary, the feeling that there was nowhere to hide, or anyone to shelter behind.

'Why don't we go out for a cup of coffee in town now and again?' Chris asked, keen to divert her friend's melancholy mood.

'Yes that would be lovely dear, I'd love to. And you can tell me all about your work on 'bore hole gravitational anomalies'. Nandini smiled warmly at her friend.

'And your new Mr Mike'.

Chapter 128: tired of wanting

(California)

After a while, they came in and hauled him to his feet, leaving Aziz marooned in a standing position arms outstretched, suspended from above, the tail of the rope tied around his neck with the bag still over his head. Several hours later, they cut him down and beat him again, this time leaving him on the floor, hands tied behind him.

Aziz did not need his eyes to appreciate the monkey high on the beams above him. It was a tiny creature, perfectly reproduced in miniature, each component of its face completely different yet unmistakably equivalent to its human counterpart. Its head reoriented frequently, like a sparrow, the precision and rapidity of the movement reflecting its scale, but unlike the similarly-sized bird, the monkey would occasionally vibrate with a frantic burst of scratching as it strummed on the hair of its midriff.

Aziz felt comforted. He felt himself thinning, his spirit growing more and more distant, fatigue rising as a fog to insulate him from the incessant noise, and a weary calm cushioning him from the anxiety that on the edge of consciousness, sometimes buzzed for his attention. For a while he was that monkey, looking down at the supine human body beneath it, enjoying the energy, the separation, the immediacy of its preoccupation.

When the men came in to beat him again, he offered no resistance. He saw no point. Fearing he might be hurt permanently, he didn't wish to provoke them, trusting in his resilience and the power of the human body to recover, given the time and the space. They untied him, and removed the bag from his head, leaving him on the blood-smeared floor. One eye was swollen and near shut. He turned painfully to lie on his back. The little monkey had gone.

There was a larger monkey in its place or maybe, he thought, an ape. An orangutan. It had a kindly concerned demeanour, relaxed and amiable. He reached out an arm to extend a finger. It swung down to hang beneath the beam, its own arm extended, and when its finger touched his, he felt a jolt of love, a surging well of compassion for himself, for the world, for the futility and fragility of existence. The great ape came down, cradling him in its arms, rocking him like a child.

Is this what I am, thought Aziz, *no more than pain?*

Sinking to his knees, Aziz began to pray.

'I have tried to please. I have looked for forgiveness in service. I have been loyal to the causes of others. I have helped the powerful, sometimes against the weak. Lord, rid me of this guilt I cannot explain. Free me from my fear.'

The tears came slowly at first and then in a flood of feeling. The great ape supported him as he rocked to and fro, then, hearing a disturbance at the door, climbed methodically onto Aziz's shoulders and up to its perch above.

A narrow trap opened in the door, and an eye peered in briefly. The guard made some notes on his pad, adjusted his earpiece to improve the sound quality from his player, and returned to his room.

Chapter 129: sleight of hand

(11.00 am)

'Beautiful sunny weather this morning isn't it?' said Detective Ben Simmons. 'Thanks for coming in Dr Reynolds, I know you must be busy.'

'Yes, I am . . . there's a lot to prepare and I've got a very early start tomorrow; really more like the middle of the night,' Chris replied. 'How can I help you?'

'Follow me ma'am please.' Simmons raised the hinged part of the counter that separated him from Chris, and slipped through to join her in the foyer. He knocked briefly on a door marked 'Interview Room' and receiving no reply from inside it, opened the door and gestured for her to enter. Chris sat one side of the desk, and Simmons the other. 'Not so long since you were last here . . .' began the young policeman.

'And why am I here now Detective?' Chris asked impatiently.

'It's about that finger we found in your fridge, and the second one you dropped off when you picked up your car.'

Chris felt an immediate shock of panic. There were the other fingers in her freezer that she had not mentioned to the police.

'Turns out, they're from different people. Forensics took DNA samples from Dr Lineker's kitchen. The first one belongs to Dr Lineker. The second one doesn't.'

'What are you saying Detective?'

'The tests match the second finger to a torso pulled out of the Grand Union Canal in Willesden. It belongs to a Brazilian drug mule who went missing about a week ago. We haven't found the head yet.'

'Oh - I see,' Chris was surprised, unsure how to react. 'I'll bring the others in,' she said. 'How long will it take you to test them?'

'The others?' asked the detective. 'What 'others'?'

'Another four - they've arrived every morning,' she said.

'Four!! Jesus Christ, Dr Reynolds. Why haven't you reported this before?'

'I've been very busy - I've stored them in the freezer for micro-surgery.'

The detective was wondering whether to make anything of this. He decided against it. 'Okay – we'll call by to pick them up within the hour if you don't mind. It takes about a week for the results to come back.'

'So Ian might have lost only one finger . . . this could be wonderful news couldn't it?'

'Every cloud Dr Reynolds . . . every cloud.'

She was heading for the exit.

Simmons suddenly remembered he had been dealing with a celebrity. 'And good luck tomorrow with the show.'

Chapter 130: monkey business

Two men in suits were standing over Aziz.

'So this is the scary hairy SAS,' sneered the guard, 'fucking pansy.' He kicked Aziz hard in the stomach. The orangutan grimaced, looking concerned.

'It's okay sir, you can enter now,' the other man said loudly, 'we have a zero threat situation.'

The door opened with a theatrical bang. Baedeker swept in.

'We meet again Mr Aziz.'

Baedeker looked good, authoritative, in control, his deep tan shading to slightly orange in the subtle greenish hue of the fluorescent lights.

'Last time you recorded our private conversation - that was really very rude. And you threatened to kill me.' Baedeker's expression switched from stern to confiding. 'I've come to see you because I wanted you to know your daughter withdrew the allegations she made against me. So did the other girl. Did you know your daughter is a lesbian - that's why she hates men?' His face was close up to Aziz, sneering and goading.

'I am about to leave for the UK and when I am there I will be meeting your friend Dr Reynolds. She is a beautiful woman. I'd like to get to know her better, and I am told her video confirms she is a woman of passion - passion for men. I wanted you to know this.'

Baedeker's head was slightly raised, his face suffused with haughty animation, as if he was addressing a crowd from the pulpit. 'I cannot be hurt by the servants of the Devil - God is on my side - I am but an instrument of his will.' He turned his attention back to Aziz, a crumpled bloodied heap on the floor. 'I wanted you to know all of this.'

Aziz squinted up at Baedeker's gloating face, the white teeth brilliant in the symmetry of his smile. Beyond him, as if looking over Baedeker's shoulder, the dark outline of a great ape was staring down from the rafters.

The gorilla was huge, its head tilted as if trying to make better sense of what was going on below. It held its massive arms wide to either side, dark eyes flashing, and yellowed teeth occasionally revealed in a snarling mask of fury. Suddenly, as if it had made up its mind, the gorilla beat its great chest, the thundering echoing through the room.

Oh shit, thought Aziz. *Trouble time . . .*

Falling in slow-motion, the beast leapt toward Aziz, curving out to him, looming ever larger through space, as primal and savage as nature itself. Aziz's chest was crushed to nothing, the hollow shell of his body folding away as the huge weight pinned him to the floor. The spasms were immediate, wracking him with convulsions. Aziz moaned with pain as power exploded in his every cell, an orgasmic flood of energy contorting him like a spring that flipped him to his feet.

The first kick to the shin of one of the guards felled the man in a sea of agony, his pain peremptorily extinguished by a second kick to his head. In the same moment the other man, unconscious from a chop to the throat, crashed heavily to the floor, one leg twisting away from his body, with the arbitrary awkwardness of flotsam jettisoned by a subsided flood.

Baedeker's mouth was already open with surprise when Aziz grabbed his balls, yanking and twisting the scrotum, the pain so immediate and total that Baedeker's voice was strangled in his throat as effectively as his testes were crushed in their little sack of skin. His expression remained cast in horror, the interplay of excruciating pain and utter panic suspending him in what might have been an impersonation of a gargoyle, the grotesque devil-mask that stares lifelessly from the gutter of a medieval Cathedral, but in fact was the human face of trauma.

Aziz led him by the balls, slowly toward the door, confiding in his ear with an almost tender whisper. 'We're going to free my daughter. I want you to know that. Then we're all going to London in your shiny Gulfstream 550 - I want you to know that. And most of all, you should never take God for granted - my guess is He would like me to mention that too.'

we're all going to London in your shiny Gulfstream 550 - I want you to know that. And most of all, you should never take God for granted - my guess is He would like me to mention that too.'

Chapter 131: ten green bottles

(California)

As they walked across the quadrangle to the dormitory wing, Aziz held Baedeker's hand. It was the same hand Clinton Schwartz had held just two days earlier, only this time, the circumstance was different. Baedeker's little finger was bent over, nestled in Aziz's palm, ready for Aziz to crack it into two with little more than a flex of his wrist. Were it not for the security men following them from a distance, the incongruous pair could easily have been mistaken for a couple of gay lovers out for a stroll, enjoying the tranquillity of a sublime Californian mid-afternoon.

Isabel was shocked when she opened the door, cringing backwards as she saw Baedeker, but seeing from his pallor and deflated reticence that this was a man transformed from the strutting and intimidating presence she had learnt to fear.

'Isabel,' said Aziz. 'It's me - your Dad.'

She looked at him closely, unsure how to respond, surprised at the numbness that offered no guidance on what would be appropriate.

'I've been expecting you . . .' she said, her voice tailing off as she realized she had anticipated her rescue not with the dispassionate vision of a seer, but with the faith of a little girl. Suddenly Isabel burst into tears, but Aziz, prickling with failure, could only look away.

'We must get Cindy,' said Isabel, wiping her eyes with back of her hands, as the shell of brittle independence quickly repaired. 'I'll take you to her.'

Minutes later the party of four were moving steadily across the white marble gravel toward the helicopter.

'There's a sniper on the roof. Tell him to lower his weapon,' said Aziz quietly to Baedeker.

'How can I possibly do that . . .?' began Baedeker, the habit of control reasserting itself.

The small cracking sound was barely audible. Mouthing emptiness like a gold fish flipped from its tank and gasping for air, Baedeker was sinking toward the ground but was prevented from reaching it by Aziz's support under his arm. Almost affectionately, Aziz now cupped a different finger in his fist.

'Get back, get back, do what he wants,' screamed Baedeker, 'for God's sake get back.'

September 29th

Chapter 132: the show begins

(5.00 am)

'An inferno a million times the mass of the earth – a miasma of inconceivable heat and a boiling vortex of orange incandescence bubbling from a billion hydrogen bombs a second, roil and churn in an Armageddon beyond imagining. With the power to transmute gas into gold, and realize the wildest dreams of alchemists not yet born, this is the energy of creation. Its light can challenge infinity and pierce the blackness of the void as far as the furthest reaches of the Universe.'

The voice-over attempted to lend a sense of scale to the image of the face of the sun appearing on the back drop framing the stage while, speaking last minute instructions into a tiny microphone held next to his mouth, the producer stared at the monitor and began the countdown on the fingers of his hand to queue the crowd for its applause.

'Imagine a hundred billion galaxies, each with a hundred billion stars,' the narrator's voice continued, rich and deep, the booming declaration of the blockbuster trailer with its familiar invitation to another dimension.

'And from this tiny speck we know as earth, the human mind can travel to the furthest reaches of the universe and unlock its secrets.' Now the screen was showing Saturn tilted to enhance its unlikely rings of gas, the apparently solid multi-coloured bands circling its equator like hula-hoops around a circus artist.

A dapper figure appeared on stage, the audience clapped, on cue. He gave a graceful twirl and a skip, sliding to a halt on the last beat of the introductory drum roll.

'Hi everybody.'

The audience cheered.

'This is Anton Belluci - your host for another and very special episode of TruthSayers, where we divide 'myth' from 'fact', separate 'wishful thinking' from the 'absolute gospel', and separate the 'bull' from the 'shh, whisper who dares.' The crowd roared its approval.

'It's just five o'clock in the morning here in downtown UK so let me remind you the show is going out live to our US audience, and can I thank you for turning out in such numbers. Especially for a such a chilly start to the day here in little ol' London.'

Again, on cue, the crowd shouted its encouragement.

'Let me introduce our technical moderator, Dr Williams from the Jet Propulsion Laboratory at NASA,' continued Belluci. 'Dr Williams is here to referee what has been accurately described as the 'Flight of the Century'. Let us take a moment to 'give it up' for our sponsors here tonight - PORTAL - a New Church for a New Age.' The audience clapped and cheered.

'Can you give us a bit of background please Dr Williams? Can you tell us what we will be seeing here tonight on TruthSayers, where the 'sword of science' will slice through the 'web of wonder', and the 'beam of truth' will illuminate the 'dark clouds' of superstition?'

'Indeed I can, thank you so much,' replied Dr Williams. 'Time and space,' he continued, 'the nature of reality itself, this is our subject tonight, the ultimate test of a century old theory that transformed our understanding of the natural universe as radically as Newton had done two hundred years before. The man whose name is synonymous with genius, Einstein - Albert Einstein - the man who gave us the Theory of Relativity, today is challenged by a team from the Malvern Research Institute in the UK. I have to declare my hand here - I fully expect the Theory of Relativity will be vindicated here tonight. But,' he paused, '. . . and this is a 'but' on which the future of the world may well hang.' The audience were hushed, waiting expectantly, 'this is Science, ladies and gentlemen and,' he paused again, '. . . the evidence will have the final say. I am here in my capacity as moderator to make sure there is no cheating or deception, and everything is done by the book.'

Taking instructions from concealed earpieces, the several employees planted amongst the crowd led them to cheer and clap again.

'Thank you, thank you, Dr Williams. I'm pleased to see we have so many truth seekers in the audience here tonight,' Belluci observed, beaming warmly at the assembled hordes.

'These latter day heretics from the UK, from the same town I'm told where radar was first invented, have a radical new theory - they believe that despite its many successes over a hundred years, Einstein's science was - and I quote - 'a colossal bungle.''

The audience cheered.

'Representing Einstein I will call Dr Arjun Patel, Professor of Theoretical Physics from Delhi University and opposing him, better known perhaps as a recent YouTube star but appearing here in her other role, her day job, the sensational, the stunning, the super sexy scientist, Senior Research Assistant Dr Chris Reynolds representing the Malvern Research Institute.' The crowd was jeering and cheering. The screen flashed a quick overlay of Professor Patel and Chris Reynolds, each encouraged by their minders to wave energetically and grin at the camera.

'So something to look forward to,' Belluci calmed the crowd. 'If I can just say that none of our experts here tonight are members of PORTAL - 'a better way for a better future' - and success for either side will not imply endorsement by the Church of anything else about our guests, for example, how they might choose to spend their leisure time.' He paused, raising his eyebrows in a crude caricature of disapproval. 'I think you all know what I might mean. So while our experts are putting their finishing touches to their arguments, or perhaps their make-up,' again, on cue, the crowd hooted with derision, 'let me first call on Dr Williams to give a brief rundown of some of the science behind this.'

Back stage, Chris was annoyed. 'For God's sake,' she said, turning to protest to Benny Wiseman the producer, 'was that really necessary? It's bad enough wearing this dress.'

'I'm sorry Dr Reynolds - PORTAL insisted on it - they believe it will help audience figures if you are presented as a .. . well . . . you know . . . a celebrity.'

'And where the hell is Ian?' continued Chris, 'surely he should be here by now?'

'We've been assured Dr Lineker will make an appearance later in the show,' said Wiseman. 'You're expected to kick it off - better for ratings believe me.'

Grafton was walking toward them quickly, gesturing to Chris. 'The machine's ready, we finished the installation checks, Janbir is still over there now.' He was fidgety and nervous, clearly excited by the whole experience. Clinton Schwartz too, was approaching, carefully picking his way through the cables and drapes. He was accompanied by a fit-looking man in a dark suit, with the signature haircut of the PORTAL security team.

'Dr Reynolds, long time no see,' said Clinton as he drew near. 'You look absolutely lovely.'

Chris was wearing a simple black evening dress, two narrowing bands of material crossing her stomach before passing over her shoulders as straps, loose and low enough to clearly emphasise her breasts, precariously concealed behind the flimsy fabric.

'Mr Baedeker would approve.'

Chapter 133: who's who

(5.10 am)

'I'm wearing this ridiculous dress because I believe it will improve the chances of securing Dr Lineker's safety - not to impress Mr Baedeker, if he were able to be with us.' Chris rolled her eyes and shook her head from side to side in a gesture of undisguised contempt. 'Though I understand from the news the reason he is not here is that he has been detained for assault on a child.'

'His accusers withdrew their hysterical allegations and Mr Baedeker was released immediately without charge.' Clinton's face reddened as he struggled to contain his anger. 'We're taking legal action against the TV station who reported this calumny and the corrupt police officer who took money to spread these lies.'

'Ahem. Let's worry about the matter in hand shall we?' Keen to defuse the rising tension, and impatient to ask the question that had preoccupied him since he first arrived, Grafton had ostentatiously cleared his throat. 'I'm Dr Grafton, acting as technical advisor to Dr Reynolds,' said Grafton.

'Dr Grafton, we've spoken on the phone - Clinton Schwartz, personal assistant to Mr Baedeker,' said Clinton, extending his hand. 'Pleased to meet you in person sir.' Clinton appeared to have completely recovered his composure.

'Likewise I'm sure,' replied Grafton. 'Is Cindy Lopez here by any chance?' he asked, as casually as he could muster.

'No, Miss Lopez didn't qualify for a trip at this point in time.' Clinton's delivery was smooth and relaxed.

'Oh . . . I see.' Only Chris noticed Grafton's disappointment, as he made his excuses and left to re-join Janbir Chatterjee still hunched over the Interferometer, on the same stage as Belluci, but hidden from the audience by a screen.

'So - what's the latest on Ian?' demanded Chris.

Clinton's companion volunteered a reply. 'I'm Bradley Hicks ma'am - CIAO liaison officer for PORTAL. We're working closely with the Brits on this - we'll be ready ma'am, don't worry about that.' His voice was deep and measured. 'Something I need to ask you - would you happen to know a big man with a prominent nose by any chance? He was trying to gain access to see you. He didn't have a pass. He said you would know him as 'Beaky?''

'I know of him, yes,' replied Chris. 'Where is he; can I meet him?'

''Fraid not ma'am. He . . . he got away.'

'Well that was not very clever of you Mr Hicks was it? He might have been of great assistance to us in recovering Ian,' replied Chris.

'Perhaps ma'am, perhaps,' continued the agent, an unattractive smirk on his face. 'By the way, can I say that was a smart move with your YouTube angle - gave our profilers a real surprise - they never expected that one.'

'Your reaction is none of my business and certainly no interest to me whatsoever.' Chris continued speaking clearly and emphatically. 'The absolute priority here is Ian's safety - we need to be properly coordinated. The other side will go with their vacuum experiment first. I will demand that Dr Lineker is called so as he can renounce our physics - or that is what we want his captors to believe. It's vital that as soon as he shows, you make him secure. As soon as he is safe, we can continue with our version of the experiment using fibre optics. When we run our experiment I would expect the 'shit to hit the fan', to borrow from your American vernacular, so he must be secured before our experiment. I must be told he is safe. Is that clear?'

'Don't worry ma'am,' said the agent. 'Our people are in place to grab him as soon as they produce him. RAW are notoriously slippery, but between us and the Brits we've got enough boots on the ground to cover whatever move they make.'

'RAW?' asked Chris. 'And who or what is that?'

'The Indian Secret Service,' said the agent.

'The Indian Secret Service?' queried Chris. 'I thought we were dealing with a commercial corporation - Sampatti.'

'How so Dr Reynolds?' asked Bradley Hicks.

'Sampatti are an Indian multinational bidding to build the next Hadron Collider. They bought out Konkreton, a Russian company who were originally chasing the concrete part of the contract. Ian was seized by Russians, with a link to Konkreton.'

'Interesting theory ma'am,' said the agent. 'Of course most governments have a role in commercial deals if they're big enough – and international trade is always a legitimate concern. Government departments and the secret service can sometimes overlap, especially in developing nations you understand. A connection between RAW and your Sampatti is quite plausible.'

'And why do you think it's RAW who have got Ian?" asked Chris.

'We don't know who has 'got' your scientist friend ma'am, but routine surveillance of the Indian embassy in London uncovered a link between embassy staff and Dr Lineker's kidnappers. As we all know, 'embassy staff' can be code for security agents with diplomatic immunity. In this case the Brits cross-checked a series of calls between a known RAW agent at the embassy and a man called Emelienko, the original bag-carrier. Seems that this Emelienko guy had a taste for sleaze - drugs, girls and gambling, made him easy to follow. But the whole operation went kind of pear-shaped. Emelienko had an air ticket to the West Indies in his pocket but he never got to use it. His goons turned on him when he bet their wages on a roulette wheel - and lost. We also know that since Emelienko dropped out of the picture, liaison for this show has been through a man who sounds of Indian origin, but we haven't been able yet to establish exactly who he is. What's the source of your information about this Collider contract, if I may ask?' added the agent.

'I just googled the right questions,' Chris replied.

Bradley raised a sardonic eyebrow, registering no other emotion at her lack of cooperation. 'In case you're wondering, ma'am, that would be the same Emelienko who was murdered by a renegade ex-soldier a couple of days ago,' Bradley observed, affecting a casualness inconsistent with the stare he had fixed on Chris. 'We think maybe this 'Beaky' who seemed reluctant to answer our questions, was one of the two-man team who assassinated Emelienko. We're not sure why exactly – they killed a bunch of Emelienko's gang at the same time – maybe they were after Dr Lineker. Our people are looking forward to interviewing the other guy . . . what's his name - Mr Aziz isn't it?' Bradley's pretence at uncertainty was unconvincing. 'I'm told you've been seen together a couple of times. He's a good friend of yours as I understand it?'

'I can assure you, Mike Aziz was not responsible for Emelienko's death and if I may observe it, 'our people' as you put it, or the CIA, as I think they are more widely known, seem to have a poor track record in keeping up with Mr Aziz.' Her condescension was short-lived.

'Perhaps you've not heard, Dr Reynolds?' asked Clinton, twisting his lips in a parody of a smile.

'Mr Aziz has been interviewed at out headquarters in Pasadena and even as we speak is being returned to the UK in Mr Baedeker's personal jet. They will be landing in less than an hour at which point when the security situation is resolved, he will be handed over to the appropriate authorities.'

The news hit Chris like a hammer blow, her head spun and she felt suddenly nauseous and dizzy. A smartly dressed young woman was hurrying toward her.

'On in two minutes Dr Reynolds.'

Chapter 134: vacuum wars

(5.20 am)

'Let me talk you through what we're doing here today - and some of the issues in the science,' began Dr Williams. He beamed at the audience, exuding an aura of relaxed authority. 'The proposition we're testing is that whatever the relative motion between the source and the receiver of light, does light always travel at the same speed? Just dwell on that innocent sounding question for a moment.' He stopped, staring at the audience, allowing the words to sink in. 'Nothing else behaves like that, certainly not in our everyday world.' Again he was silent as he strolled back and forth across the stage, poised, in control. 'It's as if I have a magic ball and however fast you run away from me, it will always overtake you at the same speed. You could be sitting in a jet travelling at 20,000 km/h and if, as you zoom by, I throw it at you when you are just 100 m away, it would catch you as quickly as if you were sitting stationary at the end of a 100 m race track, even though you're rushing away from me at colossal speed.'

'Surely that is not what we would expect,' observed Belluci.

'Absolutely correct' replied Dr Williams. 'That's why there is so much resistance to Special Relativity. It does appear completely counter-intuitive.'

'And this is what all the scientists say is true, is that right? asked Belluci.

'Yes, and we will prove it to you today, it is what is happening,' Prof Patel, a small Indian man with a bald head and glasses piped up, eager to secure his own contribution to the debate.

'That's what the Interferometer is for,' he said. 'It's throwing light in two directions at right angles to each other to check if there is any difference in their speeds. Imagine one of the beams of light is in line with the direction of orbit of the earth so we can test if the light speed is affected by the orbit speed of the earth. If there isn't an 'ether', a fixed frame of reference, then we won't detect any difference in light speed whatever the relative motion of the source and receiver,' Prof Patel added.

'So same speed is a 'Yes' to Mr Einstein. Different speed is a 'Yes' for Dr Reynolds. But why is any of this a big deal? Why hasn't this been done and dusted a long time ago?' asked Belluci.

'Good question,' replied Dr Williams. 'Many would argue it has - well most actually - including me - I have to say. The problem is that the difference, if there were one, would be incredibly small because the speed of orbit at 30 kilometres per second is so tiny compared with the speed of light at 300,000 kilometres per second. Just 0.01%. Solving the problem of how to detect such an incredibly small effect is what makes the Interferometer one of the most ingenious bits of experimental technology ever invented. Way back in 1887, the Michelson Morley experiment named after the two guys who put it together, became one of the most famous experimental tests of all time,' finished Williams.

'Prof Patel - over to you to explain how your machine is put together and what we should look out for,' Belluci gestured to Dr Patel.

'Thank you Mr Belluci and good evening ladies and gentlemen,' began Patel, pleased to be finally offered the floor in his own right.

'Light is bounced back by a mirror to its source from the end of the identical arms of the Interferometer set at 90 degrees to each other. If light travels at different speeds in each of the arms, it will put the beams out of phase, like waves in water from two stones dropped simultaneously cancelling or adding to each other as they fan out and meet.' That's why this wonderful device is known as an 'Interferometer', it measures interference.'

'And if we don't see any difference in the speeds, we see what?' asked Belluci.

'This is what made the experiment all the more remarkable in the history of scientific advance,' intervened Dr Williams. 'It found nothing.' Patel looked cross, staring at Williams with undisguised annoyance.

''Nothing' you say, Dr Williams?' repeated Belluci, extracting every last ounce of drama from the unnatural occurrence of a non-event.

'Rather I would say - a 'null result,'' interjected Prof Patel, insisting on being heard. 'We are looking for either of two results, 'bands of dark' on a screen if the light waves are out of phase and have added together, or a white screen if the light beams have travelled at the same speed and remained in phase.

Sensing this was not riveting TV and anxious that they were losing the crowd, Belluci intervened, 'While we allow the machine to run,' Belluci started, 'I understand we have a short film to shed some more light,' he smirked, 'on the background to tonight's contest. Over to you Dr Williams.'

'Thank you Mr Belluci.' Williams was looking pleased with himself again. 'This clip was put together at NASA as part of its educational program. The film will show how Relativity has been crucial to our understanding of the universe. Just consider, without Relativity we wouldn't even have the GPS system and of course, central to the Special Theory of Relativity is the fact that light travels at only one speed,' explained Dr Williams. 'Relativity is regarded as one of the greatest achievements of the human intellect ever, and has been universally accepted as true for more than a hundred years - well almost universally,' concluded Williams.

'Except of course for the occasional crackpot or kook,' added Belluci with a teasing tone to his voice, 'is that what you're saying Dr Williams?'

'Look, I am here as the moderator. The right to free speech is the greatest pillar of our society, Mr Belluci. It's what distinguishes America from the rest of the world.' A cheer went up from the PORTAL members in the audience, but this time was not endorsed by the mainly British majority, as the film started on the screen.

A quick introduction was rapidly succeeded by a glossy tour through the cosmology of the modern era, hosted by a cheerful Dr Williams, shown in laboratories or on mountain tops in exotic locations about the world. The script concluded its tribute with a description of the indispensable role of modern science in bettering the human condition and as the closing credits rolled by, Belluci once more bounced onto the stage.

'Thank you Dr Williams.' Belluci waved Prof Patel across to the podium with a cheerful invitation. 'And what is the result of your little experiment Dr Patel. Have you found the nothing that will prove everything - or the something that will prove nothing is full of something?'

Belluci raised his arm to summons a blaring fanfare of trumpets, building to the contrived climax as curtains were pulled back from the smaller screen that displayed the results from the Interferometer.

'Let us see,' said Patel sarcastically as he looked at the defiantly white screen. 'Ah yes - a null result.'

Belluci seized the moment. 'Rien, zilch, nada, niente, and in English - SFA. So what does this mean Dr Williams? Please spell it out to us in goodol' plain-speaking American English.'

'As the whole of the physics community, well, almost all of the physics community could have told you,' Dr Williams affected a token cough of correction, 'what this shows is that there is no ether, no fixed frame, nothing is nothing - there is only one speed for light - and Einstein, who produced equations of manifest beauty and elegance to account for this result, is hereby vindicated. I call on the other side to renounce their position and admit that their theories are arrant nonsense.'

'Looks like the beautiful Christine Reynolds has received a knockout punch at the end of round one. She may be down -

but is she out?' Belluci's performance was increasingly exaggerated as he leered into the camera.

'Can the current YouTube sensation, the star of the small-screen, the woman we know and lurve as Dr Chrissy 'The Missy" Reynolds - can she come from behind!' he winked preposterously at the audience who jeered and hooted their appreciation to confirm this was more the type of entertainment they wanted. 'Yes, good people, yes, yes,' Belluci was shouting now, 'Give it up for Dr Chris Reynolds!'

Chapter 135: dark matters

(5.30 am)

As Chris walked towards the podium, furious at Belluci's description of her, the crowd started wolf-whistling, clapping and chanting. Distantly she heard him finishing his introduction.

'Once more for Dr Chris Reynolds of the MRI in Malvern.'

Chris acknowledged the audience with an awkward wave, and with ill-concealed irritation allowed Anton Belluci to kiss her on the cheek. She turned to the camera speaking in a clear and decisive voice.

'Well it looks as if we might be wrong.'

There was a shocked sigh from the audience, followed by intermittent booing.

'But to avoid any doubt, let's first of all hear what Dr Ian Lineker has to say, the originator and mastermind behind Process Physics.'

Sensing the opportunity for added drama, Anton Belluci waved on the crowd, which joined in his chant like a Roman audience baying for the blood of a fallen gladiator.

'We want Lineker, we want Lineker.'

The screen switched to show an image of a Zeppelin tethered above the studio like a fat cigar in the sky, the moon massive behind it and the words 'PORTAL' emblazoned on its silvered sides to make a shameless advertisement for the Church.

Belluci seemed surprised, but recovered immediately. 'And let us not forget our sponsors for tonight - bringing the Celestial to all the World - PORTAL,' he trumpeted and the crowd roared on cue. The image of the zeppelin was replaced by the interior of a room, and as the camera zoomed slowly in, the final shot focused on the back of a man's head, seated in a chair. Suddenly the chair swung round. It was Ian Lineker.

'My God!' Chris burst out, shocked at how gaunt he looked.

'And now all the way from Australia where he was unexpectedly delayed on his hiking trip,' Belluci was taking instructions from his ear piece, 'we have Dr Ian Lineker, the genius behind the new physics and the well-known friend, can I say close friend, of our very own Chrissy Reynolds.'

'No, this is not right,' Chris spluttered. 'We need Ian here - he must be with us.'

Belluci too had expected Lineker to appear in the same studio. He skipped elegantly off the stage intent on confronting Wiseman in person to demand an explanation for why he had not been notified that Lineker was broadcasting from a different studio.

'Chris, lovely to see you again . . . you look . . . different. Sorry I can't be there in person,' said Ian, his voice still with the hint of humour that in Chris's recollection so typified him, and made the sudden change in his tone even more painful.

'Are you safe Chris? We'll cancel if you're not . . .'

'I'm safe Ian, surrounded by good people, don't worry about me - how are you?' Her anguish was obvious in her voice, and in her face. 'Your hands - show me.' The crowd was hushed. Though its ingredients were unknown, they sensed with the tribal wisdom of the herd that here was an authentic drama, an intense communication with real emotion, rather than the contrivance of suspense and climax that Anton Belluci delivered to placate his employers.

'I'm in good shape, Chris.' Lineker waved both hands at her, like the closing valediction in a Broadway musical. One of his fingers was crudely bound with gauze. 'All the better for seeing you. The science is the important thing here and there will never be another chance like this. We must proceed whatever my own circumstances. I'm sure you've come up with something for our side during my . . . umm . . . disposition?'

Chris was fighting back a tear, a tear of relief to see him and of agonized frustration he was still out of reach. A tear that acknowledged too why she respected him, with the courage to sacrifice his own wellbeing for the truth that he had already risked so much to pursue.

Belluci, who had quickly realized from the pandemonium backstage that Lineker's absence was unplanned, was hurrying with his trademark dancing elegance to re-join Chris in front of the camera. Lineker's appearance on the screen from another studio had sparked frantic activity amongst the assembled security service personnel, like the feeding frenzy of a school of fish. Several of the senior program managers were rapidly detained, including Benny Wiseman who was frog-marched to an interview room where two Special Branch officers repeated his interrogation on every possible contact he had made in the lead-up to the show.

Another man was watching Chris from the wings. He was tall with a prominent nose, and wearing an ill-fitting uniform belonging to a private security officer, now locked in the boot of his own patrol car.

Fighting to control her emotions, Chris replied to Lineker's query. 'Yep Ian. We've been busy. Bill Grafton and Janbir Chatterjee have a fibre optic Interferometer design that I think you'll like.'

'Bill and Janbir - my, oh, my - things have changed while I've been away - can't wait Chris. Fibre optic - known refractive index - I get it - nice.' Lineker seemed to be enjoying himself.

'Forgive me for interrupting guys, what exactly is going on here,' asked Belluci 'Are you saying that Dr Lineker isn't going to retract his theories - that you have a reply?'

'Absolutely - we have our own design and will run our own experiment,' replied Chris.

'Bring it on. Looks like we do have a contest after all,' said Belluci.

'Bring it on.'

Chapter 136: right to reply

(5.40 am)

Dr Williams appeared irritated.

'I'm interested to hear what you have to say for yourselves Dr Lineker. But first let me put some questions to you.'

'Very pleased to answer them,' replied Lineker, his face displayed on a screen suspended over the stage, giving him the unintended appearance of a visiting god presiding over an earthly stage.

'We have seen a convincing case that shows there isn't an ether, or a fixed frame against which the speed of light can be measured,' said Williams. 'This implies that light will always travel at the same speed, irrespective of the relative movement of its source or any movement of whoever receives it. This is consistent with the Theory of Relativity. We have also heard a lot about the technological advances and scientific insights of the last century, that have come about because of Relativity theory. And yet, you still argue it is wrong?'

'Thank you, err . . . Dr Williams, wasn't it? Thank you again for the opportunity to clarify our position. Let's get this straight from word go, no-one is denying that Relativity works. No-one is denying that there are relativistic effects as speed increases; time running slower, light bending in gravity, the contraction of fixed rods and so on. Fitzgerald and Lorentz explained all that before Einstein. So yes, relativity works - at least - most of the time.'

Belluci had decided he would best serve his role of entertainer by providing stage whispered headlines to underline the argument for the crowd. 'So Dr Lineker admits Relativity works.'

'Notice I said 'most of the time,' added Lineker.

'But what is the value of seeking to refute a theory that has proved so useful and from which so much has been achieved?' asked Dr Williams, in a tone of voice both reasonable and enquiring.

'There are several reasons,' began Lineker. 'First, there are things the theory cannot explain. Worse, there are observations recorded which the theory says should not happen and finally, Relativity suggests a version of reality which is entirely inconsistent with the other great theory of the last century - Quantum Mechanics. Arising from this confusion, is a deeply flawed cosmology, which to correct the failures of the maths to explain or predict differing effects, requires the invention of increasingly unscientific concepts, and the invention of more and more imaginary particles and forces.'

'The scientists don't understand how the universe works, so they make things up,' repeated Belluci, getting increasingly excited at the escalation of disagreement.

'As I was saying,' continued Lineker, the camera zooming in closer to enlarge his face on the screen, 'the failure to find these things is often attributed to the convenient property that they don't interact with us. Vast expenditure goes into looking for fantasy energies and non-existent figments of the imagination – look at the Hadron Collider nonsense.'

Prof Patel interjected his voice wavering with anger. 'The Hadron Collider is the most advanced engineering project of . . .'

He was cut off by Belluci, beaming widely, as he rubbed his hands together, 'Fantasies – the scientists are chasing apparitions.'

'Gentlemen please,' insisted Lineker, 'if I may just finish. It's turned science into a faith-based belief system rather than an evidence-based search for truth where your funding seems more related to how media-savvy you are than the potential for good work.'

'Well, that's quite a claim, Dr Lineker.' Belluci bellowed melodramatically. 'Did I forget to mention that the good Doctor is no stranger to the internet entertainment industry himself,' he smirked. 'I think Chrissy Reynolds can confirm - isn't that right?'

'I'm sorry, I haven't got a clue what you're talking about . . .' began Lineker but was interrupted by Chris, her voice heavy with concern, 'I'll explain later, Ian - don't worry about any of that bull . . .' she was saying when her microphone was cut off, enabling Belluci to talk over her.

'Can you give us an example, Dr Lineker, of what precisely you're talking about - in practical terms that is?' Belluci's mood was improving by the minute as it became evident the drama was ratcheting up, a struggle he was intent on magnifying.

'Okay. Thank you Mr Belluci,' Lineker replied politely and calmly. 'The speed of galaxy rotation at the edges is greater than can be explained by general relativity's account of gravity. So classical science doesn't say 'oh, maybe the theory has an error somewhere'. What it does is invent 'dark matter'. But there is no other evidence for this. We can't even detect anything that might be 'dark matter'. So classical science says 'Don't worry that we can't detect it - one of its properties is that it's undetectable'. And how much of this invented Dark Matter do they need to balance the books? Do they need a little bit or a lot, you may be asking yourself?'

'I don't know,' exclaimed Belluci. 'We don't know', he added, lifting his arms in a gesture of implied inclusion of the audience.

'Well . . . they say, dark matter makes up 25% of everything there is.'

'They say a quarter of everything is stuff we can't see or measure,' said Belluci.

Lineker continued. 'It's even worse with Dark Energy that they needed to invent to account for the observation that the universe is expanding. They say that another 70% of everything is made up of that.'

Belluci was enjoying himself. 'The scientists who look at and measure the Universe say that it is 95% composed of stuff we can't look at or measure - is this a gigantic 'Fail' for the Physicists?'

'This is preposterous.' Dr Williams shouted out but was immediately cut short by Belluci. 'A moment please . . . Dr Lineker has the stage.'

Belluci continued evenly. 'Even allowing for a bit of Australian hyperbole, Dr Lineker - is it really that bad?'

Lineker was about to reply when a hand appeared on his shoulder, and the dark features of an Indian man were visible, seemingly remonstrating with him.

'I've got to go I'm afraid . . .' The screen was suddenly obscured, as if something had passed in front of the camera lens. There was the muffled sound of scuffling before Lineker reappeared.

'No its okay,' said Lineker, 'Looks like I've got a few more minutes. I seem to have acquired an unlikely ally here.'

'So you can do better than everyone else - is that your claim Lineker?' Professor Patel spoke up, his voice cracking with anger.

'Of course,' replied Lineker, 'too easy.'

Chapter 137: draw a blank

'Hold on a minute Lineker,' Dr Williams protested. 'You attack science for becoming 'faith-based' as you put it - but we have just seen an experiment that shows light always travels at the same speed - the cornerstone of Einstein's Relativity. It is you who is denying the evidence to support your 'conviction' that somehow Einstein got it wrong. How do you account for that?'

'Okay, it's surprisingly simple,' started Lineker, the camera again panning close to show his face magnified on the screen. 'The experiment we have seen is not conclusive. As the light travels through the arm, the arm itself is moving as the earth travels through space, so the light had further to go. But the movement contracts the length of the arm in the direction of travel, it shrinks a bit. If the light travels through a vacuum, the extra distance exactly equals the reduced length of the arm - these effects cancel out.'

'Rubbish,' shouted Patel 'You don't get length contraction effects in the same inertial frame.'

Chris intervened, 'Absolutely you do, it's a physical consequence of the interaction with space itself,' she said.

'Baloney,' shouted Patel, 'there's nothing in space.'

'Apart from dark matter, dark energy, neutrinos, Higgs bosons, anti-matter, missing string dimensions, or anything else you have to invent to balance the equations, is that right, Dr Patel?' Lineker barked. 'If the light travels though air or gas, or as in the case we are testing, through fibre optic cable, the effects don't exactly cancel out because the light is slowed a bit to start with. We can work out how much because we know the refractive index of optic fibre.'

'Okay, that's enough from the men of science,' Belluci cut them short. 'Never mind the complicated arguments, the results of the experiment are quite simple. If we see lines on the screen Lineker is right, if we see a blank he's wrong,'

Belluci trumpeted. 'Everyone got that; 'Lines for Lineker', Blank for 'Blown it."

"Lines for Lineker', 'Blank for 'Blown it," the crowd chanted.

'Quiet now,' demanded Belluci. Hush descended, and Belluci yanked on the tassel to expose the screen. The crowd gave a collective inhalation of astonishment.

The screen was blank.

Chapter 138: poles apart

'You must understand this is not personal.'

Baedeker seated next to Aziz in a plush armchair of his executive jet, said nothing.

'You've seriously lost the plot, but I imagine you don't see it that way, and if you did, you probably wouldn't behave like such a prick,' continued Aziz, trying to be charitable.

'I am on a mission greater in scale and significance than you could possibly conceive,' replied Baedeker.

'I could kill you if I wanted,' said Aziz, 'how does that square with your 'mission?''

'I would become a martyr. I cannot predict the future, but I know my death would play its part in the transformation I am destined to portend.'

'Portend?' queried Aziz, 'I think you might mean pretend?'

'My soul vibration is another frequency from yours, but in each of us is the spirit of God - you are not yet lost, though the world you inhabit is coarse, brutal and ugly.'

'Okay, I get it - you may be right. Some of my best friends have been pigs, some still are,' he added, with a slight smile, 'though I don't want to insult the porkers I've known and loved. Problem I have with all this is while you enjoy yourself, other people die.'

'In this world we all die, Mr Aziz.'

'Well, we agree on something anyway,' Aziz smiled. 'I'm afraid I need the loo - come on.'

The two men raised themselves awkwardly from their seats, one bedraggled and unkempt, the stains of blood camouflaged by the ingrained dirt in the deep creases that lined his face, the other occasionally wincing as if in passing discomfort, but still upright, neat and tidy, an aura of wealth surrounding him. Arm in arm they made their way gingerly down the aisle, fellow travellers on fate's unlikely journey like cartoon characters sketched from opposing palettes, but each attended in equal measure by the strange intensity of the abnormal, and the possibility of madness.

As the two exited the toilet a few minutes later, the captain's voice came over the speaker; 'Cleared for landing at RAF Northolt in twenty minutes, Mr Baedeker. I understand they've organized quite a reception for us, sir.'

'I'll need you to pop this on for me,' instructed Aziz.

'I don't think I need a life jacket to land at an airport,' Baedeker replied haughtily.

'No, but this is a bomb,' said Aziz. 'I swallowed a bit of semtex - enough to take your head off. I've just retrieved it. 'The piece that passeth' in your language, eh?'

Aziz chortled to himself, comforted by his own scurrilous humour, and the moment's distraction it gave him from the thought of the mayhem that awaited.

Chapter 139: taking stock

(6.00 am)

'Sorry Malvern, but it's just not your day,' shouted Belluci. 'Blank for 'Blown it.''

There was silence, the shock palpable as the audience looked at the empty screen, before a chance snigger unleashed the blood lust of the mob that sensing its prey is mortally injured, bayed like a pack of dogs circling for the kill. Banners and flags with PORTAL started to appear and the howls, boos and jeers gave way to a more sinister current that flowed and eddied amongst the crowd with cries of 'Judas', 'Slut', and 'Traitor'.

'This was your idea,' Clinton was pulling Chris to the back of the stage, his voice haranguing and urgent. 'You said it would work, we got our Followers here so they could witness a new beginning - and you give them this - nothing - can't you do something?'

On the large screen, Lineker was seen adjusting his earpiece, 'What's happening, what's going on?' he was saying, his voice trailing off in confusion, before his screen too blanked out.

Chris felt the panic surging as she struggled to think clearly. Every forward possibility seemed couched in chaos and there was no going back, like a chess game where any move can only worsen the position – but the player is required to move. Distantly, she heard a crashing sound from the auditorium and the harsh confused scuffling of a brawl spreading across an aisle near the back.

Try to relax – breathe - just breathe.

The solution came in an instant.

Of course . . .

'Cue me in,' she demanded of the producer who scrabbled with a number of switches and gave her a nod of approval then pointed to the back of the stage where a spotlight illuminated a small circle in anticipation of her appearance. A riffing guitar accompanied by a stentorian thumping drum made the sort of music a stripper might use as an introduction, blasting a crude and deliberately ambiguous welcome over the loudspeakers.

'She's a real good liar,' were the only words that Chris caught. At first, she was incensed, her anger immediately dissolving as she played catch-up realizing what the producer had known by instinct, that it would take 'woman magic' to quell the turbulence of the crowd. Now thankful for his decisive action in choosing something appropriately sleazy, she felt her hips swinging to the beat, her stride lengthening into a feline zig-zag and sensed rather than heard a stutter in the roar of the crowd. She knew how visible she was and could feel her appeal in a way she had never known before; untouchable, teasing - an avatar of delight - the power of beautiful women throughout the ages. Involuntarily, her body swung with a barely perceptible exaggeration, the movement lending accent to the jostling sway of her breasts. She understood the impulse of the exhibitionist, tempted for one intoxicating instant to tear off her top and expose herself to the mob, to offer herself sacrificially to the mindless libido of the crowd, now simmering with prurient anticipation.

'I give you the goddess of 'ss'. . .' Belluci affected a stutter. 'Sssss,' he repeated, goading the beast he hoped to tame. The hum quickly subsided to an occasional titter, eager to hear how far Belluci dared go to satisfy their hunger.

'Science,' he shouted and the crowd gave a collective sigh before resuming its breathless attention, as Chris sashayed to the microphone. The audience knew her strength, could sense her indecision, and was transfixed.

'Well hello everyone,' she shouted.

'Hello,' they shouted back.

She gestured toward Grafton and Chatterjee hunched over the Interferometer at the side of the stage as they began dismantling the machine. 'While Bill and Janbir check the equipment let me point out what's at stake here.' She smiled, now languid, relaxed, the stripper transformed to the genial hostess, the mesmerizing narrator of story.

'Buying and selling of most share trades are done by computers and happen in a fraction of a second.'

The crowd exhaled, disappointed. Someone hollered 'Get 'em off,' but without the previous consensus was hissed silent by the women around him, eager to stifle any recurrence of male vulgarity.

'Did you know that certain investment banks have moved their offices to be nearer the stock exchange?' asked Chris. They didn't, and didn't care, the bubble had burst and this was poor recompense.

'Turns out they reckon a delay between their computers of a thousandth of a second costs them one hundred million dollars in trades every year.' The interest of the crowd was rekindling, provoked by the improbability of what she was saying, and their place in history as its witness.

'That's right - one hundred million dollars – in an instant - think about it.'

A buzz of appreciation rippled through the ranks, suggesting each of them, as instructed, was imagining how they might personally benefit from such a sum.

On impulse, inspired by the effect her words were having and the example set by Belluci, she abandoned her normal measured delivery and punching the air declared: 'So you better believe, it's going to be worth it to get this baby to run.' As if rehearsed, the producer cued a drum roll.

'One hundred million dollars - by designing the networks to account for the siting of the computers and the changed speed of light at different times of the day and year - we can save many times that amount.'

Like a man on a military parade, Dr Janbir Chatterjee's head shot to attention.

Chapter 140: fixed

The sound of disquiet was growing again in the audience, like the groan of a pebbly beach as a storm-blown wave drains back into the sea. The producer hit the buttons and a second NASA film, 'Miracles of Creation,' appeared on the screen. The crowd quickly calmed, captivated by the succession of beautiful images showing the birth and death of stars, and lulled by the calm and humorous voice-over, the incongruous Yorkshire accent oddly pleasing in its parochial reassurance.

Dr Chatterjee spoke briefly to Grafton then leaving him to continue his inspection of the Interferometer alone, he crossed the stage to Chris.

'Dr Reynolds,' said Chatterjee when he reached her, the excitement apparent in his voice. 'We were discussing your observation that networks can be made more efficient by allowing for the earth's movement - very interesting, very interesting. It could be worth billions.'

'Yes it is a remarkable idea isn't it,' Chris replied.

'And you really think it could work?' asked Chatterjee.

'I'd have more confidence if we could get the experiment right,' replied Chris 'Any ideas what might be the problem with the machine?'

'Oh yes, I have a theory,' replied Chatterjee. 'Excuse me Dr Reynolds, I'll return to help Dr Grafton.'

Williams and Patel were speaking to each other, and from the angry glances they were directing at her, Chris deduced neither was happy at the extra opportunity extended to her team to try to fix the machine. She ignored them, as Bill Grafton too, was hurrying across the stage to join her.

'Janbir has already found the problem. He really is first-rate that man, absolutely top-drawer, wonderful mind,' Grafton told her. 'We are running the machine again.'

'Good work Bill,' she said. 'So what was the problem?' she asked as Grafton joined her again at the back of the stage.

'It was the PDA36A - the amplified silicon photo-diode detector - Janbir replaced the unit and it just fired up fine.'

'Look this isn't the right time to split hairs, but didn't you check it?' asked Chris, her disapproval apparent in her voice.

'Absolutely - the component must have failed - just bad luck I suppose.' Grafton was sheepish, conciliatory, like a schoolboy who knows he should have done better. The screen above their heads flickered and Lineker reappeared, the arms of a technician visible as he frantically attached a microphone to Lineker's lapel.

'Thank God Ian's still there,' Chris blurted out.

'Hang in there, Chris.' Grafton squeezed her arm. 'We'll find him,' Grafton continued, with an optimism which though she did not share, she found reassuring. 'I'll re-join Janbir okay?'

'Sure Bill,' she said, 'thanks.'

When the film had ended, the ritualized drama of checking the outcome of the experiment was repeated, though after the previous results of two blank screens, this time the climax felt contrived and unconvincing. But as the curtains fell away, clear bands of darker shading were visible running vertically from top to bottom of the results screen.

Bill Grafton smiled at Chris with a thumbs-up, and Chris returned the gesture, though all she could feel was the emptiness of failure. *What will they do to Ian now?*

'A positive result. Give it up for the scientists from Malvern,' intoned a frantic Belluci, waving Chris and Dr Williams forward to join him at centre-stage, as the crowd once more made a half-hearted attempt to show enthusiasm.

'La Bella Reynolds has stripped away the covers of convention and revealed the naked truth,' shouted Belluci. 'She certainly seems to have blown your argument - wouldn't you agree Dr Williams?'

Chapter 141: truth is in the mind

(6.17 am)

'Yes, we have seen a result on this machine, whereas we saw no such resolution on the other machine. What is going on - who do we believe?' began Dr Williams. His tone was measured, at first. 'You must realize his result suggests an orbit speed of the earth far less than the thirty kilometres per second we know it to be. The answer is quite simple. Dr Lineker's machine is displaying an experimental error.'

Once again audible on the loudspeaker, Lineker interrupted, his voice high pitched with excitement. 'That is completely wrong - this is a remarkable outcome. You have to calibrate the machine to allow for the length contraction effects and the changed speed of light in the fibre-optic cables. If you do that properly, it confirms the speed of the earth through space as about 420 kilometres per second - about fifteen times the orbit speed of the earth, showing that the whole solar system is moving too.'

'How very convenient,' snorted Dr Williams. 'Lineker is obviously not familiar with the margin of error in very fine experimentation,' he sneered. 'Dr Lineker says his theory explains why Patel's vacuum machine gives a false null reading. But when his own machine gives a null result, he says it doesn't work.' Williams looked around him, exasperated, his hands opened to the audience as if appealing for common sense to prevail.

The crowd were unsure who to believe in the cut and thrust of technical argument and Belluci, eager to give them the resolution that they craved, was looking from Lineker to Williams in exasperation.

'When he gets very small 'margin of error results' from his second go with his own machine,' Williams was pressing on, 'he says his theory can amplify these discrepancies to miraculously give the result he's looking for and derive the extraordinary conclusion that the whole solar system is moving too. In other words, 'Believe in my theory and it will prove my theory'. Sorry Doctor. This is not science - this is pathetic.'

Chapter 142: old haunts

(6.18 am)

Even before they boarded the plane, Aziz had found little opportunity to talk to Isabel, with Baedeker's constant presence making any attempt at reconciliation impossible. Aziz had separated from her mother when Isabel was little, and he assumed that the resentment flowing from his ex-wife had created a distance too wide to be bridged by casual chatter. Aziz and Isabel remained acutely aware of each other even though she had chosen to sit with Cindy, well away from Aziz and Baedeker at the back of the aircraft. Aziz understood why – he knew both he and Baedeker were on the border of the grotesque, each of them a different but equal source of embarrassment to the young women.

Aziz had told the negotiators to prepare for a landing of the helicopter that had transferred them from RAF Northolt on Shepherds Bush Green, but knowing that the small triangle of unwelcoming parkland would be guarded by the police and perhaps soldiers too, he had changed his instruction to the pilot at the last moment, redirecting him down the road nearer the core of the bustling metropolis.

'I'll see you later,' Aziz assured Isabel as he left the young women at Marble Arch next to the landed helicopter. 'And take this,' he said, handing her Baedeker's phone. 'I'll phone you.' It was a promise he was unsure he could keep, nor one that he was convinced she believed. He watched as she deliberated whether to risk thanking him as 'Dad', her hesitation distilling the failure of their relationship so far and giving each of them time to acknowledge their regret in shared discomfort. She settled instead on 'Mike'.

As the helicopter clattered into the sky, lifting up from Marble Arch to sweep in an arc high over Hyde Park, Aziz knew the time for reflection was passed, though he spared a moment to remember the last time he had been there, a time that already seemed a century away when he had met with Chris and she had seized the wig from his head.

Aziz was relieved that the fine autumn afternoon had attracted so many people to Marble Arch and confident that with the crowd as a shield and the threat of the instant decapitation of the head of PORTAL, their safe passage was assured as he began the slow shuffling escort of Baedeker towards the nearby tube. The prisoner seemed a pathetic figure with the wreath of death around his neck, and his shabby captor a desperate man.

In the underpass, Aziz made Baedeker relinquish his jacket and trousers, a difficult manoeuvre in the cramped photo booth. He offered a busker 1000 US dollars taken from Baedeker's wallet to exchange Baedeker's $5000 Jon Green suit for the musician's heavy ex-military great coat, jeans and guitar. The youth offered little objection. Aziz was a frightening sight, injured and battered, and with an intensity that suggested the tortured isolation of insanity, and the rate of exchange was more than attractive.

It was in his power to fulfil the intent that had formed way back in Llanthony - to dispose of Baedeker by killing him, but Aziz decided he would let him live, choosing instead to leave Baedeker in his underwear, tied to the railings at the entrance to the tube, clutching the wire in his fist that if released would detonate the charge around his neck.

When he had secured Baedeker, Aziz exited the tube on its northern side with the guitar slung on his back over the coat, dumping his own clothes in a bin before he hobbled across the road to hop on the Number 12 bus in the direction of Acton. From the top deck he could see the police arriving, clearing the area to quarantine the exhausted Baedeker, who was slumped over with his head hung low and arms outstretched.

Aziz felt a wave of pity for his adversary. He barely noted the sensation, assuming it was an aberration rather than anything authentic, so never consciously registered that yet again the certainties of his training were being softened by the hesitations of kindness.

But Aziz had other reasons for not detonating the bomb to decapitate the Church. He had seen the scale of the Church's influence and the affluence of its headquarters. He realized this was not a battle but a war, and winning it would require more than disposing of an enemy figurehead and creating the martyr that Baedeker had predicted; it would require the discipline of an attack on several fronts, coordinated by a strong and determined leader. It was not a role in which Aziz had any personal interest, but he had formulated a plan for a rear-guard action of his own.

But first he would visit the woman he loved.

Chapter 143: PDA36A

(6.19 am)

Dr Grafton appeared again at Chris' side, just as Lineker started his reply to Williams' dismissal of the Interferometer results.

'Not now Bill please,' she said, annoyed with his interruption.

'Chris, I've got to go.' He was breathless and seemed worried.

'Why on earth?' she asked, 'can't this wait - what are you talking about?'

'Well the failed component - it was a PDA36A-EC.'

'Not a PDA36A?'

'Absolutely!'

'So it wouldn't work, are you saying?' asked Chris.

'No it could have worked,' replied Grafton.

'So what's the problem Bill?' she said impatiently.

'It isn't the one I fitted - I fitted a PDA36A - the other one, the faulty one, was swapped in - but only Janbir and I had access to it since my tests, and I just saw Janbir making for the exit. I'm going to catch up with him. I'm going to find out what the hell is going on.'

Chapter 144: square pegs

(6.20 am)

Isabel and Cindy were seated in the back of a police van. They had been questioned briefly by a plain clothes detective, a woman, but the interview had been cut short abruptly when she had received a call on her phone. They were tired but euphoric, their escape from the Church still sustaining their mood, and the excitement of another country feeding their optimism. After a few minutes a handsome young man, dressed casually in jeans and jacket swung the rear door of the van open. He explained he was their Case Officer, Simon Wilkie, and worked for British Intelligence, before cheerfully inviting them in a posh British accent to accompany him, indicating with a wave of his hand the sleek black Jaguar saloon car parked nearby.

They could see Baedeker in the distance still tied to the railings, and men in the massive armour of the bomb disposal squad like nineteenth century deep-sea divers, plodding slowly toward him with the resigned heroism of the dutiful, to risk everything for the promise of a pension and the thrill of cheating catastrophe.

'Poor Saul,' said Cindy, wondering if she would ever be close to Baedeker again with the confusion of a jilted lover, as she vacillated between acceptance of the obvious and the self-delusion of denial. 'He's not all bad you know; he has a wonderful playful side to him when you get to know him. Your father shouldn't have done that to him.'

Isabel said nothing at first, troubled by her own reaction and unsure what to think of her father. The habit of a lifetime's resentment had poisoned the seeds of any admiration she might have felt while her interest in knowing him better was inhibited by her revulsion at his appearance, and fear that he might not be sane.

'No, he shouldn't have done that,' Isabel said, knowing immediately she had betrayed him, as she followed Cindy into the back seat of the car. Simon Wilkie waved his identity card and shouted 'Whitehall' out of the window at a uniformed policeman, and the Jaguar was allowed through the police cordon, screeching into the road to weave swiftly through the traffic on Park Lane.

'Can I call a friend?' asked Cindy. 'My cell phone's not working here.'

'Sure, use mine,' replied the young man, casually throwing his phone onto the back seat next to her. 'First time in England?' he asked, looking at them in the mirror.

'We lived in Hereford, then mainly in Australia since I was ten,' replied Isabel. Cindy, speaking on the phone, ignored his question.

As they sped onwards, Isabel capitulated to her tiredness and lulled by the motion of the car dozed fitfully in the comforting embrace of the leather seat. Cindy, also exhausted, gazed expressionless at the succession of stacked apartments and grey office buildings, and at the pallid men in suits who strode quickly past groups of tourists either huddled over maps or photographing each other in front of the relics of empire that lend purpose to the central London bustle. As Big Ben loomed into view Cindy gave Isabel a nudge to wake her and share the experience, before the car crossed a bridge over the Thames and swung left, halting briefly while an automatic door opened to give access to the basement of a towering blockhouse monolith, its windows receding into the sky like a wedding cake might appear to an ant.

'My office,' smiled the young man. 'Welcome to the nut-house.'

Cindy and Isabel were interviewed together and separately, sometimes by one person, occasionally by two. They were visited by a kindly grey-haired woman who said she was a trauma specialist and who took them to a canteen where they were given cups of tea and offered a meal, then they were returned, to sit together in a warm room with no windows.

For a second time Wilkie looked cheerfully round the door where they had waited unattended for fifteen minutes. 'Ladies, you wouldn't believe how difficult the paperwork is proving on this.' They looked back at him, without responding. He continued smoothly: 'Firstly your case Isabel. You're British as well as Australian which helps. We're taking the view that you were coerced by your father into accompanying him. You have stated you do not wish to go back to the US, or Australia.'

'Not till I'm ready. I want to stay here for now . . .' replied Isabel. 'I want to start again.'

'I can understand that,' Wilkie agreed. 'But the Australian authorities have requested we send you there to attend an inquest over the death of a member of PORTAL, a name that keeps cropping up, as I'm sure you understand. You'll be given a lawyer if there is a hearing date to start any extradition process. Pending that we're keeping you in custody for a little while longer, then you're free to go.'

'Okay,' said Isabel, deflated by the interrogation she had already endured.

'Cindy - more complex for you. There are officials scheduled to arrive in two hours to take you to the airport and return you to the States.'

'What sort of officials?' asked Cindy 'I don't want to go back to the Church.'

'We appreciate that, and it puts us in a bit of a bind. You can apply for refugee status here on the basis you will be persecuted if you return home. There were already concerns about the Church that predate your stories - Israeli sources flagged them some time back. But the simple fact is we can't say 'no' to a direct request from the Americans. So, if you were to apply, you would certainly lose the application to be accepted as a refugee. A regular visa presents certain difficulties now you're already here. We have sympathy with your predicament. Of course, if I can say you're helping me with my enquiries into the Church, then these arrangements can be much more flexible. You could go 'missing' while you sort things out back home. We'll think of something to tell the Americans when they get here.'

'What's going to happen to my Dad?' Isabel blurted out suddenly, as if unable to suppress the concern that had been festering inside her.

'Doesn't look good for your father I'm afraid. He's wanted for a raft of very serious charges but I think if he survives this, the consensus is emerging that he is in need of some serious psychiatric care.'

"What do you mean 'If he survives this . . .?" asked Isabel, her eyes brimming with the tears she was fighting to restrain.

'As I was saying . . .' his tone was uninterested, avoiding engagement with the issue. 'Cindy.' He paused. 'I don't suppose you know anyone here in London, so we can arrange temporary accommodation for you. In the interim, it's best not to be here when your embassy officials arrive. If you like you can stay at my place.'

He was an attractive young man, tall and athletic looking. A whiff of arrogance reinforced his masculine air of competent ease, and he made no attempt to disguise his interest in Cindy. The emotional gale that had buffeted her for the past couple of weeks had left her even more appealing. Her body was rangy, long-limbed and fluid, her hair wild and flowing, and her eyes clear in a handsome face that now carried the hint of something more serious, with occasional filaments of anxiety just perceptible in an otherwise untroubled complexion.

She wavered.

'You'll be safe with me,' he said and somehow the offer was credible, the appeal of a sanctuary from which to recover and the implied possibility of romance in a foreign capital with a denizen keeper of its culture, hard to resist. They would make a good couple.

As if in thought, Cindy crossed her hands behind her neck, breathing in deeply, an action that emphasized her shape, as she considered the proposition. The man, and Isabel too, inhaled in sympathy with her, both equally absorbed and lost in apprehension of her reply, each enslaved by desire for a future she had the power to influence; he in hope, Isabel in despair.

Cindy crossed her legs. She gave him a smile, cheeky, flirtatious, her head slightly bowed, stealing an upward glance at him through a screen of near-tremulous eyelashes.

'Thank you,' she said, in the husky, sexy drawl of the American southern states. His heart missed a beat, another puff of self-congratulation inflating an already buoyant self-regard.

'But I have a good friend here - Dr Bill Grafton,' she continued. 'I think I'll stay with him.'

Chapter 145: to the cleaners

(6.16 am)

As Bill Grafton left the studio the sun was not yet up but through the gloom he could clearly see the outline of Janbir Chatterjee hurrying toward another hangar-like building across the car park, some seventy metres away. Chatterjee stopped briefly to punch numbers into an access pad next to the glass and steel entrance door and within seconds had entered. By the time Grafton reached the same entrance he was panting from exertion, his breath casting vapour trails in the morning chill like a racehorse cooling from a frolicsome gallop. Grafton noted the camera looking down on him and moved aside quickly, hidden from its gaze by a battered Transit van parked some three metres from the entrance and as he did so, the thought that had niggled at his subconscious suddenly resolved.

There was a zeppelin floating over the studio building he had just left. Grafton had noticed it, but had been too anxious to catch up with Dr Chatterjee to have allowed its significance to register in his mind. He stepped back from the van. Sure enough there it was, the words 'PORTAL' prominently visible on its silvered side. Surely this was the same airship that had introduced the video hook-up with Dr Lineker, just twenty minutes earlier?

The rear doors of the van he was hiding behind, had been left wide open, displaying a collection of ladders, buckets, mops, clothing and other cleaning paraphernalia that the driver had judged were not worth stealing. Looking inside the van, Grafton made a decision that was so out of character, he was excited not only by the risks of breaking the law, but also by the potential of reinventing a life that until recently had known only routine. He reached inside the van, slipping a white coat off its hanger and over his business suit, the words 'Silly Suds' now emblazoned across its back. He found a used hair net discarded on the floor and hesitated for only a second before pulling it onto his head then clambered into the van to recover a bucket, mop, heavy rubber boots and matching rubber gloves, which he retrieved from a sliding draw at the back. He slid his tie off with one hand, and strode purposefully toward the entrance door, determined to gain access and find answers to the questions forming in his mind: *Was Dr Lineker in this building? Was the reason Chatterjee had been able to fix the interferometer so quickly because he had installed the faulty component himself. Did he know it was faulty or was it his intention to sabotage the experiment and if that was the case – why on earth would he want to do something like that?*

'Silly Suds,' Grafton announced, ringing the buzzer on the intercom.

'I thought you were already inside,' came the response.

'I'm taking over,' Grafton replied, his tone forceful and deep. His interrogator could not have guessed at the wider significance to Grafton of those words, or how satisfying it was for him to say them out loud.

'There's been an emergency' - to himself this time, experimenting with a tone of voice which though different, he found equally pleasing. Grafton stood in full view of the camera, then turned his back to the lens to offer up the logo for inspection.

'There's been an emergency . . . I'm taking over,' he repeated, admiring but still unsure of his reinvention, as the buzzer sounded and a clicking noise confirmed the door was now unlocked.

Grafton pushed his way in and seeing a public toilet off the foyer quickly entered to use the toilet. He was nervous, and splashed some water on his face, then took a sip to relieve the dryness of his lips. He was about to leave when it occurred to him that he would look more credible if the bucket contained water. He filled it and more unevenly than before, the weight of the near full bucket impeding his easy progress, pushed the swing door open and re-entered the lobby. There were three closed doors and a short corridor off the foyer. Grafton chose the easiest option following the corridor. He continued past a door marked 'Studio 7', and turned the corner at the end of the corridor. He was on a landing, overlooking a spacious atrium, two gentle flights of stairs descending to the level below, the space tastefully filled with mature pot plants, the lustrous waxiness of their fanning leaves adding to Grafton's sense of the exotic and the unfamiliar.

Three men were walking briskly up the stairs, their backs to him and nearly at the end of the first flight. They turned 180 degrees onto the second flight and now, facing him, were clearly visible, all three grim-faced and tight-lipped, with the tension of conflict written in their walk. One of them was Dr Chatterjee, the other was a dapper Indian man dressed in a dark blue suit and the third man . . . Grafton felt his stomach drop away, the almost instantaneous shivering in his body anticipating the fear that paralyzed his mind a moment after. *It's . . . Shirov.* The three would be upon him in less than a minute.

Grafton stumbled back down the corridor, fumbling for access to the first door he came across. It was the door he had passed just before - Studio 7. He almost fell into the large darkened space, lit only by night lamps that cast a reddish glow over a jumble of cables, lighting stands, a small stage and the complex web of gantries and spotlights overhead. At the side was a smaller room, a glass window separating it like a fish tank from the main area.

Abandoning his mop and bucket, he rushed into the soundproof room, diving under the panel with the parallel arrays of sliding knobs that formed the controls of the mixing unit, his shivering now an uncontrollable tremor that ran through him as he crouched in a foetal position under the desk. The door swung shut behind him and the silence was complete. He could taste the relief in his mouth - like vinegar. Risking a peep over the desk, his nose aligned with a knob, larger than the rest, with the warning 'Studio Sound' beneath it in prominent letters.

Suddenly the door to the corridor was opening. Grafton scrabbled out of sight, straining to hear what was going on, like a blackbird will hunt a worm. *Nothing,* he thought *Of course, this room's soundproof.* Reaching up, his hand skittered across the surface of the control panel and found the knob he had seen that controlled the microphone in the studio. He turned it to the left. *Still nothing.* He turned it to the right and was rewarded with the immediate intrusion of voices, clearly relayed to him, as again he curled up under the desk.

It was Janbir Chatterjee who was speaking. 'I am telling you this share network idea will be worth billions. The concreting contract doesn't matter anymore - this is clean money, the way of the future, there is money for all in this.'

The Indian man in a black suit joined in, 'Our priorities have changed - this is from the highest top. It is imperative the scientist is not harmed, he is instrumental in the future.'

The reply was instantly recognizable, a deep guttural voice, lazy and insolent. 'Concrete, no concrete. Shares, no shares. Fat pig Emelienko, runt rat Chaudhry - no difference. To us - no difference. You want him, you pay now,' Shirov was saying.

The dapper man, Chaudhry, was clearly annoyed. He replied angrily, a high pitched singsong cadence at odds with his intent. 'We paid Emelienko already. It is not our responsibility if he did not pay you. As a favour we agreed we would pay half again - and we will, if the scientist is unharmed - after the show.'

'Emelienko, fat pig, greedy pig. You want - you pay. You pay now. Not after show - now. You no pay - then we keep Lineker. For a while . . .' The sentence was never completed.

There was an animated chattering in Hindi. 'Okay - I'll bring you the money,' said Chaudhry. 'But I don't have it here . . . I must fetch it.'

'Pay now - I give him to you now.' Shirov sounded angry.

'Wait here - two minutes,' Chaudhry demanded.

'Chatterjee stays - two minutes to bring money - then I kill Chatterjee too,' Shirov chuckled, the menace somehow amplified by the casual simulation of humour.

For Grafton it was an eternity. *What has Chatterjee got himself into?* Grafton was repeating to himself. *He must have deliberately sabotaged the Interferometer. Then he changed his mind when Chris came up with the share trades idea.* Grafton was appalled. Part of him, a part he was nearer accepting was no less authentic, was also admiring. *Well who would have guessed it - Janbir working for someone else, some Indian-type outfit - and for us too.*

Chaudhry was returning. He rattled something off to Dr Chatterjee in Hindi.

'Lineker is speaking - I have to go – for the science,' Chatterjee said, the sound of the door opening and closing, confirming his exit.

'I have the money, in this case . . . here,' Grafton heard Chaudhry say, the muffled thumps and scrapes suggesting the case was being opened on a flat surface, immediately followed by a sound Grafton could not recognize; 'phut, phut' like a spitting cat, and a huge crash. *What the . . .* Grafton thought, an involuntary shockwave coursing through his body. Then a banging and grunting, the sounds of tortured breathing - a chilling soundtrack of someone fighting for their life, that concluded with a shout; muffled, plaintive. For a moment Grafton heard nothing more, until the silence was interrupted by the sound of the door opening and closing again. Still Grafton waited, tasting the fear again in his mouth, still acid but stronger than before like bile, too afraid to risk raising his head where he might be seen as he tried to suppress the shivering from the overflow of adrenalin pumping through his body. Could he still hear breathing, and the gurgling sound of a whisper?

When he was certain there was silence, he peeked over the counter, horrified at what he saw, and the guilt that he had done nothing to even try to prevent it. Chaudhry was seated in a chair, his lifeless eyes bulging in frozen terror at the far wall. In his hand, restrained by a finger caught in the guard, was a pistol, a silencer lending it an unlikely length; and through his neck was a dagger, thick blood oozing from it in pools onto his chest.

Oh my God - Shirov's killed this man and now he's gone after Lineker, thought Grafton. *I have to do something.* Though his plan was still unformed, as he ran to the door Grafton stopped to grab a length of electric extension cable, seizing the bucket and mop as if each were of equal importance. He realized with a panicking nausea the responsibility that confronted him; Lineker's life was at risk and only he could save him. And his enemy was no less than the sadist who had inhabited his nightmares since their first encounter just a few days previously on the Malvern Hills.

Grafton hurried down the staircase to the floor below and entered the studio with the red warning light that said 'Recording', the sweat pouring from his face and the ammonia smell of fear soaking into his clothes. His phone rang. He jerked it out to silence the tone and looked at the display - it told him the caller was Cindy.

Chapter 146: the next big bang

(6.20 am)

Dr Williams was just finishing off his tirade against bad science, his flushed face an unmistakable indicator of his disgust.

'Well we do seem to have touched a nerve,' Lineker observed wryly. 'People can feel personally threatened with anything perceived as new. If you've spent a lifetime studying something - and this stuff isn't easy to understand even if it's wrong - you are going to be reluctant to start again at the beginning. Especially if you've made a career out of it, written books about it, taught it to countless students for decades and have established a very comfortable income from supporting it - it's no wonder they say you can only get a paradigm shift when the old guard is finally dead,' added Lineker.

'All irrelevant and offensive, Lineker and you know it,' Dr Williams spat the words.

'So Dr Williams for the benefit of our audience who may be somewhat confused by these learned discussions,' asked Belluci, 'where are we at here - does Einstein live on or have Dr Lineker and the lovely Chrissy Reynolds rewritten the science books for us?'

'The best I can offer you - Dr Lineker's experiment is totally inconclusive' Williams said emphatically. 'Why would you reject good science for no good reason? Of course Einstein is right.'

'Okay good people. Not a result we welcome on this show but it happens now and again. I declare the result is . . .' began Belluci.

'Wait,' demanded Lineker. 'What would you accept as proof?'

'When he,' Williams seemed so angry he was reluctant to pronounce Dr Lineker's name, 'can show that a physical effect, gravity for instance, travels faster than light. Then that would be a conclusive experiment - until then, there is no case to reject proven science.'

'Let's think out loud for a moment,' replied Lineker, an edge of impatience to his voice. 'Just bear with me. Okay.' He drew a deep breath. Imagine we assemble as many of the world's atomic weapons as we can get from the stockpiles accumulated in the Cold War. We shoot them into the sky all collected in one place in a geostationary orbit around the earth. In other words, they are motionless in relation to the earth. We put a clock on this weapons pile that is synchronized with a clock on earth.' His voice was speeding up, running with the idea.

'At a predetermined time - bang - we detonate them in the mother of all explosions. All that mass is converted into energy. With the loss of mass, they lose their gravitational force. If on earth we detect a change in gravity before the light reaches us, we have proved our point - gravity travels faster than light.' Lineker's face was beaming down from the screen. In the control room the producer was frantically signalling to the soundman to be ready for the next drum-roll.

'And how would you possibly measure a gravitational effect that small, Lineker?' sneered Williams.

'We trap an electron in a nanotube . . .' said Lineker.

'A nanotube is something you feed your granny with?' asked Belluci, feeding off the tension and delighted the drama had reignited.

'Err no - it's a tube made from a one-atom-thick sheet of carbon. Really tiny,' explained Lineker. 'The nanotube is then pointed straight at the explosion. We devise a shield in every other direction except for where the tube points. If the electron moves before the light hits a photon detector, bingo, we've proved it. The effect of gravity, or in this case its removal, was transmitted quicker than the speed of light.'

'How do you propose trapping the electron or measuring its movement?' Williams, in spite of himself, was becoming interested, his tone had lost the hectoring sneer.

'Didn't I read of something about measuring how round an electron is by anchoring it to a molecule of ytterbium fluoride and examining it with a laser beam - maybe something along those lines - or suspending it in a magnetic field and measuring any changes to the electric current that generates the field - it will be a technological challenge but these are all details we can work out later,' concluded Lineker.

'The cost would be astronomical,' Williams was protesting, but somehow the vitriol was missing from his voice, almost as if he was working through the difficulties rather than presenting them as insuperable problems.

'Not compared to the seventeen billion for the next Hadron Collider. Cancelling that will go a long way to paying for everything we've discussed here,' said Lineker.

'Do you realize how much effort has gone into the Hadron Collider project?' objected Patel. 'It is unthinkable you would risk such investment for . . .'

'This is about the 'truth', not securing fancy jobs in universities. The funding must be applied to finding the truth.' Lineker was in the flow now. 'Or the Alpha Magnetic Spectrometer - how many billions did that cost - weren't you involved in that project Dr Williams?'

'I was - and I am. It's a crucial step in locating dark matter particles.'

'Well the AMS could be a model for this experiment. Lots of countries doing their bit,' Lineker's tone was more conciliatory, realizing that Williams was softening. 'Don't you have several countries collaborating on the AMS, Dr Williams?'

'Fifty-six institutes from sixteen countries, yes we do. It's been an extraordinary model for international cooperation on a project of global significance.'

'Fantastic - well how about a similar effort for this. For starters the U.S. could develop the nanotech, how to align the tube and configure the detection devices,' said Lineker.

'We in India would be happy to be doing the computer systems and atomic clocks,' piped up Prof Patel, concerned to recover something in the event he lost the Hadron Collider.

'And PORTAL could do the publicity and promotion,' trumpeted Belluci, reminded over his headphones to include the show's sponsors and new majority shareholders.

'Well I imagine the politicians would all have something to say about who did what and of course who provides the bombs,' said a smiling Lineker, recognizing that serious opposition had dissolved.

'And think of the party when the bang went up - the biggest star in the sky ever,' added Chris.

Lineker was glancing over his shoulder, his smiling relaxation suddenly replaced by a look of intense concentration, the look of a trapped animal, not yet resigned to its fate. 'I'm afraid I have to leave, I'm being summoned from the wings here,' he said anxiously. 'Look, before I go let me just add this could be a great thing for world peace. Think of it as the greatest disarmament initiative in the history of mankind.' He was speaking too quickly, as if rushing to a conclusion. 'I've gotta go - see you later Chris.' He blew her a kiss, an instant before the screen went blank.

'And on that bombshell let me remind you, you heard it first here on TruthSayers,' bellowed Belluci. 'Formulated in front of your very eyes, the seeds of the biggest idea of them all for the biggest bang since the Big Bang, a new beginning for a different world.'

With the roars and hoots of the crowd ringing in her ears Chris left the stage, walking slowly under the burden of a great sadness, and realized she was crying.

Chapter 147: a real live wire

(6.21 am)

'I'm in the middle of a TV show . . . I can't really talk right now, Cindy,' Grafton whispered into his phone. 'It's lovely to hear from you of course.' He listened intently. 'You can get a cab over to Vaisakhi studios in Acton, ask for Dr Chris Reynolds . . .' He could feel the tightness spreading from his chest to his throat, choking the words so as he had to swallow before he could continue, 'if I'm not here anymore.'

'Okay!' Cindy replied cheerfully, hanging up.

Grafton could see a group of four men across the studio - one of them was Lineker. With a further spasm of terror, Grafton saw Shirov was much nearer, waiting. The cameraman and Chatterjee were speaking to each other in a language Grafton thought was Hindi while Lineker was talking directly to the camera. Suddenly Lineker was distracted by the fourth man, his arms blackened by tattoos, who had started gesturing and shouting, with a strong Russian accent, insisting Lineker come with him. The brutish square of his features confirmed to Grafton that the tattooed man was working with Shirov.

Next to the door, Grafton noticed a box of tools, part concealed under a work bench. He quickly pulled it out and slashed at the extension cord with a chisel, severing the socket at one end, a plan nascent in his mind. The cameraman, taking instructions over his earphones from his Indian controllers to keep filming, was trying to ignore the distraction of Dr Chatterjee who was remonstrating to the tattooed Russian that Lineker needed more time. Shirov's companion suddenly strode forward and grabbed the cameraman, swinging him aside and upturning the camera with a crash. He pushed Chatterjee violently to the ground then seized Lineker, wrenching his arm behind his back before pulling a knife, which he pressed into Lineker's throat as he propelled him towards Shirov, now leaning nonchalantly on an acoustic screen the other side of the studio, close to where Grafton had entered.

'Jesus Christ . . . now or never,' thought Grafton, his bowel loose and his throat parched.

As quickly as he could, armed with his bucket, mop and cord, Grafton sidled along the wall and passed behind the screen out of Shirov's view. He plugged his extension cable into an electric socket, unfolding the length of cable so as the exposed wires reached just to the end of the screen. Then he drew a deep breath and stepped out to confront his nightmares.

Just a meter distant from him, Shirov stiffened immediately, glaring at Grafton with his one good eye wide and staring, the other with an eye-patch.

'Recognize me?' demanded Grafton, standing as tall as his 5 foot 8 inches would allow in his cleaner's outfit, the hair net now slightly lopsided on his head.

Shirov sensed the challenge in Grafton's posture, and felt threatened by the inconsistency between it and the appearance of his opponent, knowing that crazy men were the least predictable. But Grafton was clearly ill-equipped to harm him physically.

'Fuck off while you can old man,' he said in his heavy Russian accent.

On impulse, Grafton tore off the hair net, the sort of gesture he might have seen many times, expecting the dramatic revelation to trigger instant recognition, as it inevitably had in the movies he had watched as a youth. Shirov looked down at the crumpled hair net and back up to Grafton. He smiled, 'Good,' he said. 'Good.'

'Malvern Hills,' blurted Grafton. 'I was flying a model aircraft.'

Shirov shouted something in Russian to his companion who was marching Lineker toward them and now just twenty metres away. Shirov laughed for a moment before suddenly, every trace of humour was gone. 'I remember . . . my little friend . . . Dr Buzz Buzz. Fuck off Buzz Buzz.' Without any warning, Shirov made another simulated attacking gesture, and involuntarily Grafton recoiled, as he had twice before.

But this time Grafton was prepared. He swung the bucket, splashing its contents over Shirov's shoes and ankles. Shirov looked down in surprise at the spreading stain on his lower legs, waiting for the effect of Grafton's attack, dreading the bite of acid into his flesh, and a pain beyond imagining. None came.

His face split into a snarling grin and his head fell back as he laughed again. 'Scary water Dr Buzz Buzz, scary water'.

The water rushed in a broadening pool, hitting the screen and flowing around its edge. Unseen by any of the men, a second wave splashing back from the opposite side of the bucket, caught the slowing current and injected its progress with renewed impetus.

Shirov had produced a barbarous looking knife from his belt which he waved in front of Grafton's face as he stared into his eyes, before pulling it back to his side, tensing his arm and smiling, in readiness to strike Grafton in the belly.

Though the leading rim of the water only just reached the cable that Grafton had laid out carefully behind the screen, in the instant that the first drop made contact with the exposed copper of the wire, the charge of electricity was announced with a banging fizz and a fantail of sparks. The lights dipped as Grafton looked down anxiously at the water lapping his own feet and the thick rubber of his yellow boots. Then, remembering his imminent plight, he looked up again, fearing the slicing arc of the knife.

Shirov's face, his eye still fixed ghoulishly on Grafton, was disfigured in agony and puzzlement. He seemed paralyzed as he sank slowly to the floor, collapsing into the smell of burning. Grafton stepped back instinctively, appalled and exhilarated at the magnitude of what he had done. He had negotiated with evil on its own terms, and this time, for the first time ever, he had won.

Chapter 148: turn table

(6.26 am)

Grafton's exhilaration was short-lived. He had not anticipated the efficiency of a fuse in the plug of his cable, that cut off the flow of electricity within a microsecond of the short-circuit, releasing Shirov from its grip, immediately before the 250 volts was able to fry his brains.

When he saw Shirov fall, the tattooed Russian threw Lineker to the ground, shouting in fury as he rushed at Grafton. Lineker leapt after his captor and with a desperate rugby tackle, clung to the man's legs, to bring him crashing down and send his knife skittering harmlessly against the screen. The man turned to land hammer blows on Lineker's head, clubbing him with his fists, until Lineker was forced to release him and his attacker scrabbled free. The Russian had taken just one stride when he faltered, then slumped to his knees, sighing quietly like a bag deflating as he fell forward onto the floor, the small hole of a gunshot wound in the back of his head hidden by the blood that was congealing like oil in the thick black of his hair.

Grafton didn't see the blade whistling toward his foot, that Shirov now sitting up had swung at him. The first he knew of it was when he heard his own terrified shriek, as honest and raw as he had ever heard, in the same instant he registered the pain travelling up his leg, as if the whole limb were torched by a flame-thrower. A man in the uniform of a security guard, a big man with a prominent nose, was suddenly beside Grafton, tugging at the handle of the knife stuck through Grafton's foot, which released suddenly by the boards beneath, popped out of his boot as Grafton screamed in agony again.

The moment after, Beaky was holding Shirov by the throat, one foot pinning his arm to the ground. Shirov's fingers were splayed across the floor, as Beaky started to saw off the first finger. Again, the screaming chilled Grafton to the bone, but this time, he knew the whimpering howls were not his own. Grafton shouted at Beaky, 'Stop for God's sake stop - Lineker is okay - can't you see - stop.'

Beaky stopped. Grim-faced he whispered, 'This is not for any friend of yours old man, this is for a friend of mine.' The wailing stopped, and Shirov's solitary eye rolled up in its socket. Beaky slapped Shirov to revive him and the babbling started again, the sounds of terror that hint at a despair beyond the reach of compassion.

'He owes me more than this but I'll settle for another three and I'm done,' said Beaky, sawing at the second finger. When the fourth finger lay next to the bloody stubs, almost casually, Beaky shot Shirov through the eye. Shirov's body jerked, and was still.

'I hope that helps . . . rest in peace old friend, rest in peace,' said Beaky, his face set with the fixed vacancy of a ballroom mask, before he grabbed Shirov's case and walked rapidly away.

As Beaky disappeared into the back of the studio, Lineker was approaching cautiously. Fearful of what agony could have caused the dreadful howling and uncertain what awaited him in the shadows Lineker called out, 'Is that you Bill?'

'It's all over,' shouted Grafton, 'yes I'm here . . . it's all over.'

'Jesus H,' said Lineker looking at the two bodies and peering at Grafton in his boots and coat. 'What in God's name happened here?'

Grafton was ashen-faced, for the moment too shocked to reply.

'I just saw Chatterjee leaving - what on earth is going on?' Lineker asked again.

'Thank heavens you're safe Dr Lineker,' Grafton was struggling to find his breath. 'Thank God - this is a nightmare - a nightmare - I must tell Dr Reynolds you're okay. She's been beside herself.' Grafton remembered the other imperative that had been troubling him. 'And I must phone Cindy.'

September 30th

Chapter 149: god only knows

(California)

The photograph made a dramatic image. Its heavily photoshopped background was dark with threat and power, a mackerel sky torn in two by a flash of lightning across the canvas. At the centre, a figure was depicted, his head tipped forward as if bowed by fatigue, but clearly not by defeat. The hair that fell gently across the brow was parted to reveal piercing blue eyes that gazed resolutely forward, in a show of strength as unambiguous as the beatific smile was tolerant and forgiving. His outstretched arms revealed lean and powerful muscles like knots in a rope of stretched cloth.

What was suggested by the concave belly and corrugated rib cage was reinforced by the smooth thighs above extended feet like a ballerina's point, and shamelessly confirmed with the artfully arranged shroud of gathered linen that protected his modesty - this was a portrait of suffering and sufferance in unambiguous homage to the greatest icon of them all - this was Baedeker as the Messiah.

The man himself was sitting at his desk, in front of the two-meter picture.

'In mysterious ways Clinton, in mysterious ways,' Baedeker was saying. 'Mark this Clinton. Why has an all-powerful Deity created evil? Can there be a clearer answer Clinton? I want this lesson incorporated into the induction program. Evil too has its place in a design quite beyond the capacity of most mortals to comprehend.'

'Absolutely sir, absolutely. Membership is already up 5.3% on a normalized average for this time last year in all regions since we syndicated your portrait with the abduction story,' Clinton replied.

'Yes, yes Clinton . . . of course,' Baedeker acknowledged the information with seeming indifference. 'If we can only bring peace to Mr Aziz - drive out the sickness from his soul - then his part in this will be sanctified and the cycle of God's love completed.'

'The CIAO team continue to look for him sir - they will find him. CIAO says MI5 - that's British Intelligence - is repatriating the daughter to Australia . . .' An outburst from Baedeker cut him off immediately.

'I have no interest in that witch Clinton.'

'I do apologize sir, I won't mention the girls again, I hadn't realized . . .'

Again Baedeker interrupted him. 'Cindy is a different creature, Clinton, surely you see that? She must be brought back into the fold. She found her separation from the source too hard to bear, that is all. But her soul is pure and her nature willing.'

'Yes I see sir. I understand she's being offered employment in the UK in the team being set up by Dr Grafton to do a feasibility study on the Big Bang experiment. They're calling it the Instant Communications Project.'

'Ah yes the ICE Project - a very interesting development. How is all that progressing?' asked Baedeker.

'There's a lot of political interest and there are many countries interested. Dr Williams from NASA is heading the committee for the Department of Energy. It seems he's become a major advocate of this new science. It's being pushed through the UN - it's seen as a wonderful opportunity for a peace initiative and to achieve nuclear disarmament all in one go. That's on top of proving the basis for a new theology of course.'

'Actually, you need to know I've been thinking about that Clinton. Paula has told me about a Multiverse theory - more convincing than this Process Physics business – we want the math to be the servant of God – not the master,' Baedeker mused.

'Yes sir, of course. We've already made a bid to do the publicity on the ICE project – but I can cancel that?'

'Not at all Clinton, not at all. I regard the project as the most extraordinary opportunity to advance our mission. It's just that in the Multiverse idea every option, every non-choice we make, is also realized in a parallel world.' The buzzer sounded on an intercom. Baedeker reached across and turned it off. 'Everything happens whatever we decide. There's no role for guilt - I like that Clinton - I like that.'

'Yes sir, it would account for many situations. Something else you should know, sir.'

Baedeker looked irritated that Clinton was not running with his idea.

'You remember our outreacher, the one who died in a climbing accident in Australia.'

'I do . . . tragic loss, tragic – they never found his body as I recall. 'Marcus' wasn't it?'

'Magnus, sir. Yes . . . that's correct. The police thought perhaps Tasmanian Devils had eaten him,' Clinton volunteered. 'Well, his father is on the Nobel prize committee and is of course, very appreciative of the work we did with his son, coming as it did at the eleventh hour. We are suggesting to the Committee that our Dr Lineker is nominated for the Physics prize. Everyone agrees it would help ICE hugely to have a Nobel Laureate involved. Your name is being put forward for the Peace prize too - it was the Church that sponsored the TV show when the idea for nuclear disarmament was first announced - without you it wouldn't have happened.'

'Very good Clinton, well done.' Baedeker smiled and breathed deeply. He rose from behind the desk, and strolled to the window to follow the near-stationary progress of a great cruise ship across the horizon, its layered decks high above the water.

'See that Clinton. Even a township of the senescent can be freed from the anchors of the past. Take heart from that Clinton, take heart. We too are about to sail again in the uncharted waters of the future. All the atomic bombs in the world - including Israel's - detonated in an immense explosion - an Armageddon on Earth.'

'In space sir.'

'Even better,' Baedeker smiled. 'Think of it - the biggest bang since the dinosaurs were wiped out by a meteor – the present day dinosaur, the countless multitude, will be extinguished too. Only the chosen will survive Clinton - the time is nigh, the time is nigh.'

"Are you sure sir. . .' Clinton was saying more quietly than usual when Baedeker changed the subject.

'By the way, that Reynolds video on YouTube.'

'Sir?'

'I watched it - it's pornographic - have it withdrawn.' The memory seemed to prompt something in Baedeker. 'And did I see a new girl in the Manna Division?'

'Yes sir, she's an accountant.'

'Have her sent up to my suite this evening Clinton, I'd like to welcome her personally.'

'Of course sir, of course.'

'I need the young around me Clinton. The old are just so . . .' Baedeker was looking again at the cruise ship as he searched for the right expression to properly express what he felt. 'Unclean. You understand Clinton?'

'Of course sir, of course.'

Chapter 150: no turning back

(2.00 am)

'Chris, it's me - don't turn on the light - it's Mike.' She jumped out of bed with a cry of relief and delight, hurrying quickly to the spectre outlined by the traces of moonlight that seeped around the blinds. She hugged him to her, pressing her body against his, her mouth eager for his lips as she kissed him, deep and hard.

Aziz let out an involuntary yelp, the sound of a pain that cannot be concealed. She jumped back, as if pushed, understanding that her exhilaration was premature, with the sudden dread of the unknown.

'What is it? What's wrong? Are you hurt?' she asked, her voice urgent with concern.

'I'm banged up a bit. Nothing too bad. Just have to treat me a bit easy that's all.'

She took his hand and led him carefully to the bed, helped him ease off his clothes and slipped in beside him, both of them naked.

'What's happened Mike?' she asked. 'Tell me.'

'Maybe later,' he answered, pulling her toward him.

She gently straddled him, supporting herself on her knees either side of his thighs, not allowing her weight to rest on his body, then lowered herself carefully so as her heat sent a thrill through him as he slipped inside her.

They made love, gently without urgency, then lay together for a while holding hands while she told him of the chaos that had shaped her life in the previous forty-eight hours. Aziz too, recounted what had happened to him, of the choices he had faced and the decisions he had made. He faltered only when he came to the part that he knew would have bearing on their immediate future.

'Beaky is in all kinds of strife, and it's on my account that Isabel may still be at risk from the Church. As it stands at the moment, I can't protect her but maybe MI5 can. I got to speak to her - she put me in touch with an intelligence officer - a guy called Simon Wilkie - about giving myself up.' Chris said nothing, listening, anxious.

'I've agreed if they give an amnesty for Beaky and offer protection for Isabel, I'll act as a prosecution witness against PORTAL.'

'I see,' she said, confused by the contradiction within her of approving what he was describing, but dreading its implications.

'I've told them they must commit to a full investigation of PORTAL.'

'Can you trust them? PORTAL have a lot of friends' she asked, her voice, quiet and subdued.

'Remember my green watch with the recording of my conversation with Baedeker in Llanthony. I've sent a copy of the audio file to the Israeli embassy as an insurance. And I've got the lawyer that Grafton recommended acting on my behalf. This Wilkie MI5 guy seems cool. He's been investigating the Church for a while apparently, and he's been good to Isabel and the American girl. The lawyer thinks I might avoid a prison term with a plea bargain . . . especially if the Israelis can get the Yanks onto it themselves. CIAO may be a child of the CIA, but not everyone in the parent organisation is a fan of the Church.'

'Okay Mike,' she said, quietly.

'I wanted to ask you before it went any further. . .' he said. 'I wanted us to have more time together, but I can't see any other way . . . they want me in a safe house.'

She interrupted him, kissing him softly on the lips. 'I understand . . . really . . . it sounds for the best. Will we meet again before . . .?' she asked, her heart heavy at the prospect.

'Before they lock me up. Oh yes. It'll take a day or two to set up. I don't think I'm being followed any more . . . but just in case, I should be going before daylight.'

'What can I do to help, Mike?' she asked, their shared sadness colouring the atmosphere of the room, as the blacks of night eased to shades of grey.

'Can you look after the watch? They want the actual watch as evidence. Only release it to Wilkie after you've heard from me and I've confirmed everything is watertight.' He handed her the heavy green timepiece, still in the plastic bag that had protected it hidden under one of the tiles in the garden of the Bellevue Guest House. Chris carefully placed it on the bedside table next to her.

'Mike, take this - it's just like yours - it might be . . . useful,' she said offering him the watch that was already there. 'Until we meet.'

He didn't question what she meant. 'Stay beautiful,' he said before a moment later the irregular footfall on the stairs confirmed he had left.

When he had gone she sat quietly for a while, her eyes occasionally moistening as joy mixed with sadness in traces across her cheek. Wiping the moisture from her lips she crossed to the window to watch the sun's first light sprinkle gold dust in the trees, and share the promise of a new beginning with the uncertainties of the past.

Chapter 151: loose ends

The hospital bed concealed a contortionist's toolkit of levers, cogs, tubes and springs in its underbelly, none of which was in use by Lineker, as he sat upright with his back against three generous pillows. When Lineker saw Chris as she peered around the door, he gave a spontaneous shout. 'Chris - how wonderful to see you.'

She rushed forward into his outstretched arms, kissing him on the cheek.

'You - you look fantastic - how are you?' he asked, now holding her at arm's length and studying her closely.

'I'm fine. Show me your hands.' She took his hands, inspecting them front and back, and one of his fingers neatly bound in gauze and tape.

'Ouch - does it hurt?' she asked.

'It still aches at night,' he replied, 'but nothing much anymore.'

'Thank God it's not worse . . . I came here yesterday . . . they said only family could visit and wouldn't let me see you.'

'Well thanks for trying,' he replied, beaming at her. 'Actually I was asleep for most of the day anyway. They gave me something to help me 'relax', as the nurse put it. Then I was interviewed by everyone and their uncle. The suits got more expensive as the day progressed.'

'Thank God you're okay . . .' she repeated. 'You can't guess how worried I've been about these hands,' she added, lightly kissing his fingertips.

'Maybe I can . . . Shirov made a point of bringing in a severed hand he kept in the freezer every morning to cut off a finger in front of me. He told me they were for you.'

They gazed at each other, her eyes moistening with tears, their hands still lightly held together.

'You look different - that skirt and your hair . . . you look more . . .'

'Well yeah,' she interrupted, 'I've had a bit of an image rethink that's all . . . not a big deal. What a crazy time it's been,' she added, pointedly changing the subject.

'Insane . . . hard to believe it really happened,' he replied. 'More like time spent in a parallel universe. You did a fabulous job holding everything together like that.'

She was smiling at him, and leaned forward to hug him again. 'Ian, I can't tell you how good it is to see you - what a nightmare for you.'

'Well . . . yeah . . . it was. I think the worst bit was not knowing what was going on - they hooded me when they moved me about. First indication of anything real was when I was handed your note telling me I was going to be on a TV show and it was going to be the Michelson Morley experiment,' said Lineker. 'They said if I didn't play ball, you would be hurt.'

'I figured they must have threatened something like that from your questions at the start of the show,' she replied. 'I was safe - surrounded by security people.'

'I assumed you'd have something up your sleeve. I have to say you make a wonderful TV 'celebrity'. But I can't quite place it - you seem kind of different, apart from your new look.'

'Different! Aren't we all?' she asked. 'The world seems a more serious place than it did a week ago that's for sure.'

'Don't it just. I've always thought the notion of evil is a question of perspective,' he replied. 'It's good to eat but it's tough being eaten, sort of thing. Still do think that in a way. But by the time we got to the show, it was more than clear none of that makes it any less real. Conflict is what it is and we are what we are and you can't change that by wishful thinking or moral theories.'

'I've being thinking about 'perspective' too, but from a slightly different . . . err . . . well . . . perspective,' she replied. 'It seems to me there are two principles or influences underlying reality. At first they might seem in opposition to each other, but that's also just a question of perspective.'

'How do you mean? he asked.

'Well firstly - reality is all about 'change' and our Physics establishes that randomness contributes to every transformation that constitutes that change.'

'So?'

'So there's a lot to suggest that there is more than just a mechanism acting from what we call the past that determines the present – there's also an unknowable pull to what we interpret as the future. Some of this is of course the 'Shit happens' type of event – at least 'shitty' from our point of view at least.'

'Yup, agreed so far,' he grinned at her.

'But the fact that everything - anything - is happening at all, itself implies an 'intention.''

'What? As in 'God's will', or the design of some overall overseeing entity?'

'No, because that would require something bigger than everything, something extraneous looking 'down' – that's just too anthropomorphic for me and well . . . childish. I'm talking about the manifestation of a principle, an essence expressed in and integral with all actuality.'

'So everything is 'It'. And 'It' is everything. Right?'

'Right,' she smiled.

'And you would call that 'God' presumably.'

'Well I wouldn't, though others might. Remember I'm not referring to anything separate from itself.'

'What would you have it called then?' he asked.

'My 'head' might just call it 'Being.''

'And what would your heart call it?' he asked.

'I suppose the heart might call it 'Love.'' She blushed slightly, thinking of Aziz and choosing not to tell Ian, not yet.

'Love . . . huh? Reminds me of an old Methodist farmer who had 'God is Love' on a milk stand.' There was a pause, both of them slightly embarrassed.

'Well Dr Reynolds . . . you have changed. And do you have an equation for this God Process Thingy? Preferably one with '42' as the answer.'

Now it was her turn to laugh. 'How about 'One divided by Nothing.''

'1/0 . . . Infinity . . . I like it.' He smiled too, swinging his legs over the side of the bed and changing the mood.

'Come on . . . let's wander down to the café. I still haven't really got a clue what all this madness has been about - talk me through it from the top - I've had enough of being cooped up.'

'Are you okay to walk?' she asked concerned.

'Absolutely . . . not even sure why I'm in here,' he replied.

Chapter 152: a.s.a.p

(10.15 am)

They sauntered down the corridor, sneaking the occasional glimpse through the open doors at the rows of beds and the mostly old people, a few sleeping, others propped up vertically against pillows. Some looked back with plaintive faces, often ghostly white, others ventured a token smile of reassurance in a noble effort to limit the contagion of hopelessness.

'Christ, this place is depressing . . .' said Lineker, 'I've gotta get out of here just as soon as possible.'

They descended the stairs to the next floor and on past a reception area with a shiny counter where the corridor abruptly widened into a room of gloomy people in vinyl chairs, waiting to learn if their luck had held, or if their reckoning with misfortune had finally caught up with them. As they strolled, Chris ran Lineker through a quick description of how Konkreton had been bought out by Sampatti, and the need for the Indians to refute Process Physics to assure the Hadron Collider contract went ahead.

'So why the involvement of Russians if the whole deal was being run by an Indian organization?' asked Ian.

'Originally Emelienko and Shirov worked for Konkreton and I assume they were still useful to Sampatti after the takeover. Emelienko was getting his instructions from a guy called Chaudhry in the Indian embassy, though Emelienko always claimed he wasn't aware of his identity - and nor were we until it was all over. Anyway, it turns out Chaudhry was part of the Indian Secret Service - they're called RAW appropriately enough. I'm told that Sampatti is big enough for the division between it and the Indian government to be very porous - a number of government officials are big Sampatti shareholders. And they were using the Indian Secret Service to do the dirty work. So it was a direct chain, Konkreton, Sampatti, RAW, Indian government - working to ensure the

Hadron contract wasn't derailed - and to make a trainload of money.'

'And how did PORTAL get into the act?' asked Lineker.

'I invited PORTAL to sponsor the show. As you know, they wanted to prove Process Physics for their 'revision of God' idea. They put up the money and ran the TV show and we planned to snatch you at the show. At the last moment the Indian contact - the Chaudhry guy I mentioned – told the producers you were in Australia and it would have to be a satellite hook-up. Ironically he seems to have got the idea from the publicity that PORTAL put out to explain your absence in the run up to the show. That was the lowest point for me - I really thought we had lost you.' Her voice choked, and a solitary tear rolled fitfully down her cheek.

Lineker turned to hug her, as the moving crowd parted and re-formed around them like the flow of a stream around a boulder. When the moment had passed, they re-joined the human current, drifting along, the unreality of the place mirroring their mood.

'It was only Bill Grafton noticing the zeppelin when he followed Chatterjee that made him realize you were actually next door and not in Australia,' Chris explained. 'Luckily, PORTAL isn't the sort of organization to overlook any opportunity for advertising.'

'Lucky too that the director in our studio was a regular sort of bloke - just a freelancer trying to add a bit of drama,' added Lineker. 'He got the cameraman to do the airship shots before the show and put them in the broadcast. They didn't notice what he was up to until after he'd done it.' Lineker ran his fingers through his hair, and gave her a big grin. 'Good on Bill for spotting it.'

They turned left and started down a flight of stairs. 'What worried me was that the more convincing our argument, the more you would be at risk,' added Chris.

'I was in trouble whichever way the show worked out if you ask me. They had to get rid of the evidence, and that was me. During the show Shirov kind of came to my rescue - for a while anyway. There was a point when the Indians wanted me off when I was arguing our case but Shirov insisted I carry on broadcasting - he was shouting about not giving me up till he got his money,' explained Ian.

'Apparently Emelienko never paid him and his gang,' Chris confirmed. 'The Indian Secret Service told Shirov they would pay him at the show, then tried to double-cross him. Chaudhry attempted to shoot him but Shirov killed Chaudhry instead and took the money.'

'It seems to me that it was the Share Trades idea that was the game changer. It set them against each other,' resumed Lineker. 'Without that it would have suited all of them to have me out of the way - Shirov to remove the evidence that might incriminate him, and the Indians not to rock the boat on the Hadron project. They would have paid Shirov and he would have got rid of me'

"Got rid of you" as in dumped you in the concrete of that building site next to the studios probably,' added Chris.

'Right - disposed of me then denied everything. But after they decided they wanted me kept alive, it left the Indians with the problem of how to explain their involvement in my kidnapping. I guess Shirov was the obvious guy to try to pin the blame on. With him killed, they could have said they were trying to save me all along and no-one could challenge their version.'

'Except Bill Grafton . . . they never knew he was listening to Chaudhry and Shirov,' added Chris.

'And of course, once he'd got his money, Shirov wanted me dead either way - Share Trade or no Share Trade. And he would have killed me for sure if it wasn't for Bill,' nodded Lineker, 'Old Grafton really came good all round didn't he?'

'Bill is completely transformed - you wouldn't believe it,' she agreed. 'By the way, about the Share Trades - the irony is, it was Nandini Chatterjee's idea, not mine. Nandini never told Janbir because she was worried about encouraging what she saw as his obsession with the share market. She mentioned it to me over coffee a couple of days before the show.'

'So the Share Trades idea was Nandini's . . .' said Lineker, musing on the idea. 'You must introduce me to Nandini again - we had an interesting chat at a party a while back - I liked her.' Chris gave him a curious glance, wondering at the significance of the remark.

They had reached the hospital's first floor cafe, and were queuing next to a stainless steel counter that supported a case with a curved acrylic lid. On its shelves were a selection of moist sandwiches, wrapped in cling-film, which having already incubated in the chiller for more than three hours, had acquired the lifeless artificiality of the surrounding plastics and lost the vitality of anything associated with actual food.

Chris and Ian looked at the display - then back at each other.

'I know exactly how those sandwiches feel,' laughed Lineker.

Chapter 153: everything's gonna be

(10.05 am)

'Who would have thought Janbir would get mixed up in a thing like that?' Lineker said with a shake of his head, as they waited to be served.

'Well that's another irony. As long as no-one took us seriously, we weren't worth bothering with, and nobody gave a damn about our work. But it was Nandini who convinced Janbir that Process Physics was going to successfully supersede Classical Physics. Of course, she had no idea what that would lead to. But Janbir was more than just mixed up with it - he was an integral part of the whole thing,' replied Chris. 'He was feeding them all their information. Bill Grafton was confiding in him everything that was happening on our side, not realizing that Janbir was working for the people who had grabbed you. Janbir was then reporting it all back to Chaudhry in the Indian embassy with terrible consequences. Poor old Stan Warner reported your kidnapping to the police after Bill went to him looking for help. Bill told Janbir that Stan had been in touch with the police. Janbir told Chaudhry, and Chaudhry had Stan killed as a warning to the rest of us.'

'Yes, Bill mentioned about Stan. Terrible business. Bill is obviously still very upset; feels he was responsible for Stan's death. He was almost in tears when he told me after the show,' said Lineker. 'Bill thinks it was Shirov who killed Stan and I can believe it, Shirov was a very spooky guy. I reckon I'd be dead too if Bill Grafton and the big guy hadn't got to me in time ... have to say ... I was very relieved to see them.'

'The 'big guy'; that was Phil 'Beaky' Jones. Bill thinks Beaky made off with Shirov's money, but there's no-one prepared officially to admit it ever existed so I think it's his now,' she explained.

'Well he's welcome to it. Coffee please,' said Lineker. They had stopped next to the cashier, who got up from her seat to jab a button on the console next to her, causing a steaming black liquid to pour into a paper cup. The flow stopped with mechanical precision, just after the cup had overflowed. The woman poured some away into a drain on the bench.

'How come this Beaky guy was there anyway - and on our side?' asked Lineker as he took his coffee from the counter.

'Beaky must have followed Bill. The guy at the front office confirmed he wouldn't let him enter and they found a broken window at the back where he got in.'

'Well 'Beaky' seemed a pretty nasty sort of fellow in his own right,' said Lineker ruefully. 'Apparently he was sawing Shirov's fingers off while he was still alive.'

'I think you saw him at his worst. Bill had told Janbir that Beaky had been asked to look out for you at the show, and it looks like they got Shirov to mutilate Beaky's dog as a warning to him to stay out of it. Beaky was very upset - very upset. He's ex SAS too, a friend of Mike Aziz - remember the man who drove us back from Llanthony?' Chris sounded casual, sneaking another sideways glance at Lineker, before also ordering a coffee from the girl behind the counter. 'Yes please. Coffee for me too please.'

'Aziz . . . How could I forget him? He was quite a character - he wanted to kill Baedeker. Is that the guy?' smiled Lineker.

'That's right. Well, he went to the US and freed his daughter from the Church - that's why he couldn't be at the show. He got the chance to kill Baedeker but, thankfully, he decided not to.' She was carrying the tray carefully to a vacant table while Ian collected small cartons of milk, and sugar in slim pencils of paper.

'Mike's got a different plan to bring down the Church but it's a long story; I can tell you later. Did you forget spoons?' she asked, 'I'll go.'

'No it's fine. I'll get them,' he replied cheerfully, setting off again to retrieve the cutlery. She waited till he was seated and looked at him intently, eager to judge his reaction to her news. 'One more thing . . .' she paused to collect herself. 'I want you to know - I'm romantically involved with him. With Mike Aziz.'

'Well . . . oh,' Lineker seemed surprised. 'Congratulations.'

'I'm in love with him . . .' started Chris, unsure if he approved or not. 'It's hard to explain.'

'No need to explain anything . . . I thought you seemed different.' Ian was smiling at her warmly. 'That's great - he seemed like a very . . . exceptional . . . fellow.'

She felt relieved. His opinion shouldn't matter - but it did.

'Mike's kinda full of contradictions. He's very effective if you want stuff done, but it's not always packaged as you might expect. He's very special - I feel we have a really unusual connection. I'd like the two of you to meet again,' she said raising the cup to her mouth for a sip. 'Ugh . . . what the . . .? Is this coffee?'

'Not the best for sure,' Lineker replied. 'I should be out of hospital in a couple of hours, it's just routine checks. Invite Aziz round to my place tomorrow afternoon if you like.'

'Great idea! Your place is safer than mine - Mike is worried people might still be looking for him,' she said, pushing the cup away from her.

'And this Beaky guy you say is his mate - I'd like to thank him. Can you ask him round?'

'Good idea, I know Mike is in touch with him. While we're at it, why not see if Mike's daughter Isabel can come too. We'll have a big reunion and celebrate the end of the madness. I'll bring dips and some salady things.'

'Two thirty tomorrow arvo sound good?' he asked, standing up from the table, the steaming cup abandoned.

'Perfect,' she replied, before kissing him on the cheek and beaming with the knowledge that for the first time in a long time, everything was going to be all right.

Chapter 154: The God Equation

(4.00 pm)

'I visited Ian first thing this morning. He seems fine,' said Chris. 'It's Nandini I'm more worried about at the moment. You know Janbir Chatterjee is in custody awaiting deportation.' Chris was standing in front of Grafton's desk. 'Nandini seems quite depressed. She's decided not to go back to India with him.' Grafton was seated, tapping away at a computer keyboard as he stared into the screen. 'Bill, are you listening?'

'Sorry Chris . . . I heard you . . . yes. I know all about Janbir, I've been talking to a chap called Wilkie - they want me to give evidence against Janbir. Apparently Janbir is claiming the Indians were just trying to free Ian.' Grafton was still tapping at the keyboard 'I've been discussing Cindy's situation with this Wilkie chap too - he is very concerned for her. Did I tell you she has been staying at my place,' Chris never noticed the flicker of pain in his eyes, as he finished, 'but Wilkie thinks she would be safer if she stayed with him.'

Chris interrupted him. 'About Nandini . . . I'm sure it would help her if she were occupied.' Chris seemed thoughtful. 'As in employed, that is. She's got her Ph.D. now and we mustn't forget it was her idea to save money by cutting delays in the computer networks for share transactions.' She lent on Grafton's desk, demanding his attention.

Grafton pushed the keyboard away from him, in a gesture that showed he was now prepared to concentrate fully on their conversation. 'And what an idea that was. The draft partnership contract with Lazenby Brokering came in this morning. It's called the TEN Project, Trade Efficiency Networking. They're putting up six million over the next three years for our research.'

Grafton eased his chair back. 'With all the new work there will certainly be room for Nandini . . . but if you want, you can take her on yourself. I'm recommending you for Project Leader of TEN.'

'Oh . . . good heavens,' Chris replied, astonished by the idea.

'Well - how do you feel about it - will you accept?'

'I'm not sure . . . it's all a bit sudden . . . what about Ian?' she asked.

'Ian will be in charge of the Big Bang experiment from our end, so you don't have to worry about him. Just have a think and get back to me.' Grafton stood up slowly. 'Dr Billings will be back on board shortly too. I was wrong to fire him like that, but I've apologised and he was gracious enough to accept the offer of my job. He'll be your boss again. Myself, I'll be retiring - time to get out and smell the roses a bit.'

'My goodness. There is a lot happening. We'll miss you.'

'Don't worry - I'll be doing some consultancy-type work, you'll still see me around – at least if the drama club leaves any spare time – I've always enjoyed a bit of theatrics . . . umm . . . as you know, Dr Reynolds.'

Grafton looked sheepish for a moment then retrieving his crutch from the side of the desk, he awkwardly worked his way across the office now cluttered with boxes and unstable towers of papers and books.

'My foot - still very sore,' he offered by way of explanation. 'Amazing Nandini never shared her Share Trade idea with Janbir - though come to think of it,' he gave a rueful smile and shrug, 'maybe not that amazing that a husband and wife didn't talk. Did I tell you Mary suggested we get back together? She says I can fly my planes if I want to, as long as she can go to London occasionally with her chums,' he added.

'That's great,' said Chris.

Grafton was staring out of the window absent-mindedly. 'I'm not completely sure I want to get back together with Mary to be honest,' he said. 'Surprising how little you can know of someone you live with, or work with if it comes to that.' Grafton's phone rang, jolting his attention back to the present.

'Of course send her right on up,' he said. 'It's Cindy,' he confided in Chris.

Grafton was straightening his tie. He ran a finger through his hair, blushing slightly. 'I think we can learn something from the PORTAL approach - science isn't just maths - it's the ontology, what it really means, that ultimately decides if it's worth pursuing.' Grafton was speaking to himself, barely glancing at Chris. 'Cindy has a lot to give us in the area of interpretation and how to use these discoveries - ethically you know.'

'I agree . . . and scientifically too. There's always a danger of over-interpreting some implication of the maths that appears logical but no longer necessarily represents anything in reality - physical reality anyway,' added Chris, but Grafton wasn't listening.

There was a knock at the door. Grafton hobbled quickly over and swung it open vigorously, as if his enthusiasm had translated directly into a slight physical excess.

'Cindy, welcome,' he said grandly, his hands wringing together. His head was slightly tilted, and his manner teetered precariously between servile and friendly as he ushered her into the room. 'Welcome to our humble workplace - how did the visa interview go?'

'Really well, thanks Bill - they're giving me the nod now I've got work here - thank you so much.' Cindy gave him an angelic smile. Chris watched his pleasure, warming to his lack of sophistication. 'And Dr Reynolds, so pleased to meet you in person,' Cindy held out her hand, a beam of genuine friendliness on her face.

'Delighted you've joined us,' said Chris. 'Bill was saying your role is to balance the maths with a more philosophical approach.'

'I do hope I can help. I find your work fascinating,' replied Cindy.

'I remember you said you were interested in Complex Systems when we spoke last,' said Chris to Cindy.

'That's right, Complex Systems and what Science can add to the old Esoteric studies.' Cindy explained.

'How do you mean?' asked Chris.

'The more I looked at the science, the more it seemed to me that 'Time', 'Now', 'God', and 'Consciousness' aren't just equivalent - they're synonyms, facets of the same inexpressible mystery.' Cindy seemed serious, lost in thought.

'Process physics starts with 'time' as irreducible, from which everything is derived with unique significance given to the 'now,'' smiled Cindy. 'Mysticism starts with 'consciousness' in which everything is manifested. In monotheistic religions everything is created by 'God.'' Maybe 'Now' is the manifestation of 'God' in 'Consciousness'?

She laughed. 'Maybe your Process Physics has found 'The God Equation.''

Chapter 155: loop the loop

(4.00 pm)

''The God Equation' - that's quite a responsibility.' Chris was smiling too.

'It is indeed,' announced Grafton. 'Let's show Cindy round the site while we talk.' With a grand flourish of his stick, Grafton opened the door to invite his colleagues to exit his office and precede him down the murky corridor illuminated only by small translucent panels cut into the curved iron of the corrugated roof.

'After you ladies,' Grafton beamed. 'Starting with this building - I think this is old enough to qualify as heritage - like some of the workers here.'

They smiled back politely.

'Talking of The God Equation, do you recall Chris, you told me over Skype about the equations that take you back to where you started?' asked Cindy.

'Yes I do remember that. Modular Forms. I remember we discussed how even randomness can generate time in a Modular Form - if you give it long enough,' replied Chris.

'Well, I've been thinking about it some more,' said Cindy.

They were slowly approaching the first in an array of radio telescopes that stretched across the complex with Grafton struggling with his sticks to keep up. The great dish, angling toward the sky, was supported by a meccano lattice of welds, bolts and metal beams, dwarfing the huts and slab buildings around it.

'When I had a conversation with an Australian girl I met at HQ, I said I didn't believe something like Groundhog Day was possible but, maybe I was wrong,' Cindy added.

Grafton had been trailing the others and had abandoned any attempt to be part of the conversation, content to watch from behind the rhythmic rolling pitch and the alternating rise and fall of the backsides of walking women.

'Groundhog Day?' he asked, raising his voice to ensure he was heard.

'You know - the film,' said Cindy, turning back to include him. 'Where you go round and round and keep waking up on the same morning with the same tune playing on the alarm clock, and so on.'

'Ah, yes - a 'time loop,'' Grafton interjected as he drew level. 'What confuses me is supposing you found yourself returned in time to where you had been before - how would you even know? This is our biggest,' Grafton added, puffing a bit, 'it's 48 metres.' The tone of his voice was raised with enthusiasm as he pointed at the great dish above them.

'Fantastic Bill,' commented Cindy, disposing of the topic before continuing, 'I guess you wouldn't know if you were in a time loop or not - your memory would be reset too, is that what you mean.'

'Exactly so - unless some detail was changed,' agreed Grafton, picking up the thread and keen to impress them. 'I know sometimes I can mislay something, car keys for instance, and however hard I search, I can't find them - then suddenly, there they are, exactly where I've looked several times before. Is that an example of a Modular Form time loop? The keys literally 'show up' where they weren't 'before', because something happened in the locp to put them there while everything else returns to exactly how it had been. You relive the same reality for a second time, but this time, you find your keys?' Grafton was on dangerous territory where an elderly man might simply be accused of carelessness.

'Who knows - but it's worth noting this is no weirder than Quantum Entanglement, with particles linked across space,' added Cindy. 'That's an acknowledged connection science can't explain and we're discussing equivalent links here - in time rather than space.'

'And just because you can't explain something doesn't mean you should dismiss the evidence,' said Grafton, nodding energetically.

You've changed your tune, thought Chris, remembering the Grafton of ten days before.

They were facing the humpback darkness of the Malvern Hills with the setting sun drawing a rim of incandescence along its top.

'And these equations are all about connections,' smiled Cindy, a distant look in her eyes. 'You know the expression 'love is eternal' - maybe love is a strong enough connection to rewrite history, to spin you round the loop again in order to be with the same person. Maybe it only looks random to us - maybe it's intended.'

'So someone's hiding my keys on purpose,' laughed Grafton. 'It beats me how it's possible with an exponential population growth, but everyone seems to have had some sort of past life experience these days.'

Chris didn't share the laughter. 'It's funny,' she said, 'I know when I met Mike Aziz I had a strong sense of 'Deja vu' - as if we already knew each other. But I still can't place where from.'

October 1ˢᵗ

Chapter 156: tea and biscuits

(2.30 pm)

The little Citroen stopped roughly half way down the hill near a small park, a typical arrangement in Malvern Wells, extending the country deep into the heart of the town. Chris collected her bags from the back seat, crossed the road and ascended the steps to the front door of an unremarkable two-storey house

'Two thirty on the nail. Punctual as ever. Come on in,' Lineker greeted her. 'That dress really suits you.'

'Well thank you - and how are you?' she replied, offering her cheek for him to kiss.

'I'm good, I'm good and you, how are you?' he asked.

'Fine just fine,' she replied, stepping through the doorway and past him into the entrance hall. She stopped and turned to face him. 'But there's something more I haven't told you yet,' she said. She looked anxious.

'Oh dear, that's sounds ominous,' said Lineker.

'The Church made a video of us at Llanthony - Cindy says they do that sort of thing - to, you know, to get control of people.'

'What do you mean . . . while we were . . .?'

'Yeah, 'fraid so,' she said. 'I published it on YouTube. I thought that would lance the boil, so to speak. YouTube took it down this morning - but it was there for quite a while.'

'Oh,' he said. 'Well, come in anyway.' His face was deadpan.

She sauntered into the living room, the current inappropriateness of the remembered intimacy creating a slight awkwardness between them as Ian continued toward the kitchen.

'Tea?' he shouted. She followed the sound, to find him at the sink filling the kettle. She noted the bare shelves and meagre mini-sized jars, more a pitstop on the circuit of necessity than a home.

'Haven't got round to shopping yet,' he smiled, briefly discomforted by her look of concern.

'That's okay - I've brought some dips and things.' She swung her wicker basket onto the kitchen bench. 'You don't mind then?' she asked. 'About the video?'

'That depends.' There was silence, a look of deep worry on his face.

'Can I have a copy of my own?' he asked suddenly, a huge smile transforming his face as he batted an ostentatious wink at her. She laughed, relieved, remembering what was so attractive about him.

A cough, coming from the laundry, posted a deliberate warning to alert them to its owner's presence.

'Jesus,' Lineker jumped, 'who's there?'

'It's me, Mike - Mike Aziz.'

Chris rushed to welcome him, but drew a sharp breath as Aziz appeared in the doorway. He was moving with difficulty and seemed bowed, his eyes blackened with bruises and his face patterned with a deep gash, criss-crossed with purple and black.

She kissed him gently on the temple. *So that's why you wanted the lights off.* Chris realized, remembering when he had visited in the night, and they had made love.

'These things always look worse than they are,' he assured her, extending an arm to shake Lineker's hand. 'We meet again - a bumpy road eh? I'd love a brew if you've got the kettle on.'

'No worries,' said Lineker, reaching for another cup. 'I've been hearing a lot about you.'

Aziz was about to reply when the back door burst open with a resounding crash. He sensed rather than knew that the uninvited visitor was accompanied by Death - and that this time, it had come for him.

Chapter 157: that awful sound

(2.35 pm)

A flurry of bullets shredded Lineker even before his body, twitching from its memory of life fell to the floor. The man swivelled, aiming his pistol at Chris as a banshee howl split the room. The sound born in terror, was other than human. It was the sound of raw fury, intent on confronting destiny and reshaping the inevitable to its will.

'No,' screamed Aziz, his defiance distilled in a final despairing leap toward Chris to intercept the bullet already leaving the muzzle of the nine mm automatic. In a parallel world, his alter ego remained calm as he watched the antics of the demon he had unleashed, knowing that it was simply a matter of time, and of place.

Aziz sensed the end, not with regret but as redemption, the natural culmination of his story in service to conflict and to his beloved, the sacrifice of fighting men that gives purpose to their nature, in gifting the future that others might survive the present.

He was smiling as the bullet smashed into his head and he never knew that the curving trajectory of his vaulting leap crashed him into Chris. She was thrown violently backwards, banging her head on the kitchen table, before she crumpled to the floor under the deadweight of his body. It was impossible to distinguish the source of the blood, the notion of ownership now cruelly redundant. It flowed into a coalescing pool, uniting them in ending, as lovers find union in beginning.

'Shit - I wanted him alive,' said the tall dark man, the arm that Aziz had broken in Llanthony still strapped in a sling, 'so as he could watch his girlfriend die.' He was trying to remove the heavy green watch from Aziz's wrist.

'Goddam buckle is stuck . . . it won't come off.'

'The Church won't be happy,' said the heavily muscled American with the blond short-cropped hair. 'You've killed their pet scientists.'

'The Church has moved on from these losers . . . they won't give a shit as long as they get their fucking watch . . . and anyway . . . fuck the Church - this is personal,' the dark man replied.

A car pulling up outside added another dimension to the drama the agents were concocting.

'Jealous ex-military psycho kills two-timing girlfriend and her lover, then tops himself, - I'd buy that if I was a local cop. Just leave the gun in his hand,' said Blondie, 'and we're out of here.' The grinding compression of gravel from the footsteps outside suggested it was a big man who was approaching the front door. The rat-a-tat of the door knocker suggested he was impatient.

'Fuck it . . . forget the watch,' said Blondie, his voice raised with concern as the other man tried to force the strap over Aziz' hand. 'She's moving - finish her - hurry,' he hissed.

Isabel was in a taxi just a mile down the road, and Beaky was banging on the door for the second time, when Aziz got off two shots from the pistol the man had thrust into his hand, an instant before the darkness claimed him for ever, and the demon, its work done, disappeared once more into the depths of the unnamed.

September 21ˢᵗ

Chapter 158: end game

(6.55 am)

There are things you know are false, but choose to believe . . . Chris was sitting huddled in a window alcove, with her back against the thickness of the cottage wall, scribbling on a piece of paper, *and there are things you know are true, but cannot prove.*

'I like that,' she said to herself, 'Gödel's Incompleteness Theorem with a social twist.'

She jammed the note down the side of the heavy cushion and swung her feet sideways to reach the floor. Slipping off her pyjamas, she crossed the room toward the full length mirror that swivelled around a midpoint in its heavy frame of mahogany, then flicked back her bob of hennaed hair to study the figure before her, rotating slightly to accentuate the shape of sculpted legs below the curves of a taut belly that she caressed gently with a painted fingernail. She noted the red varnish had chipped, a concern quickly displaced by something more pressing.

God, can I be . . .?' she sighed. *How can we have been so . . . stupid?*

She jiggled her breasts ever so slightly up and down, feeling their heaviness, her initial concern suddenly replaced by a quiver of excitement.

Too early to be sure . . . but . . . Being a mother had not been part of the immediate plan but to her surprise, this time it felt right.

Her phone sounded, the ring tone announcing her boss. She picked up the man's watch, green and solid-feeling, from the sideboard. *Unusual spelling of 'Mike Aziz,'* she thought, the old anagram habit of a Crossword Champion reasserting itself as she noticed the name 'Kim Zazie' engraved on its side. She toyed briefly with the vague sensation that the name was familiar.

7:00 am . . . very early to hear from . . . she thought as she lifted the receiver, 'Ian, hello.'

"G'day Chris, 'how's it goin'?' Like many Australians, Lineker's voice held the promise of humour. 'Look, sorry to phone like this but I want you to come in early if you can. By the way - I looked through your Modular Form stuff about time loops and all that.'

'What do you think?' she asked, excited.

'I know you're keen on the idea, and I'm sorry to disappoint, but I think essentially it's just a mathematical artifact - just a bit of fun, doesn't relate to anything real.'

'What about ghosts, premonitions, past lives, Deja vu - all the connections that can't be explained yet? If you give enough time to a random process . . .' she began.

'I understand the argument Chris,' Lineker interrupted, a hint of impatience in his voice. 'But we've only got four billion years before the sun burns out and randomness is already working overtime driving everything first time round - I think it's an over-interpretation of probability theory to suppose it can all happen again. We'll just have to let that one go - sorry. Look, the reason I phoned is to ask if you can get in by eight? I want to compare notes before the meeting. I'm assuming you managed to finish those neural network graphs?'

'Sure, pretty much done,' she replied, recovering quickly from the initial disappointment. 'I was out late last night with a friend, so I'm afraid there's still some fine tuning to do, but I can make it by eight if I hurry.'

'It'll be the new guy, Grafton, chairing the committee.' Lineker sounded worried. 'He doesn't seem to be on our side, so I don't want to give him any excuses. If they cut the budget we're buggered.'

'Don't worry about Bill Grafton, we can handle him.'

'Yeah, she'll be right. See you at eight,' said Lineker before he hung up.

I can handle a bit more of Mike Aziz too, she said to herself, catching sight of her lover in the mirror, still sleeping sprawled across the bed and remembering the feeling of familiarity when they'd first met as he'd served her drinks across a trestle table at the party in Brighton.

Like it was meant to be.

Chris crossed the room to check the approaching storm, dismissing a moment of discomfort as she noticed a man in the shadow of a tree who looked up at her as she appeared briefly at the window.

Chris pulled an umbrella from the wardrobe and sorted papers into her briefcase, before retrieving a bottle from the fridge in the kitchen. She poured some milk into a saucer, placing it carefully on the floor next to the front door as she knelt to stroke the cat that was pushing against her legs.

'See you later Mike . . . be good,' she called up the stairs, grabbing the keys to the 1970's Citroen Deux Chevaux for the quick descent from the Hills to the sprawling complex of ex-government buildings on the Worcestershire Plains 1000 feet below, and the meeting that both she and her boss had dreaded since they had received the notice demanding a progress report, just a few days before.

Acknowledgements

It has been a long and varied road. The project started in Australia with great enthusiasm and a different world view, and has concluded after a fashion in Wales, with something approaching fatigue. Some of this is described in my website www.timdub.com

As with every journey, including even the most solitary (and writing is in many respects a good example of a solo enterprise), there has been a band of accompanying characters. They divide conveniently into Heroes and Villains, so allocated on the predictable basis of either having assisted me in some way, or of having presented an obstacle to be overcome.

Heroes

Reg Cahill, Professor of Physics at Flinders University. Reg's work in many ways inspired the writing of the book

Reg pioneered Process Physics and, with stoicism and fortitude, has endured the stigma of departing from science orthodoxy in daring to show that Einstein's Relativity is deficient in accounting for several observed phenomena. He read an early draft of my book and commented on

'I appreciated very much your understanding of what this physics is all about. Your exploration of the "paradigm change" battle is most intriguing.'

Reg and a link to technical papers can be found here:
www.flinders.edu.au/people/reg.cahill

Rosie Dub read the earliest draft of my book, sighed, and observed that it had the potential to be turned into a good book. Her enduring support – emotional, financial, technical, and existential – has made the work possible.

Melanie Creedy read an early draft and offered insightful and useful advice, as did **Richard Upton** shortly after.

Kita Dub highlighted every dash in the book, a punctuation device she found particularly irritating and alerted me to the intrusion of sexism that many women readers might find off-putting.

Freda Dub specifically detailed how laddism might be removed, and was hugely encouraging of the project. She designed the cover and tolerated my obsessive indecision beyond reasonable expectation even from a daughter.

Martin Perrigo read the book, made extensive notes, corrections and suggestions and offered great encouragement.

To all of you, I offer my thanks.

Villains
I forgive you.